IT TAKES
A COVEN

Also by Carol J. Perry

IT TAKES A COVEN

Carol J. Perry

KENSINGTON PUBLISHING CORP.
http://www.kensingtonbooks.com

KENSINGTON BOOKS are published by

Kensington Publishing Corp.
119 West 40th Street
New York, NY 10018

All Kensington Titles, Imprints, and Distributed Lines are available at special quantity discounts for bulk purchases for sales promotions, premiums, fund-raising, and educational or institutional use. Special book excerpts or customized printings can also be created to fit specific needs. For details, write or phone the office of the Kensington special sales manager: Kensington Publishing Corp., 119 West 40th Street, New York, NY 10018, attn: Special Sales Department, Phone: 1-800-221-2647.

Kensington and the K logo Reg. U.S. Pat & TM Off.

ISBN-13: 978-1-4967-0719-2
ISBN-10: 1-4967-0719-2
First Kensington Mass Market Edition: March 2018

eISBN-13: 978-1-4967-0720-8
eISBN-10: 1-4967-0720-6
First Kensington Electronic Edition: March 2018

10 9 8 7 6 5 4 3 2 1

Printed in the United States of America

For Dan,
my husband and best friend.

ACKNOWLEDGMENTS

Sometimes the book title comes easily, but other times I think and think and just draw a blank. This book presented that problem, so I asked the people in the Saturday morning critique group I attend—Pinellas Writers—to help. Writer friend Warren Wilson came up with *It Takes a Coven*. Thank you, Warren!

Speaking of names, while writing the Witch City Mysteries I often think about my growing-up years in the magical city of Salem. Names of friends, classmates, acquaintances come popping up from the way-back machine and find their way into each manuscript. So I'd like to acknowledge some of the names culled from memory and from the rich tapestry of nationalities and cultures of the Witch City!

Thank you to the bearers of just a few of the names I've so liberally borrowed, in no particular order: Kowolski, Mondello, Della Monica, Dowgin, Russell, Murphy, Greene, Lalonde, Whaley, Sullivan, Wilkins, Dumas, McKenna, Stewart, Litka.

No doubt there'll be more to come!

"Now faith is the substance of things hoped for, the evidence of things not seen."

Hebrews 11:1

CHAPTER 1

I'd just finished my sample slice of almond cake with vanilla cream filling and vanilla buttercream frosting, and was about to take my first bite of chocolate cake with chocolate ganache and chocolate glaze covered in chocolate cookie crumbs, when I heard that Megan was dead.

"I can't believe it." Therese Della Monica put down her phone. "I saw her last night and she looked fine." She shrugged. "I mean as fine as anyone can look at a hundred and five."

Bride-to-be Shannon Dumas paused with a forkful of vanilla cake with hazelnut ganache and buttercream frosting halfway to her mouth. "You actually know a woman who's a hundred and five years old? I mean, you *knew* her?"

"We both did," I said. "Therese, does River know?"

"That's who called me." Therese brushed the back of her hand across misty eyes, picked up her camera, and once again focused the lens on Shannon. "Megan was the oldest witch in Salem, Shannon. She's sort of famous for that."

It was a pleasant spring Saturday afternoon. Shannon and I sat on pink ice cream parlor chairs at a round marble-topped table in the Pretty Party Bakery. We tasted wedding cake samples while Therese photographed the occasion for an album celebrating Shannon's upcoming marriage to Salem artist Dakota Berman. I'd accepted Shannon's invitation to be her maid of honor, not fully understanding exactly what duties that honor might entail.

I'm Lee Barrett, nee Maralee Kowolski. I'm thirty-two, red haired, Salem born, orphaned early, married once, and widowed young. My aunt Isobel Russell—I call her Aunt Ibby—raised me after my parents died and now we share the fine old family home on Winter Street along with our cat, O'Ryan. Therese and Shannon had each been my students at the Tabitha Trumbull Academy for the Arts, where I teach TV production. It was because of my class at the Tabby that Shannon and Dakota met and fell in love. Actually they met in a graveyard, but that's another story.

I was sad about Megan's passing, but she was, after all, more than a century old and blind, so the news wasn't altogether surprising. I'd met Megan through my best friend, River North. River is a witch too, and a member of Megan's coven. I knew she must be upset and I planned to call her just as soon as a decision on the cake was made.

"I don't know what to do, Lee." Shannon held up two forks—vanilla cake on one and chocolate on the other. "Dakota loves chocolate and so do I, but a white wedding cake seems, I don't know, like—more traditional."

"They're all delicious," I said, "so why not have a tiered cake with alternating layers—chocolate and white—with the yummy buttercream frosting on the whole thing? It'll look like a regular white wedding cake with chocolate surprises inside."

"Perfect. That's what we'll do. Thanks, Lee. What would I do without you?" She popped the last bite of chocolate cake into her mouth and stood. "Want to go pick out invitations now?"

"Maybe later," I said. "I need to call River and check on funeral arrangements for Megan. Okay?"

Theresa packed up her camera equipment. "I'm guessing it'll be a big event, even though Megan would have preferred something simple." Her eyes were still moist. The young photographer, who'd learned her craft in my class at the Tabby, had landed a part-time videography job at WICH-TV. She was also a novice witch-in-training who'd studied with the recently departed Megan. "I loved that old woman," she said. "I just want to sit down and cry, but Megan would tell me to get to work. Come on, Shannon. Let's check out that beginners' cooking class." I waited next to a display case filled with an assortment of fanciful confections, while Shannon filled out paperwork and wrote a check. Therese spoke quietly with the pastry chef, his tall white chef's hat bobbing affirmatively. She and Shannon left together, planning some cute shots of Shannon in a frilly apron holding a wooden spoon.

I was anxious to talk with River and called her as soon as I reached my car, a blue Corvette Stingray—a major and much loved extravagance.

"River, Therese just told me about Megan. What happened? Are you all right?"

"Oh, Lee. She died in her sleep. We're all so sad. Everybody loved her."

"I know. Want to come over to my place and talk about it? There's nobody home but O'Ryan and me. Aunt Ibby's training staff at the library and Pete's working a double shift. I'll leave the downstairs door unlocked for you."

My aunt is a semiretired reference librarian. She's sixty-something and doesn't look, act, or sound it. My police detective boyfriend, Pete Mondello, knew Megan too. She'd actually helped him solve a tricky case a couple of years back. They'd both be sorry to hear the news. O'Ryan, our big yellow striped cat, had come to live with Aunt Ibby and me after Ariel Constellation, his previous owner—as if anyone can *own* a cat—had been murdered. Ariel was a witch too, and some say O'Ryan was her familiar. (In Salem a witch's familiar is to be respected, and sometimes even feared!)

River agreed to join me in my third-floor apartment in the house on Winter Street. She's the late-night host on WICH-TV, the local cable channel. Her wildly popular phone-in show is *Tarot Time with River North*, where she reads the tarot cards for callers in between scary old movies. I once hosted a phone-in psychic show called *Nightshades* in the same time slot on that same station. Though I'd had a number of years of previous successful on-camera experience—both as a show host on a Florida shopping channel and as a network weather girl—*Nightshades* did not turn out well, and that is one huge understatement.

In less than half an hour, River knocked on my living room door, with O'Ryan making loving figure eights around her ankles. "Thanks for inviting me over," she said. "The coven has asked me to help plan Megan's service and I can't seem to stop crying."

"I'm so sorry. Come on out to the kitchen. Coffee's on. I have some cute little cupcakes too. Shannon and I were at Pretty Party tasting cakes for her wedding."

"Good choice. I know the pastry chef, Fabio. Great baker but a terrible magician."

"Magician?"

"Sure." She smiled. "The Fabulous Fabio. He does kids' parties in his spare time. Pulls rabbits out of his hat and does card tricks. If anybody orders a birthday cake for a kid, he tries to get hired for the entertainment."

"I guess he doesn't entertain at weddings," I said. "At least he didn't offer to. Anyway, everything we tasted was wonderful."

"Wedding planning is a lot more fun than memorial service planning." River picked O'Ryan up and followed me to the kitchen, with the cat snuggling against her shoulder. "This will be the third one I've had to go to this month."

"Really? Who else died?"

"Elliot Bagenstose, the banker. Died a couple of weeks ago. They found him dead in his own backyard under an apple tree."

"Oh, yes. I didn't know him but Aunt Ibby did. I think they attended some antiques symposiums together. She was at his funeral too. I didn't realize he was a friend of yours."

River looked away, eyes downcast, and sat in one of my 1970s Lucite kitchen chairs with O'Ryan in her lap. "Yeah. He was. Kind of."

"Here. Have a chocolate cupcake. It'll make you feel better," I said, firmly believing in the power of chocolate. I put a little cake on each of our plates, poured two mugs of coffee, and sat opposite my friend. "You said there were three?"

"Uh-huh. You remember Gloria Tasker? She used to be a waitress at one of the old diners years ago. It was a hit-and-run. She was riding her bike early in the morning down by Ropes's Point. They never found out who did it. Police said maybe the driver didn't even realize he'd hit somebody."

"I remember her vaguely." I offered River a paper napkin. "Gloria and Mr. Bagenstose were both older than Aunt Ibby and you're younger than I am. I didn't realize you had such elderly friends. Were they tarot clients?"

Tears coursed down River's cheeks. "No. They were kind of . . . associates."

"Associates?"

"I guess there's no harm in telling you now as long as you promise not to tell anyone else." O'Ryan licked River's face and she continued. "They were witches. All three of them."

"Of course I won't tell anyone. That's a very personal thing. I knew Megan was a witch, of course, but the banker? The waitress?"

River nodded. "Those two weren't ready to come out of the broom closet yet, but they were witches too—not in my coven, but I saw them sometimes at gatherings."

"Three witches in a month," I said. "Is that pretty unusual?"

"I think so. And, Lee," her voice dropped to a thin whisper, "it might be all my fault."

CHAPTER 2

"Huh?" It took a moment to process her words before I managed to form a couple of sentences.

"You realize that doesn't make sense, don't you? People die every day because they're old or sick." I refilled our coffee cups. "And poor Gloria was just in the wrong place at the wrong time."

River sighed a long, deep sigh. "I know. I keep trying to tell myself that. But . . . but, Lee," Again the whispery voice. "I've recently had bad thoughts about each of them."

"Bad thoughts don't kill people, River."

"Are you sure? I'm a witch, remember? There are such things as spells. Bad ones." She raised her chin, almost defiantly. "At least, in the old days, in the old religion, there were."

"But you don't believe in or practice such things."

"Not on purpose," she admitted, "but sometimes things happen to people that they can't control." She pointed at me. "You, of all people, must understand that."

She was right. I did understand it. River is one of

the very few people who know about something that happens to *me* sometimes—something I can't control. I'm what's known as a "scryer." River calls me a "gazer." That means that I can see things in reflective surfaces that other people don't see. Every so often, these visions, or whatever they are, can appear suddenly in a mirror or a windowpane or even in a shiny shoe. Some consider this ability a gift. For me, it's not always been a welcome one, though I'm getting kind of used to it and they don't terrify me the way they did in the beginning.

It was a sobering moment. "I'm sorry, River," I said. "I *do* understand. How can I help? I don't know what to say to make it better, except that I know you—and I know that you'd never harm anyone. What's that saying the witches have?"

She smiled. "The Wiccan rede. 'An it harm none, do what ye will.'"

"You see? You've lived by that rule for a long time and you do so much good with your readings." I put another cupcake on her plate. "Here. Have some more chocolate."

"I know you're right." She tossed her long black braid over her shoulder, sat up a little straighter, and accepted the cake. "It just seemed so creepy. Such a coincidence, that three of us would die in a row like that. It was strange, going to the first two funerals, you know? It seemed as though half the mourners there were witches."

"Of course I'm right. In a city this big, there are quite a few deaths every day," I said. "Once in a while one of them is bound to be a witch."

River nodded. "I know. I always say that I don't believe in coincidences but I guess sometimes they just happen. Even so, it's odd to see a funeral home full of witches twice in one month. And now there'll be another one."

"I suppose it is. But it probably just looks like a roomful of sad people to most everyone else. Did you all sit together at both services?"

"Pretty much. The broom closet people didn't sit with us, of course. Like Mr. Bagenstose was at Gloria Tasker's service, but he sat in the very back with one of the other secret witches. They both left early."

"Then poor Mr. Bagenstose died too. Weird. Pete doesn't believe in coincidences either, you know. But he's a cop. They just deal in facts. He still has a hard time dealing with my—um—peculiar talent."

"Huh. So do you." She dabbed at her eyes with a paper napkin but managed a little smile. O'Ryan put his paws up on the edge of the table, tilted his head to one side, and winked one golden eye—which may be the cat equivalent of a snicker.

"Go ahead and laugh at me, you two," I said. "I have to admit, though, sometimes the visions have come in handy."

"You aren't kidding. They sure have. Hey, thanks for listening, Lee." River gently deposited the cat onto the floor and stood up, brushing cake crumbs from pink jeans. "Talking to you really helped. But if I eat any more of these I won't fit into my TV glamour-host wardrobe. I have a new smokin' hot electric blue sequin number for next week and I'm not sure I can even sit down in it."

"Call me anytime," I said. "Come on. I'll go out to your car with you."

Together we walked through the short hall to the living room with O'Ryan leading the way. He scooted out his cat door onto the landing, with its "Attack Cat" welcome mat, and we followed him down the narrow, curving stairway to the back door and out into the yard.

We stopped to admire Aunt Ibby's garden, where daffodils had just begun to poke green shoots above ground and lilies of the valley had already established fragrant clumps along the fence. River paused before heading for her car. "Well, aren't you going to ask me?"

"Ask you? About what?"

"About what my bad thoughts were about them. About the dead witches."

"No, I didn't even think of it—except maybe regarding Megan. I can't imagine a single bad thought about her."

"True." River's big, dark eyes were downcast. "That one wasn't exactly a bad thought. It was more a case of jealousy on my part."

I frowned. "Jealousy? Of what? I don't get it."

She spoke so softly I could barely hear the word. "Therese."

"Therese? You're jealous of Therese? Why?"

"I thought . . . think . . . maybe Megan loves— loved—her better than she loved me!"

"River. What on earth makes you say that?"

"I know it was wrong to think it. Megan spent a lot of time studying with me too, before I was admitted to the coven." She climbed into her car. "It was Therese's turn. Now neither of us has her anymore." She began to cry again. "But I still don't care about Mr. Bagenstose. I was mad at him because once he turned me down at his bank for a tiny little loan. And Gloria was just plain mean. I'll call you later. Bye." River hiccupped, shut the car door, then rolled down the window. "I still don't believe in coincidences." I lifted my hand in a silent good-bye wave as she backed out of the driveway, leaving me standing there alone and puzzled.

A soft "merrow" from O'Ryan called me back to the garden, and after a quick circle around my left leg, he led the way back to the house. The sound of music from Aunt Ibby's kitchen told me that she must have arrived home while River and I were upstairs. O'Ryan was first into the back hall via his cat door while I entered the more traditional way. Aunt Ibby's kitchen door opens onto that hall, as does the door leading up two narrow flights to my apartment as well as one to our shared laundry room. I tapped on my aunt's door.

"Aunt Ibby? It's me. You busy?"

"Come in, Maralee. Door's open."

O'Ryan and I entered the warm, cozy room. My aunt looked up from the round oak kitchen table, which was strewn with papers, index cards, and lots of sticky notes in assorted colors.

"I'm just doing a little revision on the cookbook," she said. "There's fresh coffee in the pot. Turn Alexa down and help yourself."

I lowered the sound of Dean Martin singing "That's Amore," poured a cup of coffee, but passed on the plate of cookies on the counter. My recent cake binge had provided quite enough sugar to keep me wired for hours. The cookbook my aunt referred to was "The Tabitha Trumbull Cookbook," an updated assemblage of the recipes collected by the namesake of the Tabby—Tabitha Trumbull. The school is located in the building that long ago housed Trumbull's Department Store and Tabitha was the wife of the old store's founder, Oliver Wendell Trumbull. My aunt had discovered the cache of old recipes and planned to release the completed cookbook as a fund-raiser for the library.

"How is it coming? Nearly finished?"

Long sigh. "I keep thinking I've finished it and then another one of Tabitha's dishes sounds appealing and I'm off again—translating pinches of this and dabs of that and lumps of things 'the size of a walnut.'"

"Pete will be glad you're not finished with it. He loves being part of the taste-testing team."

She smiled. "He's not very impartial. He likes everything. Was that River's voice I heard a few minutes ago?"

"Yes. She was feeling a little down so I invited her over and fed her cupcakes from Pretty Party. I guess you heard that Megan the witch died."

"It was on the radio." She closed her notebook and gathered the assorted papers and notes into a neat pile. "Megan was a Salem treasure. No wonder River is upset by the news."

"River is involved in planning the funeral."

"I saw her at another one recently," my aunt said. "She was at Mr. Bagenstose's services."

"I know. She told me. Megan's will be her third funeral within the past few weeks. That's pretty upsetting for someone not yet out of her twenties."

Aunt Ibby frowned. "Who was the third? Anyone I know?"

"Gloria Tasker."

"Oh yes. I read about it. I didn't go to that one." She gave what I recognized as a disapproving sniff. "That witch."

CHAPTER 3

Aunt Ibby knows Gloria Tasker was a witch? I thought that was supposed to be a secret.

Maybe I'd misunderstood the comment. I tried a gentle inquiry. "Is that why you didn't go to her funeral?"

"That was rude of me. I'm sorry. Speaking ill of the dead and all that. But, Lee"—she spread her hands apart and widened green eyes, so like my own—"she was truly a dreadful woman. Nobody liked her. Well, *hardly* anybody."

I realized my aunt had meant "witch" in the generic sense. "River didn't like her," I said, "but she didn't tell me exactly why."

"Why do I dislike thee? Let me count the ways!" She paraphrased Browning. "It's really no wonder somebody ran her over."

"River says maybe the driver didn't even know he'd hit anything. I'll ask Pete about it. There must have been a police report."

"The newspaper called it a hit-and-run, but said the car had probably just brushed against her." Aunt Ibby gave another one of those sniffs. "She was getting quite broad in the beam, if you know what I mean. Anyway, the car didn't even dent her bike. What killed her was getting pitched forward over the handlebars smack into the post of a chain-link fence. Silly woman wasn't wearing a helmet."

She grew silent then. I was surprised by the harsh words from my aunt, who was usually so careful to avoid criticism unless it was of a constructive nature. "That witch," didn't qualify as constructive. Neither did "no wonder somebody ran her over." I sipped my coffee and waited for her to continue—to explain why she had such strong feelings about the dead woman.

She scribbled, "What is a 'dash' of nutmeg?" onto a bright green sticky note and stuck it to one of Tabitha's recipe file cards, then looked up at me. "Do you remember Gloria at all?"

"Just vaguely," I said, thinking back to high school days when my friends and I had occasionally frequented the old-fashioned diner on North Street where Gloria Tasker had worked. "I remember that none of the kids wanted to sit at her tables. She didn't like us. Used to slam the plates down and tell us to hurry up and eat."

Aunt Ibby nodded understanding. "That was because you didn't tip enough. She only liked to wait on the businessmen. The big tippers." She raised an eyebrow. "Gloria really was an excellent waitress—when she wanted to be." Her tone had softened.

"Guess everybody has at least a few good points," I said, hoping to lighten the mood.

"You're right. I shouldn't have said those unkind things about her. Just because I had an old grudge against the woman doesn't mean she was a bad person. I'm sorry."

"No problem," I said, wondering—but not asking—what the old grudge might be about. O'Ryan chose that moment to make his presence known with a plaintive "merrow" and a gentle scratch at the cupboard door where he knew Aunt Ibby kept his kitty treats. That cat always seems to know when an interruption is welcome.

My aunt pushed her papers aside and hurried to grab a handful of treats for our big yellow spoiled cat, then returned to the table. "Speaking of businessmen," she said, "I ran into an old friend of yours this morning. Bruce Doan. He said he'd like you to call him when you get a chance."

"Mr. Doan? Really? I wonder what he wants." Bruce Doan was the station manager at WICH-TV. He'd been my boss back when I hosted the ill-fated *Nightshades* program, and I was pretty sure he wasn't interested in repeating *that* experience. "Did he give you a hint about why he wants to talk to me?"

"Not really. He said something about 'a mutually beneficial situation.'"

"That could mean anything. I'll call him," I said. "My classes at the Tabby will be over in a week or so. He probably wants to know if I can recommend any of this year's TV production students. I know he's glad he hired Therese Della Monica from last year's class."

"A talented girl," my aunt agreed. "And a lovely person."

"She was with Shannon and me at the cake tasting today. She's doing the video for the wedding."

"That's turning out to be quite a production itself, isn't it? Did you realize that being maid of honor involved so much detail?"

"I didn't. But school will be out for the summer in a few days. Then I'll have plenty of time." I looked at my watch. "Speaking of time, Pete's coming over for dinner when his shift is over. I promised him lasagna. I'd better start putting it together."

"You said Pete's sister Marie promised to share her secret recipe. Did she give it to you?"

I laughed. "She did. Want to hear it?"

"Of course I do. I mean, if it wouldn't be betraying a confidence."

"Okay. Here goes." My aunt picked up a pen, poised to write. "First, buy a package of Prince lasagna noodles." I instructed.

Aunt Ibby wrote "Prince lasagna."

"Follow the directions on the package."

"That's it?"

"Uh-huh. Except that you have to get the fresh grated Parmesan and mozzarella cheeses from the deli, not the packaged stuff in the aisle."

"Well, thanks for sharing." She put the pen down. "Guess you'd better get started. Does Pete know the secret of his sister's lasagna?"

"Nope. He thinks it's an old family recipe from Italy. Actually, Marie got it from *her* mother. So who am I to spill the beans . . . or the sauce?"

I promised to save a piece of lasagna for my aunt, patted O'Ryan, and headed out through the living room to the front hall, where I climbed the broad, polished main staircase the two flights to my apartment.

I climbed slowly, thoughts about secrets buzzing in my brain. The secret Marie had shared—putting together packaged pasta, sauce from a jar, and some fresh deli cheeses—would, I was sure, add up to the expected tasty result. But what about River's secret—the one I hadn't shared with my aunt, and didn't intend to share with Pete either? Were the deaths of three witches—Megan, Mr. Bagenstose, and Gloria Tasker—just a strange Wiccan coincidence? Or was it possible that River might be right, that their deaths were connected somehow—though certainly not because of somebody's "bad thoughts"?

Even if that somebody *is* a practicing witch.

CHAPTER 4

The lasagna bubbled and browned its melty, cheesy, tomatoey wonderfulness in the oven; a crisp and pretty salad chilled in the refrigerator along with a bottle of Merlot; and garlic bread was ready to pop under the broiler. The Lucite table was set for two and a new Jessica Molaskey album played softly in the background.

With a satisfied glance around my kitchen, I headed down the hall to the bathroom. Almost two years ago Aunt Ibby had surprised me with this, my own third-floor apartment in the house on Winter Street. The top two floors had been pretty much destroyed by fire one terrifying Halloween night, but the restoration, under Aunt Ibby's careful supervision, was just about perfect. With the aid of state-of-the-art appliances, my meager cooking skills had improved a lot too.

Showered and with damp red hair brushed into some semblance of order, I applied a little mascara, a touch of blush, and some pinky lip gloss, then hurried back to the bedroom, wearing comfortable old skinny jeans and a brand new white silk blouse. I pinned a vintage brooch with an oval miniature painting of a yellow cat—a gift from Pete—to the deep V-neckline, then, content with my reflection in the tall oval mirror, hurried back to the kitchen.

The oven buzzer signaled that the lasagna was done just as the doorbell chimed "Bless This House," announcing Pete's arrival. He has his own key, so I grabbed oven mitts and answered the summons from the stove.

O'Ryan appeared in the living room first, with Pete close behind. (A cat door makes for a faster entrance than the old-fashioned turn-the-key, twist-the-knob system.) Pete pulled me into his arms for a warm hug followed by a lingering kiss. It was the kind of greeting that occasionally delays dinner, but the Italian restaurant aroma—and maybe the fact that I still wore oven mitts—interrupted that train of thought.

"I've been looking forward to this all day," he said. Mittless by then, I took Pete's hand and together we followed O'Ryan to the kitchen.

"The lasagna?"

"You—*and* the lasagna." With a quick peck on my cheek, he headed for the bedroom to secure his gun in one of the cleverly hidden compartments in my antique bureau, then returned and draped his denim jacket over the back of a chair while I pulled the garlic bread from under the broiler. Perfectly browned, if I do say so myself.

I could tell from his casual clothes, jeans and 2013 World Series Championship Red Sox T-shirt, that he'd gone home to change after the day's double-shift duty as a detective on Salem's police force. His dark hair, still damp from a shower, curled a little over his forehead and the T-shirt accented perfect pecs and washboard abs. I banished a few dinner-delaying thoughts, handed him the wine bottle and corkscrew, and served the salad in wooden bowls.

"Everything looks perfect, babe," he said, filling our wineglasses, then cutting the lasagna into neat, plump squares. "You've had a busy day. How'd the cake tasting go? Bring home any samples?"

"Of course. That'll be dessert. We decided on a chocolate and vanilla for the wedding cake. Therese got some sad news while we were there."

He nodded understanding. "Megan's death. She was an amazing old woman. Guess the whole city will miss her."

"River is really upset about it. She came over in tears this afternoon."

"They were pretty close, weren't they? But after all, Megan was over a century old. It couldn't have been a big surprise."

"I know. But Megan's will be the third funeral River's attended in just a few weeks. Odd for someone so young." I watched as Pete expertly served the lasagna. "Don't you think so?"

If I mention the names of the other two deceased, will he see any connection between the three?

Pete took his first bite of lasagna. "Umm. Great. Just like my mother used to make. So three friends of River's died in a row? I guess that happens sometimes. Bad things come in threes, they say. You know, like three old movie stars die in the same month. It happens."

"Uh-huh. Not movie stars, though. One was a banker and the other one was a waitress."

He put down his fork. "River knew those two? Bagenstose and Tasker?"

"Yes," I said, surprised that he knew right away

whom I was talking about, and even more surprised that he'd asked the question in what I'd come to recognize as his cop voice. "How did you know?" I asked, puzzled.

He picked up his fork and took another bite. He spoke after a moment, his tone returning to normal. "Oh, no big thing. Just that the department had to check a couple of details on each of those. No big thing. Nothing for you—or River—to be concerned about. Say, want to pass that garlic bread?"

I passed the napkin-wrapped basket. "Details? Like what?"

Does he know about them both being witches? I hope so. I don't like keeping things from Pete, but a confidence is a confidence and River said I shouldn't tell anybody about Mr. Bagenstose and Gloria Tasker being part of a coven.

Pete took a buttery round of the bread and paused with it halfway to his mouth. "You're going to eat some of this too, right?"

"Absolutely," I agreed, helped myself to a couple of slices, and waited for details.

Nothing.

So I prompted. "Aunt Ibby went to Mr. Bagenstose's funeral too. Was there something—um—suspicious about how he died? River said it happened in his own backyard."

He looked up from his plate, brown eyes all wide and innocent. "Suspicious? What gave you that idea?"

"You did. Checking details, you said."

"Oh, that. Just some routine stuff. Some of his injuries didn't seem exactly consistent with falling out of a tree. Medical examiner mentioned it to the chief. You know how Chief Whaley is about tying up all the loose ends."

I did know that. Unfortunately, I'd been involved in a couple of "loose ends" myself. I'm definitely not one of the chief's favorite people. "What about Gloria Tasker? More details?"

"Sure. That one's still an open case. Hit-and-run. We're still checking the neighborhood for security cameras that might have caught something. But it was dark and where she was riding is a long stretch of vacant riverfront with just a few houses nearby. Did you say something about cake for dessert?"

"I did. Want to start the coffee while I clear up these dishes?" I could see that Pete wasn't going to share any more information about the dead witches. He's always careful about keeping important police business confidential and the details he'd mentioned seemed pretty routine, just as he'd said they were.

I loaded the dishwasher, put a couple of squares of lasagna into a plastic container for Aunt Ibby, wiped the counters and table, and arranged the remaining cupcakes on an oval blue Fiestaware platter. Pete prepared the coffee and set our New Hampshire Speedway coffee mugs—souvenirs of the first weekend we'd spent together—onto the table. We tapped our mugs in a silent toast.

"Summer's almost here," Pete said. "First NASCAR race at the speedway is in July. Want to plan on it?"

"For sure," I said. Pete understands my love for fast cars. My late husband, Johnny Barrett, was a NASCAR driver, and I still feel quite at home at an auto race-track. "I'll put that in big red letters on my summer vacation calendar. School is over next Monday, and to tell the truth, after Shannon and Dakota's wedding I don't have much of anything to write on it at all."

"No summer theater job lined up this time?"

"Nope. Not a thing. Maybe I'll double up on the

study time and catch up with you in the criminology course." Pete and I were each taking an online course on why criminals do the things they do, but he was two years ahead of me. "I seem to be better at finding jobs for other people than I am at finding work for myself."

"Other people?"

"I introduced River to the guys at WICH-TV and now she has her own show. I found Daphne Trent for Mr. Pennington's theater group and now she's in Hollywood. Therese is a call screener for River and videographer for the TV station. I'm the one who introduced her to Bruce Doan."

"I see what you mean. Well, if nothing turns up, you could just go to the beach and work on your tan. Take it easy. Spend more time with me." His smile was broad and he reached for my hand.

"That sounds good." I returned the smile. "But speaking of Bruce Doan, my aunt saw him today and he wants me to call him."

"Maybe he wants to hire you back."

"I seriously doubt that! He probably wants to see if anyone from this year's class is ready to join the WICH-TV crew."

"What do you think?"

"I think a couple of them might be ready. The starting pay is never much but it's a real opportunity to break into the business. Here. Have a cupcake." I passed the plate, refraining from having one myself. We sat, sipping our coffees in companionable silence.

Pete's cell buzzed and he reached into his jacket pocket. "Oops. Sorry, babe, have to take this. My office." He spoke into the phone—cop voice engaged. "Detective Mondello. What's up?" He nodded, expression grim.

"No kidding. Where? Uh-huh. You sure? Can you

handle it? I've already worked a double today. Great. Thanks. I'll take over in the morning."

He tucked the phone back into his pocket. "Sorry. Where were we?"

"Come on," I said. "What was that all about?"

"Shopkeeper on Essex Street says someone took a shot at him when he was leaving his store."

"Is he okay?"

"Seems to be. Shook up is all."

"Can you tell me what shop? Just curious."

"It'll probably be on TV anyway." He checked his watch. "Almost time for the ten o'clock news." He gave a Groucho Marx eyebrow wiggle and attempted a leer. "Want to watch from the bedroom?"

"Good idea," I said. "I'll be right back." I carried the promised lasagna downstairs to a waiting Aunt Ibby, then hurried back up to my place. The TV in the darkened bedroom cast a bluish glow across my big bed, where both my boyfriend and my cat lay sound asleep. Poor Pete had worked all day and must have been exhausted. I don't know what O'Ryan's excuse was. I tiptoed to the bureau, pulled out a long nightshirt with a picture of Minnie Mouse on it, made a quick trip to the bathroom, and joined the two sleeping beauties on my bed.

The newscast had just begun. After a commercial for the new CX-9 from North Shore Mazda, the latest news anchor, Buck Covington, led off with the story about the shooting incident that had happened a few hours earlier behind an Essex Street store. The shooter had missed, but the intended victim had been taken to the hospital for evaluation. My old colleague Scott Palmer appeared on-screen with a handheld mic, doing the stand-up in front of a small shopping strip.

"The owner-proprietor of a popular downtown Salem store had a close call a few hours ago. He'd closed for the day and was preparing to enter his car, which was parked in a private lot at the rear of this building, when someone shot several times in his direction. Fortunately, the shooter missed. I spoke with shop owner Christopher Rich, who, though understandably shaken by his experience, was unharmed." A photo of Rich popped up on the right side of the screen.

He looks familiar. I know him from somewhere.

It was dark on Essex Street, of course, but the portable spots from the WICH-TV mobile unit illuminated both the announcer and the storefront. I sat up and peered more closely at the screen, straining to make out the words on the display window. *Christopher's Castle* was spelled out in Old English lettering. Below it, in smaller but still legible lettering, I read, "Your one-stop spot for psychic readings, charms, herbs, spell books, magic tricks, crystals and more."

Pete stirred slightly beside me, and I turned off the TV. I remembered where I'd seen Christopher Rich before. He'd been a guest on River's Halloween special show. One of the city's most colorful, best known (and widely advertised) witches, Mr. Rich had dodged some bullets—and River had been spared her fourth funeral in a month.

CHAPTER 5

I woke to the smell of fresh coffee brewing. Sunday morning and Pete was in the kitchen, dressed, ready for work, humming an off-key version of "Rhinestone Cowboy." O'Ryan had left the bedroom too, probably downstairs having breakfast at Aunt Ibby's. I stretched, stood, and faced my antique full-length oval mirror on its swivel-tilt stand. (River, who's an expert on such things, insisted the mirror had to be placed so that I couldn't see myself in bed. Bad feng shui.)

At first, the beveled glass showed the usual morning me with sleepy eyes and messy bed head. Then, from the center of the mirror spreading outward, a different reflection began to take shape. I saw a sunny beach. Sea grass moved in the breeze and in the distance waves splashed onto the shore. A white Victorian gazebo with a cupola and lots of gingerbread and curlicues stood off to one side.

I don't look forward to these visions. They come to me unbidden and unwanted. They've shown me scenes of death and destruction so often that I dread them. But this scene was a pleasant departure from all that. I had no idea what it meant, of course. I hardly ever know how to interpret these images. I moved closer to the mirror. "Can I get a better look at the gazebo?" I whispered. As though a camera had adjusted to close-up mode, the white structure grew larger. There was a seated figure inside, almost obscured by one of the pillars, it's back toward me.

Just as quickly as it had come the vision melted away. Once again I saw myself, and from the doorway behind me, Pete's reflection appeared in the mirror too. He retrieved his gun from the hidden cubby in the bureau and holstered it. "Did you say something, Lee? Coffee's on. Sorry I conked out on you last night. Long day."

Pete knows I'm a scryer, though it isn't something he likes to talk about. Since I had no clue about what the beach meant, I didn't say anything about it. Nor did I mention the previous night's shooting. I knew, though, as Pete gave me a good-morning hug, that he needed to know about the four witches and that it was going to be up to River—or me—to tell him about the two who'd kept their witchcraft a secret.

"Just talking to myself in the mirror," I said, returning his hug, "and you needed the sleep. I'm sorry you have to work so many weekends."

"Me too. But I have three days off at the end of next week. Maybe we can do something." I followed him to the kitchen.

"Let's." I poured a cup of coffee for myself and handed one in a to-go cup to Pete. "Something special."

"Good idea," he said. "I get off early today. How about fried clams and a movie tonight?"

"That's a good idea too. Around six?"

"Yep. See you then."

I walked with him to the living room door, where O'Ryan waited just outside. I stood in the tiny hall and waved a quick good-bye to the two as they headed downstairs, then returned to my cozy kitchen and my morning coffee. I looked at the Kit-Kat clock on the wall. River doesn't do her show at WICH-TV on weekends, but it was still too early to call her. I remembered that Bruce Doan often worked on Sundays, though.

Wonder what he wants. After I get dressed and have something to eat, I'll give him a call.

I usually have Sunday breakfast with Aunt Ibby before she leaves for ten o'clock services at Tabernacle Church. Sometimes I accompany her, sometimes not, but I never turn down the breakfast. I showered and dressed in tan cargo pants and an old Indianapolis Speedway T-shirt of Johnny's, tossed the previous day's laundry down the bathroom laundry chute, turned off the coffeemaker, and went down the back stairs to where I could already smell bacon cooking.

I'd made a good choice. Bacon and eggs and hot baking powder biscuits make a happy start to any day. Aunt Ibby had seen the news about the previous night's shooting on Essex Street and wondered if since Mr. Rich was an admitted witch he might be a friend of River's.

"I'm sure he is," I said. "He was on her show last Halloween. She never watches the news, though. Too depressing, she says. So she may not even know about it yet but I'm sure one of her roommates will tell her what's happened."

"How frightening for him. Poor man. Imagine being shot at like that with no warning. I hope the police will catch the criminal who did it soon. I wonder if it was what they call a 'random shooting' or if Mr. Rich was a target."

I'm betting he was a target and it has something to do with his being a witch.

I wanted to tell her about that, but of course I didn't. I told her about the vision, though, thinking that maybe she'd know where such a distinctive beach-front gazebo might be.

"Offhand, I can't recall seeing such a place around here, but it sounds very pretty."

"It is," I said. "I guess it doesn't necessarily have to be from around here. Could be anywhere. Even any *time,* I suppose. Darn visions never make the least bit of sense."

"At first," she said.

I nodded. "Yeah. At first."

Aunt Ibby, properly high heeled and hatted, left for church. I tidied up her kitchen, loaded my laundry into the machine, and went back up to the third floor. O'Ryan, having spotted a few cat friends on top of the side yard fence, exited via his outside cat door, leaving me alone with a long, empty Sunday to fill.

Once upstairs I poured myself another cup of coffee and sat in the chair closest to the window over-looking the yard. O'Ryan had joined his friends. There were four cats in the garden now: our big yellow striped boy, a white female I called "Frankie" who stopped by occasionally, a small gray cat I'd seen only a couple of times before, and a sleek black lady with a red collar who hadn't visited us in over a year. They made a pretty picture gathered there among the daf-fodils. Watching cats play gently together in a garden can be as relaxing as watching fish move in lazy circles in an aquarium.

By the time I stopped drinking coffee and cat watching it was nearly ten-thirty. Bruce Doan would probably be in his office. I dialed WICH-TV from memory, adding Doan's extension number—remembering that Rhonda, the station receptionist, didn't work on Sunday.

"Mr. Doan? Lee Barrett. My aunt Isobel Russell said I should call you."

"Ah, Ms. Barrett. So good to hear your well-modulated voice. Indeed, there's a matter I'd very much like to discuss with you."

"Yes?"

"Could you come over to the station? Today if possible?"

"I can. What time is good for you?"

"Let's do lunch at that little place across from the station. Say at noon?"

Sincerely wishing I hadn't just eaten that big breakfast, "Noon it is," I said.

"Looking forward to it," he said, and abruptly hung up.

I had time to change into something more respectable—a turquoise linen jumpsuit with a gold braided belt and tan sandals looked both casual and professional. I twisted unruly hair into a loose bun and secured it with a gold filigree clip. I hesitated before looking at my reflection in the oval mirror—afraid the gazebo might be there. It wasn't.

Summer was surely on the way—the sun bright and the breeze warm. I resisted the temptation to put the Stingray's top down in favor of keeping the precarious hairdo intact and headed for Derby Street and WICH-TV.

I parked in the station's waterfront lot, staying a comfortable distance away from the low granite wall where I'd once discovered a body floating in Salem Harbor, then walked along the side of the old building and climbed the three marble steps to the front door. After crossing the black and white tile floor of the lobby, I entered the brass-doored vintage elevator, which clanked and growled its way up to the second floor.

The empty reception area, with turquoise carpet, purple leather and chrome chairs, and a huge arrangement of silk lilacs (reflecting Mrs. Buffy Doan's choice of office décor) used to make me cringe, but today brought a smile. The gold sunburst clock on the wall read five minutes before twelve. Right on time. I approached the door marked "Station Manager" and tapped gently.

"Mr. Doan? It's Lee Barrett."

The door swung open and Bruce Doan joined me in the purple and turquoise ambiance. "Right on time, Ms. Barrett," he said, running a hand through thinning hair and smiling. "Time is money. Let's go."

He led the way to the elevator, punched the DOWN button, and we were on our way. The Pig is one of those places where, as they used to say on *Cheers,* everybody knows your name. I hadn't been there for quite a while, but the pretty waitress remembered me. We sat next to a mullioned window facing onto Derby Street. I glanced at the menu. "If you don't mind, Mr. Doan, I'll just have some coffee. Had a big breakfast this morning."

"Suit yourself." He waved a dismissive hand, ordered

my coffee and the soup and sandwich special for himself. (The station manager is notoriously thrifty, so my passing on lunch was probably good news.) "Now. Let's get down to business. I have a proposition for you."

I leaned forward. Interested. Waiting.

"Therese Della Monica says you're still teaching about investigative reporting in that class of yours."

"That's true," I said. "Until tomorrow. Then school's out for the summer."

"I reread your old resume." His expression was solemn. "You've never actually *been* an investigative reporter."

He was right. In addition to my short stint as a psychic, my main claim to TV fame had been a job as a second-string network weather girl and several years as a show host on a Miami shopping channel.

"True also," I admitted, "but my course material is up to date and . . ."

He held up both hands. "Oh, I have no doubt that your course is adequate. I'm not criticizing your teaching qualifications. No. Not at all."

"Then, what . . . ?"

"I want to make you an offer you can't refuse."

With thoughts of a horse's severed head flitting through my brain, I leaned back in my seat. "Go on."

"What would you say to a summer's internship as an investigative reporter on my station?" He beamed. "What would you say to *that*?"

Internship? Does that mean no pay?

My coffee and his lunch arrived, giving me a moment to think. "It's certainly an interesting idea," I spoke slowly. "Could you be a little more specific about just what an investigative reporting intern does?"

"Hey, you're the one who teaches this stuff." He

shrugged, still smiling. "Find something interesting that the public needs to know more about. Nitty-gritty. Dirt. Low-down insider straight poop. You know."

"But don't you already have people on your staff who could handle this? What about Scott Palmer?"

"Nope." He tasted his soup. "This is good. Sure you don't want some?"

I shook my head "no" and waited for him to continue. I knew this was just the kind of reporting Scott would relish.

"Scotty's already doing two sports shows, all the on-site mobile stuff, and subbing for everybody's days off. Anyway, you'd be better at it."

"How about the new guy? Covington?"

"You've seen him, huh? Let me tell you about Buck Covington. Good looking, isn't he? The camera loves him. Great set of pipes too. Can read a teleprompter perfectly. Otherwise . . . dumb as a brick. No kidding, Lee. He wouldn't know where to begin with a job where you have to think on your feet. Nope. It's perfect for you." He pointed a finger in my direction. "It's not as though you have to fill an hour every night. Nope. Just come up with something and we'll block out a spot in the evening news—fifteen minutes maybe. If it works, we'll package it and run it again in the morning. Just an occasional thing. Unless, of course, you stumble onto something really hot."

Stumble?

I finished my coffee and signaled to the waitress for another. "Do you have a budget in mind for this, Mr. Doan?"

"Well, there's no actual salary involved, of course. You'd just be an intern, after all. But the station will cover expenses." Another shrug. No smile. Mr. Doan doesn't smile about money. "Transportation. Occasional meals. Video and film production expenses. Bribes for snitches. You know."

Bribes for snitches? The man watches too many TV crime shows!

He was right about one thing, though. He'd made me an offer I couldn't refuse. And I didn't. I agreed to come up with a topic, research it thoroughly, and be ready to present it to the WICH-TV audience within the next couple of weeks.

What was I thinking?

CHAPTER 6

Although a hodgepodge of thoughts had been whirling around in my head all day, by the time I drove home to Winter Street that sunny Sunday my poor brain was in a blender. What had I just signed up for? Of course, I hadn't actually signed anything—the deal had been agreed upon with a handshake. But could I really *do* the job? As Mr. Doan had pointed out, I taught investigative reporting to others but had no actual on-camera experience *doing* it.

You can do this, I told myself.

Like a mantra, I repeated the words aloud all the way home.

You can do this.

I hoped Aunt Ibby was back from church. I was sure she'd speak those encouraging words. It would be good to hear them from another human—even one who loves me and thinks I can do anything. I pulled the Stingray into the garage, delighted to see that the Buick was already there, and hurried to the house.

I heard Elvis singing "How Great Thou Art"— appropriate Sunday music—as I knocked on the door, first gently, then a little louder to be heard above Elvis. Aunt Ibby opened the door, then turned down the sound just a tad.

"Come in, Maralee. My, don't you look pretty. You missed a lovely sermon about faith. Did you go out to lunch?"

Maybe I should have gone to church instead.

"I did," I said, "though I didn't eat anything. I had a meeting with Bruce Doan."

"Sit down and tell me all about it, dear. I was just having a nice cup of tea. Want some?"

"Yes, thanks." I accepted the tea, served in one of Grandmother Forbes's bone china cups. "He made me an interesting offer. One he said I couldn't refuse."

"What is it? Don't keep me in suspense. I've been wondering what he wanted to talk to you about ever since yesterday."

"Okay. Here it is." I leaned forward, facing her across the table. She leaned toward me at exactly the same time. We both laughed and I relaxed a little bit. "He's offered me a summer's internship as an investigative reporter for the station."

She leaned back in her chair and clapped her hands. "How wonderful! How very exciting for you." She raised one eyebrow and looked at me intently. "You *did* accept, didn't you? When do you start?"

"I did," I admitted. "I promised to have my first report within the month. But I'm having second thoughts about it now."

"Second thoughts? Why? It's a great opportunity. I suppose there's no salary involved. That doesn't bother you, does it?"

"No. Of course not. Remember, I volunteered last

summer for Mr. Pennington's theater project. No pay then, either. That's not it."

Fortunately, money isn't a problem for me. Between a substantial inheritance from my parents—well managed by Aunt Ibby's financial advisors—and the insurance money from Johnny's accident, there were no worries in that department. I could easily afford to volunteer a couple of months of my time.

"Then what's holding you back? Seems to me it's made to order for you."

"I've never really *done* it before. Teaching's one thing. Doing's another."

"That's what internships are for, silly girl." She smiled and squeezed my hand. "You can do this."

She'd spoken the magic words. I repeated them.

"I can do this."

"Of course you can. Faith, my darling child. Faith. Have you told Pete yet?" She refilled my teacup.

"No, haven't talked to anyone but you."

"He'll be happy for you. It might give you a bit of an edge, you know? Having a gentleman friend on the police department."

"Aunt Ibby! You know we don't ever discuss his work."

Again that raised eyebrow. "Do too."

"Well, hardly ever," I said, thinking about how just that morning I'd tried to figure out how to get Pete to tell me about the two dead witches without telling him what I already knew about them. "Maybe once in a while. A little bit."

Elvis began crooning "I Believe," and feeling much better about the proposed job and the world in general, I finished my tea, kissed my aunt, and went up the back stairs to my apartment. O'Ryan was already in the living room, lying on his back, feet up, on the zebra print wing chair.

"Well, you look relaxed, cat," I said. "All tired out from playing with your friends?"

He rolled over, assuming a more gentlemanly position; yawned a long, pink-tongued yawn; and went back to sleep. No conversational possibilities there. I looked at my watch. River would be up and about by now. I called her and she answered on the first ring.

"Hi, Lee," she said. "I was just about to call you. You heard about what happened to Chris Rich?"

"I did," I said. "I know he's a friend of yours. He was lucky."

"I know. I talked to him this morning," she said. "Of course, he says it has nothing to do with luck. Says he has a permanent spell of protection around himself at all times."

"What do you think?"

"Who knows? Maybe he does. Some witches have more power than others." She sounded pensive.

"At least you don't have to go to another funeral," I said. "That part is lucky. Did you talk to Chris about the two who weren't out of the broom closet yet?"

"I did. Their secret isn't a secret anymore, though. That Chris is such a publicity hound he's blabbed all about it to some reporter. Gave an exclusive interview all about how 'somebody is killing witches in Salem.'"

"No kidding. What reporter?"

"Don't know. I was mad at Chris for telling—I mean, if they wanted it known they would have gone public. Maybe they'd even kept it secret from their own families. Anyway, I gave him hell about it. He hung up on me. I don't even know what station will air it."

I'll bet anything it was Scott Palmer. He said he'd spoken with Rich. I'd turned off the news too soon.

"I'm sorry, River. You two used to be friends."

"Oh well, we'll get over it. People do. Anyway he's involved with the plans for Megan's funeral on Wednesday, so we'll be fine."

Had River had "bad thoughts" about Christopher Rich? I didn't ask. "I heard that it's going to be at the old town hall."

Her reply was soft. "All of Salem loved her, so that seemed like the right place for the public service. It's such a beautiful old building. Of course, we'll hold our own ceremony, the real one, later. We Wiccans prefer to be buried without coffins, you know, to be returned to the earth, but that's against the law so she's already been cremated. But *you* called *me*," she said. "What's going on?"

"You'll never guess who I just had lunch with."

"I won't even try. Who?"

"Your boss. Bruce Doan."

"Oh my God." Real gasp. "He's not going to fire me and hire you back, is he?"

"Of course not. He's not crazy. But he did offer me a job—sort of."

I told River about the internship I'd just about accepted. All right, I'd definitely accepted. With a handshake.

"Awesome," she said. "For you that'll be a piece of cake."

"You and my aunt have more confidence about this than I do, but I'll admit—I'm starting to get kind of excited about it. It's something I've always wanted to try."

"Piece of cake," she said again.

"No more cake please! I feel as though I've been bingeing on the stuff lately."

"Oh yeah. Shannon's wedding. How're plans coming along? It's pretty soon, isn't it?"

"Too soon," I sighed. "There's so much to do and not much time to do it. The invitations aren't even picked out yet."

"Don't worry. There are design programs that make beautiful ones in a day or two. They even make them at Walmart. Have they decided on a venue yet?"

"Just that they want it outdoors somewhere. Any bright ideas?"

A soft laugh on River's end of the phone. "Since they met in a cemetery, maybe they'll decide to get married in one."

The mental picture of such a thing was so outrageous I had to laugh too. "You're a nut," I told her. "Seriously, if you think of any good wedding venues, let me know."

Another snicker. "Gallows Hill *is* pretty this time of year."

"Bye, River." I shook my head, hung up, and went to my room to pick out something to wear on my "fried clams and a movie" date with Pete. O'Ryan eased down from his chair and trotted along behind me.

I opened my closet and pulled out a couple of possible outfits and laid them on the bed. O'Ryan, good boy that he is, jumped onto the bed, moving gracefully among pants, shirts, and sweaters without feet, tail, or whiskers touching even one garment. The cat moved to the edge of the bed then, stretching out one paw toward the cherrywood frame, craning his neck as though he wanted to look into the glass.

"Want to see yourself? Vanity, thy name is cat!" I tilted the oval frame in his direction, then selected a blue-and-white-checked cotton shirt and a pair of navy cropped pants from the items on the bed. Holding the shirt to my chest with one hand, pants to my waist in the other, I stood where I could see my own reflection.

I was about to try the navy pants with a short-sleeved yellow blouse and navy sweater when my mirror image faded. The flashing lights and swirling colors that often precede a vision spread across the glass. As usual, I didn't want to watch whatever was going to appear, and as usual, I couldn't look away.

Once again, I saw the pretty gazebo, close-up this time, and in more detail. It was in full sunlight, and although the white paint looked fresh, I could tell that the structure itself was not new. The gingerbread and intricate curlicues on the sides showed the subtle cracks of age and the worn surfaces of long usage. The person I'd seen there before was still seated, facing away from me toward the calm, sparkling sea in the distance.

I could tell this time that the seated figure was a man. He wore a black jacket. Black trousers. Formal looking.

A tuxedo maybe?

A yellow paw snaked out, tapping the mirror, and as I watched, the scene revolved slowly until my vantage point was from the opposite side of the structure. Yes, I was right. The man, sitting upright and facing me, definitely wore a tuxedo.

O'Ryan tapped the mirror again, and, like the zoom lens on a camera, the man appeared in close focus. I recognized him immediately. Christopher Rich. He sat there, unmoving, eyes wide, facing the sea.

Once again, the close-up of the man. Those wide eyes were blank, unseeing. I'd seen eyes like that before.

Dead eyes.

CHAPTER 7

As quickly as it had appeared, the macabre scene vanished. The mirror showed only a startled redhead, a yellow blouse hanging limply from one hand.

Christopher Rich. Dead?

No. He was alive. River said she'd spoken to him this morning. He'd barely escaped death, though, according to the TV. I put the blouse on the bed and sat down next to O'Ryan, who'd apparently lost interest in mirror tapping and, facing the wall, had closed his eyes.

So what was the vision trying to tell me? The mysterious, but beautiful, gazebo that overlooked a nameless beach—or maybe a shadowy graveyard—was somehow associated with witches—or a witch—or, more specifically, a *dead* witch. Of course, it was one who wasn't actually dead at all.

One of the many problems associated with being a scryer is the fact that the visions never have a distinguishable timeline. They can depict scenes from the past, the present, and occasionally the future. They also can appear on just about any reflective surface.

For me, they started out by showing up on shiny black things. Now I'm apt to see them in mirrors, store windows, even silverware or kitchen appliances.

I decided to wear the yellow blouse and navy sweater and try to forget about the vision. I knew from past experience that the thing would probably eventually make some kind of sense.

But those dead eyes were pretty hard to forget.

By the time Pete arrived I'd managed to once again focus my thoughts on what was real—not some hazy mirror image of the nonexistent. What was real to me just then—and beginning to be quite appealing—was the internship at WICH-TV. I could hardly wait to tell him about my visit with Bruce Doan.

"Hey, you were right," I said, the moment he opened the door.

"Good," he said, and gave me a brief, but sincere, kiss. "About what?"

"Mr. Doan. He actually did offer me a job. Kind of."

"What kind of kind of job?"

"Investigative reporter." I paused for dramatic effect, then smiled. "Kind of. It's an internship for the summer. What do you think about it?"

"Are you kidding? I think you should do it. When do you start?"

"I start a week from Thursday. Dube's for fried clams to celebrate?"

"Absolutely. And *Manchester by the Sea* is playing again at Cinema Salem."

"Perfect," I said. "We don't even have to do the ritual coin toss. That was my pick too."

"Movie first?"

I agreed. We headed for the comfortable neighborhood theater (where the popcorn is made with real butter) and watched Kyle Chandler and Casey Affleck as the story played out against background scenery Pete and I know well. The *real* Manchester by the Sea is just a few miles away from Salem and we nudged one another and whispered as we recognized places we knew in Beverly, Lynn, and Gloucester. There was one distance shot that took my concentration away from the on-screen troubles. The actors were on a boat, passing the typical patchwork scenery of Cape Ann's coastline—mansions and shacks, yachts and lobster boats, columning wharves and massive pilings, the old Tarr and Wonson Paint Factory and Hammond Castle. The thing that captured my attention, though, was a small white gazebo. It wasn't the one in my vision. It was a much plainer version, but similar enough to bring back the beach and the dead Christopher Rich.

After the movie we drove over to Jefferson Avenue and Dube's seafood restaurant. It's been there forever. Aunt Ibby remembers going there with her parents! We ordered their justly famous fried clams. "Hey, we're here to celebrate your new job. You okay?" Pete asked. "You're awfully quiet."

"I'm okay," I said. "It's just that, well . . . I know you don't like to talk about it, but . . ."

"You've been seeing things?" That's what Pete calls the scryer thing I do—"seeing things."

"Yes. Afraid so. Can I tell you about it?"

He reached for my hand. "Of course you can, Lee. You can always tell me about anything. And it isn't that I don't like to talk about it. It's the fact that you see these things, things that frighten you, and there's nothing I can do to protect you from them."

I hadn't ever thought about it that way. There was such sincerity, such love in his eyes that I felt tears welling up in mine. "Thank you, Pete," I whispered. "I always want to share these things with you, whatever they are—wherever they come from. But sometimes—no, *usually*—they don't make any sense."

He smiled and squeezed my hand. "Try me."

I took a deep breath. "Okay. There's been more than one in the past few days. I've tried to put them out of my mind but a scene in the movie tonight brought them back."

Our food arrived and it gave me a moment to sort out my thoughts. Since Christopher Rich had, as River said, blabbed to a reporter about Gloria Tasker and Mr. Bagenstose being witches after the attempt on his own life, I didn't have to protect their secret anymore. Pete and the rest of the police force undoubtedly knew now that someone wanted to kill witches in Salem.

What does a pretty little white gazebo have to do with it?

Pete put ketchup on his fried clams and passed the bottle to me. "Go on," he prompted. "Tell me what you saw."

I told him in as much detail as I could remember about each of the two scenes the mirror had shown.

He frowned. "So the figure you saw in the first one, the man sitting in the gazebo who had his back turned to you, turned out to be the shop owner Rich in the second one?"

"Right." I nodded. "He was dead. At least he definitely *looked* dead to me."

"He's very much alive. Whoever took a shot at him last night missed him by a mile. There are a couple of bullet holes in the wall of the building. Forensics is working on that."

"So maybe someone, even someone who's a bad shot, is targeting witches?"

"I didn't say that. I suppose your friend River must have tipped you off that Bagenstose and Tasker were witches?"

"She did," I admitted. "I wanted to tell you but River said even their families might not have known about it."

"We knew about them."

I was surprised. "You did?"

"Sure. Some of their fellow witches tipped us off as soon as Ms. Tasker got run down."

"Of course." I suddenly got it. "They were worried about their own safety."

"I didn't say that," he repeated. "Why? Is River worried?" He cocked his head to one side the way he does when he's trying to figure something out. "Did she say she was?"

Had River seemed worried about her own safety?

I paused before answering.

"Not exactly," I said.

He raised a questioning eyebrow.

"You're going to think this is strange," I began. "I know I think it is. River is worried, but not about her own safety."

"Go on."

"I don't want you to take this the wrong way"—I dropped my voice, aware of others at nearby tables who might overhear—"but River is afraid the deaths—including Megan's—could be her fault."

"Her fault? How's that? What did she do?"

"Oh, Pete, she didn't *do* anything. She said she had some 'bad thoughts' about Gloria and Mr. Bagenstose and even about Megan. She's worried that she could have put some kind of spell on them."

"Thoughts don't kill people."

"That's exactly what I told her. She said that in the old days—in the old religion—bad thoughts *could* kill people."

He was quiet for a long moment. The waitress cleared away our dishes, brought coffee and a doggie bag with a few fried clams for O'Ryan. Pete spoke in his cop voice.

"Did River have bad thoughts about Christopher Rich too?"

"She didn't say so. I'm sure they were friends, even though she was a little bit annoyed because he'd talked to the press about the others secretly being witches."

"Yeah, I thought that was a little over the top too." His normal voice was back. "Especially since their friends and relatives didn't know about it."

"They didn't?"

"Far as we can tell they didn't. The board of directors at the bank wasn't too pleased about learning that Bagenstose was one of those . . . um, people."

"I'll bet. Did Gloria have any family?"

"Not around here." He picked up the check. "Ready?"

There was no more conversation about witches, living or dead, on the ride back to Winter Street. Instead, we talked about my summer job at the TV station.

"I think you'll enjoy it, Lee," he said. "You still have friends at the station, so it won't be like starting at a brand new place." He smiled. "Even though the job description is a lot different than the last one you had there."

"You mean the 'call yourself Crystal Moon, dress up

in ruffles and beads and hoop earrings every night, consult the obsidian ball, ask people for their birthdates, and totally fake the answers to whatever they ask'? That job?"

"That's the one. You made an awfully cute fortune-teller, though."

I didn't regret everything about my brief stint as the host of *Nightshades*. After all, that was how I met Pete. "I still have some of the costumes, you know. Wink-wink."

We pulled up in front of the house on Winter Street. "If I didn't have to go to work early, I'd ask for a fashion show," he said, pulling me close for a good-night kiss. "Wink-wink back atcha."

He waited while I ran up the stairs to the front door. I turned and waved as I put my key in the lock. O'Ryan, as always, was just inside, peeking from one of the narrow side windows. Pete gave a brief wave and a tiny toot of the horn and drove away as I opened the door and entered the foyer.

"Hi, O'Ryan," I said, holding the doggie bag over his head. "Brought you a goodie." The lights were off in Aunt Ibby's living room and there was no sound of TV, radio, or Alexa issuing from the rest of the first floor, so I assumed that my aunt had already gone upstairs to her room on the second floor. I locked the front door, activating the alarm system, and climbed the stairs with the cat, pink nose and whiskers twitching, following me up to my apartment.

While O'Ryan nibbled—more or less daintily—on his cold fried clams, I changed into jammies and turned on the bedroom TV. The new guy, Buck Covington, was in the anchor chair and I was interested in watching him work. As Mr. Doan had said, he looked good and his voice was excellent. The facial expressions matched the words—happy face for the kids' lemonade stand for charity report, solemn demeanor for a four-alarm fire in Saugus. There was no further mention of the near-shooting of Christopher Rich. If Covington was really "dumb as a brick" it surely didn't show. His reading of the prompter was letter perfect. Not a flubbed word or mispronounced syllable that I could spot.

O'Ryan joined me on the bed, washed his face and paws, then curled up on the pillow beside me. Since it was Sunday, River's show wasn't on and I didn't want to watch WICH-TV's video of highlights from last summer's Topsfield Fair. Flipping through the channels, I landed in the middle of one of my old favorites, the hilarious *Hocus Pocus*, where Bette Midler led the antics of three witches back in Salem after three centuries away. It reminded me of River's warning that the old-time witches could really do some evil stuff with their "bad thoughts."

If only the deaths of three twenty-first-century Salem witches and the near-miss shooting of another were funny.

They weren't. I pulled my cat closer and turned off the TV. The deaths of Gloria Tasker and Elliot Bagenstose could easily have been dismissed as coincidental. Megan's passing was quite certainly age related. But Christopher Rich's experience led to the almost unavoidable conclusion.

Even if Pete didn't want to say so, someone out there was targeting Salem's witches.

CHAPTER 8

It was Monday morning, the last day of the school year at the Tabitha Trumbull Academy for the Arts. I dressed carefully for the occasion in a gray striped business suit, white frilly blouse, and gray heels. It's not exactly a graduation as the Tabby doesn't award degrees. The programs in the arts including music, dance, painting, acting, writing, and—in my case—TV production are open to everyone. All that's needed is a desire to learn (and the ability to pay the not-insignificant tuition). There's a commencement ceremony, though, where students, guests, and faculty gather in the Tabby's theater for school director Rupert Pennington's final address of the year, followed by a reception with tea and punch, dainty sandwiches, and cookies.

I joined my fellow faculty members on stage. We were seated in a double row of chairs behind the podium, facing the audience. Mr. Pennington, his back to us, approached his lectern raising his hands for silence. The hum of conversation stilled. I looked out over the sea of faces, trying to spot my TV production students. There'd been six of them this year—two men and four women. Dorothy Alden had already returned to her home in Alaska, but I expected that the rest of them must be part of the crowd. I spotted the Temple twins and Hilda Mendez sitting together near the front of the room. Therese would be filming the procedure, of course, and I was sure that Shannon Dumas would be there. Shannon had told me that she and her handsome artist fiancé, Dakota Berman, were coming and that they planned to bring a surprise member of the wedding party with them. I hadn't yet met Dakota's best man and assumed that would be the surprise. I looked forward to meeting him and wondered if he was another artist.

"Welcome, welcome," Mr. Pennington intoned. "We've come to the end of yet another successful school year here at the Tabitha Trumbull Academy for the Arts. Our dancers have earned acclaim, performing in venues around the country." He paused for applause, and the instructors of the various disciplines of dance each rose, looking slightly embarrassed. Theater arts, oil painting, and watercolor instructors were introduced next, with ringing words about award-winning art exhibits and smash-hit play productions. The music department was lauded with mention of the Tabby Band taking part in the St. Patrick's Day parade in Boston, and the school orchestra playing at the mayor's inauguration ceremony. The directors, instructors, and arrangers stood and bowed. The creative writing classes were next, with instructors in poetry, short stories, novels, and magazine articles praised and thanked. TV production was mentioned last and, because I was the one and only instructor, least. "Ms. Barrett's TV production classes have not only brought much favorable publicity to the school," Mr. Pennington said, "but have resulted in two generous government grants. Several of her students have already gone on to productive careers within the industry."

I stood, acknowledged the applause, smiled modestly, and sat down as quickly as I could. During that brief moment of standing, I looked over the crowd. Therese, with her video camera, stood in the center aisle focusing on Mr. Pennington. Aunt Ibby, beaming proudly, was in the first row along with the mayor and other dignitaries. Dating the head man has its advantages. I continued to scan the faces in the audience looking for Shannon—who was not known for being punctual—then settled back in my chair, concentrating on the welcoming words from Mr. Pennington—who was not known for being brief. He was about ten minutes into his speech when I became aware of some kind of commotion at the rear of the theater. The house lights were all on, so it was not difficult to see what was happening. Mr. Pennington shaded his eyes with one hand, peering toward the back door.

Shannon Dumas had arrived. The disturbance, causing a growing buzz of conversation, wasn't due to the fact that Shannon is uncommonly pretty, nor because her fiancé, Dakota Berman, was undoubtedly the handsomest man in the room. It was because there was a very large black and white bird perched on her shoulder—and the bird, nodding left and right as the couple moved down the aisle, called out quite plainly and repeatedly, "Who loves ya, baby?"

"Sorry," Shannon called out. "He'll stop in a minute. Hush, Poe!" Holding the bird by a blue leash attached to its leg, she smiled, flashing dimples, and the couple slid into aisle seats close to the rear of the long room.

The bird did indeed stop talking, although some members of the audience didn't, and the director resumed his address, picking up where he'd been interrupted, at the part about the many long years of retail success the Trumbull family had enjoyed in the old building. Could this large, talking bird be the surprise member of the wedding party Shannon had announced?

Concentrating on the speech was out of the question by then. The summer internship at the station might have to take a backseat to wedding planning for a while, I realized. The upcoming nuptials had already become more complicated than I'd anticipated. I'd been a bridesmaid before, but never maid of honor. Some honor! I'd probably have to arrange for a custom-made tuxedo for a bird along with everything else. The mental picture nearly made me laugh aloud.

A burst of applause indicated that Mr. Pennington's speech had come to a close and I once again focused on the present. Bobby Millard, one of the painting instructors and a high school classmate of mine, leaned across the seat between us. "Isn't that one of your people? The girl with the bird?"

"Uh-huh." My reply was hesitant. "Shannon Dumas. Good student." I was about to add something along the lines of "I didn't even know she had a bird. It's a surprise to me," but Bobby, grinning, continued. "It's an African pied crow. A beauty! I'd heard they could talk but I never had the chance to hear one before. Can you introduce me to—what's her name? Shannon?"

"Sure," I said. "A pid crow, you called it?"

"Right. It's spelled p-i-e-d. But you say 'pid.' It means patchy, mottled, kind of like an early Jackson Pollack.

See the random white feathers on it?" He lowered his voice. "I don't think Pennington was too happy about being interrupted but he recovered pretty well, didn't he?"

We left the stage and Bobby followed me down the aisle toward Shannon and Dakota, who were already surrounded by a small crowd. "It takes a lot to rattle Mr. Pennington," I said. "But I guess 'Who loves ya, baby' in the middle of a speech could do it."

"Ruffle his feathers, so to speak." Bobby laughed at his own bad pun and we joined the chattering group around the young couple. Therese was there too, focusing her camera on the black and white bird, which was now perched on the back of a chair while still attached by a little strap on its leg to the bright blue leather leash, tied to Shannon's wrist.

"Oh, hello, Lee," Shannon called. "Come and meet Poe. He's going to be ring bearer at our wedding."

"Here comes the bride," the bird said, fixing a bright black eye on me. "Who loves ya, baby?" On closer inspection, the thing looked enormous. It stood about a foot tall and the beak looked like a formidable weapon. I backed away instinctively.

"Does he bite?" I asked.

"He could if he wanted to, I guess," she said. "He's never bitten me and I've known him all my life."

I introduced Bobby, who stood a good distance away from Poe too. "You never mentioned that you had a . . . pet bird," I said.

Dakota spoke up. "Oh, he's not ours. Belongs to Shannon's dad. She's staying at his place in Marblehead to take care of Poe 'til her father gets back from a business trip. He'll be here for the wedding, of course.

So will Poe, so we thought we'd give him something to do. They're very social, these crows."

"You said you've known him all your life, Shannon," I said, surprised. "How old is he?"

"He's over twenty," she said. "My dad hand raised him. He has his own aviary behind Daddy's house, with heat and air-conditioning and even a TV."

"He especially likes those window glass cleaner TV commercials with the crows in them," Dakota said.

"Aren't you Dakota Berman?" Bobby asked the groom-to-be. "You do those fabulous cemetery paintings, don't you?"

Dakota nodded modestly. "Guilty."

"I teach watercolors and pastels here at the Tabby." Bobby looked hopeful. "Maybe sometime next semester you'll come and talk to my class? Maybe do a little demonstration of your technique?"

"Glad to." The two men moved to one side and continued their conversation about art, while I focused on the plan of a crow being part of the wedding party. "The idea about Poe being a ring bearer is quite original, Shannon." I tried to keep my tone level, without any hint of surprise, bewilderment, or annoyance—all of which were present at the moment. I returned the bird's baleful glare. "Why didn't you tell us about this, um, *unusual* pet before this?"

She stroked the bird's head gently. "Never thought about it. As I said, he belongs to my dad. Poe knows me pretty well, though—ever since I was a little girl. Don't you, Poe?" The bird said "pretty girl" and lifted its wings slightly.

Oh my God. The thing must have a wingspan a yard wide!

"Are his wings clipped?" I asked, backing away a little farther. "I mean, can he fly?"

"Oh sure. He can fly. But don't worry. I have him tethered." She tapped the blue leash.

"You plan for Poe here to be ring bearer then?"

"Right. My dad will be giving me away, of course, and Poe will be on his shoulder when we come down the aisle together. I'll hand my bouquet to the maid of honor. That's you, Lee." Big smile. "Poe will have the rings in a little mesh bag tied to one foot. I'll untie it and hand the rings to the minister. Then Daddy and Poe go and sit down in the first row and the ceremony goes on. Cool, huh?"

"Yes. Cool. Of course. And out of the ordinary, to say the least."

"I know." Shannon sighed a happy sigh. "Therese says it'll make a great video. Maybe even go viral."

I had to agree. "I wouldn't be a bit surprised. But look, Mr. Pennington seems to be making his way down the aisle in this direction. Perhaps you and Poe should head outside." The director was not smiling.

"Oops. Come on, Dakota." She tugged at her fiancé's elbow. "Let's go. Maybe we'd better skip the reception, huh? See you tomorrow, Lee? Gown shopping?"

"Huh? Oh, sure." I'd forgotten all about the bridal shop appointment. Oh well, I'd figure out how to fit it in. *Everything will get done on time. It'll all turn out fine,* I told myself. I watched Shannon, Dakota, and the bird hurrying toward the exit. The bird had turned his head around to what looked like an impossible angle and it seemed to me those bright eyes were once again fixed on me. "Who loves ya, baby?" he screeched. "Hey, Red! Who loves ya?"

* * *

I dutifully attended the reception that was held on the top floors of the Trumbull Building, in the handsomely restored (and reputedly haunted) suite of rooms that had long ago housed the Trumbull family. The enormous dining room, with glittering chandelier and twelve-foot-long Empire mahogany banquet table, displayed assorted food offerings to great advantage. I smiled when I recognized Fabio, the baker from Pretty Party, filling huge silver platters with a variety of gorgeous pastries, performing the restocking duties with a magician's flourish. Students, staff, family members, and guests wandered through the luxurious apartment or sat in conversational groups nibbling on the catered delicacies.

I chatted briefly with the Temple twins, two retired Boston police officers looking forward to second careers in TV, and talked to Therese's parents, who, as always, thanked me profusely for encouraging their daughter's interest in photography. (They were, however, blissfully unaware of her interest in witchcraft.)

I nibbled on a miniature chocolate éclair, and balancing a pressed glass punch cup, I strolled from room to spacious room until I found myself alone in one that had long ago been Tabitha Trumbull's "sitting room." I guess now we'd call it her home office. I pictured her at the small desk, filling out the recipe cards that Aunt Ibby had brought back to new life in her "Tabitha Trumbull Cookbook." I sat in Tabitha's chair and tried to concentrate on the present—my own personal present.

It's hard to focus thoughts when a crow you've never seen before calls you by one of your nicknames, but, turning that aside for the moment, I thought about the upcoming wedding. I did remember, once

Shannon had jogged my memory, that we had a morning appointment at Blushing Bride, in Peabody, one of the North Shore's most famous bridal salons. Finding a wedding dress appropriate for an outdoor event, and coordinated outfits for me and bridesmaids Hilda Mendez and Shannon's cousin, Maureen, shouldn't be too complicated.

I took a sip of punch and moved on to thoughts about the job I'd just accepted at WICH-TV. I'd said I could dig up my own topics to investigate. I was beginning to hope for assignments instead. I realized that I hadn't the first clue on anything interesting. Except the seeming spate of witch deaths in Salem, and I didn't feel ready, willing, or even remotely qualified to delve into that.

Just in passing, was a talking crow who called me "Red," my not-very-favorite nickname, a sufficient attention grabber? I didn't think so. My recent scrying experiences might be leading me toward something noteworthy. They usually do, but so far I couldn't figure out what they meant. What was the meaning of a Victorian gazebo and a dead witch—Christopher Rich—who wasn't really dead, but who'd apparently been shot at?

All this reverie led nowhere, so I didn't mind in the least being interrupted when Bobby Millard appeared in the doorway of the room. "Oh, here you are. Mind if I join you for a minute, Lee?" he said. Not waiting for an answer, he slid into a rose floral upholstered green wicker arm chair and faced me, his expression serious. "I just overheard something I think you might want to know about."

"Sure. What is it?"

"First of all, I think you've known me long enough

to know I'm not a nosy person. I mean, I don't go around purposely eavesdropping on other people's conversations."

"Of course you don't, Bobby."

"It's just that I happened to be standing right behind them. I wasn't trying to listen to what they were talking about."

"Slow down," I said. "Standing behind who?"

"Oh, Dakota Berman and Shannon. Did I tell you Dakota might speak to my class next semester?"

"Yes. I was there when you asked him. So you overheard something Dakota and Shannon were talking about?" I prompted.

"Right. It was about their best man."

"I haven't met him yet. I guess he's from out of town." I frowned. "I don't even know his name."

"I do." Bobby shook his head and leaned back in the chair. "I recognized that name as soon as I heard Dakota say it. Sean Madigan." He looked at me expectantly, as though he thought I should recognize that name too. Sean Madigan. I didn't.

"Sorry," I said. "Should that mean something to me?"

"It was in all the papers six years ago," Bobby said. "He went to jail."

"That was back when I was living in Florida," I said. "Must have missed it. Anyway, what does this Sean Madigan person have to do with Dakota? Why did he go to jail?"

Bobby moved forward in his chair again, looking at me intently while a new thought flashed through my poor tired brain.

I'm involved in a wedding where not only is a bird the ring bearer, but—according to Bobby—a jailbird is the best man.

"I went to some classes with Sean in Boston. Museum of Fine Arts."

Would he ever get to the point? I hoped he didn't ramble this way when he taught his art students at the Tabby. "I know. Famous school. Bobby, what did you hear?"

"I didn't even realize he was out of jail, you know? Did six years. Sentenced to ten but had good behavior, I guess. Anyway Shannon was telling Dakota that she's worried about having Sean stay at her dad's house on account of his being—you know—kind of a thief."

"What kind of a thief? What did this guy steal?"

"Paintings. He stole small, very good paintings from small, very good museums. I don't remember how he did it exactly, but I'm going to look it up. Anyway, then he copied them and put them back. Got away with it for quite a while too." Bobby's tone had slipped from worried to respectful. "Of course, eventually he got caught. Anyway, they haven't told Shannon's dad who the best man is going to be yet. But see, they have to. Sean's in Salem already and now Shannon's invited him to stay at her dad's place. Big, big house. You ever seen it?"

"No. I never have. If this Sean has—as they say—paid his debt to society, won't Shannon's father be understanding about it?" I paused for a moment, thinking of this rather peculiar crime. "Why did he do it? Steal them then put them back?"

"Sold the copies as the real thing to underground collectors. He's really very good at making copies. We all made copies at the museum. Copying the masters is part of the learning process. But later on Sean took it to another level." His tone reflected grudging admiration. "The son of a gun figured out how to do the varnishes, the brushwork, the type of canvas, the cracking of the paint. Never used pigments or binding that was introduced after the artist's death. Amazing talent."

"You said 'underground collectors'?"

"Yeah. There are people who don't care if a painting is stolen. They just want to own a real Cézanne, or Degas, or Van Gogh, or whatever."

"They must have to keep it hidden. Never show it to anybody. How strange."

"I know. Anyway. Madigan would anonymously sell copies to two or three of these collectors for big bucks—in cash—then send the original back to where he'd stolen it from."

"Uh-oh. How'd he do that?'

"Rolled it up, put it in a tube mailer, and dropped it in a mailbox. Always from another state. Then after a while, probably when he ran out of money, he'd steal another one, paint copies, find a new group of collectors—they're all over the world, you know—and do it again."

That made a certain amount of sense. "I see. And when the collectors learned that the real one had been returned, they couldn't report the fakes because knowingly buying stolen paintings is a crime."

He nodded. "Right. Anyway, Sean's the one who taught Dakota how to do those paintings that look like gravestone rubbings. You've seen them. Wonderful things." Bobby gave a low whistle. "I hope when he visits my class next semester he'll give a demonstration. You think he might? You seem to know him pretty well."

"He does them in plain sight at the cemetery, so I don't see why he wouldn't." I didn't actually know

Dakota all that well. We'd met only a few months ago, but I had to admit to myself, it'd been a pretty intense couple of months—involving one of Salem's most historic cemeteries where not all of the bodies always rest in peace. I stood, brushing a few crumbs from my skirt, and picked up my empty punch cup. "Well, guess I should get back to the reception."

"Me too," Bobby said and followed me down one of the long corridors to the Trumbull's formal parlor, with its blue moire taffeta wall coverings, antique furniture, and assorted oil paintings in gilded frames.

I wonder if the paintings are originals or copies. How can you tell?

I said so long to Bobby and looked around for Aunt Ibby. Deciding that she'd probably already left, I chatted for a few minutes with visitors, ate a tiny frosted cupcake, and took the elegantly appointed Trumbull family elevator down one floor. The old store elevators provided the rest of the trip to the street level. I liked those best. The directory on the pressed tin walls still bore the original postings: *lingerie; foundations; hosiery; sportswear; millinery . . .*

The Buick wasn't in the parking lot. Neither was Dakota Berman's pickup truck. I assumed that the engaged couple and their crow had (wisely) left the premises. I backed the Vette out and headed down Washington Street to Church Street to home.

There are lots of beautiful trees in our neighborhood— maples, oaks, chestnuts. They're always pretty. In the springtime the chestnut trees are bright with green buds and even some white blossoms. Summer brings the full display of leaves and fruit, acorns and chestnuts, and in the fall the resplendent golds and reds and browns are magnificent. Even in winter when snow and ice coat bare branches, they glisten like diamonds. But on this early summer day, after the commencement at the Tabby, when I turned onto Oliver Street the trees had a different look. It seemed that they were full of birds. Dark birds calling to one another. Blackbirds? Ravens?

They were crows. Not the black and white mottled ones, the pied crows. These were plain old black crows. Nothing rare there. But I didn't remember ever seeing them in numbers like this in our neighborhood. There must have been about fifty of them in and around the trees along the street, and their raucous "caw-caw-caw" was both loud and monotonous.

Maybe, I told myself, maybe they'd just arrived from down south, like the robins do every spring. Do crows migrate? I'd have to ask Aunt Ibby. It's very handy, having a reference librarian for an aunt. My own live-in, human Google. I tapped my garage door opener and pulled the Vette inside, hoping that the noisy birds hadn't pooped on it, and parked next to the Buick.

She beat me home. Maybe she skipped the reception. I didn't see her in the Trumbull suite.

Hurrying through the backyard, past Aunt Ibby's vegetable and herb garden, I wondered how a scarecrow might look among the pole beans and pumpkins. After climbing the back steps I unlocked the door. As usual, O'Ryan was there to greet me with loud purrs and his "cat smile," kind of a head cocked to one side, eyes wide, happy look on his fuzzy face. I bent and picked him up, disregarding the likelihood of cat hair on the needs-to-be-dry-cleaned suit. I pulled the door closed, realizing at that moment that the bird noise had suddenly stopped.

I paused for a moment, debating whether to start up the stairs to my apartment or stop to check on my aunt. O'Ryan made that decision for me, jumping down from my arms and disappearing through the cat door into Aunt Ibby's kitchen. I heard the clink of dishes and the ping of pans, so I knew she was in there cooking—or cleaning. I knocked.

"Is that you, Maralee?" she called. "Wait a second while I dry my hands."

"It's me." I answered. "Take your time. Just want to say hi."

"Come in, come in." She opened the door, wiping her hands on a red-and-white-striped apron with "Kiss the Cook" embroidered on it. "It was a lovely ceremony, wasn't it? I thought Rupert's speech was excellent, didn't you?"

"Excellent," I agreed, not remembering much of what he'd said. "But I missed seeing you at the reception. Were you there?"

"No. I skipped it." She patted her waistline. "Didn't need the calories, and besides, I had some research I wanted to do."

"Research? About what?"

"Crows," she said.

CHAPTER 9

"Crows? Like the ones in the trees out back?" I asked. "What's going on with them anyway?"

"That's what the Massachusetts Audubon Society is trying to figure out. You know I'm a member." My aunt spoke proudly.

"Of course." O'Ryan, checking out the contents of his red bowl, looked up at the mention of crows and gave a low growl. The sound surprised me. He's always shown a normal catlike interest in birds, but I've never known him to harm one. "Sounds as though O'Ryan doesn't like them in his yard."

"I know. It's uncommon for them to be here in Salem in such numbers at this time of year. That's what we're trying to figure out."

"Do they migrate here from some other place? I was wondering about that just a few minutes ago."

"Some do. We have a year-round population and then there are the ones who fly down south in the winter. They should be coming back. We're thinking that maybe these birds have come from south of here and are stopping in Salem for some reason on their way home."

"They don't usually do that?"

"I've been here all my life, Maralee, and I've never seen anything like it. They're all over the city."

"Interesting," I said. "Very interesting. In fact, do you think it might be a good topic for a beginning investigative reporter to look into?"

Her eyes sparkled and a smile lit up her face. "It's perfect! I'll bet Bruce Doan will love it."

"I'm counting on that," I said.

"I've already started digging into it, so why don't you check with him?"

"I will," I said. "Right away. And I'll see if he'll assign Therese to video the action. We'll get started first thing in the morning."

O'Ryan looked up from his bowl. "Nnyah," he said.

"No?"

"Nnyah."

"Oh, you're right. I have to go gown shopping tomorrow morning with Shannon."

Aunt Ibby laughed. "You realize you're talking to a cat, don't you?"

I nodded. "Yeah. You do it too." It was true. There's no doubt about it. O'Ryan is no ordinary house cat. I can't explain it and wouldn't even try. It may have something to do with the witch Ariel. O'Ryan, so people say, was her "familiar." We just know he's special.

"Well, you may as well begin gathering information," my aunt said, hanging her apron on a hook behind the pantry door. "It'll probably impress Mr. Doan if you have a grasp of some facts about the creatures before you propose the project. Want to see what I've learned so far?"

"I do. Let me run upstairs and change fast into something comfortable and I'll be right back."

I wasn't kidding about changing fast. O'Ryan followed me up to my apartment, where I washed my face and hands, brushed some cat hair from the suit and hung it carefully in my closet, and put on faded old cutoffs and a Police Athletic League T-shirt. Racing down the back stairs, I even beat the cat to the kitchen. Having an idea for my brand new investigative reporter gig was exciting, and getting some answers to the mysterious sudden influx of crows to Salem made the whole thing more intriguing.

I joined Aunt Ibby in her office, where she looked happily at home amid her impressive collection of the latest gadgets from the world of technology. "Look, Maralee. This is interesting. It says here that one reason we're seeing so many crows in urban areas lately is because of the plentiful food sources we humans provide for them—like parking lots and along roadsides."

"I hadn't thought about it, but I guess it's true. I mean the parking lots outside fast-food places alone must provide plenty of French fries and bread crumbs." I frowned. "There aren't any fast-food places around here, but there are sure lots of birds in the trees on Oliver Street."

"Winter Street too. Maybe they're building nesting sites." She sounded doubtful. "People all over the city are posting notices and pictures about crows in their neighborhoods that hadn't been there before. There's something unusual going on."

Thoughts of the old Alfred Hitchcock movie came to mind, but I didn't say anything about that to my aunt. For over an hour we researched crows. And ravens. And magpies. And grackles. We looked up all the black-feathered members of the family Corvidae we could think of and came up with quite a few reasons why groups of crows had chosen to congregate in various neighborhoods all over the city—but no explanation of why similar things were not happening in nearby cities. Aunt Ibby contacted bird-watchers in Beverly, Danvers, Peabody, Boxford, Gloucester, Marblehead. Nothing out of the ordinary crow-wise was apparently going on in any of their communities. In fact, the crow-tree phenomenon seemed to begin and end at the Salem city limits.

"What did you think of Shannon's feathered friend?" I asked my aunt. "Of course, Poe isn't a common American crow, so I guess he's not involved in these strange roostings, nestings, or whatever they're doing."

"The pied crow. A handsome bird. I like his name," she said. "But how did he know your nickname? Had you met before today?"

"Nope. That was kind of creepy. He's going to be ring bearer at the wedding. I just found out about it. Shannon's father raised Poe practically from an egg, I guess. He's over twenty."

"Crows are remarkably intelligent. I don't doubt for a minute that Shannon can train him to be a ring bearer. He's probably known someone with red hair before. Since he's a pet, though, I'm quite sure he isn't part of this murder of crows that's suddenly landed in Salem."

"What did you call it? A *murder* of crows?"

"Uh-huh. That's the term for a big group of them. Like a flock of sheep. A herd of cows. A murder of crows."

CHAPTER 10

I didn't like the sound of it. A murder of crows. If Aunt Ibby said it was so, it was so. But I still didn't like it. "Why not a flock? A gaggle? A swarm?" I asked. "Why on earth would they call it a 'murder'?"

"There are several theories about that," she said. "I don't believe anybody really knows. But Maralee, wouldn't it make a grand title for your investigative report?"

Bingo! She was right. I thought of what the station manager had said: "Talk about something interesting that the community needs to know about."

"Mr. Doan will love it," I said. "I'm almost beginning to love it myself. Let's print out what we've found so far and I'll put together a presentation for him."

Two hours later it was finished. Pleased with myself, I admired the typewritten pages. Footnoted dissertations on the species, copies of bulletins from the Audubon Society, an article by Roger Tory Peterson, and a couple of nice clear photos of the crows in an oak tree next to our garage. They'd all stopped squawking and cawing for a moment and seemed to be posing for my camera. The black cat with the red collar who'd been hanging around our yard lately was in one of the pictures, sitting on the back fence, making a nice contrast to the birds. Aunt Ibby had provided current Nielsen figures from shows about birds on the Discovery Channel. I put the whole thing in a clear plastic binder titled "A Murder of Crows," feeling sure that Mr. Doan would happily agree to my investigation of the "Great Salem Crow Invasion."

Pete and I hadn't made any plans for the evening. His PAL peewee hockey team had an out-of-town tournament going on, so I had plenty of time to grab one of my old college textbooks and do a little studying about my new career move. I grabbed a Pepsi from the refrigerator and sat at the kitchen table with the open book in front of me. The window was partially open, admitting a gentle spring breeze with the faint smell of roses. The raucous cawing from the birds had stopped, at least for the moment, and O'Ryan hopped up onto the windowsill next to me, peering over my shoulder at the printed words.

The chapter began with a succinct definition. *Investigative journalism is the process of researching and telling a story, usually one that someone else is trying to hide.*

Trying to hide? I knew there was a story to tell. I knew Aunt Ibby and I were equipped to do careful research. But clearly no one could hide hundreds, probably thousands, of crows. And if anyone knew the reason for this strange bird behavior, why would that person try to hide it?

I put the book down, took a sip of soda, and looked out the kitchen window. O'Ryan followed my gaze. There were no cats on the fence. There wouldn't have been room for them. Crows, evenly spaced, sat in a long silent row along the top of the wooden boards. I looked from the crows to the cat and back. O'Ryan was silent too. No low growl. No cat comment at all on the sight.

After a while, one by one, the crows flew away—some toward Winter Street, some toward Oliver—and one by one, the visiting cats appeared. The small gray cat was first. I was quite sure she came from Pete's sister Marie's neighborhood. At least that's where I'd first seen her. I thought that Frankie, the white cat, lived somewhere nearby, maybe even next door on Winter Street. I hadn't seen the sleek black lady cat with the red collar for a long time, but she looked well fed and well cared for. Maybe she belonged to one of the fine old homes on nearby Washington Square. O'Ryan watched from his vantage point as each of the three girl cats took her position on the fence. He lay quietly sprawled out full length along the sill. I returned to my reading.

A good investigative reporter is curious, determined, and possesses a well-developed sense of skepticism.

I mentally checked off those attributes, comfortable in believing I had them all, although I'm not quite as skeptical as I once was. A lot has happened in my life recently that has left some of my former beliefs turned upside down.

An internship with a local news agency is excellent preparation for this rewarding career.

"I have the internship part pretty much nailed down," I told O'Ryan, whose eyes were closed and who didn't appear to be listening. "Maybe the rewarding career will come along eventually."

He moved his ears forward slightly and gave a quick flick of his tail—which might mean "Good for you," or

"Don't bother me. I'm sleeping." Maybe even "Who loves ya, baby?"

I skimmed the pages for a few more minutes, touching on the importance of a global outlook, dogged persistence, and appropriate course work including writing, history, media, and communications. Since I was already more or less gainfully employed teaching some of those subjects, I told myself that I was good to go. "Faith," Aunt Ibby had said. *Faith!* I added faith to my mental list of needed attributes and closed the textbook.

I flipped open my laptop and typed in "Crows in Salem," figuring that I'd get plenty of responses and lots of pictures and videos. I was right. The messages ranged from funny to frightening, from silly to scholarly. But all of the pictures, all of the videos, were definitely creepy, and Alfred Hitchcock and *The Birds* were each mentioned frequently. The scariest video of all, one that had already gone viral, showed a huge cloud of birds flying in a black circle blotting out the sunlight—around and around over a small area of the city known as Proctor's Ledge. According to a team of researchers and historians, Proctor's Ledge has been identified as the probable site of the dreadful executions of 1692.

Do the crows know? How?

I quickly muted the sound. The cawing scream from the crows—that circling *murder* of crows—had reached an earsplitting crescendo. O'Ryan, whose ears are surely more sensitive than mine, had made a fast escape through the cat door into the third-floor hall. What must the people who lived near Proctor's Ledge be experiencing? I thought of the crows I'd seen in the trees behind our house, and of the silent row of them who'd perched along the back fence, and breathed a quick prayer that they wouldn't join in that hideous, screeching song.

I leaned toward the open window, listening. There was some noise, some distant cackling caws, but nothing like the sounds that had issued from the laptop moments before. I closed the cover slowly, gently, hoping that somehow it would keep the damned birds quiet.

CHAPTER 11

Once again I opened the textbook but had difficulty concentrating on the words. I'd read over the same sentence about using a compelling lead three times when my phone rang. I welcomed the interruption. Caller ID read, "River North."

"Hi, River," I said. "What's up?"

At first I thought perhaps it was a wrong number, she sounded so unlike her usual perky self. "Oh my God. Have you seen them?" The voice was a shaky whisper. "There are thousands of them. Everywhere."

"You mean the crows? Yes," I said. "There are pictures all over the Internet. Very strange, isn't it?"

"Thousands," she whispered.

"River, are you okay? You don't sound okay. What's wrong?"

The whisper changed to a strangled-sounding laugh. "Oh, Lee. What's wrong? *I'm* what's wrong. Me. It's my fault. First the dead witches, now this."

"You're not making sense. Slow down and tell me what's going on." I took a deep breath and tried to slow down myself. "Does it have something to do with the crows?"

"Something. Everything." She began to sound more like herself. That was good.

"Let's talk about it," I said. "Would you like me to come and pick you up?" It occurred to me that she might not be up to driving. "We can go for a ride and you can tell me what's made you so upset. Okay?"

"Can we go where there aren't any crows, please?"

"Yes," I said, remembering what Aunt Ibby had told me about the neighboring communities being relatively crow free. "I'll be right over. We'll go to Gloucester. Okay?"

"Okay," she said, her voice growing stronger. "Thanks, Lee. You're a good friend."

"So are you," I told her, meaning it with all my heart. "I hope I can help with . . . whatever this is."

"So do I. Listen, I'll wait for you out front."

River lives with several friends, all coven members, in an old house on Brown Street. I didn't bother changing clothes, just hurried down the back stairs and out to the garage. There was such urgency in her voice I knew it was important to get there quickly. There were still plenty of crows in the trees and on the fence although the crowd seemed to have thinned out quite a bit, and the cawing had quieted significantly. I backed the Vette out onto Oliver Street with the windows closed. I didn't want to hear those birds at all.

During the short ride to Brown Street I couldn't help looking at rows of birds on telephone wires. Were they all crows? It didn't seem so. Some of the birds were larger than others. Had the crows mobilized some of the other feathered creatures? I suppressed a shudder as once again the memory of a terrified Tippi Hedren flashed in my mind.

I parked in front of River's house—easy to identify because of the bright orange front door. (River says the color attracts beneficial feng shui.) She was, as promised, waiting outside on the small porch—what old New Englanders call a "stoop." As soon as she saw me she ran, long black braid flying; pulled the passenger door open; and slid into the seat. "Thanks so much for coming, Lee." She sounded breathless and nervously peered out the window as we pulled away from the curb. "Let's get out of here. They're everywhere, aren't they?"

"Aunt Ibby says she hasn't heard reports of any unusual activity in Gloucester," I told her, avoiding mentioning that bird-watchers in all of the neighboring communities reported the same thing. "We'll head over there and maybe you can relax a little and tell me why this is bothering you so much. I mean, sure it's creepy, but I can tell that you're genuinely frightened."

"I am. So frightened." She slid down into the seat, making her tiny frame seem even smaller.

I frowned. I wasn't used to thinking of River as "frail." But that's how she looked just then. Frail. Fragile. Breakable.

"Have you eaten lately?" I was surprised to hear Aunt Ibby's inflection in my own voice. "What you need is a good meal."

She blinked, then gave a wan smile. "You sound just like your aunt. And you're right. I guess I forgot to eat today." The wide eyes filled with tears. "I've been too scared. I don't know how I'm going to get through tonight's *Tarot Time* show."

"Okay." I headed for Route 128. "You can tell me all about it. I know where there's a great vegetarian restaurant in Gloucester. When we get there we'll talk. You'll eat. Everything's going to be all right. The show will be fine. You'll see." I spoke with more confidence than I felt, but my friend seemed to brighten just a little bit. I tried for a change of subject. "And it looks like we'll be working for the same boss pretty soon. I have a proposal all ready for Mr. Doan and I'm pretty sure he's going to like it."

"That's great! What's it about?"

Oops! This isn't a good time to speak of crows. River is already scared to death.

"Um . . . I'm going to wait until he sees the idea before I talk about it. Haven't even told Pete."

"I understand. Could be bad luck to say anything until you're sure." She smiled again, this time a real one. "But he'll love it. I'm sure. You're so smart." A little giggle. "Besides he's getting you free!"

"True. That always makes points with Mr. Doan."

We sped along 128, noticing how the temperature dropped a few degrees when we reached Beverly, like it always does. I've never figured out why.

Maybe Wanda the Weather Girl knows.

I made a mental note to ask her when I got back to WICH-TV. "It's going to be kind of fun, being back at the station," I said. "I like teaching but I've really missed the friends I made there."

"They miss you too," River said. "Marty and Rhonda talk about you all the time."

I nodded, thinking about Marty, the camerawoman on my canceled *Nightshades* show and Rhonda, the way-smarter-than-she-looks station receptionist. "We had some fun," I said, "and a few . . . uh, adventures."

"So I've heard." She seemed to relax a bit. "And I am hungry. I'm glad I called you." She turned in her seat, facing the open window beside her. "Look. Lots of trees and no crows."

She was right. I saw a few birds darting in and out of the wayside foliage, but none of the large black variety we'd seen in such numbers in Salem. Aunt Ibby had been right about that, and I was glad she'd been, but all the same, it was creepy. Why were the crows converging on one city and staying away from the surrounding areas?

I shook the bad thought away, hoping River wouldn't pick up on my doubts, my negativity. She's intuitive that way—maybe because she's a witch, or maybe because she reads the tarot.

Time for another subject change.

We rounded the rotary in Gloucester, heading for Holly Street and the good old Willow Rest Restaurant. I could almost taste the blueberry pancakes. We passed Cherry Street and I pointed to the DOGTOWN COMMON sign on the corner.

"Ever been to Dogtown?" I asked, not waiting for an answer. "When I was a kid I used to go horseback riding in there. It's full of trails and old dirt roads. Fun, but really easy to get confused and lost."

"I've never been," River said, looking back at the red sign. "Megan told me about it, though. She said witches used to live there a long time ago."

"Widows," I said. "Widows of seamen and soldiers who didn't come back from the War of 1812. They kept dogs for protection—and for company, I suppose. I guess old women living alone in ramshackle houses off in the woods with a bunch of mean dogs might get called witches." I shrugged. "At least they didn't kill them, like they did in Salem."

"Tammy Younger." River spoke in a positive tone. "Megan said Tammy Younger lived in Dogtown. She was queen of the witches there. Used to put a curse on any team of oxen carrying fish from the harbor unless the driver paid her a toll to cross a little bridge near her house."

"Poor old lady," I said.

"No. She was really a witch." River smiled. "Megan said so."

I wasn't about to argue the qualifications of a long-dead witch with a current one, so didn't comment further on the status of Tammy Younger.

I pulled into one of the parking spaces in front of the restaurant. It's not a big place, and there were already quite a few cars and several trucks there ahead of us. We hurried inside and were lucky to find a table for two near the fresh-food market section. I'd already decided on the blueberry pancakes—it was well past breakfast time but who cares? River perused the menu, exclaiming in delight over the many vegetarian choices, and decided on a field greens salad with dried cranberries, apples, candied walnuts, and onions.

"First time in Gloucester?" asked the waitress as she delivered our food. Her name tag read, "Dolores."

"No," I said, "just a little day trip from Salem. My friend is a vegetarian and I remembered that this place is famous for it."

"Salem, huh?" She looked around the room and lowered her voice. "What's up with all the crows over there? My son goes to the college and he texted me about it. Sent pictures too. Want to see?" She reached into her apron pocket.

I held up my hand. "No, that's okay. We've seen them in person."

Thanks a lot, Dolores. We came here to get away from the damned birds!

I watched River's face. The fear was back in her eyes. Things got worse. Our waitress was in a mood to chat. "It's got people around here talking about the Dogtown witches. 'Specially Peg Wesson."

I frowned, shook my head, rolled my eyes— everything I could think of to get her to stop talking about witches. To go away. It didn't work. She was just warming up to her subject.

"Yep. Old Peg. Guess you've heard about her and the silver button, huh?"

"Thanks anyway," I said. "I know you're busy. We'll just eat this lovely food and be on our way."

River had put down her fork, eyes wide. "What about her? I'd like to hear the story if you have time."

Unfortunately, Dolores had time. She glanced around the room. No one even made eye contact with her and no new customers waited at the cash register. I thought for a moment she might pull up a chair and sit down with us.

"Well," she said, her tone conspiratorial, "the story is that Peg Wesson used to fly around on a broomstick. One time she flew over a soldier's camp in the form of a big bird. A soldier took a silver button off his sleeve, loaded his musket with it, and shot the bird." Dolores leaned toward us, whispering, "At that very moment, back in Gloucester, Peg Wesson fell to the ground with a broken leg. When a doctor examined her, out popped a silver button." She raised her right hand. "True story."

I faked a laugh.

River's face had gone pale. "What kind of bird was it?"

"Ohmigosh, didn't I tell you? It was a crow. A big old black crow."

CHAPTER 12

I almost put my head right down on my blueberry pancakes and cried. The one topic I'd brought my friend here to escape had caught up with us already. Actually, River took it better than I expected. Still pale, and with the hand holding her fork shaking, she looked down at her salad and kept right on eating. When neither of us responded to her story, Dolores mumbled, "Well, have a nice day," and—mercifully—left us.

"I'm sorry, River," I said. "I knew this place was close to Dogtown, and now I remember hearing the silver button story when I was a kid, but it didn't occur to me that . . ."

She looked up. "It's okay. Really. I can't run away from what's happening. I guess nobody in Salem can. The crows, I mean—and the dead witches."

"You think there's some kind of connection? Between the crows and the three deaths?"

"Oh yes. Of course there is. And somebody's got to pay the toll."

"The toll?" I put both hands to my temples. "Wait a minute. What toll? What are you talking about?"

"Tammy Younger." She looked at me as though I wasn't quite bright. "It's just like the fisherman. If he didn't pay Tammy what she wanted before he drove across her bridge, she'd curse his whole team of oxen. So he was just stuck there with his fish until he paid. Now somebody's got to pay the toll so the crows can leave and the witches can stop dying." She scooped the last few sugared walnuts from her bowl. "Are you going to eat that last pancake? I didn't realize how hungry I was."

I was glad to see her eating, and pleased that she'd come to some sort of a satisfying conclusion about the crows and the recent deaths—even though nothing she'd just said made the least bit of sense. I slid my plate over to her side of the table. "So, Tammy collected money whenever someone wanted to use that bridge?"

"Not always money," River said, pouring maple syrup onto the pancake. "It could be a fish. A basket of clams. His hat. Whatever the fisherman had that the witch wanted. That's how it works. I get it." She sounded like herself again, and her smile was genuine.

I'm glad she gets it. I sure don't.

"Shall we order dessert?" I asked. "The pastries are homemade."

"Peanut butter cookies and coffee?"

"Sounds good to me."

After dessert, we left the cozy restaurant with River obviously in a much happier state of mind. I was pleased about that but totally confused as to exactly why it was.

I took the long way home, driving along old Route 127, delaying as long as I could the return to crow-infested Salem. The light was beginning to fade and I hoped maybe the birds would all be asleep by the time we got to River's place.

There were still a few of the big black birds on the telephone wires when we got there, but at least they were quiet. "Will you have time for a quick nap before you have to get ready for your show?" I'd worked the same schedule when *Nightshades* was the station's late movie program and I knew how much time it took to get costumed, made up, and prepared to comment on the night's scary film.

"Thanks, Lee. Don't want a nap. I'm fine. I have some planning to do and I need to have a talk with my roommates about a few things. Plans for Megan's funeral are coming along great. No worries. Love you!" Still smiling, she climbed out of the Vette and, braid bouncing, ran across the sidewalk, up the stairs, across the stoop, and disappeared through the orange door into the house.

Still wondering how and why my friend's gloomy mood and tearful pronouncements had somehow turned into a positive attitude and sunny smiles, when all I'd done was feed her a late lunch and a couple of cookies, I headed home.

I put the car into the garage, all the while looking over my shoulder at the treetops. I knew the crows were still there, silent now but were they watching me? I hurried through the yard. O'Ryan met me on the back steps. While I fumbled for my key, he washed his face and groomed his whiskers, seemingly unconcerned, or at least disinterested, in the murder of crows lurking in trees all over Salem.

Opening the door, I waited for the cat to go in first while I glanced around the yard. In the gathering dusk, the back fence was silhouetted against night shine from the streetlights on Winter Street. No birds perched, but one cat, motionless, faced in our direction. I couldn't tell at first which one of O'Ryan's friends it might be, but then I caught the glint of a silver buckle on a red collar. Some people think black cats are bad luck, but I remembered when a black cat who looked a lot like this one had helped get me out of some serious trouble. I gave her a little salute and went inside.

I clicked on the hall light and started up the stairs to my apartment. O'Ryan was already comfortably sprawled on the couch when I entered. "Guess it's just you and me tonight, boy," I told him. "Aunt Ibby has a meeting of her book club and Pete's at a hockey tournament." It was still early, but donning PJs and fixing a bowl of microwave popcorn seemed like a good idea. "I'll be back in a minute," I promised the cat.

It took a little more than a minute, but pajamaed, slippered, and carrying a bowl of fresh, hot, and liberally buttered popcorn, I returned to the living room. O'Ryan had moved from the couch and now sat facing my Mission-style barrister's bookcase. Behind its glass panels were housed my college textbooks, the set of World Book encyclopedias Aunt Ibby had given me in first grade, a set of Sue Grafton mysteries from A to Y, and my collection of miniature bronze pencil sharpeners. (They used to be lined up on top of the bookcase, but the cat had developed a habit of knocking certain ones onto the floor so I'd moved them onto the inside shelves.) Now he sat, hunched forward, clearly intent on something. A spider maybe? I put the bowl down on the coffee table, picked up a *TV Guide*, and rolled it up, ready to smack any intruding bug.

Scooching down to the cat's level, I peered into the

glass. There was nothing crawling or scampering in there. Deciding that our vain cat was just watching his own reflection, I'd started to stand up when I caught the tiniest flicker of light. Then the swirling colors. I sat on the floor beside O'Ryan and watched as the picture began to form.

No gazebo this time. No beach. I leaned closer to the glass. I was in somebody's yard. There was a lawn and a small garden. Purple petunias and pink impatiens surrounded a white birdbath. In the center of the picture was a tree. I reached for the cat, patting soft fur gently. "What kind of tree is that?" I whispered. As sometimes happens with these things, the tree came into clearer focus. "Apples," I said, recognizing it at once. "It's an apple tree."

As visions go, this wasn't a bad one. It didn't make any sense, of course, didn't mean anything to me, but at least there was nobody dead in it. I sat there on the floor with my cat, just watching. For a long moment the scene remained steady. Nothing moved. Nothing changed. Then there was a dark blur of motion. A bird flew from the tree, down into the birdbath, splashing water onto the flowers. The bird was very large. Very black.

The crow returned to the tree, where it was joined by another. And another. Before long the tree was full of them. I could tell by their open beaks that they were cawing and cackling and I was glad the picture had no sound. As O'Ryan and I watched from my living room floor, the birds rose into the air at once. They formed a tight, whirling black circle above the apple tree, then flew away. The tree's branches had been stripped bare.

For a moment O'Ryan and I looked at one another, cat nose to human nose, then back at the bookcase—

which by then was just a bookcase. No crows. No bare-branched tree. Just rows of books and pencil sharpeners behind hinged glass panels.

"Did you see that?"

O'Ryan hopped back up onto the couch and reached a tentative paw toward the popcorn bowl. "I know you're just pretending to be an ordinary cat," I muttered, moving the bowl out of his reach, taking a handful of the buttery stuff, and plopping down beside him. "I—never mind. We'll watch TV."

"Meh," he said, gazing toward the blank and silent television screen. "Merow."

I opened the slightly curled pages of the TV schedule. "Okay. *Deadliest Catch* or *Wicked Tuna*?" O'Ryan likes anything about fishing.

Tammy Younger liked fish too.

I turned on the set and tried to focus on raging ocean waves and careening crab traps—hoping to erase lingering images of death in a gazebo and a gathering murder of crows.

CHAPTER 13

I'm afraid I dozed off and missed the end of an argument between Sig and Captain Keith. I'd have to wait a week to catch up with the adventures of the crews of the *Wizard* and the *Northwestern* and the rest. I yawned, turned off the TV, and, with O'Ryan tagging along behind me, padded down the hall to the kitchen. I poured a saucer of milk for the cat, and a glass of 2 percent for myself. The Kit-Kat clock showed eleven o'clock. "Come on, cat," I said. "We'll watch the late news in bed and maybe stay awake long enough to see River's show too."

I climbed into bed, piled up a few pillows, leaned back, and turned on the TV. New anchor Buck Covington came into view. O'Ryan gave one snooty cat sniff and headed for the kitchen windowsill, one of his favorite spots for snoozing. The smiling Covington delivered local news of city hall happenings and gave a report on a Girl Scout who'd sold five hundred boxes of cookies. His facial expression changed to one of appropriate concern when a startling video of the mass of crows over Preston's Ledge filled the screen. "Senior members of the Massachusetts Audubon Society have gathered in Salem," he intoned, "to conduct a study on the recent, somewhat uncharacteristic behavior of several varieties of American crows in this area. Wildlife biologists from the United States Department of Agriculture have also arrived in Salem and will discuss methods of dispersing the crows without harming them." Close-up of a crow. "According to ornithological experts . . ." Covington didn't even stumble over the word. Doan was right. He was good with a teleprompter. ". . . the crow has great intelligence. It is adaptable to its environment. Crows will eat almost anything, and part of their ability to survive is their being omnivorous."

Wow. Ornithological and omnivorous in one paragraph without even blinking.

"They eat whatever is available," he continued, his expression sincere. "A North Salem viewer has reported that hundreds of them had roosted on a backyard fruit tree and by morning had completely stripped it of both budding fruit and leaves." The smile was back and the reporter moved on to some political news from the Boston State House, then introduced a Salem ward councilor who led a crowd opposed to a hike in property taxes. I wasn't surprised when I recognized Viktor Protector among the protesters. "Never met a protest he didn't like," Pete had said. Covington signed off wishing all a good night along with a reminder to stay tuned for *Tarot Time with River North.*

So. The denuded apple tree in the bookcase vision had a basis in reality. In a strange way, that was a relief. Most of my damned visions don't make any sense at all, like the gazebo and the man with dead eyes.

"River's on next, O'Ryan," I called. I could see the cat on the kitchen windowsill reflected in the tilted mirror at the foot of the bed. "Come on. The news is over."

He appeared in the doorway immediately, leaped up onto the bed, and positioned himself on a pillow next to my head, facing the screen as River's intro music played. An old black-and-white photo of the bandstand on Salem Common served as a background for rolling titles.

The bandstand is shaped a little like a gazebo, with the domed roof and open sides. Is that important?

A commercial for a new Amish ice cream stand at the Salem Willows Park was next. Then River appeared, seated in her high-backed rattan chair. If the events of the day had been upsetting to her, it didn't show. Not one bit. Tonight the mass of dark hair was piled on top of her head with a few strategically placed wisps framing her face. She wore a long-sleeved black velvet dress I recognized as vintage 1950s. The low scooped neckline was accented by a bright red Victoria's Secret bustier. River has a gift for mixing and matching styles and periods. This was one of her best combinations. She looked absolutely gorgeous. She began the show with a brief announcement about the time for Megan's memorial service at town hall. Including the fact that the Wiccan community would hold a private service for their beloved friend at a later date.

Tarot Time always features live card readings for viewers who call in before, midway through, and after the night's feature movie. This time, though, she surprised me—and I'm sure all of her regular viewers— with the announcement that she'd be doing her first reading of the evening for the city of Salem.

Is it because of the crows?

The answer came immediately. "We're all concerned about the mysterious appearance of thousands of crows over Salem," River said. "Perhaps the tarot can give us some answers about why these wise and ancient winged friends have chosen to visit us."

Winged friends? Try telling that to all the people cleaning crow poop off their cars!

"Astrologists tell us that Salem's birth date is September sixteenth, 1626, at 11:15 A.M.," she said with a pretty wink and a dimpled smile. "I'm not an astrologist and I'm not sure how they arrived at that date. Perhaps Salem's founder Roger Conant's writings let them figure it out. I've learned, though, that through using astrology it is possible for the cards to provide information for a city, a county, a country, a company."

She placed a card faceup on the table and the camera zoomed in on a colorful picture of a woman in a vineyard. On the woman's gloved hand was a black bird. "The Nine of Pentacles will serve as what we call the Significator," River announced, "and I've asked someone new to the city to shuffle the deck for us. Please meet our new WICH-TV friend, Buck Covington."

That was a surprise.

Covington had removed the obligatory tie and jacket of a newscaster. A fitted white shirt, collar unbuttoned with sleeves rolled up indicated that Mr. Doan's new hire's body was every bit as attractive as his face. He leaned across the table and picked up the deck of cards. She leaned toward him. I wondered if everyone watching was as aware of the look that passed between them as I was.

Yep. Something's happening there.

Without taking his eyes off River, Buck Covington dutifully shuffled, even adding a Vegas-like fanning move, and replaced the deck, facedown. "Okay?"

"Perfect," she said. "Thank you, Buck." It seemed that was his cue to leave the set, but he didn't take the hint. Just sat there, staring at River. "Well then," she said, "it's customary to ask a question at this point, and the one that seems to be on all of our minds is: What are the crows doing in Salem? And how do we send them away?"

Next came a close-up of River and the table. If Buck was still on the set, he wasn't on camera. "Dumb as a brick," Mr. Doan had said. Maybe he was right.

River began to lay cards faceup in a pattern around the nine of pentacles. It was a different pattern than the one she usually used. This time she chose twelve cards from the shuffled deck and arranged them in a diamond shape. "The twelve cards relate to the signs of the zodiac," River announced. "We'll begin with Aries. Judgment is the card that fell here. This means it will take diplomacy to handle situations at home." She put a hand, palm out, next to her lips in a mock whisper. "Mr. Covington told us that the city officials and the United States government are both working on our crow problem, so diplomacy is a good idea." She moved to the next card. "The Nine of Cups is in Taurus. Financial affairs are indicated here." She nodded. "The problem may get to be expensive for the city." Next came the Eight of Wands. "Gemini tells us here that communications make progress toward the goal. Good."

I wondered if everyone in the audience was as confused as I was. Exactly how would diplomacy, money, and communications solve the problem of a gazillion crows pooping all over the city and stripping fruit trees? River proceeded to read the cards positioned at Cancer and Leo. The Star reversed at the Cancer position told her that crows are stubborn and the Moon card at Leo reversed told her that the problem in question would take imagination along with a practical approach.

That makes sense.

Virgo was next and River held up an ominous-looking card. The Devil. River gave a delicate lift of one velvet-clad shoulder. "This is an odd one. It indicates the need for balanced meals and plenty of rest. Oh well, as Buck told us earlier, crows will eat anything."

Libra, it turns out, is the house of marriage, lawsuits, and open enemies. The card, faceup, showed a knight in black armor. The Knight of the Pentacles. "This handsome knight is the lord of the wild and fertile land," River said. "He's a methodical man, trustworthy but unimaginative. He loves nature and is kind to animals." She tapped the card with a slender finger. "Maybe this man has the answer to our crow problem. We'll see."

Marriage? Methodical, handsome, trustworthy, unimaginative man? Was she seeing Buck Covington in her own future? The thought made me smile.

Scorpio showed the Knight of Swords. I knew that card. It was the one River had always chosen to represent Pete in my readings. "He's the knight of the spirits of the air," River said. "Perhaps this card brings the involvement of police."

I'm pretty sure she threw that idea in because of Pete.

I knew it was almost time for the break leading to the movie. Sagittarius, Capricorn, Aquarius were covered in fast succession. River wound up the reading with Pisces, the sign for secret enemies and secret desires. The card displayed was the Lovers. I thought of Shannon and Dakota and remembered that I had to go maid of honor dress shopping in the morning.

"Shall we go to sleep now, O'Ryan? I have a busy day planned."

"Mlah," he said, golden eyes still focused on the screen.

"What? You want to watch the scary movie? Okay. Let's see what it is."

Of course it was *The Birds*.

"Forget about it," I said, clicking off the picture even before the title had finished rolling.

"Mlah," he repeated and stalked off toward the kitchen window.

CHAPTER 14

I'd arranged to meet Shannon, Therese, and the two bridesmaids at nine-thirty in the morning at Dunkin' Donuts on Newbury Street in Peabody, just a few blocks down from the bridal shop. I awoke early, showered, and dressed in jeans and a blue chambray shirt, being sure to wear a strapless bra in anticipation of the current trend in bridal wear. I clicked on the kitchen TV while I sipped orange juice and fed O'Ryan. Scott Palmer appeared on-screen.

"They call it a 'murder of crows,' ladies and gentlemen," he said. "That's the correct term for the astounding number of the birds who've been roosting here in Salem during the past two days and nights. Audubon officials estimate that the birds gathered in the city number somewhere between thirty and forty thousand. City officials are in consultation with wildlife biologists from the USDA. Sources have told WICH-TV that pyrotechnics may be used to safely clear the various roosting spots. Similar to Fourth of July fireworks, the devices look and sound like bottle rockets. Hopefully, this will cause the crows to disperse into smaller groups and spread out over a broader area."

The now-familiar video of the birds over Proctor's Ledge aired again and Scott continued with the voice-over. "At an emergency meeting yesterday, members of the City Council discussed the possible health risk involved due to the high concentration of excrement caused by these birds. Oddly enough, though, despite the extraordinary number of crows in this video, little damage of that type has been noted at the Proctor's Ledge site. Residents are asked to assist the dispersal project by calling the number at the bottom of your screen to report the locations of large groups of crows."

"What do you think about that, cat?" I asked. "Why would the darn birds poop on everything else in Salem but keep the place where the witches were hanged clean?"

O'Ryan kept right on eating his kibble, but I saw his ears move forward the way they do when he's listening. "I'm going to add some information about the pyro-technics to my proposal for Mr. Doan. I hope they do it. That would make for some good video. Everybody likes fireworks."

He looked up, golden eyes unblinking. "Except crows," I said. "And maybe cats. Well, I've got to get going. Maid of honor dress shopping today." I put my glass in the sink and picked up my purse. "I hope Shannon isn't thinking along the lines of pastels and ruffles."

Together we walked down two flights of stairs. O'Ryan darted through the cat entrance to Aunt Ibby's kitchen and I left the house via the back door, wondering if maybe we should consider painting it orange. The yard was quiet. I hardly dared to look toward the trees, but of course I had to. Among the leaves there were only a few birds visible. Most of them must have left the roost and flown somewhere else. What do crows do during the day anyway? Look for food, I supposed. Wherever they'd gone, I was pretty sure it was somewhere in Salem.

I backed the Vette out of the garage, glad both of our cars were safely sheltered during most of the crow's roosting periods. At least the car washes in town are benefiting from all this, I thought. It would probably be a good idea to pitch some of them a few ideas for commercials. I'd be sure to suggest it to Mr. Doan. I smiled when I realized that I was back to thinking like a WICH-TV employee.

Hilda Mendez's Jeep and Therese's Mazda Miata were already in the parking lot in front of the familiar pink and brown Dunkin' Donuts shop when I arrived. Hilda waved to me from a booth next to a window. Shannon, Therese, and a young woman I presumed to be Maureen were seated at the table. I hurried inside and joined them.

"Hi! I'm not late, am I?"

"No. You're right on time. Therese hasn't started taking pictures yet." Shannon slid out of the booth and hugged me. "We just got here. Haven't even bought our coffee yet. We stopped at a car wash and had to wait in line." She made a face. "Doggone birds. Anyway, this is my cousin Maureen. All the way from Florida for the wedding!"

I stuck out my hand. "Glad to meet you, Maureen," I said. "Shannon talks about you all the time."

"Talks about all the trouble we used to get into when we were kids, I'll bet." Shannon's cousin was a petite blonde with blue eyes. Without a speck of make-up, she had a complexion so smooth, so flawless, so perfect it probably glowed in the dark. Her handshake was firm. "I was just telling everybody about the time we took her dad's riding lawn mower and crashed it right into the summer house."

"You had a special house for summer?" Therese asked.

"No, not a real house," Shannon explained. "It has open sides. My dad calls it the pergola."

I'm sure I gasped out loud. I'd heard Aunt Ibby use the term *pergola* before. "A gazebo," I said. "A pergola is the same thing as a gazebo. Right?"

"Guess so." Shannon nodded. "Are you guys going to have a donut? I am. Probably the last one before the wedding. I think I want one of those skinny mermaid gowns. White, of course."

Therese had moved a short distance away and was quietly filming the four of us. "I'll pass on the donuts," she said. "When we were in the bakery I got frosting on my lens."

"I love frosting." Hilda pointed to a chocolate-frosted donut with colored sprinkles. "I'll have one of those. What about the bridesmaid dresses? Do you think we should have mermaid dresses too, Shannon?"

"If you like them," Shannon said. "But you don't have to. I don't want you to get something you hate. I'd love it if it was something you'd like to wear again."

Hilda groaned. "I know what you mean. I've given at least three bridesmaid dresses to Goodwill. Are you going to have a donut, Lee?"

I was still thinking about that gazebo. "Huh? Oh, sure," I said. "I like the cinnamon ones."

"That's my favorite too," Maureen stepped up to the counter and the rest of us fell into line behind her. "Have you picked a color yet, Shannon? I hope it's not pink. The last wedding I was in the bride had pink for everything. Even the invitations and the cake. Pink just washes me out."

"Definitely not pink," Shannon declared as we carried our coffee cups and donuts to the booth. "I do have an idea for the color scheme, though. It's a surprise. I hope you'll all like it."

"What's it going to be?" Hilda smiled. "Blue, I'll bet. To match Dakota's pretty eyes."

"Not blue," Shannon said, "though he does have fabulous blue eyes."

"I'm glad you're still planning on a beach wedding, Shannon." I tried to get the vision of the gazebo out of my mind. "We'll probably have to reserve a shelter. Any idea which beach you'd like?"

"Oh, didn't I tell you, Lee? There's a pretty little beach right behind Daddy's house in Marblehead. I don't know why I didn't think of it in the first place. And we're picking June twenty-first for the date because it's the longest day of summer—the day with the most sunshine. Dakota picked it. He says it's the beginning of a life filled with sunshine for us. It'll be a morning wedding. Then in the afternoon we catch the cruise ship for the Virgin Islands. Honeymoon, here we come!"

"It's perfect. So romantic." Maureen licked cinnamon-sugar from her fingers. "And we can even use the summer house."

"Perfect," Shannon said.

The gazebo. Oh, yes. Perfect.

Hilda looked at the donut-shaped clock on the wall. "Almost time for our appointment. Shall we head for the bridal shop?"

She was right. We finished our coffees and we each ate every crumb of our donuts. I followed Hilda's Jeep down Newbury Street and pulled up in front of the shop window, where faceless black-lacquered mannequins posed in white dresses—ball gowns and sheaths, trains and ruffles, long and short, strapless and sleeved. There was something here for every bride. And hopefully something not pink for every bridesmaid and maid of honor.

We were greeted enthusiastically at the door and escorted to a long, plush couch, where our bridal consultant introduced herself as Corina, and Shannon introduced the three of us. Therese's camera focused on the group while Corina asked Shannon to describe the groom, the venue, the date, the kind of gown she liked, along with the price range she had in mind. Other than the woman's audible gasp when she heard the weeks-away wedding date, the ambiance was so much like the bridal gown–shopping television shows I felt as though there might be a couple of studio cameras there in addition to Therese's handheld Panasonic.

Corina smiled and nodded throughout Shannon's answers to her questions, but she wasn't able to disguise amazement when Shannon told her about Poe's part in the festivities.

"Oh my goodness. A crow? A live crow ring bearer. How . . . original!"

"He's a pied crow," Shannon explained. "He's black and white." She extended both arms, indicating the rest of us sitting with her on the couch. "Here's my surprise. I'm going to have a black and white wedding! I want my attendants in black, me in white." She clapped her hands together. "It'll be fabulous!"

It was a revelation to me. I rarely wear black. I have the obligatory little black dress, but that's about it. I looked at the faces of my fellow bridal attendants and saw surprise mirrored there too. Corina's smile grew broader and, I thought, more sincere. "I love it!" she said. "I've done several black and white weddings before and they were all fabulous. But none of them had a crow!"

"It was Lee's idea that inspired me," Shannon said, pointing at me.

"*My* idea?"

"Sure. The chocolate and white cake. Black and white."

"I saw a black and white wedding once on TV," Maureen offered, "and all the guests wore black and white too."

"That would look amazing in the pictures," Hilda said. "What do you think, Therese?"

"I love it. How about you, Shannon?"

"Awesome idea. We haven't ordered invitations yet so we can easily include that. Something like 'the bride and groom request that guests wear black or white.'"

Having the guests dress to match Poe the crow was fine, but the idea of the bridal party wearing black was a new idea to me. "I guess another black dress is always useful," I said hesitantly, "but I have kind of a thing about black shoes. I never wear them. Can I wear something else?"

"Of course you can," Shannon said. "How about

silver or white? I want everyone to be comfortable. At least we won't have to deal with those awful dyed-to-match things."

Later, as I turned back and forth in front of a dressing room mirror, I tried to decide between a strapless black polished cotton sheath with a side slit and a narrow rhinestone belt and a halter top black satin mermaid number when the import of all the wedding guests wearing black and white actually hit me.

Maybe that explains the black tuxedo on the dead man in the gazebo.

CHAPTER 15

We left the bridal shop after about four hours of decisions and fittings. Hilda and Maureen had opted for identical short black chiffon strapless dresses, which, fortunately, were in stock and required only minimal adjustments. I found a strapless black polished cotton on the sale rack that fit perfectly. I knew I'd never wear it again anyway because I hate black, but everyone agreed it looked good enough. Shannon's simple white silk crepe Vera Wang sheath with spaghetti straps and a curvy little lace train was a bit more of a problem, but Corina reluctantly promised that it would be ready in two weeks. Therese promised to photograph the final fittings. Maureen volunteered to help select the invitations, and since the venue, the cake, and the date had been decided, it appeared that I didn't have a great deal more wedding planning to do right away. That left me time to work on prep for my upcoming debut as an investigative reporter.

I passed on Shannon's invitation to join them for lunch. Therese declined too. "I have to go to town hall and help firm up the plans for Megan's memorial tomorrow. It's not a Wiccan service, you know. We'll do that later. But since everybody knew she was a witch, Chris Rich will say a few words, and the mayor will talk about what a good citizen Megan was and how she helped to promote the city." Therese looked ready to cry. "It won't be anything too fancy. Just some nice music and some words from people who loved her." She wiped her eyes with the back of her hand.

It was going to be a difficult day for River. For Therese too. Megan had been an important influence in both their lives. I hugged Therese; said good-bye to Shannon, Hazel, and Maureen; and headed the Vette back toward Salem. I was so deep in thought about crows and dead witches and how to investigate the one without involving the other that I forgot to turn my phone back on and missed two voice mails, one from Aunt Ibby and the other from somebody named Sean Madigan I was already parked in the garage behind the house when I read the names.

I knew I'd see my aunt in a few minutes since I was already home so didn't bother playing her message. Madigan. There was a familiar ring to it. Took a moment, though, to remember where I'd heard it before. Dakota's best man. Sean Madigan. The art thief.

What in blazes does he want?

Quick debate with self. Should I treat it like any ordinary voice mail from a virtual stranger—play it back later, whenever I got around to it? Or would I sit here in a hot garage and listen to Sean Madigan's message immediately.

Curiosity won.

"Hello, Ms. Barrett?" The voice was warm and pleasant. "Sean Madigan here. I guess the kids must have told you I'm Dakota's best man in the upcoming festivities. I understand you're going to stand up for the bride. I wanted to meet you at the commencement at the Tabby, but I was running late and got to the reception after you'd already left. Anyway, since we're going to be walking down the aisle together at some point, I'd like to meet you in person. I'm staying at Shannon's dad's place. Dakota's apartment was kind of crowded." He left two phone numbers, one for his cell and one for the home in Marblehead. Nothing urgent or particularly interesting there. I'd call him back later.

I tucked the phone back into my purse, locked the car and garage, and started up the path to the house. I looked into the branches of a nearby maple tree and tried to avoid walking under it, aware of the likelihood of roosting crows. All was quiet in the yard, and if there were crows loitering among the bright green leaves I didn't see or hear any.

O'Ryan poked his head through the cat door, then came out and sat on the top step. I patted his fuzzy head. "Coming back inside with me? Or waiting for your girlfriends to show up?" He moved to one side but made no move to follow when I turned the key and stepped into the back hall. "Okay. See you later," I said, closing that door and knocking on Aunt Ibby's.

"It's me," I called.

"Come on in. It's unlocked." My aunt sat at her kitchen table, laptop in front of her, surrounded by books, many of them open.

"You look super busy," I said. "What's going on?"

"Didn't you get my message?"

"Had my phone turned off. Sorry." I waved a hand toward the book-laden tabletop. "Was it about all this?"

"Yes. Oh, my, Maralee. I had no idea that crows

could be so interesting. I've learned so much about them just this morning. I guess you knew the city is consulting all kinds of experts to figure out how to get rid of them—at a reasonable cost."

"Scott Palmer said they're thinking of some kind of fireworks."

"It's one of the ideas. Of course, some folks are worried about that being a fire hazard. Don't want to restart the Great Salem Fire of 1914 you know. I have some notes here that you might want to include in your presentation for Mr. Doan." She waved a sheaf of papers. "That's what I called you about."

"Great. Thanks. What would I do without you? I'm planning to polish up my own notes and maybe go over to the station later this afternoon to make my pitch. I've been giving the whole crow thing a lot of thought."

"Everyone is. I guess you didn't have a chance to watch the noon news."

"No. Busy with wedding dresses. What's happened?"

She closed one of the open books and gathered her papers together. "I'm dying to hear about what you girls have chosen. Did you get pictures?"

"Of course I did. Snapped a few with my phone. Not Therese quality but you'll get the idea. We all really like our dresses. Now tell me, what's new on the crow scene?"

"You remember Claudine Bagenstose, the woman who lost her husband a few weeks ago?"

"Yes. The banker who fell out of a tree."

"An apple tree. In his own backyard."

The apple tree.

"What about her?"

"That tree that the crows picked clean? The apple

tree in North Salem?" She leaned forward on her elbows, her chin propped in one hand. "That was in the Bagenstose's backyard. Over on Dearborn Street."

"No kidding?" I was truly surprised. "This whole thing gets weirder and weirder. Mr. Bagenstose was one of the closet witches that Christopher Rich ratted on."

"That was a mean thing to do," she said, shaking her head. "Mean spirited. I'll bet poor Claudine didn't know a thing about it until that Rich person blabbed about it on television. She's such a sweet person and so devoted to her husband."

"It's all so sad. Bad enough that she lost her husband, then found out on television that he was a witch. Now more publicity she doesn't want." I felt real sympathy for Mrs. Bagenstose. I know how painful, how heartbreaking it is to lose the man you love to a sudden death.

I finished my tea, showed my aunt the pictures of us in the dresses we'd chosen, and picked up the pile of crow info she'd printed out. "I'll look this over and add some of it to my presentation. Thanks so much for helping with this."

"My pleasure. Good luck with your interview. I'm sure Bruce Doan will be impressed and pleased with your industry."

"And my inexpensiveness," I added and headed for the front stairs with O'Ryan close behind me.

Once in my own kitchen again, I looked over the material Aunt Ibby had provided. I learned that crows are extremely trainable. They have great intelligence and they have a reputation for stealing things. "Look, O'Ryan," I said, pointing to the printed page. "Crows rob food from each other, and they've been known to steal shiny things, even jewelry. They can predict tornadoes by the way they fly." I decided to save most of Aunt Ibby's information for my actual broadcasts and to go with what I'd already prepared for my "show-and-tell" for Mr. Doan. My chambray shirt and jeans still looked okay. I fluffed up my hair, changed to blue kitten heels and a pair of gold hoop earrings, took a final look through my plastic-covered presentation, and I was set to go.

I phoned the station to be sure the station manager was in. "Mr. Doan said for you to come right on over," Rhonda said. "He sounds really excited about having you back on the team."

"That's good. I've missed you guys. I'll be there in a few minutes."

I parked in the employees' parking area, carefully avoiding the part of the seawall where I'd looked down into the water one fall morning and discovered a body. After taking the clanking elevator up to the second floor, I enjoyed an effusive greeting from my old friend Rhonda, then found myself standing in front of the purple door marked STATION MANAGER.

I wonder what a purple door indicates in the feng shui world. Must ask River.

I knocked.

"Come right in, Ms. Barrett."

I'd expected to see Mr. Doan seated behind his enormous stainless steel desk. I didn't expect to see almost the entire WICH-TV news team seated in chairs on either side of him. Scott Palmer, Phil Archer, and the recently hired Buck Covington all stood as I entered the office.

"Please join us, Ms. Barrett." Mr. Doan indicated a high-backed mahogany chair positioned in front of his desk. I did as he asked and the three men resumed their seats. "I'm sure you remember Phil Archer and Scott Palmer. The new face is Buck Covington. We stole him from Channel Nine. I understand you have a proposal to share with us."

Covington stood again, reaching across the desk. We shook hands. "Hi, Buck," I said. "Saw you on River's show last night." He sat, and I held up my folder. "I didn't bring copies for everybody, but that shouldn't matter. We can pass this one around if there is something special you'd like to see. Mr. Doan and I spoke Sunday about my doing some occasional short investigative news segments this summer. We'd cover things of interest to the community as a whole, topics that require a little more depth than the regular news cycle allows." I watched their expressions carefully. Phil Archer nodded in an approving sort of way. Scott frowned and looked out the window. Buck Covington smiled and looked from me to Mr. Doan and back. I held up my folder so that they could see the title. "My choice for the first report was, I think, an obvious one. Everyone is talking about the crows. Let's dig into it."

"A murder of crows," Phil Archer read. "Catchy."

"Short segments? Just occasionally?" Scott Palmer's frown was still in place.

"I don't get it." Buck Covington looked puzzled. "You want to murder them?"

"It means the same thing as a flock of crows, Buck," Phil Archer explained gently. "It's just a term they use for a big group of them. I don't know why. Good idea, Lee."

Bruce Doan leaned back in his chair, hands behind

his head. "Damned good idea, Ms. Barrett. I see that you've already begun your research. I have every confidence that you can pull this off in great style. Let's see what you've got so far on the crows."

I'd read through my notes enough times so that I could rattle off crow facts pretty well without looking at the script too much. I held up photos and charts when appropriate (feeling like a first-grade teacher with a picture book at story hour). By the time I finished with details on methods of dispersing the roosting birds, including making scarecrows, hanging a dead crow in tree branches, and shooting off fireworks, I could tell that all four men were interested, engaged, and perhaps even a little bit excited by the idea.

"Good job, Ms. Barrett." Mr. Doan reached for the folder with one hand, hit a button on his intercom with the other, summoned Rhonda to make four copies, then stood up. "That's just for starters, gentlemen," he said. "Just for starters. I believe Lee here can do a series of investigative reports for us this summer. Once the city figures out how to get rid of the miserable creatures—and it had better be damned soon— she'll move on to something else."

So that was that. I had a summer job. Sort of a summer job. I stood to leave. "Thank you, Mr. Doan," I said. The three newsmen stood, murmured polite good-byes, and left. Scott was the first one out the door.

"How about Thursday for your starting date. You seem to be ready, and with news we strike when the iron is hot, as they say." Mr. Doan held a pen poised above a large desk calendar "That okay?"

"Sure," I said, only half believing it myself, "I can do that."

"Let's see. This is Tuesday. That'll be the day after tomorrow. If you need footage get with Therese. Okay? Are we all set?"

"All set," I repeated. "Thursday."

"Right. We'll start with a live segment on the late news with Covington. Then run the short taped package Friday morning with Phil. Okay?"

"Okay. Fine. Thank you, Mr. Doan."

My first investigative report with two days to prep and deliver.

I felt something like opening night stage fright sweep over me and hoped my hand wasn't clammy when I shook his.

CHAPTER 16

Aunt Ibby had some more news to deliver when I returned home. She must have been waiting for the sound of my key in the back door because she appeared in the hall even before O'Ryan did. "Guess what, Maralee! The crows ate up a tree in Gloria Tasker's yard too. What do you think of that?"

"I don't know what to think," I said, picking up the cat and carrying him through her open kitchen door. "Did you hear that on the news?"

"No. One of my book club friends, Bertha Barnes, phoned and told me. She lives right next to Gloria's place in North Salem and she saw the whole thing. Videoed some of it too. Crows flew down onto Gloria's quince tree and stripped it bare in a matter of minutes." My aunt didn't sound particularly sorry. "Gloria was awfully proud of that tree. Used to enter her quince jam at the Topsfield Fair every year. Usually won a blue ribbon too, though I always thought she used a touch too much cardamom."

I sat in one of the captain's chairs, O'Ryan on my lap. "Slow down and back up a little please," I said. "Is anybody living in Gloria's house now?"

"I don't think so. I didn't think to ask. But if the station doesn't have film, you can get my friend's video and scoop everybody! I asked her to e-mail it to me and not to tell anyone else about it and she said she would."

Having an exclusive piece of film like that is a big plus and I was pleased. Doan would be too. "What would I do without you," I said for the millionth time. "Couldn't happen at a better time. I'm on the air on Thursday night. And maybe we can use her video for a promo tomorrow or even tonight."

"That came fast, didn't it?"

"I know. I'm a little nervous about it. But the crows are here right now, so the program has to be timely."

"You're right, of course. She's probably sent me the video by now. Better check it for quality and put together a short script and see what Mr. Doan wants to do with it." She started for her office. "Come on. Let's take a look." I carefully eased O'Ryan down to the floor. He hates getting dumped from a lap without warning. He followed my aunt, and I brought up the rear.

Within seconds the video flashed on the screen. Aunt Ibby's book club friend was a darn good photographer. With steady hand and appropriately used zoom, she'd documented a textbook demonstration on how determined birds can denude a blossoming quince tree in minutes.

"This is great stuff." I wasn't kidding. It was going to make excellent TV. "Is that Gloria's house in the background? Nice place."

My aunt agreed. "Easily the best house in the neighborhood, I'd say. Not sure how she could afford it on a waitress's salary. Want to watch this again?"

"Sure." It was even better the second time. "This is going to be perfect. I'll slam together a few words about Thursday's investigative report segment and send the whole package right over to the station."

"Good idea. The video made me think about the trees and plants in our yard. I think I'll try my hand at making a scarecrow." She put one fist under her chin, the way she does when she's thinking. "When you get a minute, would you run up into the attic and get a few things for me? There're some old jackets and pants on a clothes rack up there and I'm pretty sure there's a floppy old straw hat in one of the trunks. Would you mind?"

"Not at all," I lied. I hate going into that attic. Partly it's because of the terrible fire that almost trapped Aunt Ibby and me up there. Even more frightening was the memory of the spell book that I'd consigned to the flames that awful night. It was the real deal, the property of Bridget Bishop, the first Salem witch to die by hanging back in 1692. The book didn't burn. It should have but it was unscathed by that inferno. The damned thing was evil and I knew it. I hadn't told anyone but River about it, and I'd given it to her, with a warning to hide it well.

"If Pete comes over later we'll run upstairs and gather some scarecrow finery for you," I told my aunt. "Meanwhile I'll get this footage over to the station."

So that's what I did. Mr. Doan was, as we expected, delighted with the neighbor's footage—who asked to remain anonymous so the rest of the people on her street wouldn't think she was peeking over *their* fences with her camera. (Which maybe she was.) I hurried home, I changed my shirt for a red silk one, and drove back to the station, and did a quick taping with Marty explaining what my planned occasional investigative reports would attempt to do for the WICH-TV audience. There was, naturally, a special emphasis on Salem's current murder of crows problem, with mention of the recently deceased owner of the tree and her prize-winning quince jam. I voiced the hope that the tree would recover and that the crows would depart, resisting the temptation to report that both the apple tree and the quince tree stood on property owned by witches.

By the time I'd parked the Vette in the garage for what I hoped would be the final time for that long and busy day, sunset approached. Already the flapping of wings, the sudden motion of leaves and branches, and the cackling cawing of the birds signaled a return to the roost. I ran—literally ran—along the path, through the garden, up the steps, and into the house, where O'Ryan waited in the hall. Closing the door, I took a quick glance at the side fence. Three cats looked back at me, six eyes reflecting silvery circles in the dying light.

I ducked into Aunt Ibby's kitchen for the fourth time since morning. "Just wanted to tell you how it went," I told her. "It's a three-minute spot and they're going to start running a thirty-second teaser on the half-hour breaks tonight, then run the whole spot on the late news tonight and several times tomorrow."

"Wonderful," she said. "I expect that a good deal of tomorrow's local news will be coverage of Megan's service at town hall, so that should be just enough exposure to create interest in your report."

"River says that tomorrow's service will be a memorial for Megan, but later there'll be a real Wiccan ceremony."

"Somewhere more private, I expect," my aunt said.

"Somewhere where they can safely return her ashes to the earth. I've been doing a little research on the subject. It's a very special ceremony, a sacred passage leading from one life to the next. I expect that's why Elliot Bagenstose left word that his remains be cremated. Claudine told me that at his funeral, although, of course, she didn't know then about his being—you know—one of them."

"I wonder if Gloria Tasker was cremated too. Pete might know." I decided I'd ask him, even if it was a nosy question. "River says they can hold the ceremony anytime they choose."

"Wiccans often hold the funerals on Halloween. Maybe Megan's will be then—or maybe not. She may have expressed her wishes about it to the members of her coven. Of course, if Gloria and Elliot hadn't admitted to being witches, I guess they didn't get any special ceremony."

"Guess not. I'll be glad when all this is over. River is so stressed out." O'Ryan stood beside the kitchen door, looked up at me, and meowed his impatient meow. "Okay, big boy," I said. "Let's go upstairs and relax. I'm tired. It's been a long day."

"Is Pete coming over?"

"Don't know for sure. He's been working a lot of hours lately. He's probably tired too." I kissed my aunt on the cheek, and yawning I followed the cat up the curving wooden stairs to the third floor, through the living room, down the hall to the kitchen. O'Ryan headed straight for the open window, turned around a couple of times, then sat on his haunches, facing the screen as he peered into the darkness. I started a fresh pot of decaf, nibbled on a graham cracker, and stood behind him. "What are you looking at out there? Are your girlfriends still on the fence? It sounds as though the crows have quieted down. I suppose they go to sleep after the sun sets."

O'Ryan swiveled his head around, blinked in my direction making no cat comment, then returned his attention to the outdoors. I bent down so that my head was next to his, trying to see what it was that had captured such rapt concentration. At first I didn't see the black cat. She lay very still, all alone, along the top rail of the fence. She'd made herself small in that clever way only cats know how to do, facing Oliver Street and the trees where God only knows how many crows roosted.

"What's she doing there all by herself, O'Ryan?" I whispered. "Guarding them? Guarding us? Or is she just curious?" Again, no cat comment. The coffee-maker signaled "ready" and I poured a mugful just as O'Ryan left his windowsill perch and streaked past me toward the living room, his signal that someone was coming. I followed, reaching the door just as Pete's key turned in the lock.

I was glad to see him. His kiss told me that he was happy to see me too. He stepped back, holding my shoulders, and gave me an admiring up-and-down glance. "You look beautiful. Were you going out?"

"Thanks," I said. "I just got here myself. Seems like I've been going in and out all day. It's been a busy one. Come on in. I just made coffee."

"I could use it. I don't know why people think the police department can do anything about crow crap but they do." He took off his jacket and, slipping an arm around my waist, steered me back toward the kitchen. "Tomorrow will be busy too, what with Megan's funeral at town hall. Lots of traffic snarl-ups, parking problems."

I filled his mug, topped mine off, and put out a

plate with a few almond biscotti while he hung his jacket in the closet and stashed his gun in the bureau. O'Ryan returned to his observation point and I sat in the Lucite chair next to him, while Pete took the one beside me. "What's the cat looking at?" he asked, leaning toward the window, shading his eyes with one hand and peering out. "I don't see anything."

"I think he's watching that black cat on the back fence. See her?"

He moved his chair closer to mine and looked past the cat, his face almost touching the screen. "Nope. I don't." He squinted. "Oh, yeah. There she is. Not moving a muscle. Think she's waiting to nab a crow for her dinner?"

"Strange," I said. "I hadn't thought of that. To me, she looked as though she was some kind of watch cat. Like a guardian. A sentinel."

He sipped his coffee, reached for a biscotti, and shook his head. "I love the way your mind works, babe. But a cat is a cat." He looked in O'Ryan's direction. "Oops. Present company excepted, of course."

"Of course." I agreed. "Everyone knows O'Ryan is special. I'm thinking maybe the black cat is too."

A skeptical "maybe," then taking a bite of the almond-flavored treat, he deftly changed the subject. "This is okay, but is there anything a little more substantial to eat around here?"

"Nothing interesting," I admitted. "I feel like pizza. You?"

"I was thinking the same thing. Extra large pepperoni with extra cheese?"

"And a chef's salad?"

"How about a side of those fried mushrooms and those little bread stick things?"

"Good thinking. I'll call the Pizza Pirate," I said,

tapping in the familiar number. I recited the order, adding a couple of liters of Pepsi. "It'll be here in twenty minutes," I reported. "One of us should wait in the downstairs hall. The delivery guy always comes to the front door."

"I'll go down," Pete volunteered. "Should I ask your aunt to join us, since he'll be ringing her doorbell?"

"Yes, let's. She didn't mention that she had any plans for the evening."

"There was music playing in the kitchen when I passed her door." He smiled his cute, crooked smile. "So unless she's entertaining Cyndi Lauper in there, I think she's free."

"Good call. Why don't you and O'Ryan run down and invite her while I set the table. And if she offers to bring dessert, say yes."

"Did I ever turn down one of your aunt's desserts? Come on, O'Ryan."

The two stepped out into the front hall and started down the long, curving polished stairway to the first floor. I turned my attention back to the open window and the black cat.

She was still there but had moved closer to the maple tree. The sounds from the roosting crows were muted by then, a kind of trilling with an occasional clicking sound. The temperature had fallen with the setting of the sun. It wasn't summer in Salem yet. I closed the window.

I changed the silk blouse for a Boston Celtics T-shirt and, quite sure Aunt Ibby would join us, set out silverware, three blue Fiestaware plates, and three cobalt thumbprint tumblers. Pizza calls for paper napkins instead of cloth and I had some bright orange ones left over from Halloween. I stepped back from the table, admiring the contrasting colors, just as the downstairs doorbell chimed "The Impossible Dream."

Perfect timing.

Within minutes O'Ryan dashed back into the kitchen via the cat door. Aunt Ibby, bearing a round covered dish with one hand, held the kitchen door open for Pete with the other. He balanced four boxes topped with two soda bottles and carefully set them all on the counter. "Smells good, huh?"

It certainly did. Aunt Ibby and I hurried to dump the salad and mushrooms into serving bowls and the breadsticks into a basket. We decided to leave the pizza in the box and Pete plopped it unceremoniously onto the center of the table. O'Ryan returned to the windowsill, where he watched the proceedings.

"I'll just put the ambrosia in the refrigerator," my aunt said, opening the cover to display one of my childhood favorite desserts, resplendent with whipped topping, shredded coconut, walnuts, cherries, marshmallows, and other lovely things. "Pete says his mother used to make it too."

Sometimes an impromptu supper with loved ones—a blue jeans, paper napkins, pizza box on the table, sugary homemade dessert, and Pepsi in blue glasses meal—easily beats a dressed-up, fancy wine list dinner at Mistral. This felt like one of those nights.

"Seems as though all anyone in Salem talks about these days is the crows," Aunt Ibby said, accepting a slice of pizza. "I suppose you've heard about the quince tree that they stripped."

"Sure did," Pete poured soda into her glass. "The

tree belonged to that woman who died in a hit-and-run. Gloria Tasker. One of her neighbors reported it."

"Maralee has a video for her TV debut day after tomorrow," my aunt said, smiling broadly. "Don't you, dear?"

"Your TV debut? So soon?" Pete's dark eyes widened. "Why didn't you tell me?"

"We started talking about cats and pizza and I just didn't get to it, I guess. This day has been crazy busy."

"Oh, babe!" He reached for my hand and squeezed it. "I'm sorry. Here I'm whining about crow poop and traffic jams and you've got important news. Tell me everything." Then a sudden frown and a quick switch to cop voice. "What do you mean you've got video?"

I had to laugh at the transition. "Hey, I'm an investigative reporter now, remember? Confidential source. Anyway, Doan and the whole news crew approved my pitch on a murder of crows and Doan wants it for day after tomorrow. The anonymous video just landed at the right time. I'll show it to you if you like."

"Of course. Sounds interesting. So, what else happened on this busy day?" Normal Pete voice was back.

I put a spoonful of fried mushrooms on top of my pizza and took a bite. "Oh God, this is good. Well, we picked out all the wedding dresses this morning, but I guess you don't want to hear about that. Later I had a phone call from Dakota's best man."

The frown was back in place. "Madigan?"

"Yes. He wants to meet me before the wedding."

"Meet you? Why?"

I shrugged. "Just best man, maid of honor protocol, I guess. Says we'll have to walk down the aisle together so we may as well get acquainted."

"What did you say?"

"It was a voice mail. I haven't called him back yet. What do you think I should say?"

"Tell him you'll meet him at the rehearsal," Pete growled, tearing a bite from a breadstick. "Or at least get Shannon or Dakota to introduce you."

"In some proper public place," Aunt Ibby offered. "After all, the man is an admitted thief."

"Okay. I'll ask Shannon to set up a meeting at the Hawthorne coffee shop or maybe at the Pig's Eye."

That earned a grudging "Okay," from Pete and Aunt Ibby commented that the Pig's Eye would be convenient to the TV station.

"Should I be worried about him, Pete? Is there anything I should know?"

"No." His smile was back. "I'm just a little overprotective where you're concerned. We've been keeping an eye on him ever since he got here."

"Has he been in Salem very long, Pete?" Aunt Ibby wanted to know.

"About a month or so," he said. "Clean as a whistle as far as we can tell. Staying away from museums. But now that he's moved to the Dumas place in Marblehead he's out of my jurisdiction."

"The wedding is going to be at the Dumas place," I said. "I guess it's really nice, beachfront and a pretty gazebo, according to Shannon. It's going to be on June twenty-first."

Pete's eyebrows shot up. Cop voice. "Gazebo? *That* gazebo?"

"I can't be positive, but I'm pretty sure it is."

"Oh dear," Aunt Ibby said, retrieving the cut glass bowl from the refrigerator. "Let's talk about more pleasant things—like dessert. Then maybe after dessert and coffee you two could go up to the attic and select an appropriate outfit for my scarecrow."

"Not going to wait for the fireworks, Ms. Russell?"

"I believe in being proactive, Pete," she said. "Scarecrows work wonderfully well sometimes. Couldn't hurt to try it. Apparently our garden doesn't have the protection that Proctor's Ledge enjoys."

"That's a strange thing, isn't it?" Pete picked up the empty pizza box, clearing a space for the ambrosia, and started a fresh pot of coffee. "Almost like the witches are protecting the place where they died."

"Bridget Bishop was the first to go," I said, hardly realizing that I'd spoken the words aloud. "Oops. Sorry. We weren't going to talk about that stuff."

"Poor Bridget," Aunt Ibby said. "All of them suffered such dreadful indignities. And you're right—Bridget was the first. It's no wonder she was so angry with her accusers."

"Angry enough to cause peculiar accidents and mysterious deaths for some of them," I said. "Ariel Constellation claimed that Bridget was most certainly a witch."

At the mention of Ariel, his late mistress's name, O'Ryan flattened his ears and his golden eyes seemed to grow larger. "Mmrrup," he said, nodding his big fuzzy head. "Mmrrup."

"O'Ryan seems to agree about that," my aunt said. "Sometimes I wonder."

"What did she do that was so bad that she got accused of . . . you know . . . witchcraft?" Pete asked, taking a spoonful of dessert. "Oh, wow. This is just like my mom used to make."

"Glad you like it." Aunt Ibby tasted hers. "Haven't made this in years. To answer your question, Pete, I think Bridget's main problem was that she was pretty, she owned a couple of successful taverns, liked to party, and when she tended bar wore a bright red corset over her puritan black dress."

My brain clicked into overdrive. *Like the bright red bustier River wore over her black velvet dress?*

CHAPTER 17

After Aunt Ibby left, Pete and I finished off the pot of coffee, put the cartons into the recycling bin, and loaded the dishwasher.

"That was fun," he said. "I love spending time with you like this. You and your cat and your aunt too. It's so . . . easy, you know?"

"I know exactly what you mean," I said. "Easy is the right word."

"We're good together." He pulled me close.

"Yes," I said, "we are."

O'Ryan chose that moment to interrupt with a long bit of cat dialogue—something like "mow-mow-mow-mow" while repeatedly slipping in and out of his door.

"What's up with him?" Pete still held me but seemed fascinated with the cat antics going on across the room.

"I know what he's doing." I sighed. "He wants us to go upstairs and get the clothes for Aunt Ibby's scarecrow."

"Oh, yeah." He kissed my forehead and stepped away. "Let's get it over with."

I knew I was right about O'Ryan's intention. We followed him out of the kitchen and down the carpeted hall to the door leading to the attic. I paused, closed my eyes for a moment, and grasped Pete's hand. "Thank you for coming up there with me. I still dread this place. I know it's crazy after all this time, but . . ."

"No. Not crazy at all. You damn near lost your life up there. When I think of how I almost lost you, I feel sick."

"Well, anyway here we go on a scarecrow suit hunt." I managed a smile, pulled the door open, flipped on the light switch, and together we started up the stairs. O'Ryan lay down beside the door, not making a move to join us. He doesn't like the attic either. The smell of smoke and scorched wood had long ago been replaced with the pleasant smell of pine floorboards and fresh paint. The hodgepodge of odds and ends of old furniture, trunks, and boxes and bags of miscellany spanning generations were all gone. Nothing could have survived the heat and flames of that Halloween night.

Nothing.

Except Bridget Bishop's spell book.

I shivered and Pete put his arm around my shoulders. "You're cold. Want to do this some other time?"

"No. Let's get it over with. It shouldn't take long. Look at all these racks and bureaus." The attic was much more orderly now, well lit, with clothes in neat plastic garment bags on rolling clothes racks and a row of identical bureaus, each with eight drawers. A long metal cart like the ones they use in airports held an assortment of suitcases, briefcases, and backpacks. Some of the bureau drawers were even marked with labels indicating their contents. "Here. This one says, 'Hats.' We can start dressing our guy from the top down."

Pete pulled the drawer open and we selected a bright yellow wide-brimmed straw hat I remembered Aunt Ibby wearing on a trip to the Florida Keys. "A little effeminate for a scarecrow, I guess, but it'll flop nicely in the breeze." I agreed and we moved on to one of the racks. The next few minutes produced a man's suit in navy blue polyester. What was my maiden aunt doing with it? Don't know and will never ask, but we decided it would look fine stuffed with straw. A red silk ascot tie provided a jaunty touch.

"Do scarecrows wear shoes?" Pete asked, holding up a pair of black-and-white wing tips.

"I don't think so, but take them anyway. Let's get out of here."

Pete rolled the clothes up and tucked them under his arm along with the shoes, and plunked the yellow hat onto my head. "Job well done. He'll be the coolest scarecrow on the block."

"Hope he does his job and scares them all away." We started down the stairs with Pete in the lead.

"If he doesn't, I have a few cherry bombs left over from last Fourth of July," he offered, "and a couple of giant sparklers."

"Might take you up on that," I said, turning off the light switch and firmly closing the door. O'Ryan stood, stretched, and trotted down the hall ahead of us. "Especially the sparklers. They're so pretty."

"Not supposed to be pretty. Supposed to be scary. Remember? We're trying to scare crows, not entertain them," he teased.

Bridget Bishop was pretty yet she really frightened people. Why else would they have killed her?

Back in the comfort of the apartment, surrounded by familiar things, I began to relax. We put the suit, scarf, and shoes into a paper bag, topped off with the yellow hat. I put the whole thing next to the living room door with a reminder to Pete to drop it off in the downstairs hall when he left for work in the morning.

"You want to tell me about the gazebo at the Dumas place now?" he asked. "I guess your aunt didn't want to hear about it."

"There's really nothing to tell," I said. "I haven't actually seen it yet. Maybe it isn't the same one. Maybe it's just a coincidence that there's a gazebo at the site of Shannon's wedding. Maybe it's a coincidence that guests are going to be wearing black and the dead man in the vision is in a black tux. I don't know. I'm too tired to even think about it anymore."

"I'm beat too," Pete said. "It's probably all a big coincidence."

He doesn't believe in coincidences. And this time I don't either.

I looked at the Kit-Kat clock. "Time for the late news. We can watch my promo from bed."

"Works for me."

The quince tree–stripping sequence was even creepier than I'd thought it would be. Marty had sped up the action so it appeared as though that poor tree had been denuded in seconds. I looked all right and sounded as though I knew what I was talking about. It was, I thought, a darn good thirty-second promo for my debut as an investigative reporter.

Pete agreed enthusiastically. We turned off the TV without watching the rest of the news and I fell happily, safely, confidently asleep in strong, loving arms, where no crows, no witches, no visions could touch me.

Wednesday morning was quite another matter. At first, everything seemed normal enough. Pete was the first one up and started the coffee. He makes it better than I do anyway. I grabbed my robe and went downstairs to my old bathroom on the second floor to shower while Pete used the one in the apartment. O'Ryan passed me on the stairway on his way down to Aunt Ibby's, where he preferred the breakfast menu. It wasn't until I was back in my own kitchen that I noticed the silence.

The coffeemaker gurgled, the Kit-Kat clock's tail tick-tocked back and forth. Otherwise, the room was still. I opened the window. No cawing or cackling. Not even a peep. Where were the birds? I lifted the screen, stuck my head out over the fire escape, and looked toward Oliver Street and our maple tree, where a crowd of crows had gathered the night before. Green leaves ruffled by a slight breeze. No crows. Had the city fathers—and mothers—learned how to make them go away so soon? How? I'd have to figure it out before my broadcast, that was for sure.

I closed the screen and went back to the bedroom to dress for the day—for Megan's town hall service. Maybe I'd watch the early news while I decided what to wear. I pulled my old standby little black dress from the closet, held it up in front of me, and studied my reflection in the mirror. I really dislike black, so the LBD is the only black item in my wardrobe.

Maybe with a gold belt and a blue silk scarf. Megan liked blue. . . .

The swirling colors and sparkling lights began immediately. I sat on the edge of the bed and watched the vision come into focus.

It was Megan. But such a different Megan! The bent and wizened body was upright and supple, and the thinning hair, now a snowy white nimbus, framed an unlined, fine-boned face. Bright violet eyes sparkled where dull unseeing ones had been. She stretched a smooth, unblemished right hand toward me, and a crow, wings fluttering, alighted on her wrist. She moved her hand back slowly until the bird sat on her shoulder, where she stroked shining black feathers. Her smile was kind, benevolent, as it had always been.

With her left hand, she made a graceful motion toward the bird. Instantly, it disappeared. Didn't fly away or fade away. It simply disappeared. She looked straight at me and winked one of those startling violet eyes.

CHAPTER 18

I sat there on the edge of my bed leaning closer to the mirror. Megan waved her hand again, and the crow reappeared on her shoulder. Then they both disappeared just as rapidly and completely as the crow had moments before. Once again, the only reflection there was my own—a puzzled redhead in a bathrobe.

What are you trying to tell me, Megan?

Pete walked into the bedroom, shirtless, hair wet from his shower, humming a slightly off-key version of "Rhinestone Cowboy." He selected a white shirt from the armoire, then turned toward me. "Do I have any decent neckties here, babe?" He cocked his head, studying my face, then sat down next to me. "You okay? You look—um—a little confused."

A handsome, shirtless, nice-smelling, well-muscled man on your bed can snap you out of muddled thinking immediately. "I'm fine," I said. "Just deciding what to wear for Megan's service." I gestured toward the LBD, now draped across the pillows.

"Yeah. That's why I need a tie." He looked from me to the mirror and back. "Uh-oh. You've been seeing things again." He sat beside me, putting an arm around my shoulders. "Want to tell me about it?"

"Yes, I do," I said. "But as usual, I don't know what it means." I tried to describe what I'd just seen, aware as always that I was talking to a detective, attentive to every detail.

"The crow was there, on her shoulder," he repeated what I'd told him, "then it disappeared."

I nodded. "Yes. Then she waved her hand again and it came back."

"And disappeared again."

"Yes."

"So Megan made it come and go by waving her hand?"

"Yes." I stood up then, excited, understanding. I took his hand. "Yes! Come on and look out the window. You'll see. They're gone. The crows are gone. They've disappeared, just like the crow she showed me."

He followed me and once again I raised the screen. "Look over toward Oliver Street. The trees were full of them. They're gone now. See?"

He stuck his head out the window, just as I had. "You're right." He lowered the screen. "Let's turn on the news and see if it's happening anywhere else."

I clicked on the kitchen TV and Pete poured us each a cup of coffee. The commercial for The Gulu Gulu café seemed to go on forever. "Come on come on," I muttered. "Tell us about the crows."

Phil Archer did just that. "City officials, representatives of the Audubon Society, and biologists from the USDA are meeting at this hour in an attempt to understand what's happened to the giant influx of crows that have plagued this city for several days." Behind the veteran newsman the video of the Proctor's Ledge roost played, complete with the grating, raucous sounds of the crows. "According to the mayor, none of the suggested remedies for dispersing the roosts have yet been employed, although individual citizens have tried various means on their own. Officials are attempting to gather information on these methods to determine whether one or more of them may have had the desired effect."

"Your aunt hasn't even had a chance to make her scarecrow yet." Pete shrugged into his shirt. "She'll be disappointed."

I'd found a few of Pete's neckties in my closet. I handed him a blue-and-white-striped one. "Here. Megan's favorite color was blue. Let's give Aunt Ibby the scarecrow outfit anyway. The crows will be back."

"You think so?"

"I do." I pointed to the TV. "Look. He's going to show my promo."

Phil Archer gave a quick introduction to the video, explaining that my investigative reports would be a continuing feature. Marty had provided a wonderfully creepy title screen with Gothic lettering proclaiming, "A Murder of Crows."

"It looks good, doesn't it?"

"Are you kidding? It looks amazing. So do you." He leaned down and kissed me. "Do I look all right?"

I straightened his tie. "Perfect," I said, meaning it. "I'll look for you at town hall."

"There'll be a crowd. Boston TV stations, even the big networks and all that. Megan was pretty famous for being Salem's oldest witch."

"She'll be missed," I said, thinking again of the way I'd seen her in the mirror, "not just because she was old."

"I know. I've got to get going. I'll grab breakfast later." He retrieved his gun from its hiding place, adjusted his holster, and donned his jacket. "I'll take the bag of clothes down to your aunt on my way out. Megan's service is at ten. It's nearly eight-thirty." He tugged on the collar of my bathrobe. "Better think about getting dressed yourself, sleepyhead."

"Yep. I got distracted there for a minute."

He pulled me close again. "I understand." His voice was gruff. "I wish you didn't have to see those things."

"Me too. But I'm starting to get used to it. They don't freak me out as much as they used to." I realized as I spoke the words that they were true. I was actually getting used to the visions. That didn't mean I liked them, though.

I walked with Pete and O'Ryan to the living room and watched from the doorway as they disappeared down the back stairs. Back in my kitchen once again, in my bathrobe, I sat in the chair next to the window. The TV was still tuned to the news. My coffee was nearly cold, but I sipped it anyway. Phil Archer had moved on to coverage of the school committee's annual budget requests, but I barely heard his words. In my mind I replayed the scene in the mirror—Megan stroking the crow's feathers and giving me that conspiratorial wink as the bird disappeared and reappeared and disappeared again.

I stood and once again lifted the screen and leaned as far out of the window as I could. First I looked toward Oliver Street, then in the other direction, toward Winter Street. No crows, either way. I knew they'd be back, though. That's what the vision meant. I smiled. I may not welcome the visions, but I was getting better at figuring them out.

Aunt Ibby and I had decided to walk to town hall, rather than try to find a parking space on downtown Salem's crowded streets. It was a perfect day for a walk, cloudless and cool. The street sweepers had been out early, so the long Essex Street pedestrian mall between Hawthorne Boulevard and Washington Street was reasonably free of bird droppings. I'd paired my LBD and baby blue silk scarf with the blue kitten heels. My aunt, wearing a beige linen pantsuit and tan sandals, looked stylish and trim as always. Essex Street offers some super window shopping. There are antiques and gift stores, clothing boutiques, the ubiquitous witch shops, and even a world-class museum.

We chatted about the absence of crows and she thanked me for the scarecrow duds, saying she'd decided to make one anyway. "There's always a chance they'll be back. After all, apparently nobody knows what scared them away."

It seemed like a good time to tell her about the Megan vision. So I did. "I'm sure it means they'll be back," I told her when I was through. "Sooner or later."

We paused in front of an art gallery, admiring an Emile Gruppe harbor scene. "Have you arranged a meeting with that Madigan art thief person yet?" she asked.

"No, I haven't. Actually, it slipped my mind. So much has been going on."

"True. I guess it can wait. The wedding is still a couple of weeks away, isn't it?"

"Right. June twenty-first. Shannon got the invitations done at a quick-print place. Sent them in overnight mail. You should get yours tomorrow."

She made a "tsk-tsk" sound. "In my day, the properly

engraved invitations were sent at least two months in
advance."

"I know. It all seems kind of rushed, but it had to
be at a time when Shannon's dad would be in town.
He travels a lot. Dakota likes the date because it's the
longest day of sunshine."

"The Dumas house is beautiful, as I recall. Saw it
on a tour of Marblehead homes once."

"Did you see Poe's aviary? Or maybe a gazebo on
the property?"

"No. They just show you certain rooms, then move
on to the next mansion."

"Well, you'll get a good look at the whole place at
the wedding."

"I'm looking forward to it."

We emerged onto cobblestoned Front Street, where
the old town hall stands. The publicity brochures call
it "the jewel of Derby Square." It's been there since
1816, and though it's not used for official city business
anymore, it's often the scene of weddings and other
celebrations. Pete was right about the traffic. It was
bumper to bumper and mobile units from a couple of
Boston TV stations along with one from WICH-TV
crowded the parking spaces near the building.

"We're half an hour early," I said, "but I doubt that
we'll get a seat inside."

"Oh, didn't I tell you? Rupert reserved two seats for
us in the VIP section." My aunt pulled two tickets from
her purse and handed one to me. "Here. Better hold
yours in case we get separated." Mr. Pennington seems
to rate VIP treatment at many Salem events, and he
often shares his good fortune with Aunt Ibby. This
particular ticket was especially appreciated. I'd always

been fond of Megan, and I felt honored to be part of the city's farewell.

Our seats were near the front of the Great Hall, a bright, sunny room, with Palladian windows, gleaming wooden floors, and antique chandeliers. Its simple elegance made it seem just right for the city's homage to its oldest witch. It appeared to provide seating for around two hundred people, too small, though, to accommodate the number expected on this day, so large TV screens and folding chairs had been set up on the large brick-paved plaza adjacent to the main structure.

"Lucky it's a pretty day outside," my aunt whispered, "and a blessing that the crows have left."

"For now," I said. "They've left for now."

CHAPTER 19

The ceremony was every bit as lovely as I'd expected it would be. There were many tributes to Megan, some calling her "an ambassador of goodwill," "a true historical treasure," and "a woman of great strength and character." There were few references to her Wiccan faith, and music from a string quartet was pleasant, classical, and nondenominational. Camera people, including Therese, worked as unobtrusively as they could while capturing the event for viewers. I spotted a few people in the audience I knew to be witches. Some, like Christopher Rich, were seated with us in the VIP section. I couldn't help wondering how many people in that light-filled room were broom-closet witches, as Elliot Bagenstose and Gloria Tasker had been.

We filed out in an orderly and solemn line while the quartet played Strauss's "Blue Danube Waltz." Mr. Pennington caught up with us on the front steps and offered his arm to Aunt Ibby. "Fine send-off, don't you think?" he asked. "I'd met the dear woman a few times. A good person despite her . . . um . . . unusual religious leanings."

"She was a witch, Rupert," my aunt teased. "It's okay to say it out loud. 'Begone, before a house drops on you!'"

Aunt Ibby and Mr. Pennington have a longstanding competition in trying to stump one another with old movie quotes. This one was almost too easy.

"Glinda, the good witch, in *The Wizard of Oz*." he said. "Nineteen thirty-nine. I know it's all right to say witch, but . . ." He looked over his shoulder and dropped his voice. "You never know who is and who isn't these days."

"I was just thinking the same thing," I admitted. "Who would have thought a serious senior citizen like Elliot Bagenstose would turn out to be a member of a coven?"

"You're right, of course," my aunt said. "A most unlikely suspect. I know I never suspected such a thing and Elliot and I have for years shared an interest in fine antiques. He and Claudine have a marvelous collection, you know. Gloria Tasker was quite another story. Not hard to picture her on a broom."

Mr. Pennington smiled. "Ah, yes. Ms. Tasker. She applied for work in the diner at school when it first opened, you know. A most attractive woman."

"You think so?" My aunt slipped her hand away from his elbow. "Gloria?"

"Certainly not nearly as lovely as you, dear Ibby," he said, "nor as cultured and intelligent." He pulled her hand back into the crook of his arm. "But she had a great deal of experience."

Aunt Ibby gave a little sniff. "I'm sure she did."

"What do you think about the crows leaving town so

suddenly, Mr. Pennington?" I hurried to change the subject before things became volatile between the two.

"I was chatting with the mayor about that very subject earlier," he said. "The folks at city hall believe it all has to do with climate change. Gulf stream currents and such. They're hoping we won't have to use pyrotechnics after all. That the creatures have returned to their normal flight patterns."

"One can always hope," Aunt Ibby said, her tone a bit less frosty. "Oh look, Maralee!" She pointed across the street. "There's Pete. Doesn't he look handsome in suit and tie?"

"Sure does," I said, watching as Pete escorted the mayor and several other officials toward a waiting limo. "I picked out his tie. Blue, because it was Megan's favorite color."

"Oh, was it? That's nice. And isn't that River with that group of pretty girls over by the outdoor TV screens? They're all wearing blue too."

"Those are her housemates. They have a two-story over on Brown Street."

"Are they all witches?"

"Yes. Coven mates too." I waved in River's direction and she started toward us. "Mind if I leave you? I'd like to talk to River for a minute."

"Go right ahead. Rupert and I are going to Gulu Gulu for lunch. I saw a commercial this morning for their chicken salad wrap and it looked delicious."

"I saw it too," I said, not mentioning that I hadn't the slightest recollection of what had been advertised, I'd been so anxious for it to end. "I'll see you at home later, Aunt Ibby. Enjoy your lunch. Good to see you, Mr. Pennington. Thanks so much for our tickets. I'm saving mine as a special memento of Megan." I patted my purse, where I'd placed the VIP pass with its City of Salem gold seal. I walked across the brick plaza toward my friend, hoping that she'd realized that Megan's passing had nothing to do with her imagined "bad thoughts" and neither did anything else in the real world.

River greeted me with a warm, patchouli-scented hug. "It was a good service, wasn't it?" she said. "I think she'd have liked it that so many people cared about her. I heard there was even a representative from the governor's office here."

"The service was just right," I said. "How are you doing? I worry about you."

"I'm fine," she said, her smile bright. Maybe a little too bright. "Can we go somewhere quiet and talk for a few minutes?"

"Of course. Take a walk on Pickering Wharf?"

"Yes. Nice day for it. I'm so glad the crows have left." She gestured toward the sky. "Look. Just regular birds. I saw Pete. Did you?"

"I saw him. He's working. We'll get together later today sometime." I walked with my friend along the shop-lined wharf, neither of us talking, River studying the sky, me studying River.

There are old-fashioned park benches here and there on the long wharf, most situated where there's a view of the harbor. "Want to sit down?" I asked. "Shall we take this bench in full sun or would you rather find a shady spot?"

"This is good," she said. "Full sun shining on things is good." She looked down at the ground. "Some things can't stay in the dark forever."

Uh-oh. This sounds ominous.

I didn't respond, waiting for her to continue.

"This involves you, you know."

I didn't know. So I waited.

"Remember when I used to read tea leaves for the tourists, back before I got the TV show?"

"Sure. It was in the old Lyceum building." The handsome old building houses a restaurant now, but back in the 1830s the Lyceum was where some of the most famous people in America came to give speeches and lectures. Alexander Graham Bell even gave his first public demonstration of the telephone there.

"It's right where Bridget Bishop's apple orchard used to be," she said, looking out toward the ocean. "Did you know that sometimes you can still smell apples there?"

"I know. Every ghost tour guide in Salem tells that story."

"And you know for sure that her ghost appears there." It was a statement, not a question. And it was true. River is one of the few people I've told about it, but I'm one of the people who have definitely seen that ghost.

"She was there," I said. "I was at one of your readings and I saw her through the window."

"You contacted Bridget Bishop, right?"

"Not on purpose," I said. "I certainly didn't do it on purpose. I saw her through a steamed-up restaurant window on a dark night. Didn't even get a good look at her."

"Okay." She gave an impatient little wave of one hand. "That doesn't matter. You saw her. She contacted you. But do you know why?"

"No. Except that it had something to do with Ariel Constellation."

"Yep. Ariel was there right beside her. That's what you said. Remember?"

"Right." *Do I remember? How could anyone forget a double dead witch ghost sighting?*

"I know why you saw them. It was the spell book. You had Bridget's spell book."

I frowned, confused. "Ariel had it before she died. I didn't have it. Didn't even know where it was."

"Doesn't matter. It was in Ariel's stuff and you had all of that."

I was beginning to see where this was leading, and it was a disturbing place. "You have it now. You have the book."

"You gave it to me." A nod and a little smile. "I have it now and Bridget wants it back. It's the toll I need to pay. I'll give it back and then the witches will stop dying and the crows won't come back." She shrugged. "I probably can't do it alone. It might take a whole coven."

That would have sounded crazy to most people, but it made a certain amount of sense to me. I knew from reading old transcripts of the witch trials that Bridget Bishop was believed to be a very powerful witch, with the ability to appear as a crow, and sometimes a cat, among some other, more hideous, apparitions.

"I get it about the crows, but what about the dead witches?"

"I had the bad thoughts while I was reading some of her spells aloud."

"You read the spells? Aloud? Oh, River!"

"I know. I shouldn't have. But what's done is done."

She fluttered her hand again. "Now what I need to know is how do I get in touch with Bridget Bishop?"

I didn't have a ready answer. I was silent for a long moment while I thought about what she'd asked of me. "I don't know, River," I said. "But I think Megan might—and I might know how to get in touch with Megan."

CHAPTER 20

"A promise made is a debt unpaid." That's one of Aunt Ibby's favorite sayings. I'd more or less promised my best friend that I'd try to help her contact a witch who'd died three centuries ago so that she could return a long overdue book.

Ever since I'd learned that I'm a scryer, I'd tried only once or twice to deliberately produce a vision. It had worked on those occasions, so chances were that I could do it again, however reluctantly. Megan had recently "crossed over" and hadn't yet been properly buried, so she was probably closer to our present time than Bridget Bishop was. Or at least, so I reasoned, not that any of this was even remotely reasonable. None of it was anything I'd be able to explain to Pete or Aunt Ibby. No one except River even knew the spell book existed. I'd have to do this by myself.

After my visit to Pickering Wharf with River I walked home, taking the long way across the common and around Washington Square. I needed time to think. I decided that my best chance of contacting Megan was to use the bedroom mirror, where she'd already appeared to me. I'd seen Bridget Bishop and Ariel through a window in a restaurant full of people, but I couldn't count on that ever working again.

When I arrived home, O'Ryan greeted me at the front door with enthusiastic purrs and mrrows. I peeked into Aunt Ibby's living room and determined that she hadn't returned from lunch, which reminded me that I was hungry. The cat and I climbed the stairs together. Once inside my kitchen, he headed for his empty red bowl while I stood staring into the almost empty refrigerator. No inspiration there. One of the overhead cabinets yielded a can of chicken with wild rice soup and some saltine crackers. Another held a full bag of kibble.

I didn't turn on either the TV or radio, so O'Ryan and I ate our lunches in relative silence. I put my bowl and plate into the sink, changed from black dress into Bermuda shorts and crop top, then sat on the edge of my bed. O'Ryan remained in the kitchen. The mirror was tilted at the proper feng shui angle, reflecting the kitchen window instead of me. I watched as the cat put both paws on the sill, then—as though changing his mind about sitting there—he turned and trotted to the bedroom.

I knew what I had to do but didn't make a move to do it. As long as the mirror was tilted away from me, I didn't have to see what it might hold. For what seemed like a long time I sat there on the edge of the bed, big yellow cat beside me, and did nothing. O'Ryan made the move for me. With one swift swipe of a big paw, the mirror tilted my way.

I didn't have to speak or even to concentrate. Megan

was already there. She smiled that beneficent smile and held up both palms. Within seconds a round ball filled with smoky mist appeared in her hands. A crystal ball? Yes. Just like the one in *The Wizard of Oz*.

Am I seeing this because of Aunt Ibby and Mr. Pennington's silly movie quote game?

I leaned closer to the glass. The mist in the ball cleared. I saw a beach where a small fire glowed red, reflecting on white sand, and in a circle surrounding the flames were people, men and women, all clothed in black. I counted them. Thirteen. A coven.

River said it might take a whole coven to return the book.

From a tall tree at the edge of the scene, a bird flew over the circle, then alighted on the sand. It was large and black, with a huge wingspan. A crow, of course. Why wouldn't it be?

As I watched, the crow changed shape. A tall woman in black velvet appeared where the crow had been, her arms outstretched like wings. Over her gown was a corset, as red as the flames. Then, very small, in the distance, I saw the gazebo.

In a blink, the scene was gone. The crystal ball seemed to melt. Megan smiled her lovely smile, waved her hands, and disappeared.

What had just happened? O'Ryan climbed into my lap. I'd seen a vision for sure, but, unlike my other visions, this one was more like a dream—the kind of dream where familiar things from the recent past find their way into the subconscious. As usual, it didn't make a lot of sense. O'Ryan licked my chin in a loving way and headed back to his windowsill.

I'd contacted Megan just as I'd intended to do. But had I learned anything that would help River in her quest to return the spell book? Was the woman in the black dress with the red corset supposed to be Bridget Bishop? It seemed likely.

"Yoo-hoo! Maralee!" It was Aunt Ibby's voice from outside the kitchen door. "Are you here?"

"I'm here." I stood, smoothed the bedspread, and tilted the mirror back to its usual position. Starting for the door, I felt exactly as though I'd just awakened from a confusing, and more than slightly disturbing, dream. It was comforting to see my dependable, stable, no-nonsense aunt standing in the hallway. I hugged her. "I'm glad to see you," I said.

She patted her hair. "My goodness. What a welcome. I'm glad to see you too." She stepped inside. "I just came by to remind you to watch the five o'clock news. I saw Therese and she said there'd be a nice report about Megan's service."

"Wouldn't miss it for the world," I said. "And I hope that Megan is somehow aware of how much Salem loved her, wherever she is now." I thought of the vital, beautiful Megan I'd so recently seen in my mirror.

"I heard several people say that they could actually feel her presence." Aunt Ibby sounded pensive. "Of course, I guess you'd have to be a particular kind of person to sense things of that nature. Like River, perhaps. Or you. Did you feel anything like that?"

"Not while I was there, no," I said truthfully. "Maybe River did."

"Well then," her tone was matter of fact. "Megan was a good person, so I'm sure she'll get along just fine wherever she is. Now about Shannon and Dakota's wedding gift. Has she selected china or sterling patterns?"

I smiled at that. "I'm sure she hasn't. Shannon's dad has invited them to live at the house in Marblehead. He's away much of the year so it saves him from hiring caretakers and gives them a beautiful home. They've asked guests to make donations to the new charity Dakota is heading up for the restoration of Salem's old cemeteries. You know the two met in a graveyard and they're concerned about the terrible condition some of the old graves and markers are in."

"Grand idea. I'll write them a nice check. Glad to help out. I'm sure Rupert will want to help too. By the way, lunch was delicious. And you'll never guess who I saw there."

"I give up. Who?"

"Claudine Bagenstose. And you'll never guess who she was with."

"I know you're going to tell me."

"I didn't recognize him at first. I mean, I knew I'd seen him somewhere, but it wasn't until Rupert said his name that I remembered seeing his picture in the newspaper."

"Aunt Ibby, slow down. *Whose* picture?"

"Why, it was that man who called you. The art thief. Sean Madigan."

Madigan? With the Bagenstose widow?

"You're right," I said. "I never would have guessed. What's the connection there?"

"I don't know," she said, "but if you haven't returned his call yet, perhaps you could—politely, of course—find out."

"Hmm. Maybe I will. They certainly make an odd couple, don't they?"

"They do, but I don't mean to infer that they're a couple in *that* sense. I'm sure it's quite innocent. Claudine is such a lovely person and so recently widowed. I'll bet it has to do with one of Elliot's collections."

"Paintings, maybe? I imagine Mr. Madigan has some expertise in that field. Did Mr. Bagenstose collect paintings?"

"Oh, the dear man collected so many things. Furniture, china, valentines, jewelry, books, textiles." She ticked off the items on her fingers. "I'm sure there are valuable paintings among his treasures. You should see the inside of their house. Like a museum."

"Really? Did you see it on one of those house tours?"

"Yes. It was years ago, but I remember it well. It's an old home, facing the river, on at least an acre of land. It was in Claudine's family, you know. Belonged to her grandmother—and several generations of great grandparents."

"Is that where all the antiques came from?"

"That's right. Elliot and Claudine added to the collections. Exquisite taste, both of them. Kind of elegant hoarders, you might say." She pulled the door open. "Claudine even had her great grandmother's clothes. Dresses, hats, dear little high-button boots. Her great grandmother traveled with Inez Milholland."

"Who?"

"Inez Milholland was a famous suffragette, a very beautiful woman. Kind of a turn-of-the-twentieth-century Gloria Steinem. Well, dear, I'll be going along now. Just wanted to remind you about the news. You say Pete's coming over?"

"Uh-huh. He's bringing dinner. Going to surprise me."

"Lovely. Coming downstairs, O'Ryan?" The cat, who'd been watching, and apparently listening, from his windowsill perch, hurried across the kitchen and followed her into the hall.

I thought about returning Sean Madigan's call but decided to wait. I wasn't in any hurry to talk to him and there was plenty of time before the wedding. Pete had said he'd be here with dinner at around six and it was getting close to five. He'd miss seeing the report of Megan's service, but they'd probably repeat it on the eleven o'clock show anyway and we could watch it together then. I turned on WICH-TV, watched the end of a public service announcement about adopting shelter pets, poured myself a Pepsi, and waited for Buck Covington and the early news.

The story about Megan was the lead item. With all the hoopla about crows, to say nothing about ongoing local political skirmishes and relevant national happenings, it was gratifying to see that Salem recognized how much she'd meant to the city. I knew too that Bruce Doan had the final say on what the lead story would be. *Good call, boss!*

There was an opening shot of people filing into the town hall, then one showing the musicians. Buck Covington did the voice-over, giving a little of Megan's background as a lifelong resident of the city and of her fame as a witch. "A worthy ambassador of goodwill to people of all religions," he said, and noted that clergy from several of Salem's many places of worship were among those present for the service. Therese's cameras showed the lectern on the stage, where a series of prominent Salemites had praised the departed witch.

Therese panned the camera around the room showing the simple beauty of the place. There was even a brief shot of the VIP section where Aunt Ibby and I were seated, but it went by much too fast for me to recognize anyone. Covington mentioned the names of some of those who had been speakers, then closed with a clip of one of them who was interviewed leaving the town hall, Christopher Rich.

"What a publicity hog," I mumbled aloud, forgetting that O'Ryan wasn't there to hear me. "You might know he'd figure a way to get his face on camera."

Rich spoke slowly, enunciating each word carefully, undoubtedly relishing his moment in the spotlight. "I will miss my dear, dear friend Megan," he said. "She was such a joy. Such a comfort to all who knew her. She goes now to join her fellow witches, Elliot and Gloria, who have also left us suddenly this very month. I, too, have nearly fallen victim to that dreaded specter of death, that shadowy apparition that even now may be stalking the witches of Salem, much as that recent hideous gathering of crows have so recently stalked this fair city."

"Oh crap," I spoke out loud again. Never mind that there was no one around to hear me. "Nice going, Rich. Get everybody freaked out about somebody in Salem killing witches!"

Buck Covington took the bait. "Viewers may recall that just a few nights ago Mr. Rich was shot at while leaving his shop. There were apparently no witnesses to the incident. Police have extracted bullets from the wall of Mr. Rich's popular magic shop and they are being examined to determine what type of weapon was used."

I certainly didn't wish him any harm, but it occurred to me that if anyone was thinking "bad thoughts" about witches Christopher Rich's name ought to top the list.

CHAPTER 21

I'd calmed down quite a bit by the time Pete arrived at my living room door. When I saw a large brown paper bag marked "Bertini's" in his arms I even felt almost relaxed. Amazing what the anticipation of a perfect veal parmigiana from a fine old Italian restaurant can do for a troubled mind.

It didn't take long for me to set the table and for Pete to transfer the fragrant bounty from foam containers onto Fiestaware platters and bowls. During the time we'd known each other, conversation between Pete and me had become easy, and the happenings of this day had provided lots to talk about.

"A nice big turnout for Megan, wasn't it?" Pete passed a plate piled with still warm mozzarella sticks. "I think she would have been surprised."

I agreed. "She was such a modest person. I don't think she had any idea how many lives she'd touched in Salem. And did you notice? None of the usual 'witch protesters' showed up."

"We spotted a few of them in the crowd," Pete said, "but at least none of them was carrying those 'Death to Witches' signs. Guess they knew better, what with everybody talking about the witches dying around here."

"Christopher Rich climbing up on his soapbox didn't help any," I grumbled. "Hey, try this antipasto. It's wonderful." He leaned in for a bite.

"We're going to have another talk with Rich," he said. "You heard we got the bullets out of the shop wall?"

"It was on the news. The new guy, Covington, mentioned it. Did you learn anything from the bullets yet?"

He smiled. "Just that they're .380 caliber and that whoever the shooter was had terrible aim."

"Bad shot, huh?"

"About a mile over Rich's head."

I nibbled on a piece of garlic bread. "You'd think that by the way he's been carrying on about it he escaped within an inch of his life."

"I know. When we took him to the hospital that night he acted almost hysterical, he was so scared."

"Well, did you learn anything else useful from the bullets themselves?"

Cop voice activated. "Working on that."

I tried again. "Does the chief think somebody is targeting witches? Rich seems to be trying to promote that idea."

"He does, doesn't he? Want some spumoni? I put it in the freezer."

I realized I wasn't going to get any more information, so I settled for spumoni. After all, Megan was old, Bagenstose fell out of a tree, and whoever bumped Gloria probably didn't even know they'd hit anyone. But a gunshot aimed in a witch's direction, even if it misses, is probably of interest to the police—and something Pete's not going to want to talk about. I tried another topic. "Aunt Ibby saw Mrs. Bagenstose having lunch with a man today. Sean Madigan."

Pete stopped with his spumoni midscoop. "Are you two playing detective again?"

"No. She just happened to see them and thought it was interesting. It is, don't you think? The widow and the art thief?"

"We're keeping an eye on that situation. Nothing for you to worry about. Did you call that guy yet?"

"No. Maybe I'll do it tomorrow. Anything special you'd like me to say?"

Long pause. "There are a lot of things I'd like to know about Mr. Madigan, but nothing I want you to be involved in. Just say how do you do, be polite, and have as little to do with him as possible."

"You sound serious. Is he *dangerous* or something? Should I . . . should Shannon and Dakota, be worried?"

"I don't have any real reason to think so." *Uh-oh. Cop voice.* "Just be careful."

"I will," I said. "I promise." I helped myself to another half scoop of ice cream. "Speaking of promises, I promised to tell you about any new visions."

"You've had another one? Already?"

I nodded. "Megan was in it." I told him about the *Wizard of Oz* crystal ball, the witches around the fire, the crow turning into a woman wearing River's dress. "Make any sense to you?"

"Sorry, no. But it seems like it wasn't one of the really creepy ones. Right?"

"Right. In fact, it was different. More like a dream than a vision, if you know what I mean."

"Babe, I'm sorry. I don't even know what a vision is like." He spread both hands in a helpless gesture. "I think I get the dream part, though. Megan because of today's service. The witches because they've been in the news. The woman is wearing River's dress because you just saw that dress. The crow is obvious. *The Wizard of Oz?*"

"One of Aunt Ibby's movie quotes today."

He nodded. "Got it. Still doesn't add up to much of anything yet, does it?"

"Nope. Maybe this dream/vision *doesn't* mean anything. Indigestion, like in *A Christmas Carol.* 'A blot of mustard, a crumb of cheese, a fragment of underdone potato . . .'"

"Maybe. But if you figure it out, let me know." He stood and carried his dishes to the sink. "You've had a busy day and you have a busy one tomorrow too. Ready for your TV investigative reporter debut?"

"I think so. I know more about the habits of crows than I ever thought I would, and I've come up with a few different theories on why they're behaving the way they are."

"The way they were," Pete corrected. "They're gone now."

"I think they'll be back."

"Because of that other vision? The one about Megan making them appear and disappear?"

"Yes."

"You're not going to say anything about *that*, are you?" His anxious look made me smile.

"Don't worry. There are some logical reasons in the ornithological world for their strange behavior."

"Ornithological, huh?" Pete raised an eyebrow. "That's a fifty-dollar word."

"Like it? I picked it up from Buck Covington."

"Oh yeah. The new guy." He snapped his fingers. "That reminds me. Let's watch the late news. I want to see how they covered Megan's memorial. I was working so I didn't get to see everything."

"I think Therese did just as good a job as the Boston stations. Maybe better," I said.

"I caught some of the Boston coverage this afternoon. Pretty brief. I'm hoping the local station grabbed more footage."

I heard a tiny hint of cop talk in those words. "Sounds like you're looking for something in particular," I said. "Or someone?"

"Who, me?" Big innocent smile. "Let's clear up the rest of these dishes, then go fire up that big-screen TV in the living room."

CHAPTER 22

O'Ryan joined us in the living room via the cat door. After climbing into the zebra print wing chair, he sat up straight, ears forward in listening mode as the opening credits for the late news began to roll across the screen. Pete and I sat together on the couch, me with a cup of decaf, Pete with notebook and pencil. He might not want to talk about whatever—or whoever—he expected to see in Therese's video of the memorial service, but nothing said I couldn't look over his shoulder while he took notes.

Phil Archer sat at the anchor desk. He began the newscast with a video of a jam-packed city council meeting where various methods of crow deterrent were still being discussed. Ward councilor Lois Mercer motioned that the city consult with a pyrotechnics expert immediately about exactly what fireworks would be needed so that Salem could be prepared in the event that huge numbers of crows came back. After some lively discussion, the motion carried. Phil used the topic of crows as a neat segue into my up-coming appearance the following evening on Buck

Covington's show. He played my little promo and made several flattering comments about me and the upcoming occasional investigative reporting I'd be doing throughout the summer.

"I think your friends at the station are glad you're coming back. I wouldn't be surprised if you wound up working there again full-time." Pete said. "That video you made is really effective. I'll bet it draws a good audience. Everybody in the whole city wants to know what's going on with the crows."

"I want to know that myself," I said. "And after we figure that out—which I'm pretty sure we will—I want to know what's up with the witches. I mean, what if the deaths all in a row *aren't* coincidental?"

"At least we know Megan's was just old age." Pete pointed at the screen. "Look. There's an outside shot of the old town hall." He leaned forward, holding his pencil poised over the notebook the way he does when he's interrogating somebody.

"Want to tell me who we're looking for so I can help?" I asked.

Either Pete didn't hear me because of an announcer's voice-over describing what was going on at the memorial, or he was avoiding the question. "Look," he said. "There's the little group of the regular witch protesters. Oops! I was wrong about the signs. Therese spotted one, though. See it?"

I did. One of the men carried a small poster—maybe eight by ten. I squinted to read the hand-lettered message. "Thou shalt not suffer a witch to live. Exodus twenty-two eighteen," I read aloud. "They use that one every time," I said "but it's in particularly bad taste today. Also, it's out of context. You know that guy? The one with the sign?"

Pete scribbled something in his notebook. "We know him. He calls himself Viktor Protector. Shows up at all kinds of protests and marches. Not always about witches. One of those people who never met a protest he didn't like."

"Do you think he'd harm a witch? Or two?"

"Not really. But you never know about people. We'll invite him down to the station for a chat with the chief."

It was my turn to lean close to the screen. "Oh, look, Pete! Do you see her? She's standing right behind Viktor. It looks as though she's touching his back. It's the same woman. I'm sure of it."

"Where? I don't see anybody near him. What woman?"

I reached out to touch the screen when the scene changed to the interior of town hall. "Never mind," I said. "She's gone now. You must have seen her. Long black dress? Red shawl?"

"Sorry, babe. I missed it. Must have been looking in the wrong place. Who did you think she was?"

So I saw a woman in a funeral crowd wearing a black dress. Half the women there wore black. Including me. "Nobody. Never mind. Couldn't have been her anyway."

"Okay. Here comes the service inside. Wish I could have gone in to see it. Everyone said it was really nice."

"It was. Lovely music. Beautiful speeches." Pete's full attention was on the TV again. I felt he wasn't hearing me and it looked as though my cat wasn't either. The two of them were practically nose to screen as the camera panned around the light-filled room, pausing to highlight the front rows, where city officials were seated, and more briefly on the VIP section, where

Aunt Ibby and I were. On the podium at the lectern was Christopher Rich. I listened once again to his speech, at the same time aware of the scritch-scratch of Pete's pencil as it moved across the pages of his notebook.

Pete didn't notice my rapid intake of breath at what happened next. But O'Ryan did. The big yellow head turned, facing me, golden eyes wide—frightened. It took a moment to find my voice, and the words tumbled out, sounding jumbled and distorted, even to me.

"It's her! There she is again."

It was the same woman. I was sure of it. She wore a long black dress. This time her arms were outstretched, the bright red shawl giving the appearance of wings. She stood directly behind Christopher Rich, enveloping him in a tall, unwavering shadow.

I was there when Rich gave his speech. There was no one behind him then.

At the sound of my voice, Pete turned toward me, dropping pencil and notebook to grasp my shoulders. "Lee! What's wrong, babe? You look as though you've seen a ghost."

CHAPTER 23

Pete was exactly right. I had seen a ghost. No wonder I was confused. This was the first time the scrying thing had involved anything powered by electricity. The visions up until then had always involved inert reflective things: shoes, mirrors, windows, silverware. This was my first experience with my totally unexplainable pictures superimposing themselves onto electronic media.

It took a moment before I could recover my voice. Then I just blurted it out. "The woman in the black dress—the one I saw standing behind that witch protester? I saw her again just now, standing behind Christopher Rich, only I know she wasn't really there." I put my fingers on my temples, trying to sort out my thoughts. "Pete, it was a vision. But this time it was on the TV screen. On top of what was really there. That's why you couldn't see the woman."

Do I dare tell him that I believe the woman may be the ghost of Bridget Bishop? That I'm supposed to contact her somehow so that River can give back the spell book? Do I dare?

He pulled me close, stroking my hair. "Shh. It's all

right. I'm here. See? I turned off the TV. No ghosts."
He rocked me back and forth like Aunt Ibby used to
do after a childhood nightmare. O'Ryan had found
his way onto my lap and snuggled against me. I closed
my eyes, willing the memory of the tall woman in black
to go away. Slowly, safe in Pete's arms, and with a
warm, soft cat close by, the tension began to lessen.

Pete's words were low, comforting. "Did you see
something terrible? You were really frightened. What
was it? A woman, you said?"

"Yes. It was the same woman I told you about in the
dream/vision. She was behind the protester with her
hand on his back. Just now she stood behind Chris
Rich spreading her arms like a big bird, covering him
with her shadow. As though she was protecting him."

"Did you feel that she was threatening you somehow? You were really terrified." He looked into my
eyes. "I've seen you in some tough spots before, babe,
and I don't think I've ever seen you so scared."

He was right. Bridget Bishop, or her apparition,
frightened me on some very deep level. "It wasn't anything directed at me," I reasoned aloud. "She doesn't
even seem to notice me in the visions. But there's
something so terrifying about her. . . ."

"What does she look like? Is she ugly? Mean looking?"

"No. Not at all." Reluctantly, I called the memory
back. "She's quite tall. Taller than the protester or Rich.
She's not ugly. Not beautiful. Kind of an ordinary face.
Not smiling, but not scowling either." I relaxed slightly
in Pete's arms, while O'Ryan moved out of my lap to
lie beside me on the couch. "There's something about
her, though. Something . . . something . . . dangerous."

"Dangerous," he repeated. "Does she remind you of
anyone in—um—in real life?"

"She doesn't look like anyone I know." That was the truth. I paused to think. "Nope. Not like any living soul I've ever met." That was true too.

I don't know exactly how to tell Pete I'm planning to inter-act with a long-dead witch.

Pete was quiet. We sat there, close together in the silent living room for what seemed like a long time. "Feeling a little better?" His voice was a ragged whis-per. "Jesus, Lee. You scared me."

"Scared myself too," I said, "but yes, I feel okay now. I'm awfully glad you were here. It was just so different, you know? Seeing something on TV that isn't there. I hope that's not going to happen often."

"Hope not. There's enough weird stuff on the reg-ular shows and the news without having spooky women on top of it all." He leaned back against the couch cushions, keeping one arm around my shoul-ders. "Want to give it one more try? Climb back on the horse? Almost time for River's show." He reached for the remote. "If you see anything you don't want to see I'll shut it right off. Okay?"

I took a deep breath. "Okay." The screen came to life beginning with River's opening credits. This time camerawoman Marty had used a sunset-on-the-beach scene for the backdrop. River's theme music played, softly at first, then reached a crescendo as the camera focused on River.

"Wow!" Pete and I spoke the word in unison, then laughed. Wow indeed. River wore the skintight electric blue sequin number she'd told us about, and her long black hair hung loosely around bare shoulders. "If Covington is hanging around the set tonight," Pete said, "he's a gone goose."

"I think he is anyway," I said, "whether he knows it or not."

"You're not seeing anything that doesn't belong there, are you?" There was concern in his voice.

"Nope. Everything is back to normal. Really. Sorry to be such a drama queen. But . . ."

"But what?"

"Will you stay with me tonight?"

"Silly question."

We watched the first part of *Tarot Time.* River was at her smiling best, reading the cards for her first caller with sincerity and humor. The second caller had a scratchy, whispery voice, a bit hard to understand.

"Could you speak a little louder, caller?" River asked. "You don't have to give your name and birth date if you don't want to. Do you have a special request or wish I can help you with?"

The answer was still whispered, but perfectly understandable. "I've started a job and it's not finished yet. I'm going to—" The words came to an abrupt halt.

River frowned, then looked in the direction of the control room. Her smile was hesitant, and there were a few seconds of the kind of silence that's not good for live TV. Dead air. "Come on, River," I said aloud. "Keep the show moving."

"What just happened?" Pete looked at me.

"From the context I'd say the caller said something inappropriate. The call screener caught it before it went on the air. All the calls are delayed a few seconds. It happens. It used to freak me out too. She'll be okay." I pointed at the screen. "See?"

River's smile was back. "Oops. Lost that caller," she said. "Let's take the next call."

The show continued in the usual smooth manner.

We decided we'd skip the movie. River was showing *The Lazarus Effect*. "Not a good time for a horror movie," Pete said, tapping the remote. "Shall we go back to the kitchen and finish that spumoni?"

I didn't answer right away. Something about that interrupted call bothered me. The "I'm going to . . ." had sounded to me like a threat. "Pete," I said, "Therese is River's call screener. I'm going to text her. I didn't like the sound of that call."

"I didn't either," he said. "Sounded like the beginning of a threat, didn't it?"

"It did. It's probably nothing. Most of the time it's something sexual." But I was already texting, asking Therese what the whisperer had said that made her cut the call off. She answered right away. "She says the caller said, 'I'm going to get that witch next time and he won't be the last.'"

Pete and I looked at each other. "Ask if she has the number the call came from."

I did as he asked. "She has it," I told him.

"It sounds as though the threat is against our friend Christopher Rich," he said. I agreed.

"Christopher Rich and more. And poor River thinks these deaths are somehow her fault. Can you do anything?"

"Yes. I'll check out the phone number, though chances are it's a throwaway. Maybe between us we can ease River's mind about the crazy idea that she's responsible."

"Some people think Chris does these things himself, to get publicity," I said.

"I've heard that too," he said. "Nothing we can do right now. How about we dig into that spumoni?" That's exactly what we did. We ate ice cream, drank decaf, listened to soft rock on the radio, and talked about summer plans. We'd catch the NASCAR series in New Hampshire for sure. Maybe we'd rent a cabin in Maine for a weekend. Maybe we'd go on a windjammer cruise or take a day trip on a fishing party boat out of Gloucester. Neither of us mentioned crows or witches or visions. O'Ryan sat on the windowsill, not looking outside, but keeping his half-shut golden eyes focused on us.

"It's way after midnight, babe," Pete said, stifling a yawn. "Call it a day?"

"I think so. Thanks for staying with me."

"My pleasure." He did his Groucho Marx eyebrow thing. "I mean *really* my pleasure."

"You're a nut." I went to the window to pat O'Ryan and looked out into the silent yard. There was no moonlight, but the streetlights from Oliver Street cast a pale glow over Aunt Ibby's garden. The back fence seemed to be empty of cats, for a welcome change, but as I watched, a lone bird flew from the direction of Winter Street. It circled the yard—once, twice— casting its shadow across the herbs and sunflowers, budding hydrangea, and Queen Anne's lace below, then disappeared into the darkness.

Shouldn't birds be asleep in their nests at this hour? It looked black. Was it a returning crow?

Pete stood in the bedroom doorway, the look of concern still on his face. "You okay?"

"I am." I hurried across the room. "I just saw a black bird out there. Isn't that strange at this time of night?"

"A blackbird?"

"No. A black bird. A bird that is black. Shouldn't it be home in its bed?"

"Don't know. But we should. You have a busy day

ahead, Miss Investigative Reporter, and so do I." He was right, of course. I tried to put all the scary things out of my mind and was almost successful.

Aunt Ibby always used to tell me to "think happy thoughts" when I was frightened or sad. So, safe in my own room with my own special man, I thought of happy times, happy people, happy places. But over it all I kept seeing that circling black bird casting a long, wavering shadow across bushes and flowering plants. Was it my imagination or had that shadow of the bird with wings outstretched been shaped exactly like the one cast by the woman in the red shawl? The one who looked as though she was protecting Christopher Rich? The woman I believed to be the long-dead witch Bridget Bishop?

CHAPTER 24

Thursday was a day I'd anticipated, dreaded, embraced, worried about, and finally welcomed. The day of my debut as an investigative reporter—an intern, a beginner, but still an investigative reporter, one with some answers and more questions.

Since Christopher Rich's rant about somebody stalking witches had aired, there was no longer any point in keeping the death of three witches and the attempt on Rich separate from the murder of crows story. They were somehow intertwined. I knew it and I was pretty sure that since the stripping of the trees in both Elliot's and Gloria's yards much of Salem at least suspected it. Some of the national radio talk shows, especially those with a paranormal bent, had picked up the story as well.

I awoke with the realization that although I'd done plenty of good solid research on my topic of choice I'd done precious little actual investigating, other than a few phone interviews with city hall, the Audubon Society, and a representative of the USDA. It was time to remedy that and I had only a few hours to do it.

For a change, I was awake and dressed in white shorts and a Boston Strong T-shirt before Pete was up. I even had the coffee brewing and a pan of blueberry muffins—from a mix—in the oven. If he was astonished by this unusual display of domesticity, he took it in stride. "Smells great in here, babe," he said, kissing the back of my neck as he passed through the kitchen on his way to the shower. "Where are you off to right now?"

"I think I'll go and take a look at those trees the crows stripped."

He frowned. "You can't just go into somebody's yard without permission, you know. We had to get a warrant to look at the Bagenstose tree. Hated bothering the poor widow, but we had to do it."

"I figured I'd just knock on the door and introduce myself. She's an old friend of Aunt Ibby's. I don't think she'd mind my taking a peek at her apple tree."

"She probably won't. A friend of the family is a lot different than a cop with a warrant knocking at your door. Planning to check out the quince tree too?"

I nodded. "Yep. Nobody home there, right?"

"A Tasker cousin is there. She came from out west somewhere to clear out Gloria's personal stuff. I don't think she'll mind you looking around the yard. What are you looking for anyway?"

"I don't know. I'm just investigating. That's what we investigative reporters do." I shrugged. "I think. Don't forget to see what you can find out about that creepy phone call to River's show. Okay?"

"I haven't forgotten. Already got somebody on it. River will be fine. Don't worry. I'll be back in a minute." He sniffed the air. "Smells like the muffins are almost done."

It would have been nice to linger for a while over

breakfast—I don't bake muffins very often—but we each had plans for the day. Pete was heading for a meeting with Chief Whaley and a forensic firearms expert. It took a little digging, but I got him to tell me it was about the gun used by whoever had shot at Christopher Rich. He didn't say so, but I figured that maybe this also had something to do with that witch protester who called himself Viktor Protector and maybe even River's mysterious caller.

I'd decided to drive over to Southwick Street in North Salem first to see what I could learn about what had happened to Gloria Tasker's tree. And, hopefully, to learn about what had happened to Gloria. After that I'd go to Dearborn Street and call on Mrs. Bagenstose.

I knew it would be easier to talk to the cousin than it would be to ask the widow to let me view the sad scene of her husband's demise, but I was determined to do both. I hadn't forgotten my promise to River either. Maybe she could make more sense out of the dream/vision than I had. I felt that since Megan had shown it to me it must contain a clue on how to reach Bridget Bishop. It was much too early in the day to call on Mrs. Bagenstose or the Tasker cousin, and my friend wouldn't be awake for hours yet. By late afternoon, though, I'd have the tree business attended to and still have plenty of time to talk with River before the late news.

Pete kissed me, wished me a good day, and said he'd watch my debut, then come over to my place with champagne to celebrate. He had to work Friday but had managed to get Saturday and Sunday off, so we had a weekend to look forward to. I filled O'Ryan's red bowl with kibble, then sat at the table going over my notes for the show. I had my crow facts straight, I was sure, and the society had provided plenty of history on crow invasions similar to the one Salem had just experienced. It happened more often than I'd supposed, and "a murder of crows" was a much more common expression among birders than I'd imagined. I decided that it had a cool ring to it and decided to use the term frequently during the broadcast. I'd just added the addresses for Gloria and her neighbor to my notes when my phone buzzed. I was surprised to see a text from River.

What's she doing up so early?

I got the answer to that right away. She hadn't gone to bed yet. Apparently Buck Covington had been on hand to observe the electric blue sequin gorgeousness and they'd stayed up talking all night and she was finally about to get some sleep. She didn't mention the whispering caller. I didn't either. Maybe she hadn't talked with Therese yet. Probably a long talk with Buck was more interesting than finding out what some nutjob wanted anyway. I wished her good luck and happiness and resolved to watch the noon news to see if the River-smitten announcer was still letter perfect in his delivery. The phone immediately buzzed again, and thinking River had more to tell me, I answered without looking at the caller ID. It was Sean Madigan.

"Good morning, Ms. Barrett. So glad to speak to you in person. This is Sean Madigan, Dakota Berman's best man. Got a minute?"

"Uh—sure. Sorry I haven't had a chance to return your earlier call. Been crazy busy."

"I understand. Thought maybe if you have time I'd drop by and take you to breakfast. Get acquainted." His tone was pleasant. Impersonal, really. "Shannon thought it would be a good idea for us to meet before the wedding."

"Well, I guess . . ."

"Nothing fancy. Come as you are." I could detect a smile in his voice. Or was it a smirk? It's hard to tell over the phone. "Thought we'd just go to the diner that's attached to your school. I'll ask the kids to join us if you can make it."

"The kids?" I guessed he meant Shannon and Dakota. My mind was racing. *Go to some public place,* Aunt Ibby had advised. The diner would qualify. *Come as you are,* the man said. I looked down at my shorts and shirt. All right for a warm spring day in Salem. "Okay," I heard myself say. "I'll meet you there. What time?"

"How's right now? I hoped you'd say yes, so I'm parked in front of your house."

None of my windows face Winter Street so I couldn't confirm his statement—but I believed him. What nerve! My annoyance was undoubtedly obvious. "That's taking a lot for granted, Mr. Madigan," I said. "How do you know where I live, anyway?"

"Shannon gave me your address. I guess I'm just too impulsive." Smiley voice again. "It's such a nice day I thought it would be fun. Spontaneous, you know? Please don't be angry." The voice was softer now, appropriately little-boy repentant. What a con man! I felt my temper rising.

I don't do the temper thing on purpose and it doesn't happen often. I've been told it's a redhead thing. Aunt Ibby says she has it too, although I've only seen hers on display once or twice in my whole life. Anyway there it was—full-on, redhead, ice-cold, I'll-show-you,-you smarmy-bastard fury.

"I'll be right down," I said. I hung up, slid my feet into flip-flops, jammed a Guy Harvey visor cap over wild hair, slapped on some pink lip gloss, and, without even a kind word or good-bye pat on the head for my surprised cat, headed out of my kitchen and down the stairs to the Winter Street front door. I thought about taking my own car for two seconds but that would just be chickening out.

A smiling Sean Madigan stood on the curb, holding open the passenger door of a green 2010 Toyota Corolla. I returned the smile with a teeth-gritting grimace of my own and slid into the car, noting that there was bird poop on the roof even though the crows had been gone for a couple of days. *Hmph. Not bad looking, but still a crook and a con man and a slob too.*

"Hi there," he said. "Happy to finally meet you. You're even prettier than you look on TV."

"Oh, thank you so much," I said, trying hard to sound like the simpering wimp he apparently thought I was. "Were you able to get in touch with the kids?"

"Uh, not yet. No answer on either phone. Probably busy with wedding stuff." He started the Toyota and pulled out onto Winter Street. "But that gives us all the more time to get to know each other, right?"

I couldn't fake-simper my way past that dumb question, so I looked out the window and didn't answer it. "Are you planning to relocate here to Salem, Mr. Madigan?" I asked, after a few seconds of silence. "In spite of your recent . . . um . . . unpleasantness?" *I'll start with a few little digs, then lower the boom later. This might even be fun.*

Surprise showed on his face for the briefest instant, but he covered it quickly with an eyes-downcast expression of pure innocence. "Oh, Lee. May I call you Lee? The darkest days of my life. I've shamed my family, my friends. I'm so blessed to have a friend like Dakota who trusts me to stand with him on the most incredibly important day in his young life."

That first blast of anger had calmed down enough so that I was beginning to question the wisdom of accepting an invitation to break bread with a man I neither liked nor trusted. "Yes," I said. "You're lucky to have faithful friends like Dakota and Shannon. I understand that Dakota thinks of you as something of a mentor. With his painting, of course." I gave him a sidelong look. "Not that other thing you do."

"Did," he stated flatly. "The thing I did. No more. Learned my lesson. Jail is not fun." He gave a puzzled glance in my direction. "I'm beginning to think that you don't like me much, Lee."

Maybe I'm being a little too obvious. Tone it down.

"I don't mean to offend you, Mr. Madigan," I said. "All I know about you is what I read in the papers."

Solemn nod. "I understand. Can't blame you for that." We pulled up in the parking lot next to the diner. "Let's have a nice breakfast and talk about the wedding, the weather, the state of the union. Okay? We can try to get along if only for the sake of the kids. And that damned crow."

It was my turn to look surprised. "Poe? You don't like him? He seems like a remarkably intelligent creature."

"I'm sure he is." Sean hurried around the car and opened my door. "But the guest room where I'm staying at the Dumas place is right next to the aviary. Damned bird talks all night. 'Who loves ya, baby? Here comes the bride. Pretty pretty. Shiny shiny.' Babbles on like that for hours. Seems like hours anyway." I ignored his proffered hand and got out of the car unaided, walking a couple of steps ahead of him toward the curvy, chrome-trimmed door leading into the vintage diner–styed restaurant.

The place was uncommonly uncrowded. "Looks like we have our choice of seats," he said. "You have a favorite spot?"

"We must be late for the early birds and early for the breakfast regulars," I said, looking around, not seeing a single soul who looked familiar except Jenny, the waitress. "One of the small booths next to the windows will be fine." I walked ahead of him and slid onto the red vinyl upholstered seat, being careful not to leave enough room for him to sit beside me.

Jenny hurried over, handing each of us a plastic-covered menu. "Hi, Ms. Barrett. We have a nice fresh batch of those cheese Danish you like."

"I'll have one of those, Jenny, and coffee, please. Have you been here before, Mr. Madigan?" I didn't wait for an answer. "Everything is good."

He seemed to be studying the menu, then ordered the two-egg, two-pancake, two-sausage special and coffee. "Yes. I came here after the commencement ceremony, after I missed seeing you. Had a cheeseburger. Those little pastries they served up in the Trumbull suite weren't very filling." Another smile, this one more genuine than his previous attempts. "You missed a funny scene when the pastry chef tried to pull the tablecloth off the banquet table without disturbing the dishes."

"That would be The Fabulous Fabio," I said. "Great baker. Terrible magician. Did he break anything?"

"No. Fortunately, Mr. Pennington intervened in time."

Our coffees arrived and I took a sip and decided to say what was on my mind. After all, what did I have to lose? This guy meant nothing to me. After the wedding I'd never have to see him again. "My aunt tells me that you're acquainted with her old friend Claudine Bagenstose." I leaned forward, looking him straight in the eyes. He had brown eyes, the kind you can't see behind. "Is that right?"

Again, the look of mild surprise, then a frown. "I've met the lady, yes. I'm surprised if she discussed our relationship with your aunt, though."

I surely didn't want Mrs. Bagenstose or my aunt to get on the wrong side of this man. I hurried to correct that impression. "Oh no. There was no discussion. My aunt happened to mention that she saw you together at lunch one day recently, that's all."

He leaned back in the booth, brown eyes narrowed, body language suggesting negative feelings. About me. Maybe I'd pushed too far. It occurred to me that maybe this wasn't the kind of man one should push.

My anger had suddenly been reduced to a cold, hard lump in the pit of my stomach that felt a lot like fear. I forced a happy face. "So, tell me, Mr. Madigan, have you ever been a best man before?"

CHAPTER 25

The remainder of that breakfast date was uncomfortable—probably for both of us. Mostly, we concentrated on the food, avoiding eye contact and speaking only of, as he'd suggested, the weather—beautiful—and the wedding—a wonderfully happy occasion and, yes, this was his first experience as best man as well as my first as maid of honor. We agreed that the food in the diner was good. We didn't discuss the state of the union, wisely avoiding politics altogether.

After what seemed like hours, but was in fact only an agonizing forty-five minutes, we returned to the Toyota and started for home. "Pretty street," he said, as we passed the Civil War monument on the corner of Winter Street. "Nice trees. One of the things I missed most in jail was the green things." The simple statement, delivered so sincerely, surprised me. He parked in front of the house; politely walked with me to the front door; said, "I'll see you at the wedding rehearsal"; hurried down the steps; and drove away without a backward glance.

O'Ryan waited for me just inside the front door, as

usual, and seemed extra pleased to see me. Had he been worried about me? Why not? I'd been worried about me too. By then, though, I was no longer worried, nor angry, nor frightened. Mostly, I was confused. Was Sean Madigan a sneaky snake-oil salesman? A hardened criminal? They say jail changes a person. Had he simply been behind bars so long he didn't know how annoying he was? Or were my first instincts correct? *Jail or no jail, wedding or no wedding, art thief or not, I don't trust the man. I don't like him. And that's that.*

As I passed through the foyer on my way to the stairs, I heard the whirr of a blender coming from Aunt Ibby's kitchen. I cut through the living room and the dining room and, not wanting to startle her, called her name. "Aunt Ibby! It's me. Got a minute?"

The whirring stopped. "Maralee? Come on out to the kitchen. I have something to show you." As soon as I rounded the corner of the dining room and stepped into the kitchen my morning brightened. There, leaning a bit crookedly against the pantry door, was Aunt Ibby's scarecrow.

"It's wonderful," I said. "Absolutely wonderful." And it was. The floppy yellow hat, accented with a few plastic roses, topped its smiling pink pillowcase face. A bright red scarf blossomed from the breast pocket and yellow rubber gloves formed hands. She'd added red-and-green-striped socks to the wing-tipped shoes, and the traditional straw stuffing was just enough to give an authentic look to the whole project.

"Do you think he'll scare the crows?" she asked.

I shook my head and laughed. "No. He's much too friendly looking. But he'll definitely give the garden a touch of New England nostalgia. He's a beauty!"

"Looks like he scared O'Ryan." She pointed toward the cat, who was in his belly-to-the-ground, ears-flattened crouch position. She picked him up and carried him closer to the scarecrow. "See, big sissy cat. It's okay. He's not real." O'Ryan gave a genteel sniff in the direction of the red scarf, then jumped from her arms and stalked from the room. "I'm sure he'll scare the crows too. I'm calling him Theodore."

"You could be right," I said. "Speaking of being scared, got time to hear about my breakfast date?"

"I didn't know you had a breakfast date. Wait just a sec while I finish mixing my banana–peanut butter smoothie." She tossed a few ice cubes into the blender and it whirred again for a moment. "There. It's a new high-protein recipe. Would you like one?"

"Sure. Why not? I've already had breakfast twice. What harm can one more do?"

"Oh? Two breakfasts? And you said something about being scared?" She poured the frothy drink into two stemmed goblets, motioned for me to sit down at the kitchen table, and took the chair opposite mine. "Tell me all about it."

"I got a phone call this morning from Sean Madigan. He invited me to breakfast."

She put her smoothie down so quickly a little of it splashed onto the table. "I'm surprised that you accepted. You took your own car, I hope."

"I didn't. He was so sure I'd accept that he was already parked in front of the house. Can you imagine the nerve?"

"Oh, Maralee. You must never get into a car with a stranger!" She repeated the same admonishment she'd given me when I was a teenager. I had to smile.

"I know. But he was so condescending, so sure of

himself, such a phony baloney con man he made me mad! Really mad. I just wanted to storm downstairs and put him in his place. Know what I mean?"

"I think so. Did you do it? Put him in his place, I mean?"

I sipped my smoothie and thought for a few seconds. "I don't know. I wasn't very nice to him, I guess."

"You said you were scared. Why?"

"You know, I'm not exactly sure. There's something intimidating about him. It wasn't so much what he said, but the way he said it." I thought back to how Sean Madigan had responded when I mentioned Claudine Bagenstose. "I mentioned that you'd seen him with Mrs. Bagenstose and his reaction gave me a chill."

"Did he seem angry? Annoyed? What?"

"He was cold. Polite and cold. I hope he doesn't call me again."

"I hope he doesn't too. Look, O'Ryan's back." She patted her lap. The big cat approached, giving the scarecrow a wide berth before accepting her invitation to join us at the table. "He still doesn't like Theodore, though."

"I know how he feels," I said. "O'Ryan doesn't believe that polite smile. He knows that inside Theodore is a big fake."

I thought about telling her that I'd had another vision. I looked at the kitchen clock. If I was going to do all the things I had planned and still show up on time at WICH-TV, I needed to get going. "I'm going to do a little investigating today," I said. I gave her a quick rundown of my plans to visit the scenes of the tree strippings and asked permission to mention her name when I introduced myself to Claudine Bagenstose.

"Of course you can, and do give my love to Claudine.

By the way, have you told Pete yet about your encounter with the Madigan person?"

"No. I came right here. I'll tell him tonight. He's bringing champagne to celebrate my new career."

"He's not going to be pleased."

"Maybe I overreacted. Maybe I shouldn't have been so angry. Anyway, right now I need to go and change into something more presentable," I said, then added, "And for some reason I feel like taking another shower."

CHAPTER 26

I decided to try for a businesslike look for my impromptu interviews. I selected an ivory two-piece silk shantung outfit I'd bought on sale at Nordstrom's and hadn't had a chance to wear yet. Low heels were in order if I was going to be stomping around in other people's backyards, so I wore brown flats. After twisting my hair into a reasonably neat chignon, I added pearl earrings, tucked pen and notebook into my favorite Kate Spade handbag, and I was good to go.

I headed for North Salem, consulting Google for directions to Southwick Street, an L-shaped street just off Dearborn that made the Bagenstose and Tasker households almost neighbors.

I'd had a glimpse of Gloria's house in her neighbor's video and of her backyard in my vision. Neither one did justice to the real thing. "The best house in the neighborhood," Aunt Ibby had said, and it appeared to be true. A neat white picket fence surrounded a perfectly manicured lawn. Bushes were trimmed into rounded shapes and bright tulips marched along a

paved path leading to a beautiful little Cape Cod
cottage, its silvery weathered shingles and blue shut-
ters completing a real estate agent's dream of curb
appeal. The only jarring note was the quince tree, its
bare, bone-like branches a stark contrast to the perfection of the picture.

I parked next to a U-Haul with Nevada plates, made
sure my notebook was in my purse, and approached
the front door. I pressed the doorbell, smiling when I
heard chimes play "Fly Me to the Moon." "Be right
there," came a voice from inside, followed by a brief in-
terval of barking. The blue door opened just enough
for me to see a woman with short salt-and-pepper hair
and brown eyes, and enough for a very large Doberman
to stick his head through. "Hello," said the woman in a
friendly way. "Can I help you?"

"Hello," I said, handing one of my brand new
WICH-TV business cards through the opening. "I'm
Lee Barrett, WICH-TV. I wonder if you have time to
speak with me for a few minutes about your cousin."

Accepting the card, she pulled the door open wider
and poked her head out, looking toward the driveway.
"I don't see no cameras," she said. The dog, seeing an
opportunity to get out, ran into the yard and rolled
happily in the lush grass. "Come back here, Zeus," she
called, shoving my card into the pocket of what Aunt
Ibby calls a "cobbler's apron," She clapped her hands.
"You naughty boy."

Zeus stopped rolling and walked very slowly, head
down, toward his mistress, then sat obediently on the
top step. She rewarded him with a treat from one of
several apron pockets. "Good dog." She patted his

head, then turned toward me. "Now, what were you saying, honey? Something about Gloria?"

I repeated my name. "I'm an investigative reporter for WICH-TV." It was the first time I'd introduced myself with the title in a face-to-face situation and it sounded strange, even to me.

"Oh yeah, sure. I don't know how much help I can be. I hadn't seen her for years. Want to come in? I'm Gloria's cousin Jane. Trying to pack up her stuff to take back home. She left everything to me." She pushed the door open. "It's not that we were big buds or anything. It turns out I'm the closest living relative she had. Our mothers were sisters." She pulled my card from her pocket and looked at it. "Lee Barrett. Okay, Lee. Come on in. We can talk while I finish packing up dishes." She held the door open. "Come on, Zeus." The dog followed me inside.

The house was just as attractive inside as it was on the exterior, even with packing boxes stacked on the floor and piled onto tables and chairs. I followed Jane through a living room decorated in muted blues and grays. Crisp white organdy curtains fluttered at an open window framing a view of pink and white hollyhocks outside. "It's a lovely home," I said, as we emerged into a Martha Stewart–worthy kitchen. "Are you planning to sell it?"

Jane opened a cabinet door and pulled a step stool into position so she could reach the top shelf. "Oh, she didn't leave me the house. Just the things in it." She lifted a teapot from the shelf and lowered it carefully to the counter. "You drink tea? You can have this if you want it."

"Thanks anyway. It's beautiful but I'm a coffee fiend.

I'd probably never use it. Anyway, it's too valuable to just give away."

"I won't use it either. Not my style." She sighed. "I'm just getting tired of packing. She had some really pretty things. Top quality. You should see her jewelry. I'm pretty sure it's all real."

I'm supposed to be asking questions about Gloria. Never mind the teapots and trinkets.

"Your cousin had lovely taste," I said.

Jane nodded solemnly. "She liked *expensive* things but thank goodness she didn't leave me any bills. Her funeral was even prepaid, and one of those societies that cremates the body and puts the ashes in the ocean took care of all that."

I wrote, "Gloria was cremated. Returned to the earth." Jane wrapped porcelain plates in newspaper before placing them into a box. "I guess she made a good living waitressing; she always sent my kids nice presents at Christmas."

I remembered what Aunt Ibby had said about Gloria only liking to wait on the businessmen. The big tippers. "My aunt remembered your cousin. She told me Gloria was an excellent waitress." *Well, she did say that. Right after she called Gloria a witch.* I scribbled, "generous to young relatives." "Did you know about Gloria's . . . um, religion?"

"You mean the witchcraft thing?" I had no freakin' idea. Our mothers must be rolling over. But my kids think it's the coolest thing they ever heard."

"How do you feel about it?"

She wrapped a teacup slowly, looking thoughtful. "You know? I don't mind it. If it made her happy, it's perfectly okay with me. I just hope that's not what got her killed." She put the cup into a box. "What do you think? Is somebody killing witches? That's what you're investigating, isn't it?"

The question surprised me, though I suppose it shouldn't have. I had, after all, told her I was an investigative reporter. "I'm doing a report on the crows," I said. "My next question was going to be about the quince tree."

"God. It looks so ugly like that. If it were up to me I'd chop the thing down, but like I told you, I don't own the place." She wrapped a stack of saucers, one by one. "It would have made Gloria sad, though. She was proud of that tree. Sent me a couple of jars of homemade quince jelly every year." I made a note to mention Gloria's quince jelly.

"Were you here when the crows did it? Stripped the tree?"

"I was right here in the house. I heard all the commotion. That awful screechy noise they make about drove poor Zeus crazy." The dog acknowledged his name by moving close to Jane. She reached down and patted his head. "He barked and whined the whole time. He finally went and tried to hide under Gloria's bed. I watched the whole thing from the window. Say, if you want to see a picture of it, that nosy old bat next door was making a movie of the whole thing."

"No kidding! How do you know?"

"She's not very good at hiding it. She just holds the camera right on top of the fence. I guess she does it a lot. The lady who lives on the other side of her told me the camera is aimed at her yard just about every time she goes outside to work in her garden." She shrugged. "I was going to call the cops on the woman, but everybody around here says she's harmless. It's not like she puts the stuff up on YouTube or anything."

"I wouldn't like it," I admitted, a little ashamed that I'd already used some of the illicitly obtained footage. "I think I'd probably tell her to stop or I'd report her for snooping."

"Oh well." Jane sealed the box with a wide strip of tape. "I won't be here much longer. Maybe somebody should tell the next tenant." She opened another cabinet. "I wonder sometimes, though, how many videos she's shot of Gloria's goings-on."

I wonder too.

"I guess you know that the crows stripped another tree in the neighborhood," I said.

"You mean the Bagenstose's apple tree." Jane pulled several cake pans from the shelf and put them on the counter. "These can go to Goodwill. I have enough pots and pans. Unless you can use them?"

"No thanks. Do you know Mrs. Bagenstose?"

"Not really. She saw the U-Haul and stopped by to say hello. I guess she must have known Gloria. I showed her the tree and she said hers had been stripped exactly the same way."

"I'm going to go over to her house after I leave here. I hope she'll talk to me."

"She's really nice. Awfully sad, though, because of her husband dying like he did. Did you know he was picking a branch with buds on it as a surprise for her? She wanted to try forcing blossoms in warm water like you can do with forsythia."

"I didn't know that. What a sweet story. I'll ask her to tell me about it. Thanks, Jane."

"You're welcome, Lee. When is your show going to be on?"

"It's not really my show, just a segment on the late news. It's tonight. I'll be on with Buck Covington."

"Oooh. Lucky you! He's a real doll."

"Yes. He's good looking all right. Thanks for your time, Jane. Sorry for the loss of your cousin." I patted Zeus, who gave my hand a friendly lick. "I'll let you get back to your packing."

"You're welcome. Zeus likes you. Do you have a dog?"

"No. I have a cat, though. His name is O'Ryan."

"We have a cat too. I had to leave her home but I brought Zeus along to keep me company. Gloria didn't have any pets, although there's a cute stray black cat who's been hanging around ever since I got here. I've been putting out saucers of milk for her once in a while."

"That's nice. My aunt and I like to feed strays too. Thanks for talking with me, and please give me a call if you think of anything to add to what we've talked about—or if the crows come back."

"God forbid!" she said. Jane and Zeus escorted me to the front door and watched as I walked down the path to my car. As I unlocked the Vette I looked back, once again noting how the bare branches of the quince tree clashed with the perfection of the house and grounds. The small black cat moved so quickly if I had blinked I would have missed seeing her. She peeked from behind the trunk, then ducked back behind it as though she were playing hide-and-seek with me. I waved to her and, still smiling, headed for Dearborn Street.

CHAPTER 27

The Bagenstose house was very different from the little Cape Cod I'd just left. It was an imposing mansion, set well back from the street with a tall wrought iron fence surrounding a lush front lawn. Flowering bushes and several trees dotted the landscaped property. It was every bit as lovingly maintained as the Tasker property was, just a heck of a lot bigger. A gate closed off the driveway. I opened my window and pressed the indicated button. "Name, please?" requested an automated voice.

"Lee Barrett," I said. "WICH-TV. To see Mrs. Bagenstose. I don't have an appointment."

The voice didn't reply, but the gate swung open, so I drove slowly toward the house. Should I go to the front door? Or did media people use a servant's entrance in the Bagenstose world? I parked in front of what appeared to be a four-car garage and climbed out of the Vette. The question of where to go from there was answered when the front door opened and a woman stepped out onto a wide granite terrace. She paused for a moment, then, smiling broadly, walked toward me. "Lee? Lee Barrett? You're Ibby Russell's niece. I remember when you were a little girl and your aunt used to bring you into Elliot's bank."

She was tall with steel gray shoulder-length hair asymmetrically cut. She wore a short black dress, which, as she drew closer, I recognized as vintage French lace—probably 1920s. It was what collectors call a "flapper dress." And while it was certainly attractive on her slim figure, it struck me as an odd choice of clothing for midafternoon in Salem. I didn't remember the early childhood bank visits at all but accepted a hug and air kiss.

"Thanks so much for seeing me, Mrs. Bagenstose." I handed her my card. "I know I should have called, but it was a spur of the moment idea. I'm doing a report on the crows for the station and I understand you've had an unfortunate experience with them."

"A dreadful experience. Simply dreadful." She held the door open and motioned for me to enter. "Come in, dear child. I'll tell you all about it."

The foyer was carpeted with an exquisite Oriental rug in red tones. Mrs. Bagenstose tossed my card onto a silver tray atop a bombe chest with gold drawer pulls. Rows of paintings lined the walls. "Like a museum," my aunt had told me. She wasn't kidding. The woman directed me into a large, fireplaced room that I'd call a parlor. Massive furniture, another Oriental rug, this one in tones of blue, and more paintings. I resisted the urge to gawk around like a tourist at the Louvre, and notebook and pen in hand, I sat in the gilt carved Louis XV armchair she indicated.

She sat facing me in a matching chair, arranging the short lace skirt over slim legs. According to my aunt, Claudine Bagenstose was in her early sixties. If that was true, she was maintaining her looks extremely well. "It was the apple tree," she began. "But I'm sure you know that. It was in the newspaper and on television too. The crows came in a great black cloud one afternoon and descended on the poor, dear tree." She produced a handkerchief from somewhere and dabbed at her eyes. "Elliot loved that tree. It was just beginning to bud, you know."

"Were you here when it happened?" I asked, pen poised. "Did you see the crows?"

"Not at first," she said. "One of the maids called to me to come to the window. I heard them before I saw them. They make such horrible noises. Filthy creatures."

"But you saw them destroying your tree?" I prompted.

"It only took them a few minutes. They devoured everything. Leaves, buds, everything. Then they rose up in a big black cloud and disappeared."

"Disappeared?"

"It seemed so to me," she said. "They were there, then poof! They were gone. I'm glad my darling Elliot wasn't here to see such destruction. It was his favorite tree. Did I tell you that?"

"Yes. I spoke earlier with Ms. Tasker's cousin. She told me a very touching story about your husband selecting a branch from that tree for you."

"It's true." She dabbed at her eyes again. "That dear man's very last act on this earth was something to please me. He must have climbed on that shaky old ladder to get a branch—a spray of apple blossoms to put in my pink vase." She waved a French-tipped manicured hand toward the fireplace. "There's my pink vase on the mantel," she said, "right beside the urn holding my darling's ashes."

I hoped she was planning to return his ashes to the earth, per Wiccan teachings, but didn't comment on that. "Would you tell me the story about the apple blossoms?" I said. "I'd like to share it with the viewers of WICH-TV."

Please say yes. If there's anything Mr. Doan likes better than blood, it's pathos.

She hesitated and glanced around the room. "Oh, I don't know. The only person I've mentioned it to was Jane, that poor woman's cousin. It was quite a personal moment."

"I understand," I said. "I really do."

She put the handkerchief aside and stiffened her posture. "I believe you do," she said. "So I'll tell you how it happened. We'd had breakfast together as usual. Cook had prepared a lovely spinach omelette and we had our morning coffee afterward on the patio overlooking the backyard. It was the housekeeper's day off and cook was going to market, so Elliot and I were looking forward to a quiet day together." She dabbed at her eyes with the lace-edged handkerchief. "'It looks as though the tree is about to blossom, darling,' he said." She leaned forward and dropped her voice. "I told him I'd love to have a branch or two to put into warm water so we could watch it blossom indoors. I didn't think about it again that morning. Then later I happened to look out the window and I saw that the ladder had tipped over." She looked down at the rug and grew silent. I waited for her to finish. She looked up. "I ran outside. He was on the ground. I don't know how long he'd been lying there. I held him in my arms and told him I loved him. He was cold.

I knew he'd already gone to be with the Lord. His last act in this world was to cut that lovely budding branch for me." Her eyes glistened with tears and she touched them with the handkerchief once more.

"It's a beautiful story," I told her. "I'd be proud to share it with my viewers, with your permission."

"Of course you may, my dear," she said, then looked at her watch, a Rolex with a diamond pavé face. "I'm sorry. Time has slipped away. You must excuse me. I have an appointment shortly." I put my notebook away and stood. She ushered me politely, but firmly, toward the foyer. "It was a joy to see you, my dear. I'll try to stay awake to watch your program. I'm usually sound asleep by that time, though. Give my love to your dear aunt."

"Thank you so much for seeing me today," I said. "Perhaps someday you'll allow me to interview you about your wonderful antiques. I know the viewers would be fascinated."

"I'd be delighted to do that, dear. Someday, after my grief has lessened." She opened the door and I stepped out onto the terrace. "Bye-bye now," she said and did a little-girl twirl back into her house, lace flapper dress flaring.

I headed to my car, then realized that I hadn't seen the apple tree. She'd said it was in the backyard and I thought it would be okay if I just took a quick look behind the garage. I hurried along the edge of the long building and there it was. It was bigger than the quince tree, and much taller, which made the winter-like leaflessness all the more startling. There were other trees nearby, green and healthy, some of them bearing fragrant white blossoms. I wished then that I'd brought Therese along with her camera. It would have been good TV. I stood there quietly, thinking of Elliot Bagenstose's last sad moments. I didn't hear the man approach from behind me until he spoke.

"So we meet twice on the same day. What a surprise."

I'm sure I jumped. "Mr. . . . Madigan," I stammered. "Uh—hello." He wasn't smiling. I took a step backward.

"What are you doing?" The question was asked in a polite tone of voice, but the look on his face was chilling.

I began to answer. "I was just . . ." when I felt the tiniest flare of temper begin to rise.

It's none of your damned business.

"I'm looking at the apple tree," I said flatly. "Why do you ask?"

"This isn't a good place for you to be," he said.

CHAPTER 28

Sean Madigan's tone was no longer polite—or even friendly. "Good-bye now. Have a nice day," he said, eyes narrowed, voice cold.

I had a strong feeling that he was right. This wasn't a good place for me to be. I didn't reply, just walked a little faster on my way back to my car. That's when a window on the side of the garage gave me a glimpse of the green Toyota parked inside, next to a pair of shiny matching black his-and-hers Cadillacs.

What the hell is going on here?

When I'd told Pete about Aunt Ibby seeing Sean and Claudine Bagenstose together, he'd said, "We're keeping an eye on that situation." What situation was he talking about? What did the widow and the art crook have going on that rated him access to her garage? Was the appointment she'd mentioned with him? It certainly looked that way to me.

I peeled out of the driveway onto Dearborn Street, then slowed down to a more decorous pace on the way to North Street and home. I tried to concentrate on the new notes I'd taken about the two stripped trees, to think about the behaviors of crows, to organize my thoughts and focus on show prep for my debut broadcast just hours away. By the time I pulled into my own garage I still hadn't entirely succeeded in erasing intruding images of the art thief/best man virtually chasing me away from the Bagenstose place, but just being home again gave a sense of security, of safety. So did being greeted at the door with purrs and loving ankle rubs from our wise and loyal cat.

I picked up O'Ryan, pressed my face into soft fur, and carried him all the way up the two flights to my apartment. Such pampering was an infrequent occurrence. He clearly enjoyed it and rewarded me with dainty pink-tongued licks to my chin. Once inside the kitchen, I released the cat, tossed the notebook onto the table, kicked off my shoes, turned on Mr. Coffee, and prepared to do some last minute organizing of information. I didn't plan to count on the teleprompter but had decided to make a few backup notes to keep me on track.

After about an hour of condensing, combining, and sorting the varied pieces of information I'd gathered about crows in general—and Salem's recent murder of crows in particular, along with the "human interest" angles I'd picked up from Jane and Mrs. Bagenstose— I was confident that I had material for a good, tight, entertaining fifteen minutes of airtime. I stacked my notes, leaned back in my chair, drained my coffee cup, and looked at Kit-Kat clock. I'd had a busy day— most of it positive, some of it downright weird. There was still plenty of time for a well-deserved nap before dinner. Then I'd be off to the station, where Wanda the Weather Girl's personal hair and make-up guy had promised to work his magic on me before I appeared on camera.

I exchanged the silk shantung for my Minnie Mouse nightshirt, set my alarm for seven o'clock, and pulled on a pink satin eye mask I'd used for day sleeping back when I hosted *Nightshades*. I crawled between the covers and was sound asleep within what seemed like seconds.

A sound awakened me. I lay quietly for a moment, puzzled because it wasn't the expected monotonous buzz-buzz of my bedside alarm clock. More like a scritch-scritch. I lifted the eye mask just enough to see the clock face. Ten minutes after six. I slid the mask up onto my forehead, sat up in bed, and listened. Nothing. Whatever it was that woke me up had gone silent. I sat up, stretched, took off the mask, and put both feet on the floor, still listening. Still nothing.

"Must have been dreaming or imagining things," I said aloud, then looked around for O'Ryan so I wouldn't feel so silly about talking to myself. "Are you here, cat?"

A soft "mmrrrow" from the kitchen answered my question, then O'Ryan appeared in the doorway, head cocked in his "What's up?" position.

"Did you hear that?" I asked. "That scratchy noise? Did you do it?"

He turned around, facing into the kitchen, then looked back at me.

"Okay. I'm coming." Barefoot, I followed. He climbed onto the windowsill, sat on his haunches, nose against the pane. It was still light outside, that pretty late-afternoon kind of golden light that happens sometimes before dusk. I pulled up a kitchen chair and sat directly behind him and peered over his fuzzy head.

"What are you looking at? Did that sound come from outdoors?"

I didn't have to look far, and I didn't have to listen hard for the scratchy noise. The answer was right in front of me. Literally. I've heard crows' eyes described as "beady" and the term is accurate. A crow's eye close up looks *just* like a round, shiny, black bead. And this one was definitely close up. So was this crow's foot, long, black, sharp talons scratching rhythmically on the screen.

"I hope it doesn't think I'm going to let it into the house," I told O'Ryan, who seemed to be taking the presence of this intruder on his turf remarkably calmly. "What does it want?" The creature stopped scratching and bobbed its head forward, beak open; picked up something shiny from the fire escape; and dropped it onto the outer sill. Then it repeated the action.

Some of the sources I'd consulted said crows like shiny objects and have been known to steal them. Was this visiting crow a thief, depositing stolen goods at my kitchen window? The thing lifted its wings, which made the already oversized bird look even more gigantic. It headed toward Oliver Street, not stopping at the maple tree, but wheeling high above it and disappearing into darkening blue sky.

Naturally I was curious to see what this visitor had left for me, but mostly I wondered why it had left me anything. Thoughts of Peg Wesson and Bridget Bishop popped into my head. Legend had it that each of them could turn into crows, among other creatures. Was I seeing a recycled witch scratching at my window?

I shook away the silly thought, lifted the screen, and retrieved two shiny brass cylinders. I recognized them immediately. Shell casings. I held them in my palm, then turned one over. "380 AUTO" was incised on the base.

Three eighty auto. Wasn't that the caliber of the bullets the police had dug out of Christopher Rich's magic store wall?

Oh boy. Had I just destroyed fingerprints on evidence? I opened a kitchen drawer with one hand, removed a plastic zippered bag, and dropped the casings into it. Why had the crow brought these particular casings to me? I didn't know the answer to that, but I was pretty sure Pete would want to know about it.

Okay, so I call my straight-arrow, nothing-but-the-facts-ma'am police detective boyfriend and say something like, "Hi, Pete. Listen. This big crow came to my window. I mean, I think it's a crow but it could be a witch in disguise. But anyway, it left me something on my windowsill. No, not poop. It was two shell casings. You want to see them?"

I shook my head, closed the screen, picked up my phone, and hit Pete's private number. He answered right away. "Hi, babe. I bought the champagne for tonight. Are you all ready for your first report?"

"I am, but, Pete, I called about something else. Something strange has happened. Did you ever find the shell casings from the gun used to shoot at Christopher Rich?"

"Not yet. Why?"

"I think I may have them. Somebody—something—left them here. I don't know why, but I'm pretty sure they're the ones you're looking for."

"I think maybe I should come over. Okay?" He sounded confused and who could blame him?

"I have to leave for the station pretty soon. Hair and make-up, you know," I said. "If I'm not here, the casings are in a plastic bag on the counter. Anyway, I'll see you after the show."

Maybe by then I'll come up with a sensible way to explain this. If there is a sensible way.

I made a peanut butter sandwich and poured a glass of milk. I didn't feel like having dinner and I wanted to be gone before Pete arrived. My on-air outfit was ready in a garment bag. I pulled my hair back with a wide band and cleaned my face carefully, as per instructions from Wanda's make-up guru. I ate most of the sandwich, gulped down the milk, donned jeans and sweatshirt, grabbed my notes and the garment bag, and hurried down the back stairs. As I backed out of the driveway I looked up at the maple tree branches. About half a dozen crows looked back at me.

When I pulled into the WICH-TV harborside parking lot, I couldn't resist looking up into the oak tree on the Essex Street side of the property. More crows, all quietly watching. I guessed there might be around a dozen there, and it seemed as though those shiny shoe-button eyes watched as I walked to the front steps.

Rhonda was still at her desk when I arrived at WICH-TV. "You're early," she said. "I stuck around to watch Carmine do you."

"Carmine? The make-up guy?"

"Yep. He says he can hardly wait. Loves your red hair, your bone structure, your eyes. Says you're a blank canvas just waiting for an artist like him."

I'm a blank canvas?

Not quite sure I liked the analogy, I followed Rhonda through the soundproof door leading to the first-floor broadcast studios. As we passed the glass-enclosed newsroom it occurred to me that even though I'd been on-air talent for WICH-TV in the past I'd never yet worked in that rarified setting. *Night-shades* had been shot in a small set in the downstairs studio, across from the "Cooking with Wanda the Weather Girl" kitchen. So this night would mark the beginning of what might turn into a new career for me. Lee Barrett, news reporter. Who knows? Maybe even Lee Barrett, news anchor.

Blank canvas indeed.

The make-up room had been greatly improved in the time I'd been away from the station. Real salon-type chairs, big well-lighted mirror, shampoo station, and shelves of beauty products. Naturally everything was done in varying shades of purple, but in this environment it seemed to fit.

The man standing beside a lavender marble counter where an assortment of combs and brushes were displayed rubbed his hands together when Rhonda and I entered the room. "Ms. Barrett, you cannot imagine how delighted I am to have this opportunity."

"This is Carmine, Lee," Rhonda said, giving me a gentle push in his direction. "Carmine, here she is. Lee Barrett. Work your magic." She sat on a white wicker chair with a purple velvet cushion. "Mind if I watch?"

He nodded in Rhonda's direction, then wordlessly took my hand and led me to the violet chair in front of the mirror. He pushed a button and a beam of light illuminated every pore, every blemish, every stray eyebrow hair, every line on my face. I even saw wrinkles on my neck that I'd never seen before. I closed my eyes. Tight. "Ugh," I said.

"Ahhh," he said. "What a face. Those cheekbones,

those lips, those eyes, that complexion. And the hair! Glorious!"

He began work with cool, creamy stuff evenly spread over my face and neck. I dared to open my eyes, then quickly shut them again. "We'll let the cleanser work while I shampoo," he said. As I reclined, head over the sink, he massaged wonderful-smelling things into my hair. Darn near fell asleep. Towel dry, then back to the mirror, where he patted my face gently with a soft, warm cloth. I dared to peek at the mirror. My skin looked better already.

Note to self: Buy a barrel of that face cream.

"Now for the hair." He ran skilled fingers through the curly mess. "Maybe a little trim? A bit of straightening? Tiny highlights?"

"Uh, I don't know . . . highlights?"

Rhonda's "Absolutely! Go for it, Lee" drowned out my hesitant "maybe."

Again I closed my eyes. It would have been a totally relaxing experience, except for thoughts of the window-scratching crow, the brass bullet casings, and the most worrying question of all.

How am I supposed to explain all that to Pete?

CHAPTER 29

I kept my eyes shut as Carmine worked. I've never been very good at hair. I wash and condition regularly, have it trimmed once in a while, and do the best I can with a comb and brush. I also have a good-sized collection of "bad hair day" hats. I heard the snip-snip of scissors and felt some gentle tugging here and there. It was all so relaxing I nearly dozed off.

"A few minutes under the dryer now, Ms. Barrett."

I dared another look at the mirror. Sections of hair were wrapped in foil, spiking outward like Medusa's snakes. With a silent prayer that this guy knew what he was doing, I obediently took a seat under a lavender dome. The dryer time gave me a few minutes to think, to plot really. I needed to tell Pete the truth about how the shell casings had appeared at my window, but to explain the crow, I'd have to first make sure he was familiar with some local witch legends. Like the ones about Peg Wesson and Bridget Bishop—those naughty little shape-shifters.

This isn't going to be easy. The police are going to want to know where I got the casings. I can tell Pete about the crow and just hope he'll understand, but I'm not sure the chief will buy it. Maybe Pete will tell him someone put them there.

The thoughts were disturbing. How did "someone" get to the third-floor window? I answered my own question: It's impossible. The company that installed the fire escape guaranteed that although there's a sliding ladder leading from the second-floor platform to the ground it only works one way. Down. Maybe I imagined the crow. Maybe it was a "crow vision," appearing on window glass. Such a thing had happened before. Once a vision in a window showed me a bear. But an imaginary crow couldn't carry real shell casings. What if it *wasn't* impossible for someone to climb up to my window? That idea gave me a chill. It would mean that someone had been outside my kitchen window. It would mean that someone could have raised the screen, could have come into my apartment. . . .

Carmine's interruption was welcome. "Time for our reveal," he said, leading me back to the styling chair. He turned it away from the mirror so that I faced Rhonda. Again the gentle fingers worked on my head and again I closed my eyes. I felt the chair spin. "How do you like it?"

I opened my eyes as I heard Rhonda's soft "Oooh," and echoed it myself.

"I love it," I said. "Absolutely love it." I really did too. The length was good, the curls were tamed, the highlights were subtle. I still looked like me, but way better. Carmine efficiently cleared away the hairstyling paraphernalia and made a neat row of bottles, boxes, brushes, pencils, and tubes.

"Make-up now," he said. "We begin with the wonderful green eyes." I tried to watch the process, thinking I could learn from the master, so to speak. But he

moved so fast, wielding brushes both broad and
narrow, mascara wands (two kinds), liquid and powdered foundations, it was all pretty much a blur. He
made a grand final flourish with a brushful of bronzer,
then stepped back, tilted his head, leaned in and adjusted one lock of my hair, stepped back again, and
pronounced me perfect.

"Wow, Lee. Wait 'til Pete sees you now! I mean,
wow!" Rhonda stood behind me, gazing at my reflection.

"Perfection," Carmine said. "I've wanted to do this
since I first saw you on that psychic thing you used
to do."

"Thanks so much, Carmine," I said. "This new look
is just what I needed tonight. A real confidence
booster. What do I owe you?" I accepted the hand
mirror he handed me and admired myself from every
angle.

"This one is a gift from Mr. and Mrs. Doan," he said,
"but if you'd like me to make it a regular appointment,
just let me know."

"You'll be hearing from me," I said, holding the
hand mirror close to my face. We'd had make-up
people on the home shopping shows I'd done, but the
results hadn't been this spectacular. I handed him a
more than appropriate tip and looked at myself in the
hand mirror once more. Big mistake. The flashing
lights, the whirling colors are even more intense on a
small surface. I knew I was about to see a vision. I
didn't want to see it but couldn't look away.

No more glammed-up Lee Barrett. Instead I saw the
face of another woman. I recognized her right away.
Bridget Bishop. She smiled directly at me and lifted
one hand. In her palm she held two bullet casings.

Then her brown eyes turned black—black and beady. She turned into a crow before my startled eyes. The vision blinked off and once again I saw myself.

Rhonda's words seemed to come from a distance. "Come on. You can admire yourself later. Let's go see how you look with your outfit on. I hung it up in the dressing room. Let's go." I put the mirror facedown on the marble counter, picked up my handbag with my notes in it, and hurried to catch up with Rhonda.

The dressing room hadn't changed much since I'd last seen it. A rolling clothes rack, a couple of mis-matched tables, a brown vinyl-covered club chair and hassock, a vanity table with a mirror surrounded by round lightbulbs. I avoided looking into the mirror and looked instead at the clothes rack. My garment bag was the only one on it. Rhonda unzipped it and handed me the soft jade green silk dress.

"Thanks, Rhonda," I said. "I'm glad you're here with me."

"Wouldn't have missed it," she said. "Did you bring shoes to go with this?"

"They're in the bottom of the bag," I said as I pulled off my sweatshirt, being extra careful not to mess up my hair, and unzipped my jeans. "I think they'll only be shooting from the waist up, but I bought new shoes anyway."

"Holy crap, Lee," Rhonda said. "Are these Jimmy Choos?"

I admitted my extravagance. "Couldn't resist."

"Well, get dressed. Let's see how you're going to look. You'll be on in less than an hour."

Surprised, I checked my watch. "All that fussing with hair and make-up took longer than I thought." I

slipped into dress and shoes, then did a slow turn for
Rhonda. "What do you think?"

"Take a look in the mirror," she advised. "See what
you think."

I didn't want to look into that mirror—or any mirror.

"I can't," I said, picking up my notes. "I'm too nervous. I'm going up to the newsroom now. Do I look
okay?"

"Definitely okay."

The newsroom buzzed with the usual hour-before-
broadcast activity. When I entered the room Buck
Covington was already seated in the anchor chair, sipping on a Coke and chatting with one of the lighting
men. Marty McCarthy was my favorite camera operator
and I was happy to see that she was part of the crew for
my debut. I recognized, but had never met, the current
audio engineer who sat in front of an intimidating (to
me anyway) bank of screens and control panels. The
station's field reporter, Scott Palmer, was there behind
the glass pane too, in the news director's usual seat.
Bruce Doan likes to get as much work from every employee as he possibly can, and it appeared that he'd
found an added duty for Scott.

Heads turned in my direction as I walked to the half
circle of red and black laminate that formed the
anchor desk. A panoramic view of Chestnut Street—
sometimes called the most architecturally perfect
street in America—provided the background shot.

"Hi, Moon," called Marty. I'd been "Crystal Moon,
psychic" when we'd worked together. "Looking good,"
she said.

"Darn good," offered Scott. "Going to tell us all
about the crows?"

"I'm going to try," I said, pausing in front of the

anchor desk. "Hi, Buck. What's the plan? Do you call me up here during a break?"

He turned on that million-dollar smile. "Right. What time does Lee come on, Scott?"

"Lee gets fourteen minutes at eleven thirty-one, right after the shopping mall commercial. You'll do the teaser for "A Murder of Crows" at eleven twenty-seven and the one-minute intro at eleven-thirty. I have the crow videos ready to roll. Then we go to weather with Wanda on the green screen, sports roundup at the desk, and close. Got it?"

Buck wrinkled the perfect brow for a second and consulted a printed schedule. Big smile. "Got it."

"Come on over and sit by me, Lee," Scott offered, patting an empty chair next to him. "You can help me direct this party."

I accepted and shuffled through my notes for the hundredth time that day.

Scott put a restraining hand on my arm. "You don't have to look at those now. You know the material and the teleprompter has all the bullet points you sent over. Just relax. You're going to be fine."

Scott's not one of my favorite people, but sometimes he's right. If I didn't know the material by now I was in the wrong business. I stuffed the notes under my chair and watched the opening credits for the Nightly News roll.

CHAPTER 30

Once the on-the-air sign lit up, and the theme music played, my nervousness melted away and professional show host, weather girl, call-in psychic Lee Barrett took over. Well, maybe not that last one. Anyway, I was able to focus on Buck Covington's words, Scott's hand signals, the multiple screens facing the broadcast tech, and—most of all—the studio clock. The WICH-TV late news runs from eleven to midnight, then comes *Tarot Time with River North*. I wondered if Therese was in the building, if I'd have time to ask her about the previous night's interrupted phone call. No time for that just then. Although fifteen minutes out of the news hour doesn't seem like a long time, when those minutes have to be filled with your own words, accompanied by appropriate facial expressions, when you know you must not cough, scratch your nose, or say anything inappropriate, those minutes can seem like a very long time.

Buck read, flawlessly of course, an entertaining piece about the Dragon Boat festival on the Charles

River, then switched to a more serious note with a report on the increase in arrests for local vandalism. He gave a brief update on the Christopher Rich case, describing the finding of two spent bullets in the back wall of the magic shop. There was a brief clip of Rich himself, describing his ordeal. A touching segment on Megan's funeral included Scott Palmer's earlier interviews with some senior citizens who told about Megan's cheerful weekly visits to area nursing homes. Buck did the teaser for "A Murder of Crows" at eleven twenty-seven, and during a commercial for Liberty Tree Mall I took my seat beside him at the anchor desk.

At eleven-thirty Buck turned on the megawatt smile full blast. "I'm honored to introduce a brand new feature here on WICH-TV. Tonight our own Lee Barrett takes over as investigative reporter. She'll be joining us occasionally this summer, presenting in-depth facts on topics the community may find puzzling or even troubling. Something that has puzzled and troubled all of us lately, Lee, is the phenomenon you call a murder of crows. Tell us about it."

I took a deep breath, smiled, turned on my own carefully cultivated on-air voice—throaty and a little bit sexy—and began my new career.

"Thank you, Buck. I'm delighted to be with you tonight. Let's discuss what we've all been talking about for a couple of weeks now. Crows. Thousands of them. So why do I call this a 'murder of crows'? That's a real ornithological term. And it comes from a time when groupings of many animals were known by colorful and poetic names. How about an ostentation of peacocks? A parliament of owls. A knot of frogs or a skulk of foxes?"

With the help of the bullet points on the tele-prompter and some well-placed and prompted questions from Buck, I led the viewers through much of what I'd learned about the strange springtime roost of what the United States Department of Agriculture's Wildlife Service estimated to be 20,000 to 30,000 birds.

"Most of the crows have been noticeably absent for several days," I said. "They may have broken up into smaller groups, but there's a strong likelihood that they may reorganize, and plans are in effect for the use of more fireworks, spotlights, and perhaps electronic recordings of crow distress calls." I made it clear throughout my talk that these methods wouldn't harm the birds.

We showed the stripped apple tree and I repeated Mrs. Bagenstose's touching story of the blossoming branch her late husband had cut for her. When the video of the crows stripping Gloria's quince tree came on-screen I talked about Gloria Tasker's famous quince jelly. Mentioning the witch connection was un-avoidable, but I kept it to a minimum. "Some have associated the deaths of several members of Salem's Wiccan community with the sudden appearance of the crows, perhaps because crows and witches often appear together in folklore and paintings. The crow has long been associated with magic and the power to manipulate physical appearances." I touched on the bird's reputed penchant for carrying off shiny objects. "Many experts agree that even though stories about crows stealing rings and coins persist, there isn't much evidence that this is true."

Hey, Mister Expert, I know of one that probably carried off a couple of shiny bullet shell casings!

I closed by noting that scarecrows were beginning

to reappear around Salem, with a reminder that the birds are protected under the federal Migratory Bird Treaty Act.

Buck thanked me for the "informative and interesting report," hoped I'd be back again soon, then asked—off script—"So you think the crows will be back?"

"I think they're already on their way," I replied.

Cut to Wanda the Weather Girl, and my debut performance was over. Buck Covington shook my hand, Marty gave a thumbs-up from behind her camera, and Scott offered a fist bump as I passed his chair on my way out of the newsroom.

Rhonda had waited for me on the other side of the window. "You were great. Looked fabulous too, even though your shoes didn't show. Didn't you see River and me waving at you through the glass? She's gone downstairs. Time for her own show." She paused for breath. "Is it true about the crows? Coming back, I mean?"

"Sorry, I didn't see you in the window. Those lights are too bright. And yes, I think with everything I've been able to learn about them the crows will be back."

"It sounds like you know a lot. Hey, can you believe that Chris Rich? Getting his face on the news again? For free? What a mooch."

"What do you mean?"

"Oh, he's such a publicity hound. Only he never wants to pay for airtime. He calls here every other week trying to get us to cover some event he's having at his store." She shook her head. "I wouldn't be surprised if he shot those holes in his wall himself, just to get on TV. Well, gotta get downstairs. I'm sure I'll be seeing you around here a lot."

Maybe it wouldn't be surprising if he'd made an anonymous phone call to River, threatening his own life.

"Thanks, Rhonda," I said. "I sure appreciate your being here for me tonight. By the way, is Therese around?"

"Nope. I'm screening. Therese has an early morning video shoot. Gotta run. See you."

I wished her a good night and headed downstairs to the dressing room to pick up my jeans and sweatshirt, thinking about what she'd said about Christopher Rich. The idea that he might have fired those shots hadn't occurred to me. But there were no witnesses, so it was possible. Making a sneaky phone call was possible too. I'd surely ask Pete what he thought about it. And I'd also like to know what he thought about Sean Madigan being at the Bagenstose house.

Yeah. I'll ask him about those things right after I figure out how to explain those shell casings in a sandwich bag on my kitchen counter.

Pete's car was already in the driveway when I got there. I pulled into the garage, parked the Vette, grabbed the garment bag, locked everything, and hurried past the garden toward the house. The sensor lights along the path glowed just enough to illuminate the smiling pink-faced scarecrow standing among the flowers and vegetables. Somehow the silly face on the thing, so friendly and happy in my aunt's kitchen, had a sinister aspect in the silent after-midnight darkness. I didn't linger to look around for cats or crows, but dashed up the back steps and into the welcome safety of home. Pete had left the hall and stairwell lights on for me and O'Ryan waited just inside the door. After dropping off the bag with shirt and jeans in the laundry room, and with the cat trotting ahead, I climbed the stairs.

Pete greeted me with a warm hug and a kiss that promised more, then held me at arm's length with a long, appreciative up-and-down look. "You're beautiful on TV, lady," he said, pulling me close once more, his voice sexy husky, "but you're a thousand times more gorgeous in person."

I did a little twirl, something like the one I'd seen Claudine Bagenstose do. "Like the new look?" I asked, knowing for sure that he did.

"I like," he said. Taking my hand, he led me down the hall to the kitchen. "Let's celebrate."

As soon as I stepped into the room, I felt a rush of tears. "Oh, Pete. It's wonderful!" And it was. The room glowed with soft candlelight, and a vase filled with red roses shared space on the table with a bottle of champagne icing in a silver pail. Two champagne flutes and a bowl of my favorite treat, chocolate-dipped strawberries, completed the loving picture.

Thoughts of crows and casings almost disappeared, as Pete—with a courtly flourish—held my chair, then, sommelier-like, popped the cork on the champagne. He poured the lovely bubbly into our glasses, then raised his in a toast. "To Lee and a bright new career in television."

"Do you really think so, Pete?" I asked as we tapped the flutes together. "I hope I'm good enough. I know I have a lot to learn about reporting, but . . ."

"Shh," he said. "I recorded your program. You just watch it and you'll see for yourself. You're good enough. The way you spoke about the crows almost made me like the damned things. Here. Have a strawberry."

I sipped my champagne and took his advice about the strawberry. Two strawberries, actually. Glancing across the room to the long granite counter, where a few more candles glimmered, I saw a corner of the plastic sandwich bag peeking out from behind the sugar bowl. I knew we'd have to talk about it soon, and I could tell that Pete wanted to put that moment off every bit as much as I did.

"More champagne?" he asked as I licked one last bit of Belgian chocolate from my lips.

I put a hand over my glass. "No thanks. This was a wonderful celebration, Pete. The roses, the champagne, the strawberries, the candles. It's all perfect and I love you for it, but we do need to talk about those shells, don't we?"

He nodded. "We do. How about I put some coffee on and we go into the living room and you can tell me all about where they came from. Okay?"

"Okay," I agreed, still not sure of what I was going to tell him—not sure of *how* I was going to tell him. So much of it didn't make any sense even to me. Pete turned on the overhead lights and together we snuffed out the candles, put the few strawberries that were left into the refrigerator, and rinsed out our glasses. Then with a cup of decaf in one hand and the sandwich bag in the other I followed Pete down the hall to the living room and reality.

CHAPTER 31

O'Ryan snoozed in the zebra print chair, barely blinking as we entered the room. Pete and I sat side by side on the couch, our cups and the bagged shell casings on the coffee table in front of us. I was first to break the silence.

"You know that I *see* things in unexpected places," I began.

"I know." His tone was sympathetic. "Did *seeing things* have something to do with these?" He gestured toward the shell casings.

"Yes. At least I'm pretty sure it did."

"Can you . . . do you want to tell me about it?"

I nodded. "Someone—something—left them on my windowsill."

He frowned. "That would mean someone was on the fire escape. I don't like this, Lee." He began to reach for my hand, then paused. The frown grew deeper. "What do you mean *something*? Something left them on your windowsill?"

"Maybe."

"Come on, Lee. This is serious. I've told you

before—you can tell me anything. I'm not judging you. Not doubting you. You need to tell me exactly what happened." His voice slid into cop mode. "These shells . . ." he pointed to the bag. "These shells may be evidence in an attempt on a man's life. That's serious business."

"Rhonda thinks Chris Rich might have shot the bullets into his shop wall himself. For publicity. I'm even wondering if he made that phone call to River."

"Rhonda may be right. Maybe not. We don't know. We don't have a weapon yet. And we've sent River's phone tape to a police lab for voice analysis. If it was Chris we'll find out. But I need to know what you know about these shells. I need to know now." He took my hand and squeezed it. "Please trust me, babe."

"I do trust you, Pete. I do. It's just that the damned visions complicate everything. Sometimes I don't know what's real and what's not." I fought back tears. "Okay. Here goes."

I blurted out the whole thing, barely pausing for breath. I told him about the crow-shadow woman I'd seen in the yard and about the crow on the fire escape dropping the shells onto the outside sill. I tried to describe how the crow's face had turned into a woman's face and how the same woman had looked at me from the hand mirror at the station. I reminded him that I'd seen visions in window glass before, and he'd been with me when I'd seen one on the TV screen, so he knew that the surfaces where the things appear had evolved over time. "Whatever I saw from the window," I cautioned, "might not have been there. I mean, the shells were there. You have them in your hand. But how they got there I don't know."

He looked worried. "Then it's possible that

someone—someone real—could have been out there on the fire escape sometime during the day. That would mean they'd have managed to pull down the escape ladder that goes from the second floor to the ground."

"Yes. I've been thinking about that. It's supposed to be foolproof. Guaranteed, Aunt Ibby said so, and you know how she is about security."

He stroked my hair, looking into my eyes. "Jesus, Lee, I worry about you."

I had no answer for that and the tears started again. O'Ryan left his chair, climbed onto my lap, and gave my cheek a friendly lick. That made me smile. "I'll be okay," I promised. "I'll keep the window locked until we're sure the escape ladder is secure."

"Good idea. Now, what about the woman you keep seeing. Do you know who she is?"

"I think so. But you're not going to like my answer."

"Try me."

"Bridget Bishop," I said, speaking very calmly. "Well, the ghost of Bridget Bishop."

He stopped stroking my hair and leaned back against the couch cushion. "You mean the old witch that's supposed to haunt the Lyceum?"

"Yep. But now she's haunting me."

He couldn't help smiling at that idea. "Wow. Listen. Maybe I can tell the chief that somebody figured out how to climb up on your fire escape and put these shells there without mentioning crows."

"Well, a bird really *could* have dropped the shells there, you know. They're shiny, and small enough for a bird to pick up and carry. Anyway, they might have nothing to do with whoever—whatever—shot at Christopher Rich."

"True." He took a couple of sips of coffee. "But didn't you say that the experts don't buy that story about crows? We don't have a weapon yet anyway. I'll just take these along and put them in the evidence locker for now."

"Wait, Pete," I said. "Another odd thing happened today."

He raised one eyebrow. "Odd how?"

"I saw Sean Madigan again."

Instant cop voice. "You did? Where?"

"He was at Claudine Bagenstose's house. I ran into him just as I was leaving. He wasn't very nice."

"What did he say?"

"It was almost like a warning. He said, 'This isn't a good place for you to be.'"

"Hmm. You don't have any reason to go back there, do you?"

I hadn't given that any thought. "Now that you mention it, I guess I don't."

"Okay then, I wouldn't worry about it."

That's Pete. He knows how to make the complicated into the manageable. An unknown somebody—or maybe a bird—left two unidentified shell casings, which may or may not be important, on my fire escape and an unpleasant encounter doesn't have to be repeated. So lock the window and stay away from the Bagenstose house. Seemed simple enough. I felt better.

"Thanks, Pete," I said. "I love you. I'm still worried about River, though. Will you tell me what you find out about that phone thing?"

That brought a hug. "We're on it. Don't worry. I love you too. Want to see yourself on TV now?"

We watched my fifteen-minute segment of the news together. I was happy with my performance, and pleased with the way I looked, even though nobody saw my new shoes.

It had been a very long day for both of us. We finished our coffees and shared a couple of white chocolate–covered strawberries with sprinkles. Pete locked the kitchen window and promised to check the fire escape in the morning. I didn't glance at the glass panes and even took off my sensational new make-up without looking at the mirror. Not an easy thing to do but I didn't want to risk seeing any more crows or witches, real or imagined.

Pete didn't lose any time the next morning in carrying out his promise to check the fire escape. "Think your aunt will be awake by now?" he asked. "I'm planning to go out this window down to the one at her level and see if the drop-down ladder is secure. Don't want her to think there's a stranger outside." He lifted the window sash all the way up. The cool morning breeze was pleasant. The sound of crows cawing in the distance was not.

I tried to ignore the noise and glanced at the Kit-Kat clock. "She's probably in her kitchen, on her second cup of coffee, halfway through the *Globe* crossword. I'll call her to be sure."

She picked up right away. "Good morning, Maralee! You were wonderful last night and you looked so pretty."

"Thank you. I think it went well. The reason I'm calling so early—Pete is going to check on the security of our fire escape. Just wanted to warn you that you might notice a man outside your window shortly."

"That would certainly be a surprise." A note of hesitation. "Why? Does he think there's something wrong with it? Is it unsafe?"

"No, not that." I signaled to Pete that it was all right to climb out the window. "I'll explain it all later. You did tell me that the contractor guaranteed that no one could climb up from the ground, didn't you?"

Her "absolutely" was indignant. "I wouldn't have installed it if it wasn't positively intruder-proof. Anyone would have to have wings to get to the second level!"

That's exactly what I thought in the first place. Wings. Crows' wings on a shape-shifting witch ghost.

"I know you're right. Pete just wants to be sure I'm safe up here. Love you. We'll talk later. Bye." Poking my head out of the window, I watched as Pete slowly descended the metal stairs. I sneaked a peek at the maple tree. A few crows, not a lot of them. I focused on Pete. He seemed to be inspecting every rung. When he reached the second-floor level he pulled a transparent bag from his pocket, a blue adhesive strip at its edge.

I've hung around Pete long enough to recognize an official evidence bag when I see one.

CHAPTER 32

Pete saw that I was watching and gave a little wave with the hand holding the bag. In the other, he held his evidence-gathering tool. He calls it a Swiss Army knife on steroids. It has pliers, both regular and needle nose, wire cutters, assorted screwdrivers, a lanyard, can and bottle openers, a file, and a wood saw. I've missed a few gadgets I'm sure, but you get the idea. Within the grip of those pliers, and about to be dropped into a plastic bag, was something Pete had found on my fire escape. All I could tell at such a distance was that it was small and red. He dropped the bag into his pocket and moved slowly, deliberately toward the end of the platform where the drop-down section of the escape ladder was secured. Kneeling, he took a photo of the assemblage, then stood, turned, and scrambled back up to where I waited.

I moved away from the window while he climbed inside. He brushed dust from his jeans and pulled the plastic bag from his pocket. "What do you think of this?" he asked, placing it on the table. "Looks like you had a visitor out there after all, but that ladder clearly hasn't been moved since it was installed."

The realization that there'd been no two-legged guests at my window brought a wave of relief. "Thank God," I whispered and quickly sat down. I reached for the bag, recognizing the small red collar with its silver buckle right away. "The little black cat," I said. "She's not the first one of O'Ryan's lady friends to come to the window. Impossible for a human; easy for a cat." I inspected the bag, turning it over in my hands. "You don't have to take this, do you? It doesn't look as though the collar is broken. It must have just slipped off. I'll put it back on her neck, if she'll let me."

"You can keep it," he said. "It doesn't seem to have anything to do with the shell casings."

I removed the collar and handed the bag back to Pete. "Can you reuse this?"

"Nope. Contaminated. Might have fleas," he joked. The mood in the room had become much lighter. I put the bag into the recycling bin, carried the collar into my room and placed it carefully into one of the secret compartments of my bureau, and returned to the kitchen.

"Haven't any witnesses to Chris Rich's story turned up at all? You'd think somebody would have heard the shots or have seen someone behind the magic shop," I said.

"Not much is new. We've identified the last two customers who were in the shop before he closed up that night, though. Caught them on surveillance video as they left the store."

"Two people together?"

"No. One at a time. We've asked each of them to

come and fill out some information for us. Maybe one of them saw something."

"Anyone I know?" I asked, half kidding.

"Don't think so. One of them is Viktor Protector. Last guy you'd expect to see in a witch shop."

"He's protesting a tax increase now," I said. "Buck showed a clip on the news tonight. Who's the other one?"

"Just an amateur magician. Rich says he's a regular customer. Calls himself Fabio."

"The Fabulous Fabio," I said. "He's doing Shannon's wedding cake."

Pete gave a questioning look but didn't comment on the magician/baker. "Guess I'll get ready for work, babe. You have any special plans for the day?"

"Not exactly. I need to decide what my next investigative report is going to be. I plan to ask River if it would be possible for me to do a report on the Wiccan funeral rites. Not the public one we just did at town hall. The real one."

"I'm guessing they probably keep that stuff pretty secret," he said. "Better think of a plan B."

"I've also been thinking about what becomes of stolen masterpieces. Want some breakfast?"

"Nope. Not enough time. I'll grab a sausage biscuit on the way to work. I hope you're not thinking about interviewing Madigan, are you?"

"Not really," I said. "Just a passing thought. Maybe I'll do an in-depth investigation of the wedding-planning business. I'm right in the middle of that one and the wedding is on the twenty-first."

"Got my invitation. What should I send for a gift?"

"Just like it says on the invitation. They're asking

for contributions to the fund for repairing broken tombstones in the old cemeteries."

"That's easy. I don't have to wrap it. The invitation says I have to wear black or white. Does that mean a tux?"

"Not if you don't want to," I said. "Just black slacks and a black shirt will work. We have time to figure it out."

"Well, let's not worry about it this weekend. Two whole days off. I've got tickets for the Sox and the Angels for tomorrow night. Sound good?"

"Sounds perfect." I kissed him good-bye and turned on the kitchen TV. Mr. Doan had said they might use a shortened clip of my report on *Good Morning Salem*. Call me vain—I wanted to watch it again.

Someone had done a good job of editing the piece, hitting the most important bits and using the best visuals. The quince tree–stripping sequence was the most dramatic part. Downright eerie. I hoped once again that the poor tree would recover and provide more quince jelly for any future tenants of Gloria's cute house. I studied my on-screen appearance too, more carefully than I had when Pete was with me. Carmine had done a darn good job.

I knew Aunt Ibby would be curious about the outcome of Pete's morning stroll on the fire escape and I wanted to talk to her about my recent scrying episodes. Even though Pete had managed to make me feel better about the things I'd been seeing, I was still filled with questions—and dread. I needed my aunt's calming wisdom and felt lucky that she was just a couple of flights of stairs away.

With O'Ryan a few steps ahead of me, we took the

back stairs. I tapped on the kitchen door and the cat barged right on in through his cat door. "Come in, Maralee," my aunt called. "It's unlocked. I've been expecting you. What was that commotion on the fire escape all about? Come in here and tell me everything."

"That's exactly what I came here to do," I told her. "It may take a while. I've had a busy couple of days."

"Pull up a chair, my dear. Have you had breakfast?" Without waiting for an answer she filled a cup with fragrant hazelnut coffee and put a fresh, still warm corn muffin on a plate. She put the butter dish and a bowl of her homemade strawberry preserves within easy reach, then sat opposite me, fairly quivering with expectation. "What's going on?"

Where to begin? So much had been packed into twenty-four hours. I started my story with my visits to the Tasker and Bagenstose households. "Gloria's cousin Jane was very nice. Showed me around the house. It's really cute. Did you know Gloria didn't own it? Rented it, I guess."

"I didn't know that. I've never been invited over there." Again that little sniff. "But then, of course I wouldn't be."

"What do you mean? I get the feeling you and Gloria didn't get along."

"Oh dear, is it *that* obvious? I may as well tell you then, now that she's dead and gone." Slight pause. She looked down at her hands. "Once, while you were living in Florida, I became engaged."

That was a shocker. "Engaged? You?" I gasped.

"Well, you needn't act so astonished. I'm not without some sort of appeal."

"I'm sorry. I didn't mean . . ."

She waved a dismissive hand. "Never mind. I know what you mean. Anyway, Gloria deliberately set her cap for him. Outright seduced him. I gave back the ring. She promptly dumped him and moved on to her next victim." She sighed. "I've never quite been able to forgive her. Even though she's dead." She gave a shrug of her shoulders and a grim smile. "And poor River thinks *she* had 'bad thoughts' about Gloria! She should see inside my head!"

Even though I've known her all of my life, my aunt continues to amaze me. I didn't know exactly how to respond to this latest revelation, so without comment I proceeded with my own story, saying the first thing that popped into my head. "Jane has a dog named Zeus," I said, "and she has a cat back in Nevada. She says she didn't know Gloria well at all but she's the closest living relative Gloria had. She inherited all the personal belongings and she's packing what she wants to take home. She offered me a pretty teapot but I have no use for it."

"Did she know about the video her neighbor took of the quince tree?"

"She did. Apparently the whole neighborhood knows about the nosy photographer. Jane thinks her cousin must have been the subject of more than one video."

My aunt made a "tsk-tsk" sound. "Bertha Barnes is a member of my library book club. I didn't know she took her photography hobby to that extent. I wouldn't like to have anyone knowing what's going on in my own private space."

Like having crows and cats and God knows what else looking in your kitchen window.

"Jane said that Mrs. Bagenstose dropped by, to express condolences I suppose, and they compared notes on the damage to their trees. That's how I learned about Mr. Bagenstose's last gift to his wife—a spray of apple blossoms. Nice story, wasn't it?"

"It was. Did you give Claudine my regards?"

"I did. She's quite attractive, isn't she? She was wearing an exquisite lace dress from the nineteen twenties, and somehow, it looked just right on her."

"Yes. She has an amazing wardrobe of beautiful clothes spanning at least a century. Inherited most of them from her great grandmother, I've heard. Everything was black. The woman was widowed young, like you were, Maralee, and wore black for the rest of her life."

"I seem to be surrounded with little black dresses lately," I said. "Shannon's black and white wedding, River's black velvet gown, Claudine's flapper dress, the woman in my vision."

"Oh yes, tell me about the vision-woman. Have you figured her out yet?"

"I haven't figured her out, and I know it's important that I do. It sounds nutty, but I believe she's Bridget Bishop."

It was Aunt Ibby's turn to act astonished. "Bridget Bishop? Why on earth would you think that?"

Was it time to share the truth about that cursed spell book? The truth I'd kept secret for so long? I wasn't sure. I hesitated. "Can you, just for now, trust that I have good reason to think so?" I asked.

"Of course." She reached across the table and patted

my hand. "I have faith in you always, Maralee. But can you tell me what the woman in the vision was doing? Perhaps I can help to figure it out."

"I guess I have to back up and tell you about the shells."

"Seashells?"

"No. Shell casings. From bullets A crow put two of them on my windowsill."

"How do you know a crow did it?"

"I saw him put them there."

She nodded as though that made sense. "I see. Is that why Pete climbed out the window?"

"Sort of. They're the same caliber as the bullets they dug out of Christopher Rich's wall. Pete was worried that a person left them there. A person who could get inside. Could get to me."

She gasped. "Oh, no. Go on."

It was my turn to pat her hand. "No. It's okay. He checked. No one has been on the fire escape except a cat. She lost her collar there."

She assumed what I call her "wise owl" look. "A red collar? Was it the small black cat?"

"Yes. I'm going to try to put it back on her if she'll let me. It's not broken. Must have slipped off."

"A black crow and then a black cat," she murmured.

"That's right."

"You've been seeing Bridget Bishop dressed in black. I imagine you believe there's a connection between the three?"

It was a relief to hear someone else—especially my aunt—put that thought, that *knowledge* into words. "Of course I do. Bridget Bishop is, or was, an extremely powerful witch. She had special, uh, special methods."

"Spells? Special spells?"

"Yes, and according to the old witch trial records, Bridget Bishop used animal familiars. Quite a variety of them."

"I know," said my librarian aunt, who knows a lot about everything. "I remember reading that she used a black pig, and some sort of strange monkey with the feet of a bird." She cocked her head to one side. "I wonder if that's where the idea for the flying monkeys in *The Wizard of Oz* came from. I must ask Rupert."

"A witch needs to find an animal willing to work with her, or him," I said. "River says a witch can 'ride' a familiar. That means she astrally projects into the animal and can see through its eyes." I remembered how the eyes of the woman in my vision had changed into crows' eyes and shivered at the memory. "Call me crazy, I believe Bridget Bishop was on my fire escape. First as a crow, then as a cat."

There. I've said it out loud.

"I'd never call you crazy," Aunt Ibby said. "Have you told Pete any of this?"

"No. I mean, I've told him about most of the visions, but have I told him I really think a long-dead witch is peeking in my kitchen window? Not exactly."

CHAPTER 33

As well as I could, I brought Aunt Ibby up to speed on what was happening in my life. I told her about the brief encounter I'd had with Sean Madigan outside the Bagenstoses' garage.

"You say his car was parked inside the garage? As though he was part of the household?"

"I wouldn't go that far," I said. "I mean poor Mr. Bagenstose is barely a few weeks in the grave—or rather in the urn. His ashes are on the mantelpiece next to the pink vase Claudine used for the apple blossom branch he cut for her."

"I didn't mean *that* kind of part of the household, dear. Certainly not. Not Claudine. But Mr. Madigan does have a background in fine art. I wonder if she's consulting him about Elliot's art collection." She paused, looking thoughtful. "And, regarding the poor man's ashes, I wonder if she's aware of the witch tradition about going back to the earth. I'm sure that must have been Elliot's wish. Perhaps someone should tell her."

"I sure wouldn't volunteer for that," I said. "I think I'll take Madigan's advice and stay away from there."

"Is that what he said to you? How rude."

"That's not exactly what he said," I admitted. "He told me it was not a good place for me to be."

"Does Pete know about this?"

"Yes. He seems to agree."

"Hmm." Wise old owl look back in place. "Perhaps you should take the advice then."

"I intend to. I'll move on to other things. Any bright ideas for future investigative reports?"

"The crows appear to be gathering again," she said. "I imagine you'll be called upon to follow up on last night's report with some in-depth information on how to get rid of them for good. Humanely, of course."

"You're right. I suppose they'll use fireworks. That'll be a great visual. Everybody likes fireworks. Except crows, apparently."

"You should definitely include scarecrows too. How do you like mine?"

"Theodore is magnificent. Maybe I'll interview you for a brief tutorial on how to make one."

"Let's look outside and see how he's doing. I'll bet there aren't any crows in my garden."

O'Ryan was way ahead of us. As soon as Aunt Ibby uttered the word *outside* he scooted across the room and out the cat door. By the time we opened the door to the yard, he was at the garden gate, grooming his whiskers. My aunt was right. There were no crows in her garden, even though the branches of the oak, the maple, and the chestnut trees were dark with them, iridescent blue-black feathers glistening in the morning sun, raucous voices caw-cawing.

"See?" she said, sounding almost gleeful. "My scarecrow works just fine."

"Could be," I said, "but maybe it has something to do with the large yellow cat." O'Ryan, his tail straight up like the plume on a drum major's hat, patrolled up and down between the rows of plants.

"Between the scarecrow and O'Ryan maybe this little plot of earth is safe from those rascals," she said, looking in the direction of the clamoring crows, "but from here it appears that the city is in for another Corvus invasion, just as you expected."

"Afraid so. I think I should call River later today. This might be disturbing for her." I remembered how thoroughly frightened my friend had been by the crows after they'd first appeared in Salem. "She seemed to think that somehow it was her fault they were here, and that was in addition to blaming herself for the deaths of the three witches."

"Poor River. I hope she's come to realize that witchcraft has nothing to do with either circumstance."

"I hope so. She seems almost like her old self lately and she certainly looks wonderful. Have you seen *Tarot Time* lately?"

"I caught the beginning of her show one night when she was wearing the black velvet dress we talked about. Stunning with the red corset."

"She looked great in it, didn't she? But did it remind you of the clothes they say Bridget Bishop wore?"

"Good heavens! You're right. Did River dress that way on purpose, do you think?"

We headed back toward the house, but O'Ryan maintained his pacing in the garden. "I don't know," I said. "I haven't asked her about it. Maybe I will."

Maybe I will. Someday, when all this is over.

Aunt Ibby went into her kitchen. I thanked her for breakfast and climbed the curving staircase to my apartment and to my own kitchen—with the big window opening onto a fire escape. I'd always thought of that sturdy platform with its ladders to safety as a comforting presence in my life. Now, I didn't even want to look at it.

I'd told Pete I'd be working on ideas for future investigations for the show, and I fully intended to do it. I put the laptop on the kitchen table and began by listing possible topics.

1. Methods of dispersing crows
2. In-depth study of wedding planning
3. Theft and forgery of paintings

I'd already accumulated the general information on the methods other places had used when a murder of crows had descended on their cities. An interview with a pyrotechnics expert would be good. I could probably get an appointment with the mayor too. As for the wedding planning, thanks to Shannon and Dakota I already had contacts there. What about number three on my list? If I decided to do it, and that was a big *if*, a study of famous art heists would come first. One of the biggest, the robbery at Boston's Isabella Stewart Gardner Museum, tops the list and is still unsolved. If I did it right maybe even the big Boston TV stations would cover it. It could even go national!

Whoa. I'm getting ahead of myself. Back to the cherry bombs and bottle rockets.

I opened the folder I'd started earlier on crow dispersal methods. The point of all of them is to make the crows uncomfortable enough to get the desired result: make them move someplace else, and do it without harming the birds.

Is Bridget Bishop trying to make the witches of Salem uncomfortable enough to get what she wants—the return of her spell book? Is she harming witches in the process? Or is that someone else's doing?

I was having a hard time staying focused on my duties as an investigative reporter. I kept mixing the job up with the other things on my mind. Things like the dead witch and cats and crows and a dead man in the gazebo and the art thief I'd soon walk beside at a wedding on a beach and black dresses. Way too many black dresses.

Time to take a break. Refocus.

I closed the laptop, pushed my chair back, stood, and stretched. I faced the window and wondered if O'Ryan was still assisting the scarecrow, performing crow-watch in the garden. I lifted the sash and looked down. Yes, O'Ryan—that noble beast—still proudly walked his new self-imposed beat. So far, so good. I saw no crows in the yard although I still heard a bunch of them chattering in the trees.

I caught a flash of motion close to the edge of the window. There, approaching on dainty paws, was the black cat, sans collar. At just about the center of the wooden frame, she placed two front paws on the outer sill and looked up, straight into my eyes. I heard an unfamiliar female voice.

"Do you have it?"

I couldn't tell where the words came from. Not from inside the kitchen, yet not from outdoors either.

The voice is in my head. Am I crazy after all?

"You know what I want."

The cat's eyes held mine. I looked away to where O'Ryan paced, robot like, between the green rows below.

"Yes, yes," I said aloud. "Wait right here. I'll get it." I hurried to the bedroom, hands shaking as I pressed the button hidden in a carved curlicue on my bureau. A compartment popped open and I picked up the red collar.

The cat now sat on the sill. I put the collar on the table and lifted the screen slowly, carefully. Was it really a cat? Or was it a vision? I put a tentative hand forward. If it was a vision, I shouldn't be able to touch it, to feel its fur. The idea that the thing was real was even scarier than the possibility that the whole thing was in my imagination.

It was real. I felt behind me for the collar, fumbling for it, not taking my eyes from the cat's eyes.

"Hurry," the voice commanded. The cat stretched its sleek head toward me.

I placed the scrap of red leather around her neck and secured the silver buckle. With the briefest nod in my direction she darted to the top of the ladder, where Pete had so recently made his cautious way down to the second-floor platform. She paused for a few seconds, then with a graceful leap landed just outside Aunt Ibby's window. With one last soaring bound she alighted in a cushioning patch of rosemary. Lifting those delicate paws one by one she approached O'Ryan. He turned, facing her. With his head down, front legs outstretched, he bowed.

CHAPTER 34

I closed the window against the increasing volume of rasping crow noise and once again sat at my table. I opened the laptop and stared at the blank screen. What the hell was that? Had I had a conversation with Bridget Bishop? I was pretty sure that was exactly what had just happened and I didn't like it one bit.

We have to give the damned book back. Then she'll go away and take her crows with her. But how are we supposed to do it?

Megan—the beautiful, smiling Megan—appeared on the screen almost instantly. I smiled back at her, knowing, hoping, believing she would answer the question. Of all of the images this strange ability of mine had produced, hers was the most welcome. "Can you show me how, Megan? Please show me how." Even as I spoke, I had faith that she would. I was pleased too that she wore blue. Not black.

The screen assumed a smoky, misty look. It was like the crystal ball in my dream. When the haze cleared I saw a beach. It was nighttime with no moon at all, but a glow of firelight illuminated the scene. As I watched, a procession of black-robed men and women, one by one, approached a blazing fire. *More black!* I frowned but leaned forward, trying to memorize every detail. A woman at the head of the line held something with both hands. A few of the people following her were veiled or masked. I knew that those were witches who kept their involvement in witchcraft secret. There were thirteen of them altogether, and as they formed a loose circle around the fire, I seemed to move closer. I recognized the leader as River, and the item in her hands was an urn, something like the one I'd seen on Claudine Bagenstose's mantel. Megan's ashes? Of course. But how was Bridget Bishop involved?

The focus changed again. As the fire and the witches receded into the distance, a starkly white shape stood out against the nighttime beach. I recognized the gazebo right away. It was the same graceful structure where I'd seen Christopher Rich, dressed in black and clearly dead.

What is it doing in this vision, which I'm sure represents the return of Megan's body to the earth?

"What does it mean?" I asked aloud. "And where is the spell book in all this?"

I received an answer to my question. The parade of witches on the firelit nighttime beach vanished. In its place was a sunlit place where waves lapped on a tranquil beach. The same gazebo was there too, with dozens of black and white balloons fluttering from the gingerbread trim. The balloons were all in fanciful shapes, like whales and starfish and even an octopus. A white-spotted pied crow flew into the picture, trailing a blue leash. I recognized the ancient paper-covered book clutched in Poe's talons.

I understood. The scene of Shannon and Dakota's

wedding and the location of Megan's funeral were one and the same. It was also the place where River needed to return Bridget Bishop's long-lost spell book.

What about Christopher Rich? Does he have to die there?

More questions formed in my mind but it was too late. The beach blinked away and I was once again alone in my kitchen, staring at a blank screen. O'Ryan chose that moment to stroll into the room via the cat door. I was glad to see him. He was glad to see his red bowl and ignored me in favor of kibble.

"O'Ryan," I said, "is that black cat a witch in disguise? You can tell me."

He favored me with his blankest of blank innocent cat looks and went straight back to eating. Didn't matter. I knew the answer anyway.

I pulled up my topic list. Methods of dispersing crows was number one. I was pretty sure I had the answer to that one. Give the spell book back to Bridget Bishop and they'll leave. On to number two. Wedding planning. That one gave me an opportunity to call Shannon and get an answer to the gazebo question. Is the one on the Dumases' beach the one in my vision? It must be. I scrolled my directory and tapped her name. "Hi, Shannon. Got a minute?"

"Oh, hi, Lee. I was just about to call you. Good news from Blushing Bride!"

"Oh? What is it?"

"Our dresses are ready early. We can pick them up Monday. Isn't that great?" Her voice fairly rang with happiness. "Can you make it? We can meet at Dunks, same as last time. Nine o'clock?"

"I'll be there," I said. "By the way, I met the best man, Sean Madigan. We had breakfast together yesterday."

"No kidding. I'm glad you got a chance to meet

him. He seems nice, doesn't he? Did I tell you he's not staying here at my dad's place after all?"

"No. Why? What happened?"

"Poor guy wasn't getting any sleep. The guest room is right next to the aviary, you know, and I guess Poe talked all night." She gave a little giggle. "Anyway, Sean has a lady friend who has a spare room, so he's staying with her. Worked out for the best. My dad was a little nervous about having him here. We have some nice paintings and stuff and Sean . . . well, you know."

"I understand," I assured her. "Glad it worked out for everyone. Would you do me a favor, Shannon? Could you e-mail me a picture of the gazebo, um— your pergola? I'm working on an idea for a segment about wedding planning and Mr. Doan likes a presentation with photos."

"Glad to. I'll run outside and snap one and send it right away. I'll bet Mr. Doan was thrilled about your show so far. That part about the crows stripping the tree was so creepy and you looked gorgeous."

"Thanks. Having a professional make-up guy makes a big difference."

"Nope. It's not about the make-up. You're a good reporter. I hope I can do that someday too." She gave a happy little sigh. "I'm so glad I took your class. Anyway, I'll see you Monday morning."

"I'll be there. Don't forget to take that picture for me."

"Right away," she promised. "Bye."

"So," I said to O'Ryan, "Sean has a lady friend with a spare room, huh? What do you think of that?" He pretended he wasn't listening, but the forward-pointing ears gave him away so I kept talking. "I wonder if Pete knows about it. I'll bet he does. There's a lot about this case he's not telling me."

O'Ryan stopped eating and turned to face me. "Meh," he said, and shook his head.

"I know. I said 'case,' didn't I? Pete would laugh and call me Nancy Drew. Are you laughing at me too?"

I'm sure he was even though I've never heard him laugh out loud. I stopped talking to the cat when Shannon's picture of the gazebo came through. Several pictures. She'd shot it from every side. The one showing the beach in the background looked exactly as it had in my visions except, thankfully, there was no dead man in it.

CHAPTER 35

I chose the shot of the gazebo with the beach and the ocean in the background, and made two full-page prints on photo paper. I put one aside to use for the suggested venues part of my proposed report on wedding planning because I'd told Shannon I would. (A promise made is a debt unpaid.) The other was for me. I studied it with a magnifying glass from every angle. I hadn't realized until I'd examined the enlargement that there was a bird perched on one of the inside seats. Too dark to be a seabird, it was probably a crow. Why wouldn't it be?

I wanted to share the picture with the few people I'd told about the visions. Maybe it would look familiar to one of them and help to connect the dots for me. I didn't expect to see Pete until late evening and River would still be asleep. I was sure my ever-curious Aunt Ibby would be interested. "Come on downstairs with me, cat," I said. "Let's go visit our aunt. You can tell her all about your garden adventure with the witch-cat and I'll show her the picture." Down the two flights we went again. I'm sure most of the miles on my Fitbit come from stair climbing. I took my usual seat at the kitchen counter and O'Ryan curled up in one of the captain's chairs.

"It's awfully pretty," she said when I showed her Shannon's picture. "I don't recognize it at all. Sorry. Is that a crow inside there?"

"Afraid so. I can't seem to get away from them. I had Shannon send this over because I wanted to be sure whether or not the gazebo behind her house is the one in my visions."

"And is it?"

"Yes. No doubt."

"The visions are tied up with Shannon and Dakota's wedding then," she said.

"Yes."

She folded her arms and did that wise old owl thing again. "And you still believe Bridget Bishop is connected to our little black cat friend as well as to the murder of crows."

"Yes," I repeated. "I gave the collar back to the black cat and I swear I could hear her talking to me. I think O'Ryan knows she's Bridget too." I paused, carefully phrasing my next observation. "I also believe that there's a major relationship between Claudine Bagenstose and Sean Madigan."

Her arms unfolded quickly and one eyebrow shot up. "Relationship? As in man-woman relationship? I can't believe that. Not Claudine."

"I don't know what kind of connection there is, but I learned today why his car is in her garage. He's living there."

She brought both hands up to her mouth and her eyes widened. "Good heavens! Not Claudine! What will people think? Oh dear, I know what they'll think. They'll think she's just like Gloria Tasker, for goodness' sake." Big sigh. "Is there no propriety in Salem at all anymore?"

"Shannon says Sean moved out of their house in Marblehead because Poe kept him awake all night with his talking," I said. "The guest room is right next to the aviary. It could be true, but how did he know Claudine Bagenstose in the first place? Any ideas about that?"

"Both Claudine and Elliot were great collectors. I told you about it. Do you think it's possible that they were customers of Mr. Madigan?"

"Collectors of stolen art?" I said. "I'm afraid it's a possibility. If they bought a painting from him they believed it was stolen even if it was a fake."

She nodded. "Well at least that would mean Claudine's not a you-know-what. Like Gloria."

My aunt's priorities are sometimes peculiar. "It might mean she's an accessory to art theft," I reminded her. "That could be worse than being a you-know-what."

She reluctantly agreed. "Have you talked to Pete about all this?"

"I'll talk to him tonight and show him the picture of the gazebo." I still hadn't told my aunt about the spell book and I wasn't sure I'd ever tell her or anybody. I didn't want to cause a long-dead hanged Salem witch any more annoyance than I already had. I just wanted Bridget to get her book and take it with her to wherever she was spending eternity. It was a good time to change the subject. "Shannon says that we can pick up our dresses for the wedding on Monday."

"That was fast. I can hardly wait to see what you've picked out."

"Black isn't my favorite color, as you know," I said, "but I do like my dress, even though I probably won't ever wear it again. I can't imagine being like that ancestor of Claudine's who wore black for the rest of her life after her husband died. Not me!"

"I've seen some of the great grandmother's wardrobe. Claudine did a vintage fashion show for the Friends of the Library years ago. All black. Even her corsets and chemises and fabulous hats were black, and all of it was obviously expensive. Lots of Paris labels. She has the woman's rings, earrings, bracelets, hat pins, and necklaces too—all with real jewels!"

"By the looks of the Bagenstose place, there's still plenty of money in the family." I thought about the mansion. "Plenty of spare rooms too, in case a friend needed a place to stay. Even room in the garage for an extra car."

"Seems like you've got a lot to think about," Aunt Ibby said. "Is there anything I can help with, research-wise? I'll be at the library most of the day. Just call me if you think of something I can look up."

"I will, and thanks for listening to me and not thinking I'm crazy."

"You are not crazy. You are very special and you can talk to me about anything."

"Pete says that too. I'm blessed to have both of you in my life. Come on, big cat. Let's go home." O'Ryan dutifully followed and together we climbed those stairs again.

Back in my own kitchen, I tried to focus on things practical. I marked "9 A.M. Dunkin' Donuts" on my calendar for Monday and began a shopping list for the weekend. So far all we'd planned was a trip to Fenway on Saturday for the Sox game. I'd need to plan a few meals for Saturday and Sunday. I wondered if Shannon had called Therese about taking pictures of our final fitting. I put aside the shopping list and hit Therese's number.

"Hi, Lee. Your show was awesome. Congratulations," was her greeting. I had to laugh.

"It's not my show by any means," I said. "But thank you."

"You'll have your own news show someday. I'm sure of it." Since Therese is a novice witch, and had been personally trained by Megan, her prophetic words carried some weight. I thanked her again and asked if she knew about the Monday morning fitting plans. "I'll be there," she promised. "It's going to be a busy week. We have some coven things happening. Plans for Megan's funeral, you know. We have to figure out which covens will be involved in the gathering. Everyone wants to be represented. We all loved her." There was a little catch in Therese's voice. "I talked to Pete about that phone call, you know. He told me not to worry about it, that the police will take care of it. So I told River it was nothing to be concerned about. She seemed relieved."

"He's probably right," I said. "He almost always is. Will the funeral be soon?"

"The night of the summer solstice," she said. "Midsummer midnight. A perfect time for her to move on to the Summerland."

I remembered what Dakota had said about getting married on the longest day of the year. "That's the twenty-first," I said. "The same day as the wedding."

"I know," she said. "Same place too. We try to choose a garden or a seaside for a peaceful transition, and

Mr. Dumas said we could hold it on his private beach.
It'll be beautiful."

So my vision had been correct. The black-robed
witches forming a circle on the beach suddenly made
perfect sense. "I'm afraid I don't know anything about
Wiccan funerals," I said, "but I loved Megan too. Can
I help in any way?"

"You can send white flowers if you like, but only
family and Wiccan friends and fellow coven members
take part in the ceremony."

"I understand," I said, and I did—but I still felt
oddly left out. After all, Megan was communicating
regularly with me, not Therese. "I'll see you Monday
morning then," I said and we wished one another a
good day.

The visions had shown me the funeral and the
wedding taking place on the same beach. It hadn't occurred to me that they were both on the same date.
Midsummer. The summer solstice. Why not? A perfect
time for weddings and funerals—beginnings and
endings.

I still wanted to talk to River. I had so much to tell
her and to ask her. I decided to risk waking her and
called even though it was just a few minutes before
noon. I was surprised when my friend answered on the
first ring sounding bright and alert at this early—for
her—hour.

"Hi, Lee," she said. "I watched your show through
the window last night. Did you see me and Rhonda
waving at you like a couple of goofs?"

I laughed. "Couldn't see because of the lights. If I
had I probably would have laughed out loud in the
wrong place. Got a minute to talk? I have some news
for you."

"I have something to tell you too," she said. "I'm wide awake and starving. Want to go someplace for lunch?"

"We could grab a sandwich at the Hawthorne Tavern on the Green," I suggested. "It's a short walk for both of us."

"I'll be there. Fifteen minutes?"

"That soon? You really are hungry!" I checked the clock. "Sure. I'll see you there.

"I can hardly wait to see you." Her voice actually sparkled.

CHAPTER 36

The Tavern on the Green is a cozy little pub in the historic hotel. I was first to arrive and watched River as she practically bounced through the door. My friend looked far different than she had just a few days earlier when we'd driven to Gloucester to get away from the crows. Her long black hair was in a single braid, her pretty oval face free of make-up. With her pink mini dress and white sandals, she looked more like a high school kid on spring break than the glamourous star of a late-night TV show.

"Lee, I'm so glad you could meet me." She joined me at a corner table. "Seems like we have lots to talk about."

"You go first," I said. "You sounded so excited on the phone."

"I did? Well, maybe I am. You'll never guess who asked me out!"

I controlled a grin. Just about anybody who'd watched the interaction between River and Buck Covington on her show would know the answer to that. But I played along. "I give up. Who?"

"Buck Covington, that's who! The handsome hunk who interviewed you about the crows. We're going out to dinner tomorrow night. What do you think about that?"

"I think that's great. If it makes you happy it makes me happy too."

We ordered lunch—me a straight-up burger with Vermont cheddar, River a grilled portobello mushroom with Brie. "You said you had some news for me," she said. "Good news, I hope."

"I think it is," I told her, lowering my voice. "If this gazing thing of mine is working right, I believe I contacted Megan. I asked her to show me how to return the book."

She leaned forward, eyes locked on mine. "I knew she would help me. I just knew it. What do I have to do?"

I looked around the room. No one was in hearing distance but I whispered anyway. "Therese told me about Megan's funeral at the Dumas place in Marblehead. It's going to happen there. I saw it."

"That makes a lot of sense," she said. "I figured it would take a whole coven to do it anyway, and there'll be even more than one coven at Megan's return to the earth."

"More than one? I saw only thirteen people in a circle."

"That would be right. Your visions are getting more specific, aren't they?" She whispered too. "This will be a gathering of witches from several covens but Megan's own coven will distribute her ashes. Since Megan is gone, they picked me to balance the power as the thirteenth member."

"That's why I saw you carrying an urn," I reasoned

aloud. "I didn't actually see Bridget Bishop there, but I saw a crow carrying the book."

"She'll be riding in an animal or a bird of some kind, I expect," River said. "But wouldn't it be cool if we actually saw *her*? In person? Wow!"

"I guess I won't be able to be there, will I?"

"Not without a sudden conversion to Wicca." She smiled. "But don't worry. I'll give you a full report."

I told River about the conversation I believed I'd had with the black cat. "Does that make sense to you?" I asked. "Could she actually get into my head that way?"

She shrugged. "Bridget was powerful in the sixteen hundreds. I'm sure she still is. Maybe even more so. I just hope when she gets her book back she'll be able to move on. She might even stop scaring restaurant customers with apparitions and apple smells!"

"I hope so," I said, resuming my normal voice. "But the ghost tour guides will miss her."

"I sure won't," she said, tossing her long braid over her shoulder. "And I'll bet Gloria's and Elliot's families won't miss her tree-stripping crows." She frowned. "I wonder why she did that. Do you have any ideas about it?"

"I don't," I admitted. "But I'm pretty sure Bridget is calling attention to those two particular witch deaths for a reason."

"If you're right, she might not cross over until the reason is figured out. Is Pete working on it?"

"I think so, but you know Pete. He doesn't like to talk about police business. He hasn't even told me what he's found out about that threatening phone call you got."

She frowned. "I was scared when Therese told me what the rest of the message was. I was afraid for

Christopher Rich. But Pete said not to worry, so I'm trying hard not to. I understand about him not talking about police business. You don't like to talk about the gazing business."

"True. But speaking of crows . . ." I began.

"You told Buck that you thought they'd be back, and it looks like you're right," she said. "There were a bunch of them on Brown Street this morning."

"They're on Oliver Street too." I was whispering again. "But in one of the visions, Megan waved her hand and made them disappear, then come back, then disappear again. I think when Bridget gets her book, she'll send the crows away for good."

Lunches finished, we paid our tabs and left. I wished my friend a great dinner date with Buck Covington, and she hoped Pete and I would have a relaxing weekend. We parted at the main gate to the common and walked in opposite directions. I'd turned my phone off before lunch, and when I turned it back on a new voice mail popped up. It was from Gloria Tasker's cousin, Jane.

"Lee?" she said. "You told me to call you if I thought of anything you might like to know about. Well, something happened. Maybe it's nothing, but. . . ." Her voice trailed off. "Anyway, this guy came to the door yesterday. Said he noticed I was moving and wanted to know if I had any old paintings for sale. I'd already packed all of Gloria's pictures that I thought were pretty into the U-Haul, but there were a few in the garage I was going to send to Goodwill, you know? This guy kind of turned his nose up at them, same as me. He wanted to know if there were any more and I told him they were already packed in the truck so he left. But something happened last night you might want to know about. Oops. Have to hang up now. Zeus needs to go out. You can call me back if you want to." She left a number. I walked a little faster, anxious to get home and return Jane's call. I already had an idea of who the painting-seeking man was. Still very much aware of the presence of crows in the trees bordering the common as I hurried past, I was relieved to see that they numbered far fewer than they had in the earlier invasion.

At least they do so far.

Once at the house I got my notebook and pencil ready, sat at the table, and called Jane. "Hello, Jane," I said. "It's Lee Barrett. What's going on?"

"Thanks for calling, Lee. Like I said, maybe it's nothing, but it was strange. Kind of scary. I'm going to be glad to get out of Salem, what with the crows and the tree thing and all."

"What happened? Are you okay?"

"Oh sure. No problem," she said. "I told you about that guy, the one who wanted to buy old pictures."

"Yes. Did you get his name?"

"No. He didn't say and I didn't ask. Didn't think it was important."

"What did he look like? Young? Old?"

"Oh, around fortyish. Brown hair, brown eyes, average height. Nothing special about him. But listen. Here's what I wanted to tell you about. Something happened last night. It was real late, after midnight. Zeus got to barking up a storm, scratching at the front door, going nuts. I peeked out the window and didn't see anything, but I let the dog out anyway."

"What happened?"

"Zeus made a beeline for the truck, barking his head

off. I heard somebody cussing—like loud, whispering cusswords, know what I mean? Then running sounds, and a car took off burning rubber all the way to the corner."

I could hear the fright in her voice. "You think somebody was trying to break into the truck? The same man?"

"That's what I think. He didn't get into it, though. Zeus saw to that. Good dog. Anyway, we're heading out this afternoon. I just wanted to tell you about it."

"Did you report it to the police?" I asked.

"I thought about it, but what was I going to say? I mean, nothing was stolen. All I could have told them was that my dog barked at somebody and they took off. I didn't see who it was, and who wouldn't run away from Zeus?"

"I'm glad you called me, Jane. My boyfriend is a police detective. Would you talk to him?" I was sure Pete would think, as I did, that Sean Madigan was involved somehow in the midnight visit.

"Uh-uh. I don't have time to get involved with police reports and all that." Her voice was firm. "I want to get on my way home. I've had enough of this place. Good riddance."

"Can't say I blame you. It hasn't been a pleasant trip for you, what with your cousin dying and all the work involved with sorting and packing. Can I call you later at this number if I have any questions?"

"Oh sure. It's my cell, and listen—I saw you on TV. You looked so pretty and it was real nice to meet you."

"Thanks," I said. "Nice to meet you and Zeus too. Have a safe trip home."

After I hung up I sat still for a minute, staring at the

notebook. I hadn't made many notes—just that a man had offered to buy old paintings, that he'd learned that there were some in the U-Haul, and that the dog had chased someone away from the truck late that same night. Not much information, but I planned to tell Pete about it anyway.

CHAPTER 37

I spent almost an hour at Shaw's Market and wound up with all six of my canvas shopping bags full. I felt prepared for any mealtime possibility, from picnic on the beach to candlelight buffet to breakfast in bed. So whatever Pete and I decided to do with our weekend, we wouldn't go hungry. I unloaded the bags onto the kitchen counter with O'Ryan investigating every can, box, and frozen carton. I expected Pete to arrive early, around six. I didn't have to plan anything for dinner because we'd already decided to make an early night of it—a ride down to the Salem Willows to watch the sunset. We'd grab a chop suey sandwich and play a few of the vintage pinball games in the old arcade. A good old summer fun date.

I'd just put a half-gallon tub of vanilla ice cream in the freezer—there'd be hot fudge sundaes sometime this weekend—when O'Ryan took off for the back stairs door, a sure signal that Pete was about to arrive. I started for the living room door to greet him. Just as his key turned in the lock my phone buzzed. Jane's name popped up for the second time that day.

"Hi, Jane," I said. "Can you hold for a sec?"

Pete was all smiles, with one of those big supermarket bouquets of brightly colored flowers in one hand and a giant Hershey Bar in the other. "Happy long weekend, babe," he said, and leaned in for a kiss. Really bad timing for a phone call from an almost stranger.

Dumping the phone onto the coffee table, I accepted the flowers, the candy, and the kiss. My polite upbringing prevailed. "Sorry," I whispered, pointing at the phone. "It's Gloria Tasker's cousin. Gotta take it."

"It's okay," he said, taking the flowers back. "I'll put these in water."

"I won't be long," I said, meaning it with all my heart. I held the phone to my ear. "Hello, Jane. Are you and Zeus on your way home?"

"Yep. We're already on the Mass turnpike. I'm sorry to bother you. I wasn't sure whether to call you or not. Sounds like you're busy, but I thought this might be important." Her tone was urgent.

I sat down on the couch. "What's wrong, Jane?"

"Well, after I talked to you before, I decided to give Zeus a quick rinse with the hose. You saw how he likes to roll on the ground and this is a rental truck. I didn't want the seats messed up. They might charge more, you know?"

"Uh-huh. Go on."

Would the woman get to the point, so I could get on with my romantic weekend?

"He had something sticky in the hair around his chin. It looked like blood and I was worried thinking maybe he bit whoever was messing around with the truck last night."

"Has he bitten anyone before?" Pete had come back into the room and gave me the head-tilted, eyebrow-lifted "what's up" signal. I gave him the palm-up "I don't know" hand signal in return and put the phone on speaker mode.

"No, Zeus has never bitten anybody. He's a sweet boy. But I figured, what the hell? Somebody was messing with his stuff. He thinks he's protecting me, so they got what they deserved. Right?" She didn't wait for an answer. "Then, after we got on the road, I noticed there were little red spots on the passenger seat where he rides. I pulled over and took a look, and, Lee, he has two puncture wounds on his left shoulder."

"Oh, the poor thing. What did you do?"

"I have a first aid kit, so I've cleaned them, used an antibiotic. I'm going to bandage him up so he won't lick. They're tiny little holes, but they're still bleeding a little. I think whoever was trying to get into the truck stuck him with something. I hope he did bite the bastard. He seems to feel okay. His nose is wet and his tail is wagging, but I'll have his vet look at it as soon as we get home. I just thought you should know about it."

"I don't like hearing that, Jane," I said. "Let me know how he's doing, won't you?"

I could tell by Pete's expression that he didn't like hearing it either. He gestured toward the phone and whispered, "Let me talk to her."

That surprised me. "Jane, I think I told you that my boyfriend is a detective. He's here right now. Can you talk to him?"

"All right," she said. "If you think it's important."

Pete took the phone. "Hello, Jane. This is Pete Mondello. I'm sorry about Zeus. You said these are tiny wounds. How tiny? Does it look he was stabbed with some kind of knife?"

"Um, no. Not a knife." Jane's voice was hesitant, thoughtful. "These are little round holes. Very small holes. A knife would make a slanted cut, wouldn't it?"

"Usually, yes," Pete said. "How far apart are the punctures?"

"Oh, maybe four or five inches."

"I see. Do you think it's possible that whatever the weapon was it could have made both holes at once? Like if it was a long, pointed object? Something like a knitting needle?"

"Something like a knitting needle!" Jane exclaimed. "Yes. That's kind of what it looks like. A really skinny one that went in sideways and the point came out a few inches from where he got stuck. But what kind of nut job goes around stabbing innocent dogs with knitting needles?"

It occurred to me that a charging Doberman doesn't look all that innocent, but I didn't say so. Pete asked Jane if she could photograph the wound with her phone and send it to me and she agreed. "Thanks, Jane, I may be calling you back later if that's okay," he said. "Here's Lee." He handed me my phone.

"Jane," I said, "I'm glad you called. Please stay in touch and let us know how Zeus is doing. Drive carefully."

"I will. I'll take that picture as soon as we stop for the night, but I don't know how good it will be. Two little dots on a big black dog. Anyway bye, you two."

"What's all that about knitting needles?" I asked Pete. "You aren't telling me something."

"You know I don't tell you a lot of things. Can't. But what's all that about somebody messing around with her truck? I didn't want to question her about it until I knew what happened there. Were you planning to tell me about that?"

"Sure was. I've had three calls from Jane this afternoon, just about back-to-back. You weren't here for the first two." I repeated as well as I could what Jane had told me about the man who'd wanted to look at Gloria's pictures and the previous night's excitement in front of Gloria's house. "She didn't call the police because, as she said, her dog barked at somebody, they got in a car and drove away in a hurry, and nothing was stolen."

He nodded. "Yes, she's right. We probably wouldn't have given it much priority. But the three occurrences put together—the man looking for paintings, the attempt to break into the truck, and the attack on the dog—make it add up to something quite different."

"You're thinking it adds up to Sean Madigan, right?" I said.

"Not necessarily." He spoke slowly, deliberately. "But it may add up to a murder."

That statement didn't make the least bit of sense to me. I was sure he wasn't referring to a murder of crows, so what did he mean? What murder? Who was dead? I waited for him to continue, to explain what he meant.

Nothing. He picked up the Hershey Bar I'd left on the table. "Better put this in the refrigerator. Maybe we'll make s'mores sometime this weekend. Did you get marshmallows?" He headed back toward the kitchen.

"Whoa. Just a darn minute." I chased him down the hall. "You can't say, 'It may add up to murder,' then change the subject to candy bars. What are you talking about? What murder?"

He turned to face me, a half smile on his face. "You found something today that maybe we've missed. I'm rethinking one of the witch deaths."

"Which one do you think was murdered?"

"Elliot Bagenstose," he said. "The man who fell out of his own apple tree."

CHAPTER 38

Our date at the Salem Willows that fine June evening was a strange one. We did all the usual things we and generations of dating couples have done: rode the flying horses, watched the little kids ram bumper boats into each other, took goofy pictures in the photo booth, played pinball and other vintage arcade games. (Remember Zoltar the animated fortune-teller? He's still there!) I took a good hard look up into the famous willow trees—checking for crows. Saw a few, but nothing extraordinary. In between playing games, watching the sun set, and taking big bites of those famous chop suey sandwiches and arguably the best popcorn in the world, we talked about a possible murder.

"Remember I told you that the medical examiner found some of Bagenstose's injuries weren't entirely consistent with falling out of a tree?" Pete finally brought the subject back up.

I remembered. "Are you allowed to tell me what injuries you mean?"

"Perforated eardrum."

"Can't a hard fall cause that?" I asked.

"It absolutely can. That's why, even though the bleeding from Elliot Bagenstose's ear seemed like more than a blow to the head usually causes, it was completely plausible that a fall from that height could rupture his eardrum, could kill a man of his age. Besides, he had a heart condition. The ME ruled 'accidental death,' and released the body. I'm going to take another look at the doc's notes and X-rays."

"So if he didn't die from falling out of a tree, what do you think he *did* die from?"

"I think he *could have* died from a narrow sharp instrument being pushed through his ear and into his brain."

I almost choked on my popcorn. "Like a knitting needle?"

"Something like that. There are still a lot of questions. I'm going to do a little more checking and run it by the chief."

"Who would do such a thing? He was a bank president, pillar of the church and all that."

"I don't know if anybody did. I want to check a few things out, that's all. I probably shouldn't have said anything about it, but what happened to Jane's dog, that got me thinking in a new direction."

"Me too." I said, as another idea burst into my brain. "A new direction."

"Wait a minute." Pete stopped working the flippers on the Captain Fantastic pinball machine and the ball rolled right past the hole. "What are you thinking? No playing girl detective on this, okay?"

"I'm not a detective," I insisted, "but I am an investigative reporter. At least I'm trying to be. I promise I won't do anything to get me in trouble. Really. And what you just said about knitting needles—completely off my radar."

"Don't even go there," he said in his cop voice. "I'm serious."

"I'm not thinking about that," I said honestly. "I'm thinking about what's locked up in Jane's U-Haul that somebody wants so badly."

"Interesting," he said, moving to the Superman machine. "You might suggest that she have an appraiser take a look at the contents as soon as she gets home."

"You mean Gloria's paintings?"

"Not necessarily. Could be anything—or nothing. Trying to get into the truck could have been a random thing. Kids out of school for the summer raising hell, going around trying car doors looking for something to steal. Happens all the time."

"Kids don't carry knitting needles."

"Don't go there," he warned again.

I promised that I wouldn't and I meant it. But I would keep in touch with Jane. I wanted to know what was in that truck, and I didn't think it had anything to do with a bunch of bored teenagers trying doors.

We didn't talk much more about police or reporter business. By then I guess neither one of us wanted to go there. That didn't mean either of us had stopped thinking about the U-Haul, the apple tree, the injured dog, or even the possible murder of a witch. At least I hadn't, and the silence on the drive home told me that Pete hadn't either. We were on Derby Street, about to turn onto Hawthorne Boulevard, when he said, "It's early. Want to take a ride over to North Salem, maybe stop at Treadwell's for ice cream?"

A quick vision of a big scoop of coffee Oreo ice cream with chocolate sauce and crumbled waffle cone bits on top immediately replaced all negative thoughts. "Good idea," I said, and we were on our way.

"Mind if we drive by Tasker's place?" Pete said. He'd already turned onto Foster Street, taking a shortcut through the neighborhood.

"Are we looking for anything special?" I asked. "I didn't bring my notebook. Darn."

"I always have mine." He patted his shirt pocket. "Good habit for a reporter. You never know what might turn up."

We approached Gloria's darkened house. There were other houses on three sides of hers, left, right, and behind, all with lights beaming from the windows. Boom! Another idea.

Maybe the nosy neighbor fits in somewhere. What else does she have pictures of?

"Pete," I said. "What about the nosy neighbor? The woman who took the video of the crows destroying Gloria's quince tree. Can you find out which house is hers?"

"I'd guess from the angle of the video you showed it would be that one." He pointed to the house to the right of Gloria's.

"When I saw the U-Haul it was parked pretty close to that property line. What if the woman heard Zeus barking? What if she grabbed her camera and took pictures?" I was excited. "Jane says she was always snooping on the neighbors, but hardly ever talked to any of them."

Pete parked across the street from the empty house and turned off his lights. He pulled the notebook from his pocket and flipped the pages open. "What's her name?"

"Bertha something, I think," I admitted. "She didn't

want me to credit her at all. I guess she thinks people might say she's nosy." I had to laugh, that sounded so silly. "Aunt Ibby knows her, though. She's the one who got the video for me."

Notebook snapped shut and headlights back on. "Do you think she's still up?"

"The nosy lady?"

"No. Your aunt."

I looked at the clock on the dash. Only nine o'clock. "I'm sure she is. Shall I call and see what kind of ice cream she wants?"

"Ice cream?"

"You promised." I put on a fake pout. He turned the car toward the famed ice cream parlor on the Salem-Peabody line and my coffee-Oreo sundae. I called my aunt, took her order for hot butterscotch on maple walnut. I knew Pete would have his usual hot fudge on vanilla. Questions about over-the-fence photos, knitting needles, and, yes, even murder could wait a few more minutes.

With our three treats safely on board, we headed home. "You think I could be right about the woman taking pictures last night?"

He reached across the console and patted my knee. "I think you've been right about a couple of things, babe," he said. "You were only supposed to be investigating crows and you've managed to turn up some good information that we'd have missed."

I hadn't thought of it that way. If I hadn't gone to see Jane about Gloria's tree I wouldn't have known about the man who was looking for paintings. I wouldn't have met Zeus and learned about the peculiar wound in his shoulder that reminded Pete of Elliot Bagenstose's punctured eardrum. If I hadn't snooped behind the Bagenstose's garage I wouldn't have seen Madigan's Toyota inside, although I had a sneaky feeling Pete had already known about that.

Aunt Ibby was genuinely happy to see us. Pete handed her the ice cream and put the photo booth pictures on the table. He got right to the point, asking for the name and telephone number of her snoopy friend. My aunt obliged, scribbling the information on an index card and handing it to Pete. "She doesn't often share this kind of thing, you know. The only reason she sent it to me was because I'd told her about Maralee's interest in the crows."

"I understand that her neighbors say she photographs them all the time. Without permission." He shook his head. "I don't understand why nobody's reported her to us before this."

"Jane told me that she doesn't share her pictures with anybody. Doesn't put them online or anything," I said. "It's some strange kind of voyeurism, I suppose."

"Do you think those photos of the crow tree are important somehow, Pete?" my aunt asked.

"Not the crows, Ms. Russell." He tucked the index card into his pocket. "I think she may have photographed an attempted break-in last night."

"That would be important, wouldn't it? But I think she would have called you if she had. She once explained to us at book club that taking candid photos is her hobby. That if she took a picture of anything important, like a Big Foot or an alien spaceship or the like, she'd report it immediately."

"It's worth a shot anyway." Pete dug into his hot fudge sundae and shared a drop of vanilla ice cream with O'Ryan.

"Speaking of shots, the early news had a report that

Christopher Rich actually has a gun that uses the same kind of bullets as the ones he claims were shot at him," my aunt said. "Some people are saying he might have shot at the wall himself."

"We didn't watch the early news," I said, surprised. "Did you know about that, Pete?"

"Oh, sure," he said. "Lots of shop owners have guns for protection. His is legal. We're taking a look at it."

If it was on the news he could have mentioned it to me. He knows I'm interested.

"How come you didn't tell me about it?" I asked, trying not to sound as annoyed as I really was.

He looked surprised. "I'm sorry, babe. I meant to. We got to talking about other stuff and I forgot. Didn't think it was important. He brought the gun to us this morning. We're checking it out. He says he's never even fired the thing. It looks brand new. Chief doesn't think there's anything there. I don't either."

"River thinks he fired those shots himself. For the publicity."

"Don't think so," Pete insisted. "Not from that gun anyway."

"What about the shells I found?" I asked. "Can you tell what gun those came from?"

"Not yet. But if I hear anything new about it, anything it's okay for me to talk about, I'll tell you. But I'll bet you a pizza they didn't come from the bullets in Rich's wall."

"You're on," I said. "I'll bet they did."

Why else would the Bridget/crow show them to me?

I licked the last tiny crumb of Oreo from my spoon and sighed a contented sigh. "That was good. Going to the Willows tonight was good too. Sometimes the simplest things, like pinball games and ice cream, are the best."

"You've got that right," Pete said. "Like wearing jeans and a T-shirt instead of a tuxedo and a stiff white shirt."

"You're talking about Shannon and Dakota's wedding, I suppose," Aunt Ibby said. "I haven't decided what to wear to it myself. The invitation says black or white."

I thought about Monday's gown fitting. "If I didn't have to wear black I'd choose white for sure. Or maybe a black and white print to match Poe's feathers." I looked at Pete. "I'm glad you decided on the tux, though."

"Yeah. My sister Marie said I should, especially since you'll be all dressed up, walking down the aisle with Madigan."

"Ugh. Don't remind me. I hope I don't have to dance with him."

"If you have to, don't worry. I'll cut in," Pete promised.

"Be sure to get some pictures taken together. Nice ones." Aunt Ibby tapped the photo booth pictures— me with my eyes crossed and Pete with his tongue out. "Not like these."

"I like casual pictures," Pete said, "as long as I know they're being taken." He patted his shirt pocket. "Thanks for the address, Ms. Russell. Your friend might be really helpful."

"I think she'll be happy to help." She paused. "Maybe not. She likes being anonymous."

"According to her neighbors she's not as anonymous as she thinks she is," I said. "But what I think is amazing is that they seem to accept her anyway."

"They must believe she's harmless," Pete said. "Just another colorful local character. Look at the way we accept our Salem witches. That's a big change from the sixteen hundreds."

"You're right," Aunt Ibby said. "Those seventeenth-century people could never have imagined there'd be a statue of Samantha Stevens in downtown Salem."

"Or that Mr. Dumas would invite a couple of covens to hold a Wiccan funeral on his private beachfront," I said, still surprised about it. "But it'll be Midsummer midnight and I can't imagine a more perfect place for Megan's funeral."

"A good location," Pete agreed. "Since it's private property chances are Viktor Protector and his friends won't be gate crashing."

"That's good," my aunt said.

My phone buzzed. "Look, Pete, it's a picture from Jane. Poor Zeus's shoulder." I handed him the phone. "Can't see much on that little screen, can you?"

"Nope." He peered at the display. "It just looks like a patch of black dog hair. Want to forward it to my phone? I'll blow it up later."

I did as he asked. We disposed of our ice cream cartons, said good night to my aunt, and with O'Ryan in the lead we climbed the front stairway to my apartment.

CHAPTER 39

On Saturday morning we joined a good sized group of people for a brief annual ceremony at Proctor's Ledge commemorating the June 10th anniversary of Bridget Bishop's hanging. Therese was there with the WICH-TV mobile crew. I noticed that Christopher Rich was about to address the crowd. We left a bouquet of daisies and red roses and left quietly before his speech began. There were no crows in attendance. After that the weekend passed pretty much as we'd planned it, except I'd bought way too many groceries. Ballpark hot dogs and beer at the Sox game and Sunday dinner downstairs at Aunt Ibby's dining room table meant I'd only had to prepare a couple of lunches. Pete made us breakfast in bed twice and we made a good dent in that half gallon of ice cream. Monday rolled around much too soon.

Pete had to be at work at eight and I'd promised to meet the girls at Dunkin' Donuts at nine, so it was one of those rushing-around, fire-drill, quick-cup-of-coffee-and-a-blueberry Pop-Tart-for-breakfast kind of mornings. Pete left first, so I was alone when I passed by the garden on my way to the garage. There were a couple of crows perched on the back fence, but Theodore Scarecrow seemed to be doing his job well. I saw no evidence at all of scavenging crows among the herbs or vegetables.

The trees on Oliver Street still had quite a few black-feathered visitors among their branches, but not as many as I'd seen in recent days. Local radio and TV reported that, although the number of crows in the city was still far above the normal population, they'd scattered over a wider area. There were even some reports that a significant number of them had been observed roosting in Gloucester's Dogtown area.

So there, Peg Wesson and Tammy Younger.

If the crows kept leaving at this rate chances were there'd be no big pyrotechnical display for me to cover, and if they'd already stopped chowing down on gardens and trees any follow-up "Murder of Crows" investigative report was unlikely. It was time to put plan B into motion—if only I actually had a plan B.

This time I was first to arrive at D.D. I ordered a large coffee and settled into a booth with notebook and pen ready for inspiration to strike. I'd thought about doing a segment on an inside look at wedding planning, but a topic without fireworks and legendary witches seemed suddenly much too tame. I alternated between staring out the window and doodling on the open notebook page.

Shannon, Hilda, Maureen, and Therese all arrived at once and tumbled, laughing, through the door like a clip from a Three Stooges movie. I scooted over to make room for them while they ordered coffee and joined me one at a time. Shannon bought a half dozen assorted doughnuts and plunked the box down on the middle of the table while Therese took pictures. "Okay," Shannon said. "The dresses are a week early. That's worth celebrating with doughnuts! I was worried they wouldn't be in time. We sure didn't give them much notice."

"Good omen," Maureen said. "Everything is going to be perfect. Even the weather predictions for next week are good. Fair and unseasonably warm."

Shannon clapped her hands together like a little kid. "My perfect wedding. I'm marrying the man of my dreams, my daddy's going to give me away, I have the coolest ring bearer in the world, my dress is gorgeous, the cake is going to be fabulous, I even hired a magician who pulls rabbits out of his hat and makes balloon animals for the guests! How awesome is all that?"

The Fabulous Fabio. That explains the black and white balloon sea creatures in my vision.

"Totally awesome," Hilda declared, raising her chocolate doughnut in a toast. "To Shannon and Dakota. May they live happily ever after." We tapped our doughnuts together, creating a little flurry of powdered sugar; finished our coffees; and headed for the Blushing Bride and our final fittings.

We'd decided to put on a mini fashion show for Therese's camera, so our consultant, Corina, added jewelry, bouquets of silk flowers, and even a veil for Shannon—all to approximate the way we'd look at the wedding, just a little more than a week away. Alone in a dressing room, I posed in front of a three-way mirror. Even though the dress was black, my least favorite color in the world, I liked my reflection. That is, I liked it right up until the moment Bridget Bishop joined me in the left side of the glass and Megan appeared on the right. Megan smiled. Bridget didn't.

I turned and faced the Bridget image and mouthed, "What do you want from me?"

It was easy to read her lips, especially when I heard her voice in my head at the same time. "I want my book."

I turned to the image of Megan on my right. "How?" I whispered aloud.

Again, Megan held the crystal ball. In a swirl of mist, I saw River walk to the center of a huge pentagram drawn in the sand. Holding the book in both hands, she stretched her arms over her head. A crow flew into the scene—an extremely large one. *Even bigger than Poe,* I thought. The crow gripped the book in its talons, then disappeared into the mist. At the same instant the Bridget image disappeared from the mirror. The Megan image remained, a look of sadness replacing her smile.

In the crystal ball a line of black-robed witches began to form. I counted them. Fourteen.

That's wrong. There should be only thirteen.

There was a tap at the dressing room door. Megan disappeared. There was no one reflected in the mirror except a perplexed me. "You okay, Lee? We're ready for the pictures," Shannon called. "Let's go."

I pasted on a grin, opened the door, stepped out, and joined the others. We smiled and posed and preened for the camera. Corina fussed over us, adjusting a shoulder strap here, a fabric fold there, making sure everything was perfect.

Still, I couldn't erase the image from my mind.

Something is wrong. There should be only thirteen.

What did it mean?

* * *

With my black gown safely enveloped in a pink garment bag and draped across the passenger seat of the Vette I drove home. I was anxious to talk to River, to tell her that Megan had revealed quite an explicit picture of how the book return was supposed to happen. I also wanted to ask her about the significance of that extra witch in the picture. I checked my watch for the umpteenth time. Still too early to call a person whose TV workday begins at midnight. Been there. Done that.

The idea that I finally knew how the book was to be passed on to the original owner brought me a great sense of relief. I hadn't realized how worried I'd been about it, until Megan had shown me that crystal ball. For a long time I've alternately feared, doubted, resented this scrying thing that had somehow become part of me. But in this case I believed in Megan. I believed she had disclosed something real, something that would actually take place just as she'd shown it. It was a good feeling.

With the wedding plans well in place, my gown carefully hung in my closet, and the cat fed, I was ready to move on with plans for another investigative report. That little cruise through North Salem the previous night had stirred something in my mind besides a desire for ice cream. I had nothing on my calendar that needed attention, so I decided to take another ride in that direction. Maybe I'd stumble onto some little clue, some tiny bit of information that could become inspiration. Once again, I backed the Vette out onto Oliver Street, where the crow population had lessened considerably, and headed northwest toward Bridge Street. I had no predetermined destination in mind and I almost surprised myself when I turned onto Dearborn Street. I passed the corner of Southwick Street and, farther on, slowed down as I approached the iron-gated Bagenstose mansion until the driver in the car behind me gave an impatient blast of his horn. I finally pulled over beside the quite unlovely chain-link fence separating vehicles and pedestrians from the sometimes up-to-the-sidewalk-at-high-tide water of the North River.

The tide wasn't high just then, so I climbed out of the car and, standing beside the chain-link fence, viewed a pleasant scene of placid water, a few small boats, and some greenery. I knew from the newspaper reports and from what I'd heard from Aunt Ibby that Gloria had died when she was thrown from her bike headfirst against one of the sturdy galvanized iron fence posts. Within seconds I was joined there by—wouldn't you know it—a crow. It perched at the top of the fence. This was a big one and it had a red band on its right leg. I knew that the U.S. Department of Agriculture often banded birds, especially migratory ones. However I'd become very much aware of black creatures wearing red anything. I looked at the bird's eyes. It cocked its head and opened its beak. I knew that crows could learn to speak. Poe was a good example of that. I'd seen one at a bird sanctuary in Florida who had a vocabulary of about thirty words.

This crow looked at me and croaked one word, perfectly clearly. "Murder."

I'm sure I answered out loud, "What did you say?"

It looked at me again. Spoke again. "Murder," it said, and flew away.

CHAPTER 40

I climbed back into my car and was about to start the engine when a green Toyota pulled in close beside me. In what seemed like an instant, Sean Madigan appeared at my open window. "Thought that was you," he said, leaning against my door, one arm propped against the convertible top of the Vette. "Hard to miss this little beauty. How come you're cruising past my place again? Looking for me?"

I felt an instantaneous flare of temper. This guy had a knack for bringing that out in me and I didn't like the feeling. "No," I said, keeping my voice level. "And what do you mean, 'your place'?"

The smarmy smile. "You know what I mean. My apartment over the garage at my friend Claudine's little ranch."

I checked my rearview mirror. This end of Dearborn Street isn't much traveled and there were no vehicles, no pedestrians or bike riders in sight. "I don't like people touching my car," I said. "Back off or risk losing that arm." I tapped the gas pedal a couple of times, letting the big engine roar. He looked mildly surprised but took a step back and raised both hands.

"Whoa," he said. "Don't get hostile. I just thought you might want to talk to me."

Now I was confused. "What for? What would I want to talk to you about?"

"About Claudine," he said. "And her collections. For that TV thing you're doing." His expression was all surprised innocence. "Isn't that what this is all about? About her hiring me to appraise the collections for her?"

That was news to me. "Uh, no," I said. "I have to go now."

"Listen," he said, leaning toward me again but being careful not to touch the car. "I'm sorry if I sounded rude the other day. But Claudine doesn't like people snooping around her backyard like you were doing."

"I wasn't snooping."

"Looked like it."

I shifted to reverse and started to back up slowly. "Good-bye," I said.

"See you at the rehearsal then." He waved, then folded his arms and watched as I drove away.

So Sean Madigan was staying at the Bagenstose mansion to appraise the many collections Aunt Ibby had told me about. Maybe Sean had given me a good idea after all. "Like a museum," my aunt had said about that house, and from what I'd seen it was so. What if Therese and her camera and I got a chance to show the WICH-TV audience some of those treasures? I began to like the idea. Pete had told me that the Bagenstose house wasn't a good place for me to be, but workwise it could turn out to be a perfect place!

Thoughts of the report I could do on the contents of the great house had almost driven the memory of the talking crow out of my mind. Almost. Why had the thing said "Murder" at the place where Gloria had died? Had the hit-and-run been a deliberate attempt on the woman's life?

I drove slowly along Dearborn Street, beneath the arching canopy of fine old trees. A few crows showed themselves, not a lot of them. I thought some more about that talking crow. Maybe my visions of crows and cats and Bridget Bishop made me imagine things that weren't real. A banded crow isn't an uncommon thing even with a red band. Besides, that screechy, cackling voice could have said any number of things. Maybe it had said mother or birdy or dirty. Probably it was just cawing and had spoken no words at all.

Back to concentrating on report topics. I knew the Bagenstoses must have collected old paintings. I'd seen some of them. Why else would Claudine invite a shady character like Sean Madigan into her home? Or at least into her garage. Aunt Ibby had told me that Claudine had a big collection of late nineteenth- and early twentieth-century fashions too. The textbook on investigative reporting said that topics should be things people are curious about. Who in Salem could drive by that spooky old gated mansion and not wonder what's inside? I wondered too. What else had they collected in there?

Claudine had been gracious toward me, even re-membering seeing me when I was a little girl. Maybe now that her husband was gone she might be planning to sell some of their things, maybe thinking about downsizing to a smaller place. She might even be glad of the extra publicity my report would give. I realized

I was talking myself into ignoring Pete's advice to stay away from the place, but snooping is one thing, and serious research for one's job is quite another.

As long as I was in the area, I could call on Aunt Ibby's friend Bertha Barnes to thank her in person for her excellent video of the crows stripping Gloria's tree. I could ask politely whether she had any more interesting pictures of crows. Or whatever. Did she save all of the pictures she took? I wondered. Impulsively, I took a quick left turn onto Southwick Street.

I parked in front of the vacant Tasker house, making sure notebook and business cards were in my purse. I looked into Gloria's yard, curious about the state of the quince tree. The lawn looked a little shaggy but the branches of the sturdy little tree had begun to sprout a bit of green, making me feel both pleased and relieved.

If Pete was correct, Bertha's house should be the one on my right. Making sure my car was locked—just in case that story about bored teenagers was true—I squared my shoulders, marched right up to the nosy neighbor's front door, and rang the bell.

A querulous voice from inside called, "Just a minute. I'm coming." The door opened a crack. "Who are you and what do you want?"

I held out my business card. "Hello there, Ms. Barnes. I'm Lee Barrett, Ibby Russell's niece? You helped me out on my very first appearance on the news. I was in the neighborhood and wanted to stop by to thank you personally."

The door swung open immediately. "You're Maralee!" The plump little woman framed in the doorway looked like Central Casting's idea of everybody's grandmother. Bluish white hair in a tightly curled perm, granny glasses perched on a cute button nose, a floral print cotton dress, sensible shoes—the whole package. No wonder none of the neighbors turned her in for spying on them. She was completely adorable. "Come right in, dear." She stood aside and ushered me into the house. "Ibby always speaks so fondly of you at the library book club meetings. She's very proud of you!"

I followed her into a cozy living room—chintz slipcovers on overstuffed chairs and love seat, maple-finished coffee table and a matching hutch displaying a set of antique Quimper plates—and accepted her offer of "a nice cup of tea and some cookies." I could already smell the gingersnaps. I hadn't yet figured out how to ask politely if she'd happened to have her camera handy when Zeus caused a noisy commotion practically in front of her house. So when she returned with the tea and cookies on a tin tray with a Currier & Ives reproduction on it I just blurted it out.

"Mrs. Barnes, I imagine you must be part of the neighborhood watch program, so may I ask a question about some strange things happening around here recently?" I took a sip of tea. "I only ask because of my new job. If it's none of my business, please say so."

"Oh, sweetheart," she said. "I'm glad you asked. You must be talking about the other night when that sweet dog from next door set up such a howl. I'm going to miss Zeus. I used to sneak him doggie biscuits under the fence. I hope that nice Jane didn't mind."

"I'm sure she didn't. Go on. You were saying he made a lot of noise?"

"He did. I thought for a minute he'd been hit by that car."

"What car?"

"It's a little green car. I'd seen it around here

before. At first I thought it belonged to one of Gloria's gentlemen friends who didn't know she'd passed, you know?"

"A green car. You didn't happen to have your camera with you that night, did you?"

"Of course I did, darling. It's always with me." She reached into a pocket of her housedress and pulled out a small Minolta. I even have pockets in my bathrobe, so if anything interesting happens at night I can catch it on video. It's my hobby, you know."

"Really? Do you, um, *save* all of your video records, Mrs. Barnes?"

"Oh, call me Bertha, hon. Everybody does. I don't save them all. No indeed." She glanced around the room, as though she thought someone might be listening, and dropped her voice. "Most of them are pretty boring. This isn't a very exciting neighborhood since Gloria's gone. Now what video did you want to know about?"

"If you took one on the night Zeus set up such a racket," I prompted. "That's the one I'd like to see. Did you?"

"Sure did. Want to see it? It's kind of dark. I didn't want to use any lights and it was late at night." She stood and motioned for me to follow. "Come on into my hobby room."

It was a small room and three walls had been fitted with floor-to-ceiling shelves. Rows of old-fashioned VHS videos with hand-lettered labels filled most of them. Hundreds of DVDs in plastic cases were stacked neatly in the others. "You must have been collecting these for a long time." I tried to keep the absolute astonishment out of my voice. "A really long time."

"Not so long, hon. Ten years or so. Keeps my mind

occupied, you know? Like they say, if you don't use it you lose it." She waved a hand at the packed shelves and the two big-screen TVs on the fourth wall with DVD and VHS players lined up beneath them. A wide recliner stood in the center of the room. A single straight chair stood beside it, a box of Whitman's chocolates on its seat. "Sometimes I watch two of 'em at a time. Compare the old and the new. It's really fun." She moved the chocolates to the arm of the recliner and motioned for me to take the vacated chair. "Here. Sit."

Speechless, I sat.

"I'll show you whatever you like, dear. I love keeping busy with my hobbies. Why, if it wasn't for my pictures and the library book club I'd just be another boring old lady." She pointed to a large wicker basket next to the recliner. "That and my knitting, of course."

The basket overflowed with skeins of colorful yarns. But what grabbed my attention most was the round Quaker oatmeal box beside the basket jammed full of sharp-pointed knitting needles.

CHAPTER 41

Naturally the very idea that Bertha's knitting needles had anything to do with Zeus's injury or with Elliot Bagenstose's punctured eardrum was preposterous. But they did give me a chilling reminder that I wasn't just investigating barking dogs; nosy neighbors, however adorable; or tree-eating crows. I could be messing around with a murderer.

I charged ahead anyway. "Bertha, I'd like to see the one with the dog and the green car."

"Sure sweetheart. I'll put it up on the big screen for you." She took a DVD from the shelf and loaded it into a Toshiba player. "Sorry it's so dark. But there was a streetlight, you know, so it's not too bad. Want to hear the sound too?" She passed the chocolate box. "I like a little something to munch on while I watch my pictures. Have one?"

I passed on the chocolate and said yes to the sound.

It began with a dog barking, at first in the distance, then closer. Jane's U-Haul was in the center of the frame just beneath a street lamp. Zeus came bounding into the picture, the barking turning into a growl as he disappeared behind the truck. A harshly whispered voice said, "Get away from me." Zeus whimpered. Had the person kicked him? The whispering voice grew louder. "Shit! Get away! God damn it." The dog howled as if in pain, there was the sound of footsteps running, and then the dog ran from behind the truck. A quick view of a Toyota, its color indistinct, flashed past as the camera panned away and focused on the yelping dog running toward Gloria's house. A faint voice, which I took to be Jane's, called the dog's name. The video ended.

"Well, was it what you expected to see, honey?" Bertha asked. "Not bad, seeing as how I shot the whole thing in the pitch dark, huh?"

"It looked good, Bertha," I told her. "And I'll tell you why I wanted to see it. Somebody injured Zeus that night, and it looks as though it happened right behind Jane's truck. Would you send me a copy of this? Abusing animals is wrong and your pictures might help to find the person who hurt him."

"Okay, dear. I guess you're going to do a show about animals, huh? I like animals. I really liked Zeus. Is he going to be all right?"

I assured her that I'd spoken to Jane. "She's going to have a vet give Zeus a thorough checkup as soon as they get home." I gave Bertha my e-mail address and she promised to send the video. I was sure Pete would be interested, especially that brief shot of a Toyota. I also knew he'd have something to say about my snooping, playing girl detective. But as he'd pointed out, if I hadn't met Jane, found out about Bertha Barnes's "hobby," and made friends with Zeus, he'd be missing a lot of good information.

On my way back to Winter Street I decided to take

another little detour. I hadn't been inside Christopher Rich's shop since my Crystal Moon *Nightshades* days when I'd sometimes bought props and Halloween decorations there. I knew that just as soon as he saw my WICH-TV business card publicity-obsessed Christopher would welcome me like a long-lost sister.

I was right about that. "Lee Barrett," he exclaimed, pumping my hand and putting an arm around my shoulder at the same time. "What an honor to see Salem's newest TV star! Your report was fascinating. Just fascinating. Welcome to Christopher's Castle. What can I do for you today?"

The shop had a pleasant sandalwood incense smell and merchandise was attractively displayed. Unlike some of the many witch shops in the city, Christopher's Castle was far from gloomy or scary. Glass bowls filled with colorful crystals and polished gemstones shared space with witch-themed jewelry. Pentagram rings and necklaces, earrings shaped like dragons, silver bracelets like coiled serpents sparkled on velvet display pads. Costumes offered customers masquerade choices from fairies and elves to mummies and wizards.

I extricated myself from his grip and pretended to be fascinated by a gold bust of Nefertiti. "It's been a long time since I've shopped here. I was at town hall when you gave your lovely tribute to Megan. I decided right then to drop in the next time I was in the neighborhood," I lied. "How are you doing, Christopher? I was shocked to hear about the gunshots. You must have been terrified."

As I'd anticipated, the opportunity to talk about himself to a member of the media was too much to resist. He answered every question I threw at him and didn't object when I took notes. "I understand that the last two customers you had that night were Fabio, the magician, and a man we often see on TV protesting various things. An odd couple."

"They didn't come in together, you know." He straightened a pile of Ouija board games. "Fabio is a regular here. I have a huge inventory of magic supplies. He stops by nearly every morning on his way to work. He's a baker by trade."

"I know," I said. "A very good one. I've sampled some of his work lately. What about Viktor Protector? Is he interested in magic too?"

"A strange man. He's one of those oddballs who protests witches, yet he buys book after book about how to become one of us. I believe the police think he may have fired those shots at me."

"Do you think he did?"

"No, he didn't do it." Rich sounded positive. "And by the way, I didn't do it myself either, in case you've heard those nasty rumors. A jealous little witch named River is spreading that lie."

Oops.

"I understand that Megan's Wiccan funeral will be held soon. My sources say Midsummer night. True?"

He nodded. "You have good sources. Want to know another little secret? Off the record?"

"Of course I do." I put my pen down on the counter. "Off the record."

"Another person showed up on the outdoor surveillance camera on the building next door. Someone besides Fabio and Viktor."

That surprised me. Pete must have known about this but had never mentioned it. "Do you know who it was? Do the police know?"

"It was a woman. Hard to recognize her. She was hiding in the shadows, but the camera picked her out."

"Got a description?"

"Not a good one. Tall, wearing black. Call me crazy," he said, "I think I know who it is and why the cops can't find her."

"I won't call you crazy," I promised. "Who is she?"

"Bridget Bishop," he said. "You know who that is, don't you?"

"Of course," I stammered, brain reeling. "First witch hanged."

"Right," he said. "Psychics all over town are feeling her presence. Smelling apples over at that restaurant. They're chalking it up to the anniversary of her death. I'm sure she was out in my parking lot that night. But what am I going to tell the cops? A ghost-witch did it?"

I hadn't heard that about the psychics. I wondered if River had. I said the first thing that popped into my head. "Can a ghost shoot a gun?"

He shrugged and half smiled. "Not very well, I guess, since she missed me by a mile."

"Why would Bridget Bishop be mad at you?"

He looked around the shop. We were alone, but he whispered anyway. "I put a spell on a fellow witch. A bad spell. Killed him."

I wanted to tell him what I'd told River, that bad thoughts and witch spells don't really kill people. But I remained silent. Let him talk.

"We vow to do no harm, you know. But I used one of Bridget Bishop's own spells."

Impossible! River has the spell book.

"It was the only one of her spells I'd ever seen. Ariel Constellation sold it to me a long time ago. I paid a lot of money for it. Ariel told me I should never use it in anger. But I did, and a man died."

Elliot Bagenstose?

"Did you destroy the paper the spell was written on so it will never fall into the wrong hands?" I asked, keeping my voice level, professional. "That would seem to be the right thing to do."

"I thought about selling it at first. Couldn't do it. So I burned it to ashes. Not a scrap of it left."

If it burned, it wasn't Bridget Bishop's spell. Christopher Rich, you were snookered by Ariel Constellation!

I couldn't tell him that, of course. But when the police figured out who'd *really* killed Elliot, Christopher could stop blaming himself. So could River. Anyway, the woman in the parking lot could very well have been Bridget. She wasn't shy about appearing to me any darn time she felt like it, and I'm not even a witch. But I doubted seriously that a camera could have captured her image even if she was there.

"I understand why you might think you saw Bridget," I said, "but you must admit, a woman in a black dress is a fairly ordinary sight."

"You're right, of course, Lee. I never should have mentioned it. Well, I'm sure you have better things to do than listen to an old man ramble." He reached for a colorful brochure on the countertop and handed it to me. "By the way, I'm sure you know that I'm a bit of an expert on things magical. I'd be more than happy to be a guest on your program."

Oh, I'll just bet you would.

"Thank you, Christopher." Realizing that I'd just been dismissed from Christopher's Castle, I put the brochure into my handbag. "I'll certainly keep you in mind."

I was halfway back to my car when I realized I hadn't asked Christopher why he was angry enough with a fellow witch to use such a powerful spell—or at least what he believed was one. And I was darn sure he wasn't about to tell me who he'd cast it on.

CHAPTER 42

Pete's peewee hockey team had a night game at the Rockett Arena over near the college, so I didn't expect to hear from him until late. He always takes the team out for pizza after the game, win or lose.

I sat at my kitchen table and pulled out the notebook, realizing I had a lot to learn from Pete about note taking. O'Ryan watched from the windowsill as I ripped out the day's sketchy, messy entries and attempted to make some sense of this very strange day. My maid of honor dress was safely stashed in my closet and Megan had shown me the way to return Bridget Bishop's book, so I didn't need to record those two items. I started a fresh page.

Talking crow? Maybe.
Madigan lives over Claudine's garage, appraises
    antiques.
Bertha Barnes (adorable) DVDs and VHSs of
    neighbors. Video of Zeus. She knits.
C. Rich angry with River. Said he fired shots.
    Saw tall person in black behind shop.
    (B. Bishop?)

C. Rich used B.B. curse on man who died.
  (Elliot?)
Note: C.R. says Viktor P. reads about joining
  witches. Weird.

Okay, it looked neater, but did it make any more
sense? I closed the book and faced the cat. "Sean
Madigan must think I'm stalking him," I said. "Or is he
stalking me?" O'Ryan ignored my question and kept
the golden eyes focused on the outdoors. I kept talking to him anyway. Sometimes I think it helps to hear
my thoughts out loud.

"Mrs. Barnes is a doll. You'd like her. I saw a video
about a good dog named Zeus. River thinks Christopher Rich shot those bullets himself. I don't know
what to think. Oh yeah, I might have heard a crow say
'Murder.'"

He turned and looked at me when I said the word
and gave a slow, solemn couple of nods of the big fuzzy
head. So the crow and the cat think Gloria's accident
was not an accident. How can that be? Could someone
have followed Gloria in the early morning darkness,
deliberately forced her into the fence? It could have
happened that way. Gloria and Elliot Bagenstose, both
witches, had died a few weeks apart. Gloria had been
first.

Had anyone checked Gloria's eardrums?

I hoped Pete would call after the hockey game. I
had a lot to tell, and even more to ask.

It was nearly ten o'clock when that welcome phone
call came. I must have sounded like a babbling goof as
I tried to explain the day's happenings all at once. In
his most professional, quiet cop voice, he said, "Take

it easy, babe, relax. I'll be there in half an hour. Got to drop the nephews off. Calm down, okay?"

The advice didn't help much. By the time O'Ryan ran to the living room door and the bell chimed "Bless This House," I was in full fidgety mode. Couldn't sit still or think straight. I pulled the door open. "I'm so glad you're here," I told him. "I need to talk to you."

"I got that," he said, pulling me close. "What the hell is going on? You're nervous as a bitsy bug." I've always meant to ask Pete exactly what a bitsy bug is, but that could wait for another time.

We sat on the couch together and I told him in rapid succession about the crow, the nosy neighbor, Sean Madigan, Chris Rich, and the woman in black. He nodded, said all the right things, made me feel a lot better. It was when I got to the question about Gloria's injury that he sat up straight, frowned, and said, "Jesus, Lee. I don't know. She was a mess. Hit and run. Blunt trauma to the head with no helmet. I saw the ME's photos. I'm sure her eardrums were smashed, along with most everything else in her head. Jesus! Never thought about it. You may be onto something there."

We wound up drinking decaf in the kitchen, as usual. I told him in more detail about how Sean Madigan had followed me to the end of Dearborn Street, startled me, even leaned on my car. That last one still ticked me off. "He acts as though I'm stalking him," I complained. "Fat chance of that ever happening."

Pete's smile was wry. "Yeah. I heard about that."

It was my turn to frown. "What do you mean? Heard about it where?"

"From Madigan. He thinks you're stalking him."

I put my mug down so hard coffee splashed onto the tabletop. "*What*!?"

He leaned forward, both elbows on the table. "It's police business," he said, "but it looks as though I'm going to have to let you in on it before you get yourself hurt."

"I don't get it." And I surely didn't. "You mean the art thief is involved in police business somehow? With you?"

"Okay. Here's how it all went down. A few months ago Madigan contacted us from the minimum security prison where he was doing his time. He said he had some information about stolen paintings we might want to know about. Wanted to make a deal."

"What did you say?"

"He didn't talk to me. Art crimes is above my pay grade, but it seems that after Elliot Bagenstose died, his widow got a message through to Madigan that she had about fifty pieces of major artwork to sell. Wanted to know if he could appraise them, then get rid of them for her in exchange for a piece of the action."

"What made him think they were stolen?"

"She mentioned some titles and artists. He recognized some of them as stolen," Pete said. "The guy knows his business."

"Wow! Did he agree to do it?"

"No. He told us about it right away. Said he might be able to help us find some valuable paintings that have been missing for a long time."

"Is that how come he got out of jail early?"

"Exactly. He got his sentence shortened in exchange for finding whatever stolen paintings are in the Bagenstoses' house." Pete leaned back in his chair. "Surprised?"

"Surprised that he's on your side of the law," I said. "But I still don't like him."

"That's fine. You don't have to like him. Just stay out of the way and let him get on with what's he's doing.'

"No problem with that," I said. "Has he found any paintings yet?"

"I think I've told you all you need to know for now. Thanks for the tip about Gloria's ear. I'll talk to you tomorrow." He stood.

"Oh yeah. Mrs. Barnes is sending over the video of Zeus barking at whoever was messing with Jane's truck. You can't see much, though. The action was behind the U-Haul. All you see is poor Zeus running with his tail down and a blur of a Toyota. And somebody cussing in the background."

Pete sat down again. "A Toyota?"

"Yep. Surprised?"

"Hmm. It fits right in with something Madigan told us. Son of a gun." He stood up, smiling. "Thanks again, Lee. Good job."

"You're welcome. Can you tell me what I did?"

"Sorry. Not yet." He looked at the Kit-Kat clock and stood again. "Can't stay tonight, babe. Early meeting in Boston with some bigwigs. I'll call when I get back. When you get that video will you forward it?" I said that I would, and after a few nice kisses and a promise to call me, he went out the living room door and down the stairs, leaving me with even more questions than I'd had in the first place.

So Sean Madigan was working with the police to solve some art thefts and Claudine Bagenstose might be in it right up to her Van Cleef & Arpels earrings.

CHAPTER 43

I added the bombshell about Sean Madigan to my notes. I found it hard to believe. The notorious art thief working undercover for the police. That's the stuff that TV shows are made of.

You can't tell a crook by his cover, I wrote, then sat back and smiled at my own little joke.

The video from Bertha arrived just then and I dutifully forwarded it to Pete. There was a new text message from Jane too. She was making good time and expected to be home by the next day. Zeus seemed fine. She planned on taking Pete's advice about contacting an appraiser to check out the things she's inherited from Gloria. That seemed wise to me. Besides, it might possibly tell us what the person behind the truck in Bertha's video had been looking for. "Hope Zeus didn't catch anything from whoever he bit," she texted. I'd almost forgotten about that dog bite, but I was sure Pete hadn't.

O'Ryan had abandoned his windowsill by then and joined me at the table. He concentrated on washing his face for a minute, then, with a big pink-tongued

yawn, jumped down from his chair and trotted to the
bedroom. I yawned too and followed him. Sleep was
an excellent idea.

The next few days moved quickly. Hilda and Maureen
and I gave a bridal shower for Shannon at the Salem
Waterfront Hotel on Pickering Wharf. Pretty Party
catered and guess who was part of the entertainment?
The Fabulous Fabio, doing some wedding-themed
magic tricks. He made a giant fake diamond ring
appear on a guest's finger, then pulled a stuffed bunny
dressed like a bridegroom out of his tall white chef's
hat. His performance was surprisingly good, and when
I had a chance to speak with him for a few minutes between the cake cutting and the Bridal Bingo game, I
told him so. I also worked in a couple of questions
about what he'd seen and heard after leaving the magic
shop on the night somebody shot at Christopher Rich.

"Did you hear the shots?" I asked.

"Sure did." He put a plate full of pink-iced cupcakes
on a nearby table. "Try one of these. There's a plastic
engagement ring in one of them. Whoever gets it will
be the next one to get married."

"What if she's already married?"

"Don't know. It's never happened." He smiled and
raised both hands in the air. "Anyway, like I told the
cops, I was right at the edge of the parking lot. Then
boom boom. Shots came from somewhere in the
bushes behind me."

"You must have been scared to death. What did
you do?"

He smiled. "I'm ex-military so I hit the deck at the
first one."

"So you never saw the shooter?" I'd hoped he'd say something about a shadowy figure in black but he stuck to his story.

"Didn't see a thing. It was dark and I had my head down."

"Did you hear anybody running away?"

"Not exactly."

"What do you mean, 'not exactly'? You heard something then?"

"Birds. I heard birds making a commotion so I knew something had disturbed them. They don't usually squawk late at night." He snapped his fingers and a paper rose appeared in his hand. "Sorry. Have to go make balloon animals. Nice talking to you." He handed me the flower, then moved away. I knew without asking that the noisy birds were crows. I stuck the rose in my hair, reached for one of the pink cupcakes, then changed my mind. What if I got the ring? I wasn't ready for another marriage just yet. Why tempt fate?

The shower was fun and a big success. Shannon looked so happy, so beautiful, absolutely glowing. She'd brought Poe along with her, thinking that it might help him become accustomed to being around a crowd, and it seemed to work. She'd handed his tether to Maureen while she unwrapped gifts and he didn't seem to mind being passed from hand to hand. He did, however, single me out with a "Hey, Red! Who loves ya, baby?" He seemed to know me. Shannon said he watches a lot of television and might have seen me on *Nightshades*. Maybe she was right. I said, "Hi, Poe. Nice to see you again." No point in being rude. After all, Poe wasn't the only member of the crow community who'd spoken to me recently.

The shower was just one of many wedding-related

events leading to that special day. Hilda and Maureen, along with some of Shannon's other young friends from school, hired a limo and took Shannon to Boston for a "bachelorette party." I bowed out of that celebration, pleading age and teacher status, leaving me a welcome evening free from making table centerpieces with net and glitter, constructing beach-themed place cards, and putting custom-printed "Shannon and Dakota" labels on champagne bottles. Naturally I spent it with Pete.

We held hands across a table at Greene's Tavern. "Pete, if I ever again agree to be somebody's maid of honor," I said, "please talk me out of it."

"I'll try, babe," he said, "but in just a few more days the bride and groom will walk down the aisle and say, 'I do.' Then you'll say how beautiful it all is and be ready to do it again."

I sighed and took a sip of light beer. "I know you're right, but just now I don't care if I never even get invited to another one. Let's talk about something else."

"How about this?" He pulled the ever-present notebook from his jacket pocket and flipped through the pages. I remembered that mine was at home on my desk. "Here it is. I heard from our friend Jane this morning. She thanked me for suggesting that she get an appraiser for Gloria's things. Turns out the jewelry was worth much more than she'd thought, but the big surprise was one of the paintings."

"I thought all along it would be a painting since Madigan was interested in them," I said. "What was it? Something famous?"

"Not so much famous as stolen." His expression was serious. "It was a small oil painting of Judith Sargent Murray by John Singer Sargent. It was stolen from a private collection back in the sixties." He closed the notebook

"Wow. What will become of it now?"

"Jane returned it to the family it was stolen from. There's a reward from the insurance company involved, but mostly she wanted to do the right thing. What we want to know is how a waitress in Salem wound up with it."

Our pizza arrived, half pepperoni and half extra cheese. I helped myself to a big slice from the cheese half. "Is Sean Madigan helping with that?" I asked, knowing I was pushing my luck in the "that's police business" department, but feeling as though I deserved an answer.

I got one. "He is." Period. End of answer.

I tried another angle. "I talked to Fabio, the magician, about the night when he witnessed the shooting behind the magic shop. He says the shots came from the bushes behind him. That means Rich didn't fire them himself, doesn't it?"

"Seems to. We never thought he'd done it in the first place. He was too freaked out about it after it happened." He reached for a second slice of pizza. "Hard to fake that much fear."

"He believed in the idea that someone was loose in Salem killing witches. I think he still does."

Pete's cop voice kicked in. "He may be right about that after all."

That surprised me. I was quiet for a moment. "Did you talk to Viktor Protector about it? Chris Rich says he goes around protesting everything, but he buys books about learning to be a witch. Strange, huh?"

"We've talked to him. He gets paid for leading the various protests. Claims he doesn't personally believe in most of them." He shook his head. "Strange damned way to make a living, but he certainly has the right to free speech."

"Had he heard anything about who might be targeting witches? After all, he hangs around with those people."

"Sorry," he said. "Confidential information there."

I sighed. "I understand, but the police department rules sure get in the way of some interesting conversations."

We switched to a safer topic. Crows. We talked about the lessening numbers of them, halfway regretting that the city might not have to use the pyrotechnic system to chase them away. We both love fireworks. Although during the recent hectic days of wedding preparation Pete and I had talked on the phone every day and had lunch together a couple of times, I hadn't brought up again the matter of the talking crow who may or may not have said, "Murder," and I knew better than to ask him about the condition of Gloria Tasker's eardrums, let alone Elliot Bagenstose's. Knitting needles were not mentioned either.

But that hadn't stopped me from thinking about them.

CHAPTER 44

It seemed as though it had been a long time since Pete had spent the night at my apartment. From the way O'Ryan carried on, purring and rolling over and meowing loving cat words, you'd have thought it had been months instead of a week. It felt that way to me too. Conversation about crows and stolen art and shooting stopped at the door. I didn't even bother to look at my e-mail or check the table in the downstairs front hall, where Aunt Ibby always put whatever the letter carrier had left for me.

In the morning we had time for a leisurely breakfast, so I was able to use up some of my surplus groceries. I fixed bacon and eggs and English muffins served with coffee and Aunt Ibby's homemade marmalade. It was a wonderful start to the day. Pete kissed me good-bye at nine o'clock with a promise to call later.

The wedding rehearsal dinner was scheduled for seven o'clock that evening. Wanda the Weather Girl promised no rain, warm breezes, and a late sunset. Summer had arrived in Salem. I'd scheduled a pedicure, shampoo, and blow-dry for three-thirty, but my time was my own until then. It felt good.

I'd finished making the bed, straightening up the kitchen, and putting the dishes away when there was a tap at the kitchen door. "Yoo-hoo, Maralee, it's me," my aunt called in a soft voice. I smiled and opened the door. Who else would it be?

"Good morning. Come in," I said.

O'Ryan was first through the door, my aunt following. She handed me a stack of mail—bills, catalogs, letters, advertising flyers, a magazine or two. "These have begun to pile up in the past few days. I know you've been busy with the wedding and all, but I thought there might be something important here."

I tossed the pile onto the table and gave my aunt a hug. "I doubt it, but thanks so much for looking after me. You always have. Got time to sit down and visit for a while?"

"Of course I do." She pulled out a Lucite chair, picked up the cat, and sat with O'Ryan on her lap.

I pushed the coffeemaker's ON button, then took the chair opposite hers. "We need to catch up on things," I told her. "Shannon's wedding has been a lot more time consuming than mine and Johnny's was." It was true. Johnny and I had been married in a tiny chapel just outside of Orlando. Johnny was a rising star on the NASCAR circuit and we'd wanted to avoid the army of sports reporters who followed him around. Our attendants had been a girl who worked with me on the home shopping show and one of Johnny's fellow drivers. Johnny's mom and Aunt Ibby and a few of our closest friends comprised the guest list. I wore white and carried orange blossoms. It was perfect.

"I have a bit of an ulterior motive in bringing your mail up here," she admitted. "I've been consumed with curiosity about one of your letters ever since it arrived a couple of days ago." She pulled a cream-colored oblong envelope from the pile and handed it to me. "This one."

I accepted the hand-addressed envelope and recognized the return address immediately. "Claudine Bagenstose." I gasped. "Why is she writing to me?"

"That's what I'm dying to know too," my aunt said. "Unless it's none of my business, of course." She leaned forward. "Aren't you going to open it?"

"Oh, yes." I unsealed the envelope flap and pulled out a creamy folded sheet bearing the monogram *CB* in raised black letters. After unfolding it, I read the short message aloud.

"'My dear Lee,' it says. 'I've thought about your suggestion that some of the lovely antiques Elliot and I acquired during our many happy years together might be of interest to your viewers. I'll be at home between two and three on the afternoon of the twentieth. If you care to drop by you can see if you think it's a good idea. No camera yet, of course. Hope to see you then. If this is inconvenient we'll do it another time. Cordially, Claudine Bagenstose.'" A telephone number followed.

"My goodness." Aunt Ibby's eyes were wide. "That's today. What are you going to do?"

Conflicting thoughts flashed through my over-stuffed brain one after the other. If I went, would it look as though I were stalking Sean Madigan? If I didn't go, would I miss the opportunity to give viewers a peek inside the gates of a museum-like home most

Salem people would never see any other way? If I went, would Pete think I was snooping? If I didn't go, would I be behaving unprofessionally? If Claudine was actually involved somehow with stolen art, why would she invite TV cameras into her home? The obvious answer to that one was that she probably wouldn't.

"I heard that she was thinking of moving to a smaller place now that Elliot's gone." Aunt Ibby interrupted my barrage of contradictory thoughts. "Must cost a fortune to heat and cool that old mausoleum. Claudine's smart. I'll bet she's planning to use your TV footage to advertise the house and the antiques to prospective buyers."

"Mr. Doan would probably like the idea," I said, "and I'm sure there's an audience for it."

Aunt Ibby agreed. "Kind of a cross between *Antiques Roadshow* and *Lifestyles of the Rich and Famous*. I know I'd watch it, even if I didn't know you."

"Pete asked me not to go snooping around there, and Sean Madigan thinks I'm stalking him."

My aunt gave a ladylike sniff. "Stalking him! Outrageous nonsense. And pursuing your career isn't snooping by any means. Besides, you've been invited."

"True. I think I should do it. Let's see. If I stick to Claudine's schedule and leave there at three, I'll still have plenty of time to get my hair and nails done." My mind raced. So much for the leisurely day I'd planned. "If I can focus on the right collections, like furniture and clothes," I said, "I'll promote it as an investigation into Salem's fashionable past. A time capsule of Salem history spanning decades—all in one historic home!"

Aunt Ibby clapped her hands, startling the cat. "I love it," she said. "I can help with the research. Just take good notes. Try to get accurate dates. I can help you put together a proposal for Bruce Doan the minute this wedding is over."

The more I thought about it, the better I liked it. If the visions Megan had shown me were correct, she'd be returned to the earth and be able to go on to a beautiful place the witches call "Summerland." Bridget Bishop would have her book back from River, and the crows would be gone from Salem. There'd be no point in doing a follow-up on crows. It would be old news, and besides, without fireworks it wouldn't be much fun.

"I think I'll call and tell her I'll be there at two," I said. "And I'll call Pete too, and let him know what I'm doing. Then he can tell Sean Madigan that if he sees my car he doesn't need to worry about me stalking him. What a jerk."

"I think it's a good opportunity for another successful report for you. I'd love to go with you. What a treasure trove you'll see." She shooed O'Ryan from her lap and stood. "I can't wait to get started. I know Claudine's great grandmother was a suffragette. I'll bet the old newspaper archives at the library reported on her. Probably in a not-too-flattering way. Those brave women put up with a lot. Don't get up. I'll let myself out." She and the cat were out the door in seconds, and she hadn't even had her coffee.

I did as I'd said I would. I called Claudine and confirmed the appointment for two o'clock. I called Pete too, but it went right to voice mail. I left a message. He'll probably worry about me but what can happen at two in the afternoon on a sunny spring day in North Salem?

By one forty-five I was headed across the overpass to North Street. At one fifty-seven I was admitted through the gate at the Bagenstose house. I parked in the long driveway, far enough from the garage doors so that if anyone wanted to back out the Vette wouldn't be in the way. Making sure that I had notebook, pen, and business cards, I walked to the front door and rang the bell.

A uniformed maid answered the door, giving me a questioning look. I handed her a card. "Lee Barrett from WICH-TV. Mrs. Bagenstose is expecting me." She nodded, placed my card on the same silver tray where Claudine had put the last one, and motioned for me to follow. She ushered me into a different room this time, more of a den, with surprisingly contemporary furnishings. Claudine sat in a maroon recliner with her feet elevated on the footrest. No black flapper dress this time. She wore bright Gucci print palazzo pants with a white eyelet blouse and looked absolutely stunning.

She spread her hands in welcome but didn't stand. "Lee, dear, thank you for coming. I'm just a bit wobbly on my feet today. A bit of arthritis in my knee has been kicking up lately." She reached for a sheaf of papers on the mahogany drum table beside her. "These are notes about the collections we use for our occasional house tours. I'd like to show you around myself but I've asked my associate, Mr. Madigan, to escort you through the house." A silvery giggle. "It's easy to get lost in here if you don't know your way around, isn't it Sean?"

"Yes, ma'am," came the now familiar voice from behind me.

"Sean, this is Lee Barrett. Ms. Barrett is a reporter from WICH-TV. Lee, Mr. Madigan is an expert antique appraiser, so I'm sure he can answer any questions you might have."

"Mr. Madigan and I have met," I said, trying hard to keep the frostiness out of my voice. "We have some mutual friends."

He nodded oh so politely and accepted the tour script from Claudine's perfectly manicured fingers. "Ms. Barrett. Shall we begin? I understand you've allotted just an hour."

"If you decide to do this, Lee," Claudine promised, "you and I will spend plenty of time prowling through this old wreck of a place together. Won't that be fun?"

"I'm sure it will. Thank you for the opportunity. I hope your knee feels better soon."

"Oh, arthritis comes and goes. Just part of the aging process, I guess. Go along now. Sean, be sure to show Lee my great grandmother's suite."

I followed the silent "appraiser" from the room, wondering whether having him serve as my guide had really been Claudine's idea, or whether Pete had told him I was coming and to keep an eye on me. I didn't have to wait long for an answer.

We climbed a curving staircase, longer and wider than the one on Winter Street. Once out of earshot of Claudine, he whispered, "I told you this isn't a good place for you to be. What do you think you're doing?"

"My job. Same as you," I told him. "Are you going to show me great grandma's room or not? We only have an hour."

"It's right down this corridor. Pete called and told me that you'd be snooping around and that I should be sure you're okay. Had to talk the old lady into letting me play guide dog." He opened a door at the end of a red-carpeted corridor. "Here's the great grand-mother's room. She was a suffragette." He consulted the paper. "She traveled to California and Washington, D.C. with Inez Mulholland."

I already knew that, and how the press paid more attention to Mulholland's beauty than to her message.

The room was wonderful, the wealthy Victorian lady's bedroom from the curvy quilted headboard on the rosewood bed right down to the French Ivory comb, brush, and hand mirror on the matching dressing table. I made some notes under my escort's watchful eye, then pulled my smartphone from my handbag. "Mind if I snap a few pictures? They'd be for my own use, not for broadcast."

"All right with me," he said. "None of my business." He pulled open a closet door. "I guess you want to see her clothes, right?"

"Yes, please," I said. It was a very modern lighted walk-in closet with shelves and drawers and hangers arranged to display the great grandmother's wardrobe to its best advantage, some of the outfits displayed on vintage dressmaker's forms "Wow. I'm sure this isn't part of the original house. Too new."

"You're right. Mr. Bagenstose had it especially built for this collection." He motioned for me to step into the closet, then, oddly, put his finger to his lips and pulled the door closed.

"Hey, what do you think you're doing?" I pushed against the door.

"Shh," he hissed. "Room might be bugged. Listen. I'm only going to say this once."

I listened.

"You know why I'm here. To ID the paintings for the cops. That's all. Anything else I see here is none of my business. I'm a convicted felon. There are certain things I can't afford to be involved with. You understand?"

"I think so. Yes," I said, starting to feel claustrophobic inside that closet full of old black clothes.

"Okay. I'm going to show you another collection that's not on the tour." He rattled the papers Claudine had given him. "But I'm not going to say anything about it and you're not going to write anything down about it. Got it?"

"Got it," I said, not really getting it at all, just wanting to get out of the closet.

He opened the door and, reading from his script, returned to a normal tone of voice. "Mrs. Bagenstose's great grandmother was a young widow when she joined the women's rights movement. She never married again and wore black all of the rest of her life in mourning for her husband. That's why all of these clothes are black. All of her hats are black too. They make up a separate collection. I'll show it to you next, but first examine these outfits as much as you like. They are all perfectly preserved top-quality designer pieces and span about forty years. Mrs. Bagenstose enjoys wearing some of them occasionally."

I moved to touch a two-piece velvet suit displayed on a vintage dress form, marveling at the tiny waist the woman must have had, when Madigan, with finger to his lips once again, pushed a row of clothes out of the way, revealing a sliding panel. I had just enough time to click off one shot of the suit as he moved the panel aside, long enough for me to see what was in the two-foot deep area behind the closet's false wall. Then he closed it and repositioned the all-black, old-time high couture on the adjustable wooden hanging rods.

It was an odd contrast of collections—the rows of soft luxurious fabrics providing cover for the rows of hard metal guns.

"Okay then, we haven't much more time." His voice was brusque. Businesslike. "On to the hat collection." He pulled open the door to an adjoining room. "She actually had a whole room devoted to hats."

I still hadn't moved away from the dress closet, trying to process what I'd just seen, and why he'd shown me the hidden guns. I was aware of his voice, reading once again from the script. The words droned on about the importance of hats in women's wardrobes in the late 1880s and early 1900s. How the hunting of wild birds to harvest their feathers for the millinery trade had nearly wiped out the entire snowy egret population of the United States. The more recent hats were smaller and plumeless. Sean said early environmentalists had succeeded in stopping the bird-hunting practice.

I tried to focus on Sean Madigan's recitation, forced myself to pay attention to the hundreds of hats displayed on tall wooden stands. Wide-brimmed bonnets decorated in elaborate concoctions of silk flowers and satin ribbons vied with plume-covered hats, some of them topped with entire stuffed exotic birds. It was fascinating and heartbreaking at the same time. I had to turn away from the evidence of the sad slaughter of so many beautiful birds. Instead I looked at a round marble-topped table, where a tall, delicately painted porcelain vase was displayed. No. Not a vase. More like a large round sugar shaker with holes in its top. I had a quick flashback to a round Quaker Oats box stuffed with long, sharp knitting needles.

This round container, though, was filled with long, sharp, jeweled hatpins.

CHAPTER 45

I could hardly wait to leave, to call Pete, to try to make sense of what I'd just seen. I checked my watch and almost sighed out loud. Still almost twenty minutes to go. I struggled to pay attention as Sean narrated, with what sounded like real enthusiasm, some history about a roomful of gorgeous Oriental furnishings that a four-times-great grandfather of Claudine's had brought to Salem from China. It really was a beautiful display, definitely museum worthy. If this show idea ever actually happened, it would be good TV. I was sure of it.

My hour was finally up and I followed Sean down the grand staircase. I peeked into the room where Claudine had greeted me, but the recliner was empty. Seeing my questioning glance, he said, "Claudine has a doctor's appointment. I have to drive her there. Something about her knee. I'll let you out."

He held the front door open. "I guess I'll see you tonight at the rehearsal," he said.

"See you there," I said. "Thanks for the tour. It was interesting. It's quite a place."

"You don't know the half of it."

I stepped out onto the terrace and he closed the door firmly behind me. I backed out of the driveway, probably a little too fast. I wanted to call Pete right away but realized that we'd probably need some time to cover everything I needed to tell him. I checked the clock on the instrument panel. Three ten. I barely had time to get to my hair and pedi appointment. The phone call would have to wait a little longer.

At five, with toes pretty in pink and hair tamed, styled, and smelling good, I pulled into our garage. The Buick was there too, so I knew my aunt was back from the library. I'd already laid out clothes to wear to the rehearsal dinner. "Nothing too dressy," Shannon had said. The dinner after the rehearsal was going to be at Turtle Cove. Mr. Dumas is a big fan of their local seafood.

I'd promised to tell Aunt Ibby about what I'd seen at the Bagenstose house. There wasn't anything I had to tell Pete that she couldn't hear too, so I decided to save time by calling him from her place. I could catch her up on the details about the clothes and those hideous hats later.

"I can tell by your expression that you're excited," she said as soon as she opened the kitchen door. "Tell me all about it."

"I will," I said, tapping my watch. "I'm going to report to you and Pete at the same time. I'll put the phone on speaker, okay?"

"Good idea," she said. "Time saver."

Pete picked up on the first ring. "Are you okay? Did you run into any trouble? Jesus, Lee. Do I have to worry about you every minute? Maybe this new job isn't a good idea after all."

"Uh, hello, Pete," I said. "Haven't got time for a lecture now. I have to get dressed for the wedding rehearsal. I'm fine. Your friend Madigan watched me every second. I found out some stuff you need to know."

"Oh, babe. I'm sorry, I don't mean to lecture. I know you're smart and savvy and capable and all that. I just worry, you know?"

"I know. I worry about you too. You're a cop, for goodness' sake. I worry about you all the time. But listen, this might be important."

"Okay, shoot."

"I've got you on speaker so Aunt Ibby can hear this too. Okay?"

"Yes. Hi, Ms. Russell."

"Hi, Pete. Maralee is excited about something."

"Here it is," I said. "Claudine wasn't able to give me the tour herself, so Sean Madigan did it for her. He says he talked her into it so he could keep an eye on me. Said you asked him too. Did you really?"

"I did. What's the matter with Claudine?"

"Arthritis in her knee, she said. Sean was taking her to the doctor after I left. He had a script so he could tell me about the clothes and furniture and all. In the great grandmother's room there's a big, modern walk-in closet. He said Elliot had it built to display the clothes properly. Anyway, when we were inside the closet, he pulled the door closed behind us."

My aunt gasped and Pete cursed.

"Oh, stop it you two. It was nothing like that. He said the room might be bugged and he wanted to show me something."

"What was it?"

"Pete, there's a secret panel in the back of the great

grandmother's walk-in closet. There's another whole collection behind it."

"Collection of what?"

"Guns," I told him. "All kinds of guns. Big ones, little ones. They're mostly hung up on a Peg-Board wall. I only got a peek. Maybe just a few seconds. But it's full of guns. I took a picture of a suit that I think must show a little bit of the panel. I'll send it to your phone if you want to see it."

"Might be useful," he said. "Yes. Send it when you get a chance."

"I will. That's not all I saw, Pete," I continued.

"Go on."

"The great grandmother had about a million hats, all black mostly ugly feathered things that take up a whole room. There's a round vase thing on the table. It's full of hat pins. I'll bet some of them are a foot long."

"Hat pins," he repeated. "That fits, doesn't it? A tiny hole like that would be easy to miss. Even by the ME."

"Right. And the tiny holes would bleed on a dog, but would heal up fast."

"Oh, dear," my aunt said. "What are you going to do, Pete? About the guns and the hat pins?"

"I'd like to get a warrant right away, search the place," he said, "but I need to wait just a little longer until Madigan finds all those paintings. Claudine's been bringing them out from somewhere one at a time for him to appraise and identify. He hasn't been able to find where she's got them stashed. That old place must be riddled with secret panels, underground tunnels, God only knows what else."

"How long do you think you should wait?" I asked.

"A day or two is all we can delay. Sean thinks he

can get some information from Claudine about everything. It looks as though the old woman has a bit of a crush on him."

"I think she does," I said, remembering the flirty flapper dress, the comment about getting lost in that big house, the little giggles when she spoke to him.

"I've got some undercover guys keeping an eye on the place, watching the comings and goings. You know. We can wait a little bit."

"Oh my," sighed my aunt. "A crush on a young thief, and poor Elliot barely in his grave. Dear Lord, is there really no propriety in Salem anymore?"

Pete and I made arrangements to get together after I got home from Marblehead. I stayed at Aunt Ibby's long enough to tell her about the dresses and gowns and tiny-waisted suits, and the fabulous Oriental furniture I'd seen. I told her about the hats too, and she already knew all about the decimation of the birds.

I dressed in a long blue crinkle skirt and off-the-shoulder white blouse and added a concho belt, turquoise necklace, and beaded sandals. I put on my make-up, trying hard to remember the tricks I'd learned from Carmine. The results were pretty good. I drove slowly, only peeking at the vanity mirror a couple of times and arrived at the Dumas's a little early. Hilda and Maureen were already there, as were two handsome young friends of Dakota's I'd never met before. Both Hilda and Maureen were clearly delighted with the groom's choice of ushers. The minister hadn't yet arrived, nor had the best man. Poe was apparently ready for his duties and perched happily, untethered, on Mr. Dumas's shoulder nibbling on cashew nuts being fed him by hand.

"Lookin' good, Red," Poe commented.

"Thank you," I said, realizing that I was becoming accustomed to having conversations with a pied crow. "You look good too."

The minister arrived at exactly seven, with Sean just a few minutes behind him. It was a beautiful evening, the sun low in the sky, the ocean calm, the sand on the beach still warm. A few seabirds hopped along at the water's edge, and there were no crows in evidence at all.

After a few false starts and much giggling from the bridesmaids, we were all in our rightful places. A wooden boardwalk leading to a pretty little altar decorated with potted stargazer lilies and red anthurium had been constructed since I'd been there last. Dakota stood at the altar facing the rest of us. Hilda and Maureen walked with their escorts and I walked beside Sean. Shannon followed on her father's arm, and Poe, tethered once again, rode on Mr. Dumas's shoulder.

As a group, it turned out that we followed instructions nicely. We finished in a short time and gathered in the gazebo for a champagne toast to Shannon and Dakota before heading to the restaurant. I asked Sean politely how Claudine's visit to the doctor had turned out. "The doc says she has to use a cane," he said. "She's not happy about it, but I think she feels better."

"Hope so," I said, moving away from him and looking toward the water's edge, picturing what the Wiccan ceremony for Megan might look like from there. "That's something I'd like to see," I murmured.

"What? What would you like to see?" I hadn't realized Shannon was standing so close to me.

"Oh, I was thinking about the Wiccan funeral tomorrow night," I told her. "I've never seen one. I'd like to but I guess you have to be a Wiccan to witness it."

"Oh, I don't think so," Shannon said. "I bet I'd get a good view from upstairs in my house." I turned and looked at where she pointed. "See the window in the middle? Right under the pointed eaves? That's my room."

"Bet you could," I said. "But you'll be in the Virgin Islands on your honeymoon tomorrow night."

"I will, but you won't," she said. "I'll leave you a key and you can go up there and watch it. Why not? It'll be cool."

I was hesitant. "What about your dad? Would he mind?"

"Nope, he won't be home either. He's leaving after the ceremony for a job in Washington, D.C. There won't be anyone here overnight except Poe. The lady who takes care of him until Dakota and I get back isn't coming until the next morning. Do it. You know you want to."

"I really do. Thanks, Shannon."

"It's the least I can do," she said. "If it wasn't for you I wouldn't have met Dakota. I'll leave a key under the conch shell on the patio."

When we all left for the restaurant, the sky was beginning to darken. I looked back at the gazebo, glad that it was empty. No man dressed in black marred the view.

CHAPTER 46

Dinner was delicious, as expected. I wasn't seated beside Sean, so I didn't have to have much of any conversation with him. It was a happy group that night, as it should have been. Shannon and Dakota made a perfect couple. We all agreed on that. With promises all around to go straight home and get a good night's sleep so we'd all look good for the wedding, we headed for our cars.

I'm still not sure whether I imagined it or not, but I kept catching glimpses of a green Toyota in my rearview mirror. Of course, there are lots of them around, so I was probably just being a little paranoid.

I called Pete as soon as I got home. "I'm home. It was really nice. Can you come over so we can talk?"

"You sound serious. Anything the matter?"

"Oh, no. I mean, I don't think so," I said. "It's just that we haven't had a chance to have a real conversation in what feels like months."

"I know what you mean. Feels that way to me too." I heard the smile in his voice. "I know you've had dinner and I ate at Marie and Donnie's. Stuffed manicotti."

Yes, Pete's sister and brother-in-law are named Donnie and Marie. "Shall I bring ice cream for dessert? And should I bring my tux, so you can make sure my tie is on straight in the morning?"

"Yes, to both tux and ice cream," I said. "Chocolate this time?"

"Chocolate it is. Be there soon."

Within less than half an hour O'Ryan announced, by tearing down the hall and out the living room cat exit, that Pete's car had arrived. I opened the door, and with a garment bag in one hand and an insulated ice cream bag in the other, Pete leaned in for a kiss.

I hung the tux in my closet beside my black dress while Pete secured the ice cream in the freezer. We took time for a proper kiss, then took our accustomed seats at the kitchen table. "Tell me what's going on," he said. "In detail, not little bits and pieces."

"Better get the notebook out then," I said, only halfway joking. "So much has been happening. I don't know what's important and what isn't."

He took me seriously. The worn notebook appeared on the table along with a sharp yellow number two pencil. "Any more visions you want to tell me about? Sometimes they seem to lead in the right direction. When I talked to Viktor Protector about what he might have seen outside the magic shop, he told me the darndest thing."

"He did? About what?"

"He told me he isn't going to protest witches anymore. Claims one of them pushed him and made a burn mark on his back."

I remembered the woman in black with the red shawl. "Do you believe him?"

"He showed it to me. A damned handprint plain as

day. Right on the man's back. He claims it was a second-degree burn. You told me you saw a woman touching him when we watched the news."

"Bridget Bishop," I said. "She's angry about witches getting killed. It's not a good idea to tick off a witch as powerful as Bridget Bishop. I guess our friend Viktor learned that."

"Are there any more visions you don't understand that might lead us somewhere?" He closed the note-book. "Off the record."

There is one. Megan showed it to me. "It was at the bridal shop," I began. "You know those three-section mirrors they have?"

He smiled. "They have those in men's stores too."

"Right. Anyway, Megan gave me this vision. She was on one side of the mirror. I was in the middle. Bridget Bishop was on the other side."

"Full-length visions?"

"Yes. Life sized, full length. That was a first. This involves something that goes back a while. There's a book. A real book that once belonged to Bridget Bishop. It's her spell book."

He looked skeptical, with that one-eyebrow-raised thing he does. "The actual book? From sixteen ninety two?"

"Yes. It's true. Ariel Constellation had it at one time and now River has it. Bridget wants it back."

"She told you this."

"Yes."

"Go on."

"I asked Megan how River could give it back. She showed me in that smoky crystal ball I told you about before."

"The *Wizard of Oz* crystal ball?"

"Yes. It's going to happen on the beach behind the Dumas's house. Tomorrow night. Midnight. River will give back the book, the crows will disappear. That's what this has been about all along. The damned book."

He nodded slowly, got up, and took the ice cream from the freezer. "Want chocolate sauce on yours?"

"No thanks. Just the ice cream please. Do you believe me?"

"Have you ever actually seen this spell book?"

"Yes."

"I believe you."

"I have a chance to watch it happen," I said. "To watch when River gives it back to her."

He put the bowl of ice cream in front of me and handed me a spoon. "Can I come with you?"

"I don't think so. I'm afraid it might not happen if you're there. Bridget isn't fond of lawmen."

"That's true. Will you be in a safe place?"

"Absolutely. I'll be inside the Dumas's house. It's a very solemn religious ceremony, you know. Nothing bad is going to happen. Oh, one more thing about that vision. You know how there are thirteen witches in a coven?"

"I've heard that, yes."

"In the vision there were fourteen. That bothered me at the time. It still does."

"Did Megan explain that?" he asked, in almost cop voice.

"No. She just smiled and waved and disappeared. I don't think I'll be seeing her in any more visions. I'll miss her." I was surprised to feel tears welling up in my eyes.

Pete handed me a paper napkin and went back to the freezer. "Any more of that vanilla ice cream left?"

I dabbed at my eyes with the napkin. "Sure. There are some of Aunt Ibby's peanut butter cookies in the cabinet too."

He filled a bowl half with vanilla and half with chocolate ice cream, added a couple of cookies, returned to the table, and moved his chair closer to mine. "Don't cry, babe. If you're right about all this vision and witch stuff it'll be over real soon. And if Madigan can locate the last of those hot paintings, that'll be over too. When I get the warrant I'll find out all about the gun collection behind grandma's petticoats and we'll take a close look at the hat pins. We can concentrate on what actually happened to Bagenstose and on who took those shots at Chris Rich."

"Another thing, Pete," I said. "Remember when I told you that River blamed herself for the deaths of the three witches? Because she'd had bad thoughts about them?"

"I remember."

"Christopher Rich is blaming himself for at least one of them. He thinks he put a spell on a fellow witch."

CHAPTER 47

It's amazing what talented professional wedding planners can do with a hundred yards of beachfront property in a few short early morning hours. Pete and I arrived at ten-thirty for the eleven o'clock ceremony. A red carpet lined the wooden walkway and the altar itself now displayed an amazing canopy of white capiz shells, which spun and jingled in the breeze. The entire walkway and altar were banked with roses, red and white, all arranged in tall shiny black vases. The gazebo now housed the wedding cake. The Fabulous Fabio, in full chef's regalia, stood beside the towering concoction. Balloons in fanciful shapes of starfish and octopi and sharks dangled from the roof—just as they had in my vision—and garlands of fragrant white jasmine wound around each pillar. A huge white tent had appeared on the opposite side of the house, which I assumed must be where the brunch buffet reception would take place.

It was tempting to stand there for a while just admiring the perfection of it all, but Maureen and Hilda grabbed me by the hands. "Come on up to Shannon's room," Hilda said, pulling me toward the house. "We need to help her with her veil. Doesn't everything look amazing?"

"I hope when I get married it will be this perfect," Maureen said, "if I can ever find a guy like Dakota."

I hadn't been inside the Dumas's house before, and knowing I'd need to find my way to Shannon's room in the dark that night, I paid particular attention to my surroundings. "Where's Dakota getting ready? And the two handsome groomsmen?" I asked as we passed through a beach-themed living room toward an open staircase of knotty pine.

"They're all over in the guest room next to the aviary," Maureen answered. "Mr. Dumas is over there getting the leash on Poe. Mr. Madigan is there too. It used to be his room, you know, but he thought Poe talked too much."

"So I've heard," I said. "Poe seems to think he knows me. Calls me 'Red.'"

"That's so cute. Here we are. Her room is right at the head of the stairs. Wait 'til you see the view she has of the water."

That works out well for me. I'll bring a small flashlight, tippytoe up these stairs to the first room I come to. Perfect.

Maureen was right about the view. Even with Shannon standing before a full-length mirror in her gorgeous Vera Wang gown, it was hard not to look past her toward the panorama of ocean, sky, and beach. "Lee, can you help pin the veil a little bit back," Shannon said, "so the spray of baby's breath holds it in place?"

"I think so." I made the adjustment she asked for, then stood back, admiring the effect. "He's a lucky man," I said. "Let's go downstairs and pick up our bouquets. I can hear Poe chattering down there already."

Hilda and Maureen were at the window. "Look. The

boys are already lined up at the altar and the minister
is there too," Hilda said. "Men in tuxedos look so handsome, don't they?"

There was a tap at the door. "Sweetheart? It's Daddy.
Let's go."

Folding chairs that had been set up for the guests
were nearly filled. I looked around and spotted Pete in
an aisle seat in the last row. I've noticed that fire-
fighters and EMTs and other first responders often do
that too, in case they have to move in a hurry. Aunt
Ibby and Mr. Pennington were seated near the center
of the area. Therese, wearing a black and white print,
moved around as unobtrusively as she could, the ever-
present video camera recording the happy event.

My bouquet of red roses was tied with an enormous
white satin bow. Hilda and Maureen each carried
white roses with red bows, and the bride's bouquet
was an absolute confection of white roses and white
orchids with cascading ivy. The familiar strains of
Mendelssohn's "Wedding March" sounded, and a cute
little flower girl, Dakota's niece, with a basket of rose
petals led the procession. Smiling faces turned to
watch as Hilda and Maureen fell into step behind her.
I followed them, and behind me, Shannon, on her
dad's arm, approached the altar. Poe, safely tethered
and riding on Mr. Dumas's shoulder, bobbed his head
right and left as though acknowledging applause.

The plan was for Shannon to hand her bouquet to
me, then untie the tiny gauze bag containing the rings
from Poe's foot, take them out of the bag, and give
them to the best man. Then her dad would slip the
empty bag into his pocket and he and the crow would

sit in the front row while the ceremony continued. At the appropriate time, Sean would give the rings to the minister, the words *With this ring* . . . would be spoken, and the two would be as one.

Everything worked. It was amazing. The bird did his part and didn't make any inappropriate remarks. The rings slid onto the individual fingers smoothly. The kiss at the altar was romantic without being slushy. The bride was radiant, the groom ecstatic. The only problem for me were the dozens of shiny, black, smooth-sided vases I had to pass as we retraced our steps back toward the house.

I'd just started back up the aisle, my hand resting lightly, politely, in the crook of Sean Madigan's elbow, when the pinpoints of light and the swirling colors seemed to bounce from the vases into my line of vision. It was a really brilliant display, impossible to ignore. I tightened my grip on Sean's arm. He looked down at me, curiosity in his glance, but kept on walking. "You okay, Lee?" he asked.

"I'm okay." I wanted to get away from the vases, but couldn't. Our little procession along the narrow aisle moved slowly, as Shannon and Dakota paused every few steps to acknowledge a guest, speak to a friend. These visions were uncommonly clear. No clouds or mists. The pictures were as sharply defined as a high-definition motion picture would be.

First, I saw the young girls. There was no sound, but open mouths and contorted features showed me their screams as they writhed and rolled on a rough wooden floor. They wore drab-colored long dresses, grays and browns, and each of them pointed at me with accusing fingers.

The pictures moved from one vase to the next,

distorting slightly at curved sides and coming into clear focus on the surface of the next one. I saw a group of women. They stared at me, faces sullen. With my free hand, I gestured to them. *Help me.* They turned their backs.

I saw a man wearing a white wig with long curls. *How strange.* The girls appeared again, more of them this time, more tortured and terrified than before. The girls pointed once again, and the man banged a gavel on his tall desk. Then I was in a dark place with a dirt floor and a small, barred window. There were other women there with me. Strangers. All of them wept.

I knew I was on a beach in Marblehead. I knew I was holding the arm of a man beside me, yet at the same time I was in those pictures on the vases.

I stood in a wagon, grasping the sides to keep from falling. The sun shone so brightly I closed my eyes against it. The wagon lurched to a stop beside a tree. There were people gathered around me now, the sullen women, leering men, a few wide-eyed children. *Dear God, don't let the children watch this.* I looked up to heaven.

I saw the noose above my head.

CHAPTER 48

We'd reached the last row of folding chairs and Sean's voice seemed to come from far away. "Pete," he said. "Something's wrong with Lee."

Pete slipped his arm around my waist. "It's okay. Thanks, Sean. I've got her." He fell into step beside me and the three of us continued along the aisle as though we'd planned it that way. I felt myself smiling, nodding to guests, returning to the real world, away from whatever dark place I'd just visited. "You saw something," Pete whispered. "Something bad?"

"Yes," I whispered back. "It was in the black vases. All of them."

"You all right now? Want to go home?"

"Oh, no. I'll be fine." I turned to Sean. "I felt a little faint for a minute. I hope I didn't scare you, Sean."

"You turned pale and squeezed my arm. I thought you said, 'Help me.' You sure you're okay?"

"I'm fine," I said again. "Probably shouldn't have skipped breakfast."

Sean looked relieved, smiled, and shook his head. "Why do women do that?"

"Excitement of the day, I guess." We'd reached the tent, where a row of white-jacketed servers stood behind long tables laden with silver dome–covered food. A reception line was taking shape: Shannon and Dakota, flanked by bridesmaids, groomsmen, Shannon's dad, Maureen's mother, and Dakota's grandmother. Poe was on Dakota's shoulder doing that head-bobbing thing. Shannon beckoned for Sean and me to join them.

"Guess we have to go shake hands with everyone," I said, reluctantly moving away from Pete and once again taking Sean's arm. For the next twenty minutes we smiled and shook hands, posed for pictures, and greeted friends and strangers. Again, everything went precisely as planned. *There really is something to this wedding-planning business. Might be a good show topic after all.*

All of us in the wedding party were seated at a long banquet table overlooking clusters of smaller tables placed around the enclosure. The centerpieces we'd slaved over looked lovely and there were fresh flowers everywhere. Thankfully, they were arranged in baskets, not black vases.

Mr. Dumas, who still had Poe on his shoulder, stood. "If you'll excuse me for a few minutes, folks," he said. "I think I'll put this good boy back in his aviary. All this food in plain sight might make him forget his manners."

"Bye, Poe," I said.

"Bye, honey," he said. "See you later."

When the father of the bride returned, the congratulatory speeches began in earnest. Sean Madigan did a credible job of toasting the happy couple, and by the time the food was served it was evident that Shannon's black and white wedding was a resounding success.

The guests were invited to adjourn to the "summer house," where the cutting of the wedding cake was to take place. We dutifully trooped out single file behind the bride and groom. Pete was able to sneak into line behind me, making me feel more comfortable as we approached the gazebo. "Looks like Fabio is going to perform for us," Pete said. The baker had exchanged his puffy tall chef's hat for the tall black magician's version. He stood at the entrance of the gazebo, bowing and smiling at the crowd. Shannon and Dakota took their spots beside the cake, posed for the still photographer, then cut the first two pieces and fed them ever so gently to one another. Dakota's grandmother took over the cake cutting, passing the slices of chocolate and vanilla deliciousness to waiting guests.

Fabio moved to the grassy area in front of the structure and began creating fanciful animals from black and white balloons, then moved on to card tricks. He pulled an amazing number of black and white silk scarves from an astonished young man's ear, and produced paper roses like the one he'd given me in rapid succession, handing one to each woman guest in the crowd. I'd just joined the applause as Fabio took a well-deserved bow when I noticed the man sitting on the bench behind the wedding cake. He wore a tuxedo. I tugged on Pete's sleeve.

"What's Christopher Rich doing here?" I asked.

"I don't know," Pete said. "I'll ask him."

I watched as Pete walked around the hexagonal structure, reached across the rail, and tapped Christopher Rich on the shoulder. They talked for a few seconds, nodded to one another, then Pete returned to my side.

"What's up with that?" I asked. "He looked the way he did in my vision. Dead."

"Rich is apparently The Fabulous Fabio's mentor. At least he sells him all his magic equipment. So he's here to supervise. He wore the tux because he wants to blend in with the wedding crowd. Wasn't invited, apparently."

"Sounds like Chris," I said. "He likes to be where the action is, invited or not. Are you about ready to leave?"

"Thought you'd never ask."

"I want to tell Aunt Ibby we're going," I said, looking around for my aunt. "With everybody dressed in black or white, it's hard to tell who's who."

"Like one of those islands full of penguins," Pete said. "I'll wait for you right here near the cake. Wouldn't want you to go off with another penguin by mistake."

"Never happen," I promised and headed back to the white tent, where Aunt Ibby was in deep conversation with one of the chefs, trying to wheedle the recipe for the butternut squash soup everyone had raved about, while Mr. Pennington stood by patiently.

"Maralee," she called as soon as she saw me. "I was worried about you. You looked a bit under the weather. Are you feeling well?"

"I'm fine. Just a little headache. Pete and I are going to go along now."

"Rupert and I will be right behind you. It was a lovely wedding, wasn't it?"

"Just about perfect. We're going to say good-bye to Shannon and Dakota. I'll see you at home."

I hurried back to where Pete waited. We wished the couple happiness, I whispered a thank-you to Shannon for leaving the key under the conch, and we headed for our cars. Mine was closest to the house and Pete had parked the Crown Vic across the street. "I'll follow you home. I don't have to go to work for a couple of hours yet. Want to tell me about what you saw in those visions?"

"I do, Pete. I want to tell Aunt Ibby and River too. I know why Bridget Bishop is so angry about whoever is killing witches."

"Okay, babe. I'll see you there in a few minutes. Oops. Hold on." He pulled his phone from his pocket. "It's the chief. Gotta take this." He turned partly away from me but I could still hear his part of the conversation. "Yes, sir," he said in his cop voice. I watched his face as he listened to Chief Whaley. "I've got it," he said. "Be right there."

He leaned into my open window. "Sorry, Lee. Something came up sooner than I thought it would. Chief has a search warrant for the Bagenstose place. I'll call you as soon as I can. Love you. Bye." He crossed the road at a dead run and I heard the siren as he sped away toward Salem. I noticed that the green Toyota was still there and wondered if Sean knew about the warrant.

I drove home slowly, carefully, thoughtfully. The haunting pictures I'd seen on the vases were engraved on my mind. I hoped River could help me sort them out, and Aunt Ibby's always wise council would be welcome too.

I parked in the garage and decided that I'd ask to borrow the Buick for my planned midnight ride. The

Vette is much too recognizable. I knew that O'Ryan, who always figures out which door I'll use, waited just inside the back hall. Aunt Ibby and Rupert Pennington had gone to the wedding in his car, so I didn't know whether or not my aunt was home yet. Unlocking the door and resetting the alarm system, I listened for sounds of activity from her rooms. All was silent. O'Ryan and I climbed the stairs to my apartment. It was good to be home. There was a real sense of relief that my maid of honor duties had been fulfilled, that I'd contributed to what had turned out to be a picture-perfect wedding—except for the pictures no one but me had seen.

CHAPTER 49

I changed from gown to jeans and T-shirt, silver sandals to well-worn sneakers and called River. In honor of Megan's funeral Mr. Doan had given her a rare night off. They'd show a "Best of *Tarot Time*" rerun in her time slot, so she was probably awake. I needed to see what she thought about the vision. Besides that, I wanted to be sure she approved of my viewing Megan's ceremony from a distance. More important, how did she feel about my watching the return of Bridget Bishop's spell book?

My friend was wide awake. "How was the wedding? I'll bet it was beautiful, huh?"

"It was and the weather was wonderful too. You never know about that when you plan an outdoor wedding. But, River, I had a vision while I was there."

"While you were at the wedding? With all those people around? What happened?"

I told her in as much detail as I could remember—and I was pretty sure I remembered every terrifying second of it.

When I finished she was silent for a long minute. "Are you there, River?" I asked.

"I'm here," she said, and I realized that she was crying. "I'm here, but you were *there*. With her. With Bridget during those awful days before they killed her."

"That's what I thought," I told her. "I saw through her eyes. I saw the girls who claimed she'd bewitched them. I even saw the judge who sentenced her. I saw the people who watched her die. No wonder she's angry. No wonder she sent the crows."

"I don't think she's angry at me after all," River said. "She's not even angry at Salem. She's angry at whoever is killing witches. Someone in Salem is acting as judge, jury, and executioner and it's got to stop."

"I'm glad you're not blaming yourself anymore," I said. "I felt terrible about that."

"I know. I'm glad too. Did you tell Pete about what you saw in the vision? What does he think about it?"

"I haven't had a chance to tell Pete. He was going to follow me home from the wedding and try to help me figure it out. But he got a call from Chief Whaley to go right over to the Bagenstose mansion right after we left. Pete said the chief has a warrant."

"A warrant? To search someplace or to arrest somebody?"

"I don't know. There wasn't time to ask questions. By the way, your friend Christopher Rich was there."

"Huh. Some friend he turned out to be. I worry about him, you know, because of that phone call, but he's still a big jerk. I didn't realize he knew Shannon and Dakota that well."

"As far as I know, he doesn't," I said. "He told Pete he was there to help the Fabulous Fabio with his magic act. All dressed up in a tux too, so he'd blend in with all the other guests."

"He doesn't want to blend. He likes to be the center of attention," she said. "He's all upset now because he thinks he should be the one to carry Megan's ashes instead of me."

"What makes him think that? You and Megan were so close."

"He's more famous than I am. I'm just a little card reader and he's a witch, a magician, a psychic, a shop owner. There've been magazine articles written about him, he's been interviewed on national TV, he was once king of the Witches Ball, blah blah blah. He says if he can't carry her ashes, he's just going to sit that part of the ceremony out."

"Seems kind of childish, doesn't it?"

"Yep. And he doesn't even know about my returning the book to Bridget. That'll really frost him."

"I want to talk to you about that, River," I said. "About your returning the book, I mean. I know I can't be with you and the witches tonight because I'm not Wiccan. But if I can be in a place where I can see the ceremony from a distance, where I can't be seen by anyone else, is that okay with you?"

"You won't intrude in any way? We won't even see you?"

"Right."

"No cameras of any kind? No recordings?"

"Right."

"I don't see any reason why not then. Just don't tell anyone I said so."

"Thank you, River," I said. "Maybe when this is over Bridget can be at peace and move on to the Summerland with Megan."

"I hope so," she said. "With all my heart I hope so." Then she added, "I hope she takes all those crows with her."

"They'll go away," I promised. "I'm sure of it. Megan showed me."

"And let me know about what's going on at that Bagenstose house, will you? I always wondered what was in there." I told her that I'd call when I learned anything and said goodbye. I wondered too what was in there that had caused Chief Whaley to move so fast.

O'Ryan darted suddenly through the cat door and out into the upstairs hall, so I knew that Aunt Ibby had come home. I followed the cat down the stairs and we greeted her together.

"What a nice welcome home," she said. "Go on out to the kitchen, my dears, while I go upstairs and slip into something more comfortable. Then I want you to tell me more about what you saw at Claudine's house. All the details."

"I have a few pictures on my phone," I said. "I didn't take many, but it'll give you an idea of the clothes and hats and furniture I got to see. I'll run back upstairs and get it."

I stopped in the downstairs hall to pick up my mail, and my aunt and I walked up the front stairs together, she and the cat to the second floor, me to the third. My phone was on the kitchen table, where I'd left it after my talk with River. I slipped it into my jeans pocket, looked over the mail, flipped through the new issue of *Motor Trend*, and hurried back downstairs. My amazing aunt had already changed into a polka-dotted cotton dress and white Crocs and started a pot of tea.

Side by side at the kitchen counter, we looked at

the photos I'd managed to take, one by one. "Here's what the closet looks like. A real walk-in with a state-of-the-art closet system. Track lighting, hanging rods, pull-out shelves, lingerie drawers, the whole deal," I said, pleased with the good quality of the picture, taken so hurriedly.

"Isn't that an old-fashioned dress form?" she asked, pointing. "My grandmother had one. Remember? It was in our attic before the fire."

"I remember," I said. "Look, I took a close-up of it. The two-piece suit on it fascinated me. Claudine's great grandmother's waistline must have been about eighteen inches."

"It was the corsets," my aunt said. "Cruel things. Women fainted a lot in those bad old days." She leaned forward, peering closely at the photo. "Is that the secret panel behind the form? See? It's open just a crack."

"That's it," I said. "Sean had just pressed the button to open it when I took the shot."

"Send these over to my computer, will you? I'd like to blow them up. See more detail."

"Don't you want to see the hats?" I asked.

"Later. Come on down to my office. I think I see something interesting here." She was already across the kitchen, on her way to her first-floor room full of the high-tech gadgets she loves.

I did as she asked, sent the photos, and hurried to catch up with her. "What are we looking for?" I asked.

"Details, my dear. There's something interesting just inside that panel. I'm not sure. But it may be important. Did Pete see these pictures?"

"Just this one. I thought he might need to see

where it's located in the house. Sean wouldn't let me photograph the guns behind it."

"A person is allowed to have a gun collection," she said, "as long as it's safely secured."

"This one seems to be," I said.

The photo of the partly open panel filled the screen. We could see parts of a few of the guns I'd seen hanging on the Peg-Board. "That's what I thought I saw," she said. "And I bet that's what Pete saw too."

I squinted at the screen. "What is it? All I see is little parts of a whole bunch of guns."

She touched the screen. "That one. It's small so you can see most of it. A Walther PPK."

"Uh-huh. What about it?"

"It's a .380-caliber gun. It fires the bullets that fit those shells you found."

The mental lightbulb went on over my head. "I see. Someone in that house had access to the kind of gun that was fired at Christopher Rich."

"Exactly," she said. "Now let's look at those hats."

"Wait a minute. How do you know this stuff? About the gun?"

"*Dr. No,*" she said. "James Bond. Nineteen sixty-two."

I should have guessed.

CHAPTER 50

Aunt Ibby was right about the photo. Pete and Chief Whaley had spotted the small gun visible through the crack in the panel door. The search warrant had been obtained faster than Pete had thought it would be, which is why he'd had to leave so suddenly after the wedding. He called and gave me a hasty explanation of what was going on at the Bagenstose house, and promised more details later. "But for right now," he said, "we're busy trying to locate Claudine Bagenstose."

"Claudine is missing?" That was a surprise. "Is Sean there? He might know what her plans were for the day."

"He's here. Doesn't know where she is. She was here when we served the warrant. It kind of freaked her out. Sean was still at the wedding reception. Both cars are still here, hers and Elliot's. Anyway, like I said, she was crying and carrying on about the warrant. She excused herself to go to the bathroom and poof! Disappeared."

I knew he didn't mean "poof, disappeared," the way

Megan and Bridget Bishop did in my visions. "Didn't anyone see her leave?"

"Nope. There's a cop at every entrance. Chief is taking this gun thing seriously. We're clearing out the gun collection. There's at least one that's been fired recently."

"The Walther PPK," I said.

Surprised cop voice. "How'd you know that?"

"Double O Seven," I said. "James Bond used one."

"Oh," he said, as though my answer made sense. "Anyway, Sean says this house is so full of secret panels and hidden rooms and underground passages, she could be hiding anywhere in here. He knows about them because of the hiding places they used for the stolen paintings. Claudine kind of got around to confiding in him about those lately. He's showing a couple of uniforms around the house right now. He has all her passwords, so we're going to see what's on her computer."

So he used Claudine's "crush" to get whatever he wanted. The location of the paintings and even her passwords. I wonder what else?

"I hope she's okay," I said. "Will you let me know when you find her?"

"Sure I will. You still planning to go to that witch thing you were talking about?"

"I am. It'll be at midnight on the beach at the Dumas's place. I'll be safe and sound inside Shannon's room upstairs watching from the window. No worries."

"I know Megan was special to you and you really want to be there for her funeral. Be careful driving, babe. I'll call you even if it's late. Okay?"

"Okay. I hope Claudine's all right and she's not guilty of anything too serious. The arthritis in her knee is pretty painful, I guess. And, Pete, don't forget about the hat pins."

"I won't forget. Lethal-looking darn things, aren't they?"

Sometimes I'm braver than I know and sometimes I'm not smart enough to know when I should be scared to death. On my way from Salem to the beach at Marblehead that night I was alternately excited about the Wiccan funeral I was about to witness and, at the same time, worried about what else I might see. Maybe Megan's return to the earth, the beginning of her journey to the Summerland, was something a nosy reporter had no business watching. On the other hand, Megan had appeared in my visions, apparently happy to help me.

The return of Bridget Bishop's book was something else. That was personal to me. After all, I was the one who'd more or less, however unwillingly, inherited it from Ariel Constellation. I was also the one who'd tried hard to destroy it. Maybe it was *my* fault that the long-dead witch had unleashed such fury on Salem.

Even if it is my fault, I'm sure returning it to her is the right thing to do.

I'd borrowed Aunt Ibby's Buick and left my house early, thinking it would be wise to get there before most of the witches showed up. There were several vacant sandy lots along the street leading to the Dumas's. Some had FOR SALE signs and none of them had NO PARKING signs. I chose one where there were a few trees and slid the Buick in behind the biggest one. I locked the car and began the short walk to the beach.

I was glad I'd brought a flashlight. There was no

sidewalk and I'd deliberately worn dark clothes. I hurried along on the side of the road, my feet sinking into soft sand. Very few cars passed and I was increasingly aware that maybe this wasn't such a smart idea after all. Maybe when I'd assured Pete that I'd be in a safe place I hadn't considered a lonely walk on a pitch-black road.

When I reached the Dumas property there were already a few cars in the area where I'd parked the Vette this morning—mostly dark-colored Fords and Chevys. *What had I expected? Brooms?* I stayed well back in the shadows, skirting the edge of the house, not daring to use my light this close to the beach. I felt along the low wall surrounding the patio and found the conch shell. I slipped my hand under it and pulled out the key. On the beach below I saw the beginnings of a fire and several figures silhouetted against the white sand. I fumbled for the lock and inserted the key, then exhaled a long sigh as I closed the door behind me, realizing that I'd been holding my breath.

Feeling my way across the room, I struggled to remember where the stairway began. When I found it I flipped the flashlight on and began to climb, holding on to the smooth maple bannister all the way. Tripping and breaking a leg at this point would not be smart. Shannon had left the door to her room open for me and a nightlight burned in the adjoining bathroom, giving enough light to keep me from bumping into the furniture.

I turned the flashlight off and smiled when I saw that she'd pulled a chair up to the window. On a table a bottle of Pepsi chilled in one of the aluminum ice buckets that had held champagne at the reception. She'd also left a toy telescope marked *Pirates of the*

Caribbean. Good idea. I should have thought to bring binoculars.

I picked up the telescope and focused it on the glow of the fire. Toy or not, it worked well enough to magnify the scene on the beach below. The walkway and altar were gone, as were the tent and all the tables and chairs—not by any witch magic, but by the efficiency and coordination of the wedding planner. I was pleased to see that all of the black vases were missing too.

Carefully, slowly, I opened the window a few inches, admitting a cool breeze off the water along with the sound of gently splashing waves. In the distance I saw the occasional flash of what New Englanders call "heat lightning." It's a harmless summertime phenomenon, and it produced just enough flickering light to help me see what was going on down there near the shoreline.

Shannon's bedside clock displayed eleven-thirty. The fire had grown larger, throwing green and gold showers of sparkles into the air. The flames were contained in a large round pit surrounded by stones. Black-clad witches began to appear. One by one and sometimes two by two, they made their way toward the fire. At first I tried to count them, remembering that extra witch in my vision, but they moved around too much. I guessed there were between twenty and thirty of them, and within the fire glow, I saw that a few wore masks or veils, secret witches like Elliot and Gloria.

I picked up the toy telescope again and fiddled with the simple focusing mechanism. Christopher Rich's platinum blond hair was easy to spot, and River wore the black velvet dress with the red bustier she'd worn on *Tarot Time,* so I recognized her right away. The witches joined hands, forming a circle around the fire. They moved in a slow, rhythmic dance-like pattern, all the while chanting melodic words that had no meaning to me but gave a peaceful feeling to the scene.

Some of the faces were vaguely familiar. Perhaps I'd seen that woman at the market. Maybe that man was a high school classmate. Had I seen that one in church? About half of the crowd seemed relatively young—twenties, thirties maybe. There were some with gray heads among them too, moving more slowly than the younger ones, but no less enthusiastically. A few stood outside the circle. Therese, a novice witch, was among them—not yet coven members, I guessed, but trusted neophytes.

I watched the seconds tick by on Shannon's digital clock. 11:57, 11:58, 11:59, 12:00. At the moment of midnight, River lifted a white urn from beside the fire pit and moved to where a pentagram had been drawn in the sand. At the same time, Christopher Rich dropped from the line and, still moving in cadence with the others, walked toward the gazebo. He was really going to sit out the scattering of Megan's ashes, just as he'd said he would. What a sore loser. A gray-haired witch wearing a veiled hat, perhaps needing to rest, slowly limped along behind him.

Don't go there, Chris. Don't sit in the gazebo!

A collective joyful cry of "Blessed be" went up from the witches gathered around the edges of the pentagram. I turned the telescope back to River, realizing that Megan's ashes had been returned to the earth, then quickly looked back to the gazebo, where Chris now sat on the bench, hands folded in his lap, his eyes blank.

Go back now and join the others, Chris. Don't stay in the gazebo!

But he stayed. Even without using the telescope I knew he'd be just as he had in my vision. My phone buzzed just as a sudden cackling call came from the direction of the aviary. "Better run, Red! Better run!"

CHAPTER 51

The veiled witch was on the first step of the gazebo when she reached toward her hat. I dropped my phone, grabbed the flashlight, ran down the stairway, raced for the door. "Chris, run!" I yelled, and hit 911 on my phone. When I got to the patio he looked in my direction, still not moving. The woman drew closer to him, tossing the veiled hat to one side. I'd heard that a person could be frozen in fear. Was that happening to Chris?

"Run, run, run!" came the crow voice from the aviary. The man remained motionless The woman sat beside him. She raised her right hand and moved it toward his head. Toward his ear. I didn't have to see the hat pin to know it was there.

An echoing crow caw came from the opposite direction. Not Poe this time. This new crow appeared as if from thin air. It dove at the woman, claws tearing at her upraised hand, and raking her face. Chris still hadn't moved.

I ran toward the gazebo. "Help!" I yelled. "Help!" The woman slashed at the air with both hands. I knew that the flailing woman was Claudine Bagenstose, and that she was no match for the dive-bombing crow.

Does she still have the weapon in her hand? Too dark for me to tell.

It wasn't too dark for the crow, though. It snatched the hat pin, the jeweled top catching rays from my flashlight, reflecting shattered sparkles of red and gold, and flew into the shadows.

"Help!" I yelled again. I heard the sound of running feet pounding on packed sand as the witches streamed from the beach below and into the gazebo, surrounding the woman who lay moaning on the floor.

Is she going to melt now, like the wicked witch in the movie?

I hurried to Chris's side. River was already there. "Chris," I said, shaking his arm. "Can you hear me? Are you all right?"

He blinked a couple of times and looked around. Sirens sounded in the distance. "It's okay," I said. "The police will be here in a minute."

At the sound of the sirens, the mention of the police, the masked and veiled witches hurried away. The others stayed, looking down at Claudine Bagenstose, some murmuring words I didn't understand, others silent.

"Lee," River whispered. "What should I do about this?" She pulled the spell book from her pocket.

I looked back toward the beach, to where the fire still glowed, to where the approaching tide lapped at the edges of the pentagram etched in the sand. A large crow now circled the space where, moments ago, the covens had gathered.

"Come on," I said. "I'll go with you. Hurry." We ran then, toward the ocean. River stepped to the center of

the pentagram holding the book high above her head.
The crow swooped down, grasped it in yellow talons,
and disappeared in a blinding flash of light.

When I opened my eyes I thought for a moment I
was seeing double. River, her arms at her sides, stood
facing another woman. Each of them wore a long
black dress, each wore a red corset. The woman, with
the spell book tucked under one arm, smiled and held
up her hand. River did the same. They touched palms.

Another flash and Bridget Bishop disappeared.

River and I returned to the gazebo, where no one
there seemed to have noticed that we'd ever left.
There was no mention of the flashes of light, of the circling crow, while Christopher Rich, standing erect and
smiling, accepted congratulations on overpowering
the hat pin–wielding woman who now lay prostrate at
his feet. The jeweled hat pin, a good ten inches long,
lay sparkling on the seat, where moments earlier Rich
had sat frozen, immobilized.

A wordless look passed between River and me.
Somehow, during the few minutes we'd spent on the
beach, there'd been a shift in realities. I knew that a
crow had overcome Claudine, had flown away with the
hat pin she'd been about to shove into Christopher
Rich's brain while he sat on the gazebo bench, unable
to move. Yet now, the hat pin rested on the seat. Claudine lay on the floor of the gazebo, her face unmarked
by razor-sharp talons, and Christopher Rich stood,
enjoying the praise of his fellow witches who'd apparently all witnessed him bravely overcoming a crazed,
would-be assassin.

The police arrived. An officer helped Claudine to her feet and she shook his arm away. Another officer read her her rights from a Miranda card. *You have the right to remain silent. You have the right to an attorney. . . .* Claudine ignored her rights. Especially the one about remaining silent.

"Witches," she muttered. "Witches. I hate them all." She laughed, a short, unfunny, strangled sound. "I didn't even know they were witches until I saw it on television. I killed them because they were lovers. Can you believe it? Elliot chose that sleazy waitress over me. He even gave her my favorite little oil painting. Carried it out of the house in a paper bag and drove straight to her place. Didn't even catch on that I was following him. Stupid man. Did you know he bought that house for her?" Claudine shook her head. "I suppose I own it now." She laughed. "I sent Sean over to buy my painting back, but he messed up." She put her hands behind her, accepting the handcuffs as easily as if they were gold bracelets. She tilted her head toward Christopher Rich. "I decided to shoot him. People were starting to talk about somebody killing the witches in Salem. What a great idea. Just kill one or two more witches and nobody would ever connect Elliot and that tramp Gloria to me!" Again, the strangled-sounding laugh. "But he was the only witch I knew about for sure. He's on TV bragging about it all the time. So he had to be next." She bobbed her head in River's direction. "I even called you up and told you I was going to kill him, you stupid girl." She looked down at the ground almost apologetically. "But I missed with the gun. Had to go back to my great grandmother's hat pin."

I heard Pete's voice before I saw him. He and Sean Madigan rounded the corner of the house. Pete walked to where River and I stood. Cop voice. "You girls okay?"

We both nodded. "We're okay," I said.

"Good. I'll talk to you later." He touched my hand, then climbed the steps to the gazebo and spoke in low tones to the officer.

Claudine Bagenstose hadn't stopped talking. "Is the dog all right? I'm sorry I stuck him, but he bit my knee when I kicked him."

Sean spoke to Claudine in a soft, friendly tone. "Zeus is fine. How come you swiped my car again?" he asked. "And how did you get out of the house without me seeing you?"

"You don't know all my secrets." She spoke in a little-girl coquettish voice. "There's a nice escape tunnel under my house that I haven't shown you yet. Elliot built it. Be a good boy and I'll show you later."

Claudine was taken away in one of the police cars. Pete took statements from the remaining witches. The WICH-TV mobile unit arrived and Christopher Rich got more television face time than even he could have dreamed of. Every witness told the same story. The heavily veiled woman, Claudine Bagenstose, had approached Christopher Rich, who was sitting in the gazebo observing a Wiccan funeral ceremony. She'd threatened him with a weapon of some kind and Rich had quickly, bravely subdued and disarmed her.

Not a single one of the witnesses recalled seeing a crow dive bombing the woman while she tried vainly to shield her face from clawing talons. No one heard Poe telling me and Chris to run. No one saw the brilliant bursts of light or the circling crow or the two identically dressed women facing one another on the beach. Nobody mentioned Bridget Bishop's spell book. Not that night or any other time. It was as though it had never existed.

But it had.

EPILOGUE

Claudine just kept right on talking in spite of her high-priced lawyer's advice. Like a courtroom scene in an old *Perry Mason* episode, she talked to anyone who'd listen to her. She freely admitted to killing both Elliot and Gloria. She'd become suspicious about the increasing frequency of Elliot's after-hours business meetings and simply began following him. The path had quickly led to the little house on Southwick Street and Gloria Tasker. The decision to kill both of them had come just as quickly.

The hat-pin-as-weapon idea came, oddly enough, from her great grandmother's reminiscences about her suffragette days. Society was transitioning back then, however slowly, from expecting and advocating female dependence on men to recognizing their ability to defend themselves. A foot-long hat pin plunged into a predator's arm or eye turned out to be a popular deterrent to "mashers." Forcefully pushed into an ear, her great grandmother had cautioned little Claudine, a hat pin would likely cause death.

Gloria's habit of taking predawn bike rides was

perfect for Claudine's plan. She'd meant to simply run the woman over with Elliot's car. The hat pin was to provide insurance that Gloria was actually dead. "She made it easy for me," Claudine told a Boston reporter in the corridor of the Essex County Court House. "She ran into that post and splattered her brains all over. She was probably already dead, but I stuck her anyway."

Elliot's death was quite different. The story about the apple blossom branch was partly true, except for the fact that it had been Claudine's idea for Elliot to climb up and cut a certain hard-to-reach bough while she steadied the ladder. "I yanked it out from under him," she told Scott Palmer in answer to his shouted question as she walked the gauntlet of reporters on the courthouse steps. "The hat pin still had Gloria's dried blood on it. I showed it to him before I stuck him." Then she'd laughed her silvery laugh.

The paintings have been returned to their rightful owners. The case against Claudine is still ongoing, complicated by the "slayer law," which prohibits inheritance for a person who murdered someone from whom he or she stands to inherit; by Claudine's penchant for self-incrimination; and by questions about her competence. Both the Bagenstose mansion and Gloria's little house still stand empty, but both of their fruit trees are blossoming once again. The twin Cadillacs are still in the garage; the Toyota is not. Sean said that Claudine was in the habit of borrowing his car to go to yard sales and flea markets because her black Caddy made vendors mark the prices up, so he'd given her a set of keys. He was sure she'd "borrowed" it for other reasons too, like for an attempted U-Haul break-in. He hadn't known about the secret tunnel that had allowed her to get away with his car to follow Chris Rich on that fateful Midsummer night.

Pete had been on his way to the Dumas house even before I dialed 911. The police lab's report on the voice pattern from River's mystery call had just come in, identifying the caller as Claudine. He'd tried to call me, to warn me, but by then my phone was on the floor of Shannon's bedroom and I was in the gazebo, watching a crow attack a murderer.

Christopher Rich is more famous than ever and has written a "tell-all" book about the case, since he was one of Claudine's intended victims and was also the apparent hero of the story.

The crows disappeared that night, just as Megan had predicted. The scientists who study such things are still debating the cause of Salem's murder of crows. Theories range from the birds' pursuit of a particularly rare migrating grasshopper to the proliferation of cell towers interfering with their natural guidance systems.

Shannon and Dakota are obviously supremely happy together. Dakota's fund for repairing damaged headstones is growing nicely and made a perfect topic for my second appearance as WICH-TV's investigative reporter.

Sean Madigan has accepted a position at a prestigious museum as an art instructor and as an expert authenticator of old paintings. Pete convinced Bertha Barnes that photographing people without permission violates their right to privacy, so she has given up that hobby and now only photographs dogs and cats.

My relationship with Pete continues to develop in so many wonderful ways. Lately we've been double-dating occasionally with River and Buck Covington, whose relationship is still in the "getting-to-know-you" stage. Aunt Ibby and Mr. Pennington continue trading lines from old movies.

Rumors are flying about the station needing another field reporter, and Mr. Doan has hinted that my name is being mentioned. That was the job I applied for at WICH-TV in the first place. Wouldn't that be something!

We haven't seen the little black cat for quite a while. I like to believe she's playing in the green fields of Summerland. O'Ryan watched for her from his windowsill for many nights and I think he still misses her.

Tabitha Trumbull, Aunt Ibby, and Pete's Mother's Ambrosia Fruit Salad (updated)

1 (8-ounce) container Cool Whip, thawed
2½ cups shredded coconut
½ cup chopped walnuts
1 (8-ounce) can fruit cocktail, drained
1 (8-ounce) can pineapple chunks, drained
1 (11-ounce) can mandarin oranges, drained
3 cups miniature marshmallows
1 (10-ounce) jar maraschino cherries, drained
   (optional)
1 teaspoon nutmeg
1 teaspoon cinnamon

1. In a large bowl, combine all the ingredients.

2. Mix together well and refrigerate for 30 to 45 minutes.

Aunt Ibby's
Peanut Butter Banana Smoothie
(Aunt Ibby calls it "The Elvis")

2 tablespoons creamy peanut butter
1 cup milk
1 fully ripe banana
3 tablespoons sugar-free Maxwell House
    International French Vanilla Café
8 ice cubes

1. Blend all ingredients except ice in blender until flavored coffee is completely dissolved.

2. Add the ice and blend on high speed until smoothie is thickened and smooth. Serve immediately.

Love following Lee's adventures in the Witch City?
Keep reading for a sneak peek at

Bells, Spells, and Murders

Coming soon from Kensington Books

And be sure to catch up on

Caught Dead Handed
Tails, You Lose
Look Both Ways
Murder Go Round
Grave Errors

Available wherever books are sold

It was the first day of December in Salem, Massachusetts, my hometown. Wanda the Weather Girl had advised the WICH-TV audience to expect afternoon snow flurries and overnight plunging temperatures and, as the old song says, it was beginning to look a lot like Christmas. I've been associated with the local TV station in one way or another for a couple of years, but this December first was also the beginning of a brand new broadcasting position for me.

I'm Lee Barrett, nee Maralee Kowalski, thirty-two, red-haired, Salem born, orphaned early, married once and widowed young. I wasn't nervous about the new job. I have a solid background in TV—Emerson College graduate, worked in Miami as a home shopping show host, did a stint on a network weather channel, taught Television Production at a local school, and even spent a short time as a TV call-in psychic. (Not too proud of that one.)

My boss at the station, Bruce Doan, likes all of his employees to wear more than one hat, so in addition to doing occasional investigative reports on the late

news, I'd just become WICH-TV's newest field reporter
and I was excited about it. It meant that I'd be covering
events on location, reporting from the scene where
news was happening. It was, I thought, a dream job
come true, and just in time for Christmas.

The holiday season is a big deal in Salem. It seems
that everything that can hold a light bulb blazes
brightly, and since the year's theme was "Ring in the
Holidays in Salem," a whole lot of bell jingling was
going on too. My Aunt Ibby had even tied a bell with a
red ribbon onto our cat O'Ryan's collar. He was not
pleased about it. Aunt Ibby and I share the big old
family home on Winter Street, where I have my own
apartment on the third floor.

So far on my first morning as a field reporter, I'd
stood in front of the bandstand on Salem Common
telling the audience about the traditions involved in
the decoration of the annual community Christmas
tree there. Next, I'd visited with a group of veterans
who repaired and repainted donated used bicycles for
underprivileged kids as part of a Veterans Helping
Santa program.

There was nothing further listed on my schedule
until an eleven o'clock appointment with Albert
Eldridge. Mr. Eldridge was, among other things,
chairman of the Holiday Walk committee, overseeing
a popular walking tour through one of Salem's beau-
tifully decorated historic districts. So by nine-thirty
Francine, the mobile unit driver/photographer, and I
were headed back to the waterfront TV station on
Derby Street where a light dusting of snow had begun
to fall.

Having the opportunity to work with some of my
old friends at WICH-TV on a daily basis made this

new job even better. I checked in with Rhonda, the way-smarter-than-she-looks receptionist. "How'd you like your first morning?" she wanted to know. "I watched the Christmas tree segment. You looked good. If you were nervous it didn't show."

"Not nervous," I said. "Excited."

She leaned across the curved purple Formica-topped reception desk, pushing aside an improbable arrangement of glitter-sprinkled lavender poinsettias. "Okay, tell me everything," she said. "You still dating the hot cop?" The "hot cop" in question was detective Pete Mondello and the answer was a resounding "yes." Still dating, still a cop, and definitely, still hot.

I caught her up on recent day-to-day happenings in my sometimes ordinary, sometimes very strange life— carefully omitting the stranger parts. "Aunt Ibby is going to London for the holidays," I told her. "Her friend Nigel invited her when he was here last year."

"Oh? Good for her. But does that mean you'll be alone for Christmas?"

"Not alone," I said. "O'Ryan will be with me and anyway, Pete's sister and brother-in-law have invited me for Christmas dinner at their hose."

"That'll be nice," Rhonda said. "Did you know that the Doans are inviting everybody to a Christmas Eve party here at the station?"

"Got my invitation. I'll probably go." Sometimes Pete volunteers to work some of the holidays so that the officers with kids can be with their families. That meant There was a pretty good chance I'd be spending Christmas Eve with my friends at WICH-TV. New Year's Eve is always reserved for Pete though.

It didn't take long for Rhonda and me to catch up on each other's lives the way good friends can, and by ten-fifteen Francine already had the mobile van parked in front of the building, engine running and the heater cranked up when she phoned. "Ready to roll, Lee? If this snow doesn't let up you'll have to do your interview with the old guy indoors instead of in front of the fancy-ass mansion."

I glanced at my watch. She was right. We'd be a little early for our appointment, but if Mr. Eldridge wanted to give viewers a peek at some wonderfully decorated old homes we'd better do it right away before blowing snow made filming difficult. I said goodbye to Rhonda, pulled up the fake-fur collar of my plaid wool jacket, plunked a knit hat over red hair gone wild, and hurried downstairs. The snow had picked up in intensity. Not the soft, fluffy kind, but the icy face-stinging variety. I hurried along the sidewalk to the waiting van, pausing only to stuff a few dollars into a camo-painted kettle manned by a bell-ringing Santa with an obviously fake beard and a just as obviously genuine smile. I climbed into the passenger seat. "Let's roll."

It's not far from Derby Street to Washington Square, so within minutes we pulled up in front of a large, and what one might describe as stately, brick home. A discreet black and gold sign over an exquisite Samuel MacIntire carved doorway identified it as *Historical Charities of Salem*. The annual Holiday Walk was just one of the numerous charitable fund raisers Albert Eldridge chaired throughout the year. Some of the proceeds went to maintenance and restoration of Salem's many historical sites and buildings. Other funds supported veteran's causes, aid to needy families, a community Bookmobile (Aunt Ibby's favorite) and—especially at holiday time, toys for kids. I felt honored to be able to meet and interview such a prominent and important citizen.

While Francine made camera and lighting adjustments, I climbed the steps to that handsome front door and, following the instructions posted on the glass inset, entered the reception area without knocking or ringing. A cushy Oriental runner on a polished hardwood floor led to a massive mahogany desk where a diminutive gray haired woman welcomed me with a smile. A fragrant Scotch pine with Victorian ornaments, stood to one side of the desk and a tall wing chair upholstered in gold and green stripes flanked the other. Several comfortable looking club chairs in solid colors were arranged attractively around the room.

Only the long, white-plastic topped metal table next to the door seemed out of place. An untidy row of cardboard boxes, canvas bags, plastic tubs, all filled with a variety of items, spread across the top. More boxes were piled underneath between the folding legs. I saw canned goods, cake mixes, shampoo bottles, candy bars, detergents, packages of diapers. A pile of stamped envelopes in a wire basket marked "outgoing" beside a matching empty one marked "incoming' was at the end closest to the door. A tall barrel marked "toys" stood at the opposite end.

"Good morning. May I help you?" The smiling woman greeted me from behind the desk. I handed her a business card, one of my new ones, identifying me as a field reporter. "I'm Lee Barrett. I'm early for an eleven o'clock appointment with Mr. Eldridge."

"Oh, yes." She peered at the card through granny glasses perched at the end of her nose. "Lee Barrett.

You're Isobel Russell's niece. Maralee. She speaks so highly of you."

"You know my Aunt Ibby?" I wasn't surprised. In her position as head research librarian at Salem's main library, I think my aunt has met just about everybody in Salem at least once.

"Yes indeed. She and I are both members of the Christmas Belles, you know. We're going to start rehearsals this week for our holiday concert." She offered her hand across the broad expanse of desktop. "I'm Lillian Jeffry, Mr. Eldridge's secretary."

"How do you do, Ms. Jeffry. My aunt has told me about the Belles. Sounds like a lively group of musicians."

"We do have a grand time together." She glanced at a grandfather clock in the corner. "You're early for your appointment. Mr. Eldridge likes to keep a timely schedule so I'll announce you at precisely eleven. Meanwhile, just make yourself comfortable." She waved a hand toward the wing chair. "If you'll excuse me, I'll continue with my work while we chat. Mr. Eldridge likes to have all of his holiday cards hand addressed, and as you might imagine, a man of his stature has hundreds of friends." I started toward the chair she'd indicated. "Oh, just a moment dear. While you're up, would you add these cards to the outgoing basket? The letter carrier should be along any minute." I accepted a stack of envelopes, admiring the perfect cursive, mentally comparing it to my own back-hand scrawl, and added them to the pile.

"You have beautiful handwriting," I said. "No wonder Mr. Eldridge likes to have you address his cards." I paused in front of the table. "Are all these things gifts for needy people?"

"Yes. Sorry if it looks a little bit messy. People come in and leave donations. Then some of our people pick them up and take them to the right charities. Toys for the kids, new socks and underwear for the vets, diapers go to the battered women's shelter, candy for all of them." She smiled. "I know it looks disorganized, but it really runs quite smoothly. Things come and go from that table all day long. Look. Here comes the letter carrier now."

The postman entered, said "Hi, Lilly, stayin' out of trouble?" Not waiting for an answer, he picked up the outgoing stack of envelopes and dropped a few pieces of mail into the incoming basket and hurried away. "'Bye, Howie," she said to the already closed door.

The grandfather clock chimed eleven. "All right Lee, I think you can go right on into Mr. Eldridge's office now. I know he's expecting you. I checked just a little while ago to see if he wanted me to order some lunch for him, but he's so deep into his work he didn't even answer. A break will do him good. He's been poring over the books since I got here this morning."

"Thanks. We're going to try to do the shoot outside. He'll probably enjoy the fresh air." I walked carefully along the polished floor, hoping the heels of my boots wouldn't mar its perfection, and tapped gently on the door before pushing it open.

It was a beautiful room, as one might expect in such a house. More Oriental carpeting, portraits of distinguished men and elegant women lining cream colored walls. Ashes from a dying fire smoldered in a wonderful huge fireplace with boughs of holly and evergreen arranged on the mantelpiece. Mr. Eldridge, chin resting on his chest, red Santa hat slightly askew, appeared to be reading a book which lay open on his desk. He didn't look up when I entered. "Mr. Eldridge?" I said. "I'm Lee Barrett from the television station. We have an appointment."

No reply. I shook his shoulder gently. "Mr. Eldridge?" The chair rolled back and the man slid forward ever so slowly, feet first, until almost all of him was under the desk. Just his head and shoulders remained propped against the chair seat, the Santa hat at a rakish angle covering one eye. The other eye was open, bloodshot, unseeing.

I backed out of the office. "Ms. Jeffry," I said, trying to remain calm. "Please call 911."

Connect with
Us

Visit us online at
KensingtonBooks.com
to read more from your favorite authors, see books
by series, view reading group guides, and more.

Join us on social media

for sneak peeks, chances to win books and prize packs,
and to share your thoughts with other readers.

facebook.com/kensingtonpublishing
twitter.com/kensingtonbooks

Tell us what you think!

To share your thoughts, submit a review,
or sign up for our eNewsletters, please visit:
KensingtonBooks.com/TellUs.